Hidden Wings

MAY TOMLIN

Independently published

Website: maytomlin.com
Instagram: @maytomlinfiction
Facebook: facebook.com/maytomlinfiction/

ACKNOWLEDGMENTS

To Alyxius Young who read the very first draft and said "keep writing." To Elise Welch who said: "publish." To Lynette Sieler, Abby Little, Abigail Wennerstrom and everyone in the Beta group who plowed through an unfinished manuscript offering advice and improvement: thank you! To my editor Candie Moonshower: your patience and humor kept me going. To Hewitt, my patient husband who let me write instead of sitting by your side to watch football: you've been a great sport! And lastly to the One who imbued me with an imagination and who never tires of teaching me his ways, all glory and honor be to you, God.

CHAPTER 1

The gnawing reared up again in LaRae Gunther's midsection. She shoved the vibrating cell phone beneath the text book and caught the professor frowning at her before refocusing on the drawing. Fingers clenched around a medium charcoal stick, she contrasted the subtle curves of the vase with harsh shadows. A critter eating at her insides was the only way to describe Mother's nagging. She pushed a stubborn lock of hair off her face, then tucked it into the pencil bun on top of her head and gathered her things. As she left the classroom, a text lit up the screen: *Mom is worried. Respond to her voicemails, sis.*

LaRae donned the bargain tweed coat and stepped out of the hall, navigating a puddle at the front doorstep. Accidentally dropping her phone in water would take care of the pestering. She tramped across campus through wet snow, the icy blasts off Lake Michigan taking bites out of her face. Although wrapped in layers of newly acquired Goodwill clothing, she felt frozen to the bone. That seemed about right. Like the rest of her life. Why not add her toes inside wet leather boots to the list? A seagull swooped down and snatched a soggy crust by her feet. Enviously, she admired its audacity and proficient wings while forcing her own legs to dash towards the dorm. After digging out the ID and sliding it through the electronic lock to the building, she glanced at the bulletin board in the hallway. Among the leaflets announcing activities ranging from concerts and study groups, to occult medium consultations and vegan cooking classes a new poster snagged her attention. The Art Showcase Exhibit run by the Fine Arts Department was opening tonight. She came to an abrupt halt. Was it safe to attend or would it wake up the old longings? She shook her head, deciding on the library. When the elevator stopped on the fourth floor, she strode to suite 17 and changed out of her charcoal-dusted frock. The elective class was rough on her clothes, but oh so easy on her soul. The only drawback was that it also poked at her yearnings.

A vibrating noise emanated from the laundry hamper. Her mother's seventh attempt at reaching her. With a clipped greeting, LaRae answered.

"Where have you been, Rae? Did you get the brochure? Dental hygienist! The community college says credits from your freshman and sophomore year will transfer."

So this was the most recent in the litany of career suggestions. LaRae thought of how she had disposed of that particular brochure in the recycling bin.

"I knew we would find it someday. With the recession, it's a perfect fit. There will always be bad teeth. People part with hard-earned money for this service. Of course, I don't go. A couple of dollars' worth of dental floss is all I need. But most folks get their teeth cleaned twice a year. Extravagant, I know. But that's our society." The voice sharpened. "Are you tuning me out, Rae?"

"Mom, we've been through this. I have chosen a Bachelor's degree. Please turn off the speaker on your cell phone?"

Dishes clattered and the faucet got turned on. With Illinois cornfields in a deep freeze, Mother took her frustrations out on her house, performing another spring cleaning.

"Are you reorganizing the cabinets?"

"Been letting things slide since Christmas. With the time it's taken to find a different path for you, I haven't been as thorough as usual." Instead of turning off the speaker, her mom yelled louder.

LaRae sank down on the bed, weariness settling over her like a wet wool blanket. The idea of wearing a white coat and taking inventory of the mouths of Dresden's population caused a gag reflex. While her mother droned on, LaRae shut out the anxious undercurrent beneath the spoken words. But the current snagged her, pulling her under, leaving her clamoring for air.

"You'd better suck it up Rae. Life is hard. It is difficult to keep bread and butter on the table. I've told you before and I'm telling you again. These highfalutin' colleges have majors that prove worthless. The other day when I picked up half-priced Fruit Loops at the discount store, I asked the cashier about her education. What does she brag of having? A Master's degree in sociology."

Swooshing noises and crackling indicated the phone was being placed outside on the porch. The snapping sound of the kitchen rug being beat against the railing caused LaRae to tense. The seriousness her mother exhibited in ridding the house of pathogens reminded her of the CDC trying to eradicate Ebola.

"Sociology, my hat. Just as bad as choosing an art major. And now she is sorting dented tomato cans!" Over the yelling, a loud clunk and crash resounded. A garden pot must have been caught in the beating.

In their conversations, the "bread and butter talk" led to all kinds of suggestions on how to avoid debt and make an honest living. Hard as she tried, she could not see herself selling steel-toed work boots in the neighbor's shoe store or working as the pet groomer's assistant in order to start her own full service kennel. Shuddering at the thought of doing close-up business with God's four-legged creatures, she decided if everything else failed, she'd be a hot dog vendor on a sidewalk in Chicago. It beat tending to teeth, feet, and animals' intimate parts.

"Your dad agrees. Even with financial aid your education is costing too much. The new mechanic at the garage said his wife works as a nurse at Wilmington General. They offer a bonus for new hires. If you keep turning up your nose at everything I suggest, you could do the nurse assistant training at Heartland Community College."

"It's a quasi-miracle I got accepted at Northwestern University. I am discussing the choice of major with my academic advisor plus taking an aptitude and personality test."

Her mother harrumphed, the information stuck in her craw. Over the line the clattering of porcelain and glass increased to a crescendo.

She will break something. Once again, I'll be the source of more unhappiness.

"Your dad and I never needed a personality test to find out whether running his auto shop and me taking care of our house and children would be suitable."

Amanda was beeping in.

"I have to go Mom, I'm getting an urgent call." She clicked over to the next call but let Van Gogh's "Red Vineyard" beckon to her. The museum print lit up her otherwise sterile dorm room wall. She stepped into the scene, meandering down the rows of grapevines, the setting sun of Provence kissing the back of her neck. Her index finger and thumb plucked a grape from the heavy, drooping vines, cradling the warm, plump fruit in her palm.

"Earth to Rae. Are you there, sis?" Amanda chirped.

No. I'm on Mars, sick and tired of interference. "Don't send texts with messages from Mom, Mandy."

"Ouch, Miss Grouch. Why are you so bummed? Just because we changed our minds and want you home does not mean you need to act snotty."

LaRae rose and paced the cubicle-sized bedroom reminiscent of a doctor's office. A year and a half of inhabiting the space, and it still looked the same. As a freshman she'd envisioned Indian tapestries in rainbow colors draped over a four-poster bed, with ethnic rugs covering the floor and Moroccan lanterns spilling star-shaped light over the desk. But once the initial giddiness of moving in had faded, she'd done nothing. In awe, she trod the hallowed ground of this fine institution, studying beneath beautiful leaded windows in the warm glow of wood paneling, yet on the inside she remained an onlooker, observing but not participating. "This is my ticket out of Dresden," she protested to Amanda. "I don't care if I end up with a gazillion student loans." But her sister interrupted.

"I have a game changer. Brace yourself: I am pregnant!" The din of Zumba music that had been blaring in the background stopped, as if waiting for the squeal LaRae could not muster. "You say nothing? I just peed on a stick at the gym. Drew keeps begging for a sister and Mickey needs a playmate. It'll mean more stretch marks and saggier breasts." A pop resounded against LaRae's eardrum. Amanda was into blowing bubbles with her chewing gum. "The way Christopher's commissions are picking up I'll get a tuck or two. 'Mummy tuck' they call it. All the rage in Hollywood and the big cities."

Loud smacking filled the pause.

"I'll break it to him at Sweet Yogu's tonight. I already crave their chocolate fudge topping."

LaRae rolled her eyes. It didn't take pregnancy for her sister to develop or indulge cravings. "I am happy for you. It must be due around fall break so I'll come help you then."

"I need more than that. I am stressed out of my mind building our house in Normal. What color of granite? Brass or chrome fixtures? Recessed lighting or crystal chandeliers? I lie awake agonizing when I should be resting. Then I stress about Domingo and Jose not understanding English. I specifically asked for slate colored porcelain tiles, and they put real slate up the guest bathroom wall. A terrible mess, I tell you. You have no idea what I'm going through!"

LaRae pulled off the rest of her clothes while listening. From one harrowing ordeal to another, Amanda was the long-suffering heroine of never ending trials. "I'll come down Friday, but I'm not quitting school."

"That's quite an attitude and we will discuss this more. Make sure you bring Mom's new vacuum. Please vacuum under the beds, it'll help me. Nausea is a beast."

LaRae grimaced and ended the call. Forever a victim of her sister's persuasive charm, she'd get corralled into scrubbing the bathrooms next. Even outside of pregnancy, Mandy feigned dizziness when cleaning toilets and tubs. Fortunately, Amanda's cleanliness standards were not as unattainable as Mother's. LaRae stepped in the shower, letting the jets soothe her muscles while searching for a distraction from "Operation Repatriate Rae." After pulling on black yoga pants and a matching hoodie, she headed out the door.

The Open Art Studio welcomed visitors, offering refreshments and wine. She placed a cracker and a piece of Emmental cheese on a disposable plate. Beautifully lit spaces highlighted graduate students' works. Surreptitiously, LaRae slid a hand over the abstract sculpture to her right. It was smooth and cool to the touch. Her fingers itched to hone the Russian doll-shaped granite object. It needed something. Eying it from different angles, she toyed with various possibilities. When going to bed tonight, ideas would surely emerge and forms, shapes and colors crystallize.

She walked across the gleaming marble floor to the paintings. An oversized painting, in the tenderest shades of pinks and blues, portrayed a nude cradling an infant. Executed with a palette knife, the angles appeared sharp yet smooth. LaRae took in the texture of the canvas, sensing the buzz starting at the bottom of her spine. It never failed. Exposed to the expressions of other artists, LaRae's body started its own little jig, arms reaching out, grasping for a substance to mold or imprint. With nothing, her hands felt bereft. She clasped both palms together and watched the art students greet visitors, smiling and thanking them for their compliments. And while watching, the darkness seeped in. *Why them? Why not me?* After bundling up, she exited, treading gingerly on the iced pavers of the quad. Like life itself, one wrong step could lead to disaster.

Despite the cold, a strange heat seared through her head. *I am mad.* The realization hit her. And the more she pondered it, the more fury bubbled up. Back in the dorm, she locked the door and sat cross-legged on the floor, maniacally tapping the keyboard of her laptop until she pulled up the description. Not one item on the list repulsed her. On the contrary, like a mermaid's mesmerizing song, the proffered curriculum exerted an irresistible pull. She rose to find Starr. When her roommate did not answer the knock, she stuck her head in the door. "I just decided to major in Art Theory and Practice." Her suitemate looked up from a compromising position and Starr's boyfriend's eyes skewered her.

"Whoa girl! You just about caught us in the act. Lucky for you we still have clothes on!"

LaRae apologized profusely and backed out.

"That's great news! Glad you didn't pick anything dumb," Starr yelled from the futon in her densely furnished room. Throaty laughter followed. LaRae leaned against the wall in the hallway and pulled her left earlobe. On her mother's immaculate fridge, magnets never suspended Crayola drawings or splattered water colors. Instead, art work had mysteriously disappeared while sensible crafts like knitting and sewing were mandatory. Into that setting, LaRae was dropping a bomb.

CHAPTER 2

As LaRae's foot pressed the brakes of her thirteen-year-old Toyota Corolla, the floorboard vibrated and the rattling noises turned into a threatening roar. After gunning it down I-57 South, she eased onto the narrow lane and swiped a hand across the inside of the fogged-up windshield. The visibility improved but tendrils of smoke escaped from beneath the hood. Dad needed to doctor the car but she didn't like to inconvenience him. Surrounded by snow-covered fields, she thought of how German immigrants had taken to the flat stretches of tillable and dark soil on the Midwestern planes of Illinois. Her father's forebears had arrived in 1887 and had scratched out a living from the rich dirt.

The sign announcing the town of Dresden had been pockmarked, probably by juvenile hunters practicing their aim. Three thousand hardworking citizens made up the town she called home and except for the hullaballoo of the Corn Festival, it hummed along like a well-oiled machine. True to their stoic heritage, its inhabitants went about their daily business regardless of terrorist threats and global warming. Her father, a content middle-aged man in blue overalls, took pride in his grease-stained hands and worn overalls. Gunther's Automotive Repair serviced the pickups, vans, and compact Fords and Chevrolets of Dresden.

The town's only traffic light turned green, and LaRae waved at

Mrs. Ruth sweeping the sidewalk in front of Ace Hardware then flicked the blinker down and turned left at the Farmer's Co-Op. A Hispanic crew was applying orange paint to the chipping facade. She entered Evergreen Estates, a misleading name because this time of year it was shrouded in white. Although seasonal changes of potted geraniums in the summer, mums in fall and pansies in the winter brought variety, the solid brick of the ranch-style homes of the 1960's neighborhood remained unchanged. As she pulled into the driveway of their three-bedroom home, she saw new lace curtains fluttering in the open kitchen window. The outside air smelled of Norwegian raisin buns. With Mom's hot flashes, the window stayed cracked when she baked. The inherited recipes from the old country had been worn as thin as the papery "lefse" tortilla Mom made for Christmas and baptisms. The cakes and yeast goods did not make for thinness in the humans consuming them, however no one worried about that part.

LaRae grabbed her nylon duffel bag and entered the kitchen through the garage door. Baking racks covered in starched linen towels lined the spotless Formica counter. She lifted a corner of a towel and peeked. A dozen golden rolls and two loaves of sourdough bread spelled temptation with capital T. Bleach odor intermingled with the scents of cinnamon and anise and although dated, the kitchen appliances gleamed. Animated conversation drifted in from the living room.

"Doctor Wohler ordered me to cut bad fats and reduce the sugar." Her mother's voice rose an octave as she continued. "I was dishing out green beans at the potluck when the doctor says: 'Mrs. Gunther. As much as we love your meatballs at this church, I ask you to switch from pork to ground turkey. Be forewarned, with your husband's high cholesterol count I'll medicate him if you do not follow my orders'. So, with one sweep he marched into the fellowship hall and changed my cooking forever! The nerve of that man."

"At least your daughter will be excited you made her favorite treat!" Mrs. Stubbs's voice was comforting.

"There is no telling. She announced she is gluten-free. Of all the strange things to become! Plus, she spends her hard-earned money on supplements. Vitamins and fish oil and green capsules. As if plain food is not good enough."

LaRae moved towards the half-open doorway of the living room, feeling guilty about the trail of foot prints she left on the carefully striped carpet vacuum pattern in the hallway.

"Oh goodness! Is she becoming one of those fanatic 'vegenarians'?"

LaRae choked back a snicker. Mrs. Stubbs was leaning over her mom's blue and white willow china, sipping from a steaming cup. Apparently, the word vegetarian was new to her vocabulary. A linen cloth with an embroidered daisy pattern ironed into sharp planes covered the teak coffee table.

"Not sure. She's as skinny as a rail and just plucked at the bratwurst and vegetables during her last visit. Says bacon fat is not good to cook in. So, I stopped only to find out she has a problem with using Crisco, too."

Mrs. Stubbs gasped. "I read in *People Magazine* at the doctor's office that this famous Russian ballerina cannot have children because she starved herself as a teen."

LaRae watched her mom's permed curls bob in agreement, her cheeks flushed. "I worry just the same about Rae. As quiet as that girl is, she still has a mind of her own. I keep trying to teach her common sense but I swear she lives inside her head! She needs to grow up and apply what we've taught her. If not, I simply fear for her."

LaRae readied herself to walk in when Mrs. Stubbs answered.

"You are so right. Young folks just don't know what's good for them anymore. Take her to the donut making class tomorrow. Every woman needs to learn how to please a husband." Mrs. Stubbs bit into a second bun. "And in my humble opinion that takes more than what goes on in the bedroom! I say Charles cares as much for my donuts as for the other!"

Obviously embarrassed by the turn of the conversation, her mother flushed even more.

LaRae coughed to cover up the giggles bubbling up. If she were Charles, she'd stick to the action in the kitchen. It was difficult picturing short and overweight Frieda Stubbs in a romantic bedroom setting. As far as worry over her own body weight, her love for chocolate and butter ruled out the danger of anorexia. As to the art of acquiring and keeping a man, she decided the lure of donuts was not part of the plan. "Hi Mom, I'm here!" she said.

"Goodness Rae! Don't sneak up on people. I almost dropped the creamer." Mom rose and they embraced. "Come join us. Frieda is sharing news. Norman has saved enough to buy farm equipment." Mother arched her tinted eyebrows meaningfully and opened the china hutch to grab another plate.

LaRae sank onto the antique burgundy couch reserved for visitors and spoke to her cat laying in a sun spot by the bay window. The black long-furred kitty stretched, walked over and jumped on the sofa, purring. She stroked his silky fur while thinking of Norman Stubbs. They'd been buddies since they were in diapers at First Lutheran for Mothers' Day Out. When Norman moved on to T-ball and baseball she had cheered for him. Fond of animals, he'd raised mice, bunnies and pet pigs for 4-H. When his ambition to win the McLean County Fair pig race drove him to compete, she'd been by his side too. Who could help but admire his steadfastness and drive? LaRae had cleaned the pens and rabbit cages so he could focus on the more important tasks of weighing and training. Over the summer when Norman was turning thirteen, he grew into a pimply-faced adolescent with pants that were too short. Whether his mother was oblivious to the growing boy's needs or too stingy to buy new clothes, she'd not figured out. For a good while he'd cut a sorry figure. But today, the scraggly teen had transformed into a bearded, broad-shouldered man with new goals and plans. Frieda broke into her thoughts.

"Your father is so nice to train him as a mechanic. Our boy sure has a way with a wrench, not to mention a screwdriver. My, how he loosened the bolts of our dining room table at the age of four. Never mind the pork roast ended up on the floor, Charles said right then that we had produced real talent." Their friend nodded her head in undisguised admiration, her double chin shivering before helping herself to a waffle.

LaRae smiled and turned to her mother. "I brought ingredients from the Indian store by the school. I'm making Indian curry tonight."

Mother's body stiffened. From the memory of ingesting too many of my failures in the kitchen, LaRae thought wryly.

"I already made meatballs. Maybe tomorrow? Please run to the grocery though. The weekly specials expire today and I am too busy to go. But by all means, eat first."

LaRae lifted a bun off the imitation silver platter and savored the traces of cardamom paired with the sweetness of the raisins. A sigh of relief escaped from her mother's lips and Mrs. Stubbs motioned to the porcelain tray. "The cookies are good too. And the waffles."

"No thanks." She stood up and grasped the two-inch thick coupon folder her mother fetched from the bureau.

"Cut out the chili bean coupons from today's paper too. Be careful. Last time you cut into the UPC code and we lost 40 cents on each can. Small things in life make all the difference."

Dubbed the Coupon Queen, Mom had elevated penny pinching to an art form. Every store in the vicinity recognized Mrs. Gunther as a formidable force to be reckoned with. On Black Friday, LaRae had squirmed while shoppers pointed and snickered when her mom undertook negotiations over a toaster with the zeal of a UN representative brokering a deal between Hutus and Tutsis.

She hopped in the car and drove to the grocery but childhood memories stirred, making her feel like she was breaking into hives. Lost in a blur of checking expiration dates and matching coupons to the specials, she remembered having to return frivolous items she'd purchased that were not on the list when younger.

"If you get in trouble again kiddo, I still carry mints." Edna the cashier with frosted hair winked and bagged the loot. LaRae laughed and thought of her former humiliation when forced to return candy.

"Hopefully, there won't be any more returns. But thanks for the comforting treats in the past."

That night they watched Mom's favorite show and Dad brought home Dairy Queen Chocolate Swirls. Afterwards she started to rearrange her room when a knock on her bedroom door brought LaRae out from under her bed.

"What are you doing down there? I bought you a blouse for the upcoming square dance." Her mother pulled a pastel pink shirt out of a Kmart bag. "Don't worry, it was 50 percent off."

"It's the shade of my bedroom walls and linens."

"Your favorite, I know."

My least favorite. Upon returning from summer camp at age eleven, Mom and Dad had surprised her with a freshly decorated room. Though she hated the bland color, their effort had been touching. A decade later, she still paid for her silence. "Thanks, I may not go though."

"You stuffed the bulletin board under your bed?"

"I'm twenty-two. I don't need any more suggestions about careers or dates." LaRae pushed the offending cork board further under the bed and thought of the nursing aide info tucked into the bottom of the kindling by the fireplace. She gently ushered her mother out of the room.

"I love you." She hugged her Mom goodnight and tore the tag off the button-up shirt. $11.99. It was ugly but a bargain indeed.

The next morning she helped with the dusting and maneuvered the rented carpet cleaner around the den and living room. When she offered to wash windows, her mother's eyes turned into slits. "No long walks at the lake and no sticking your head in a book. What is going on?"

"Nothing." She hid behind the curry recipe, chopping onions, sorry to have brought up the windows. Her mother's pride and joy, Mother was a step ahead of the competition in keeping the windows the shiniest. Her window cleaner had a secret ingredient that envious neighbors tried to coax out of her but despite flattery and attempted bribes, Mother remained mum.

Two hours later, the fragrance of curried chicken and basmati rice wafted from the dining room. LaRae lit the handmade candles from a Chicago store and brought in warm chapattis. The newly purchased sari found a purpose as a table cloth and its flimsy turquoise and gold weave fabric added sparkle to the room.

Her father entered with a glint in his grey eyes. "Well, daughter. Dinner smells good this time. I feel less worried."

LaRae giggled and looked back at him through gold-rimmed glasses fogged up from dishing the steaming sauce. "Since traditional home cooking has not worked in my favor yet, I went for bold and adventurous."

They all sat down and her dad blessed the meal.

At the first bite her mother made a choking noise as the spices hit her tongue. "Let's hope the adventure does not make us suffer indigestion."

"There is rice pudding for dessert. I thought something mild might help balance out the meal." LaRae ate with them, then cleared the dinner plates and brought in the sweet treat.

Halfway through, her mother wrinkled her nose and shoved the dessert bowl away. "I prefer the rice puddings of my youth. Lingonberry jam in the center and whipped cream mixed in with the rice. How strange that Indians add licorice to their pudding. And don't worry, Rae. You know I don't waste food. I'll give it to your cat."

LaRae looked at her mother, not sure whether to laugh or cry. Dad patted her back and not so secretly popped a couple of Tums he'd fetched into his mouth.

"So did you call the community college about the nursing degree?" Her mom dropped the question while snuffing out the candles. Ominous silence filled the room.

"I'll be right back." LaRae ran to the bathroom, locked the door, and took a deep breath. The 1960's green tile wall framed the face staring back from the square, unadorned mirror. The face itself was taking on a pistachio tint too, except for the mouse brown, wild waves of hair partially draping the narrow face and angular chin. High cheekbones spoke of her Nordic genes. She stared the face down. *You can do this. It is simple. Paste on a smile. Waltz into the dining room and say: I have decided to become an artist.*

She raked the curls off her forehead and unwrinkled the knotted brow, then marched back in and took a seat. The sari had disappeared and instead her mother's stern face reflected in the polished mahogany surface. It was a jury of two, Mom and her double.

LaRae looked at her parents and smiled with trembling lips. "I signed up for the Art and Theory Practice Major. I want to be an artist."

The room's oxygen vanished. Her mother's left eyelid started twitching rhythmically.

"Did I tell you what happened to my sister Stella, the aunt you never knew?"

LaRae shook her head. Stella was a taboo topic. Mother clenched her hands and stared intently out the bay window at the dead rose bushes.

"Grounded repeatedly for getting into trouble, she ran away to a hippie community in San Francisco where they smoked pot and painted psychedelic paintings. One time we got photos of her living in a yurt like Mongols do in Asia. She ended up pregnant but the child died from a congenital disorder. So the doctors said, but I still think it was the drugs and toxic paint odors that caused it to happen."

LaRae's father put his arm around his wife, patting her shoulder. "Stella was a sweet girl. A little high-strung, yet sweet. Wouldn't harm a fly. Gifted at sewing too; remember she made that crazy quilt out of African fabrics?"

Irritated, Mother shook herself free. "She lived like a bag lady, and I will not see my own daughter go down that path. You know well how it ended too!" The chair toppled when her mother shoved it back and rushed to her bedroom. Soon sobs filtered through the plywood door.

Dad spoke in low tones. "Rae, think about it and reconsider please?"

The next morning, when mom skipped church, LaRae knew she'd caused a Gunther family earthquake. She rapped on the bedroom door, stomach convulsing and entered.

Mother's tight curls were out of place, a serious infraction in her book on etiquette. Her flannel nightgown was buttoned wrong; the pleading look in her blue eyes reminded LaRae of a little girl lost in the woods.

"Mom?" She sat down on the edge of the double bed and gathered her mother's left hand in her palms. "I promise I won't do what your sister did to you." *Even though the idea of living in a yurt is appealing...*

Her mother squeezed her fingers. "I lost Stella. Don't venture down that path. I can't bear the thought of losing you." A tear trickled and fell on the woven cotton blanket before she straightened and reassumed her usual decisiveness. "Go back and change it. I'm trying my best to curtail this wild streak in you. I'm at my wit's end."

LaRae nodded and kissed her mom's cheek then packed her bag and hugged her father before hitting the road to school. It was an uneasy ride accompanied by sputtering and clunking under the hood and a hammering of her heart even louder than the engine noises.

CHAPTER 3

Sun rays spilled over the herringbone wood floor and the utensils laid out on the work bench sparkled in the light. Because a professor had noticed LaRae excelling in an elective pottery class during this spring semester, she was able to plant her rear on the stool in the potter's studio this afternoon. Recognized as "a budding artist," her teacher had granted her unrestricted access to the studio.

As smooth as silk, the wet clay caressed her fingers. She closed her eyes and dug into the grey texture, loving its plasticity and ability to forgive mistakes. Errors and accidents could be shrugged off without panic or scolding. A vase formed between the middle and ring fingers of her two hands. She slowly raised the vessel walls with her newly learned isometric posture over the wheel. A sudden thump against the window startled her and caused her foot to press harder on the pedal. Outside, a bird flopped and tumbled. The twisted mass on the wheel leaned over precariously. With a lightning quick reflex, she tried re-centering the clay by slowing her foot on the pedal, but the vase twisted and crumpled. A wave of sadness rushed through her for the injured bird and the failed clay object. A Bible passage by Jeremiah crossed her mind. Memorizing it had won her an extra gold star in Sunday school.

"The word, which came to Jeremiah from the Lord,

saying:

> Arise and go down to the potter's house,
> and there I will cause you to hear my words.
> Then I went to the potter's house, and there he was,
> making something on the wheel."

LaRae reformed the vase and spoke over it.

> "And the vessel he made
> was marred in the hand of the potter;
> so he made it again into another vessel,
> as it seemed good to the potter to make."

Eyelids shut, she meditated on the words when once again the clay spun out of control, bits and pieces flying across the room. Embarrassed, she gathered stray lumps from the nearby wall and floor.

Is this what had happened to her aunt? Not paying careful attention but recklessly throwing herself into precarious situations? What if God had offered her a do-over but she turned him down? Was that why Stella's life imploded?

Before returning to school last Sunday, Dad had caught up with her in the laundry room. "There are things you ought to know. Your mom and Stella argued over money after your grandmother died. On the Fourth of July that year, Stella passed from a drug overdose. I think your mother blames herself."

LaRae lovingly put the pieces of clay together hoping Stella had let God do the same to her during her last moments on earth. As her niece, LaRae decided to rectify the past. She would prove that excelling in the arts was not synonymous with moral failure or financial ruin. One day her parents would beam with pride at what their daughter achieved and her Aunt's memory would be honored. At that thought, LaRae yielded to the flow of creativity, losing track of time and space, carried along by the winds of destiny—a cotton ball cloud without a care.

"Attention everyone. Notice the natural curvature of the

woman's spine? The sensual tilt of the chin? This drawing is not only anatomically correct, but imbued with emotion. What feeling is being conveyed?" The professor dangled LaRae's sketch between his thumbs and forefingers in front of the class.

"Despair," a student suggested.

"Exactly!" Professor Langschaffen yelled. LaRae's cheeks heated. Fortunate to sit in with the art major class for a live model event, she'd sketched her heart out. But the girl to her left who was selling portraits on Etsy glared at her. And the French guy named Pierre rolled his eyes. *I am infringing on their territory.* Embarrassed by the unwarranted attention, she grabbed her backpack and crossed the campus where patches of tender March grass pushed up through the snow. The fun was over; math, an essay on Al Qaeda, and an anatomy test loomed ahead. One positive aspect of studying in her room was that her mother did not control the thermostat. Feet in mismatched woolen socks, LaRae relished the heat pumping through the vent and dumped a can of tomato soup in a pot, heated it and ate in front of the TV. On a beautiful spring night, she was holed up in the washed out, flannel pajamas she was forbidden to bring back home. A flea market find, with a distinctly male opening at the front, Mom and Amanda had been aghast when she showed up for breakfast in the blue and white striped buttoned top and draw string bottoms.

After finishing the soup she made hot cocoa with organic milk and sipped from the cobalt blue mug she'd made while settling in at her desk to study math. The non-logical axioms on the Web page required more intense initiation than entry into the Zeta Tau sorority. Unfortunately, calculus, her least favorite, was necessary to obtain an official degree. She endured two hours of torture, then got up to stand on her head, legs against the wall hoping the increased blood flow would help her focus. The sudden ring of her cell phone pierced the silence.

She put her feet on the floor, pulled the strings of her saggy bottoms tighter then checked the time. *11:11pm. Mom calling late?* She seized the phone and braced herself for one more harebrained idea.

Beekeeper! People will always want honey. Plus there are big bucks in pollinating orchards. LaRae pictured herself in full beekeeper garb, fumigating hives. But Dad's voice spoke into her ear and head, the normally gravelly sound replaced by a ghostlike tone. "Are you seated, Rae?" She sunk unto the swivel chair. "Listen carefully. I want you to stay right where you are. Do not come home." At her desk, her hands gripped the edge. The sharp corners dug into the flesh of her palms.

She stared at the problem clearly spelled out on page 324: "Thus non- logical axioms, unlike logical axioms, are not tautologies." The words blurred. "Dad! What's wrong?"

Her father cleared his throat and repressed a groan. "Mother was killed in a car wreck tonight."

LaRae was sinking, phone stuck to her ear. "No! That must be a mistake. She is probably in a coma. People in a coma or on ventilators often revive. Let's hope for the best. I'm heading home."

"It happened instantly, Rae. Before the EMTs arrived on the scene."

The strange sound of a lamb bleating filled the room. Rae realized the sound was coming from her. "Where? How?"

"Returning from the Women's Club. Aaron's son hit her. He ran the red light. They suspect he was drunk."

"Your mechanic?" Aaron's pimply teenage son hitting her mom's dent free, polished Buick? Crushing it. And crushing her mother? LaRae wailed as the news sunk in. "No. No! She cannot go yet!" Blackness engulfed her. Low voices murmured, mentioning her name. A hand shook her shoulder.

"Here, take this." Starr crouched by her on the floor. "It's a Xanax." The rim of a glass touched her lips. "I know you don't do drugs. Today is an exception. I'm talking to your father using your phone. He says for you to swallow."

LaRae gulped the pill and let Starr tuck her in, then felt her girlfriend's arms wrap around her as her eyelids shut.

They lowered the formerly energetic body of Mrs. Linda Gunther into the grave on Maundy Thursday. As Amanda leaned into her shoulder and wept uncontrollably, LaRae dug her 2 inch heels into the soggy soil to keep her balance. To her sister's right, her brother in-law Christopher stared at a flock of birds, his hands taking inventory of his pockets until he located a handkerchief. Across the brown hole, her nephew Drew stood like a sentinel, his hand in his grandfather's, wide-eyed at the spectacle unfolding before his five-year-old eyes. Toddler Mickey fiddled with a straw he picked off the ground. Dad hunched over in the suit his budding paunch had outgrown. She recalled him wearing the suit at Amanda's wedding before midlife took its toll on his physique.

LaRae took in her father's anguished features. The scene appeared surreal. Yet, Amanda's tears trickling onto her own tightly clasped hands were wet and real.

When the ceremony was over, LaRae held her sister, stroking her back with no idea what to say. "I don't know how to raise my kids without her! Every piece of advice I ever needed came from Mom," Amanda sobbed.

As Christopher solicitously opened the BMW's door, LaRae watched him tenderly kiss his wife's cheek and stroke her bulging belly. Amanda and Mom had chatted daily, exchanging news, household tips and anything else under the sun. An icy numbness spread through LaRae's limbs. For herself, it was too late.

A steady flow of casseroles, congealed salads, aspics, cakes and cards kept arriving at the ranch house. They filled the garage fridge and food spilled onto the dining table because Mother had maintained a fully stocked freezer. Shocked by the tragedy, the inhabitants of Dresden rallied around the Gunther family, shaking their hands in a subdued manner and offering their help.

They used the rest of Easter break to regroup as best they could. No one had the heart to remove Mother's clothing.

Instead they skipped church and headed to Evergreen Lake, bringing drinks and a complimentary bucket of fried chicken from the Popeyes manager. Even though it had grown a soft layer of moss, their old picnic table was still standing. Except for sparrows twittering and stealing crumbs, they ate in quiet, then got up to walk to the lakeshore.

Sporting Ray Bans and a hot pink Lycra top, Amanda looked hip in her maternity yoga pants. "I remember us picnicking here when I was a senior. I'd just met you and refused to put away my phone, panicked about missing a call or text." Amanda looked at Christopher, drowning in his caramel-colored eyes framed by the silky curved lashes she swore should be illegal on a male.

Drew trudged ahead, alert and scanning his surroundings, informing his grandfather of the danger of copperheads and how to treat their bites.

"You brought a genius child into the world!" Christopher cheered up his still red-eyed partner while carrying Mickey on his shoulders.

"By marrying his father." Amanda leaned into him.

LaRae listened to the repartee and recalled when Christopher, the bright honor student, had asked her out a long time ago. Both members of the Astronomy Club, their excitement mounted at the approach of a rare blood moon. Christopher had invited her to join him for the Friday night football game before they headed to the nearby field to bring out their telescopes. To put it mildly, LaRae had been surprised. Held back from starting school at six, she pictured herself more mature than her sophomore classmates. But she hadn't imagined her maturity being noticed by the best looking senior in school. Was it the start of an intimate friendship or just sharing their common interest in the sky and its constellations, she'd wondered. Either way, the closest thing she had ever had to a date, she'd earned $15 weeding the flower garden and had gone shopping. The green chiffon shirt had matched her eyes and the skinny jeans had been a fashion statement.

Seated in the bleachers, they'd cheered for the Dresden

Panthers, while gobbling chili hot dogs. Amanda, dressed in the red and silver cheer leader uniform, performed jumps. Upon each landing, her sister squealed and waved exuberantly at them. After the game, LaRae introduced her date to her sister on the field. Amanda's face had sparkled with glitter, her clingy top and tiny skirt accentuating her developed curves and tanned, muscular legs. The violet doe eyes were lit with excitement from being tossed repeatedly in the air and beneath the floodlights, her platinum blonde hair positively sparkled. Soon, LaRae ended up relegated to the back seat of Christopher's car and the telescopes to the trunk. She'd listened to her sister's animated conversation, her own voice diminished to a pitiful croak while her eyes stung from repressed tears. These days they all laughed about it. And LaRae had become their "lucky charm". After all, Christopher had cast one look at Amanda and behaved like a moth drawn irreversibly towards a bright shining flame. He was still dancing in its light and warmth.

Trailing behind the flirting couple down to the lake, LaRae tripped over a root. She pushed herself back on her feet again when a tree branch snapped behind her fast-moving brother-in-law, stinging and snagging her wild hair. In pushing it away a blackberry thorn ripped the skin on her forearm and droplets of blood trickled to the ground. Despite the hurt, she pushed through and followed the path her father staked out.

The dark ribbon of I-55 snaked ahead.

"You have to go back," her father had prodded her. "Dresden has nothing for you right now. Finish your schooling. Make your mother proud." How could she make mother proud? That was an enigma she'd been unable to crack. Back on campus, she delved into academia, hoping to surprise family members with a good outcome. But by staring at the whiteboard without words registering or sitting listlessly in the ceramic studio, how could she become a great artist?

Unrealistic. Optimistic. Rebellious. Naïve.

Back in the classroom the following day, inner voices rebuked her choice of major. In addition, inspiration – instead of taking flight, lay at her feet, wings broken. What remained was the daily drudgery of English papers, social studies and the blasted calculus that made her head spin every time she cracked the book open. After class, LaRae entered the dorm suite, kicked off her wet boots and crashed on the purple futon. In the open kitchen Starr's two girlfriends were pouring freshly brewed tea into glass jars to let it ferment.

"Rae, you need a break! Smoke a joint with us; it'll relieve the pressure." Starr sank into the bean bag to her left and took a puff from her doobie before offering it. Her girlfriends joined and nodded approvingly. On the bamboo table candles flickered. A cloud of frankincense incense blended with the aroma of fresh hemp brownies. In a weird way, the odors reminded her of decomposing matter and death.

Trapped in a pressure cooker of thoughts, she considered the offer. Although chemically induced, would she be able to float on the cotton cloud that had carried her along in the studio? All other efforts at regaining equilibrium were failing. She stared at her roommate's outstretched hand; the Gemini wrist tattoo glinted green in the glow of the Christmas lights that stayed up all year. As LaRae lifted the smoking joint, President Bill Clinton's famous sentence, "I did not inhale," crossed her mind. She giggled at the absurdity, her lips closing around the earthy, pungent marijuana when mysterious Aunt Stella flashed on her mental screen. Abruptly, she pulled the stick out of her mouth and drowned it in the steaming coffee cup on the table.

"Whoa!" Starr put a hand on her arm. "You just ruined my Starbucks double tall mocha!"

"Sorry!" LaRae rushed to the front door and descended in the elevator. A wall of rain made her go back up to grab the umbrella off the rack in the hallway.

Starr's husky voice drifted into the foyer. "As tightly wound as a time bomb. I hope she doesn't blow a fuse. The business with her mother's accident shut her down all the way."

As LaRae stormed out the door, wet gusts from the nearby lake hit, tearing the unbuttoned coat open and slapping loose strands of hair against her face. A moment later, another gust wrung her umbrella outwards, ripping away her fragile protection. Oblivious, she forged ahead, face drenched from rain and tears while opposing thoughts sparred like medieval knights with sharpened lances.

CHAPTER 4

As a reluctant winter yielded its grip to an insistent spring, LaRae packed her stuff into the trunk and headed for Dresden. She parked by the curb on Wisteria Lane and took in the ways in which their home had changed. Weeds popped out of cracks in the driveway and beds. Gutters brimmed with rotting maple leaves. When she noticed the row of dead geraniums in the bay window, the dam broke.

Her head landed on the steering wheel, and sobs wracked her body. With a congested nose, she stumbled into the house and found Dad seated in front of the TV. A Stouffer's dinner and a can of Coca Cola sat next to a pack of cigarettes on the folding table. Upon seeing her, he stood up and reached his arms out. They clung to each other. Stoic by nature, Dad's grief was carried quietly and with dignity.

"We can do this. We just have to stick together." She looked up at his glistening eyes.

He patted her back. "Welcome home, Honey. I've missed you so much."

"I've missed you too."

She made her way to the kitchen and attacked crusty dishes too dried out to load into the dated dishwasher. After scrubbing them and even polishing the faucets and disinfecting the countertop, she took a quick inventory of the fridge. A bag of

Wonder Bread and a jar of grape jelly presided next to a moldy package of Swiss cheese. The margarine Dr. Wohler had talked her parents out of using was back in the door compartment. Dad's idea of vegetables was cans of baked beans and an occasional carrot stick. Sighing, she admitted to the necessity of learning to cook. To avoid casseroles loaded with sour cream and mayo, she'd shop at the budding Farmer's Market, grilling lean meats and steaming veggies. Female cunning was needed to get her dad on board with a leaner diet so she'd take a crash course in both topics.

As the month of June arrived, the lack of creativity and the drudgery of cooking, cleaning and doing laundry made LaRae simmer along with the vegetable soups and meats puttering on the stove. At the back of her head Mother's voice corrected the way she dusted, vacuumed and polished. "Straight lines. Go in a circle. Change rags." But like a beaver ready to fell another tree, she attacked chore after chore because the bustle served as a foil to postpone an even more dreadful task.

Finally, one steamy July morning, she faced the inevitable by entering her parents' bedroom and sliding her mother's white painted plywood closet open. The wardrobe smelled of Tide detergent and Downy softener. The rest of the day she sorted through dresses, pants, shirts and sweaters, then realized belatedly that the attic contained neatly labeled summer clothing as well. The garments were bargains from Walmart and JC Penney. An exception was the sky-blue wool dress with the mother-of–pearl buttons made by her maternal grandmother. She thought of how her Norwegian "mormor", or "mother's mother", had become a widow who supported herself by sewing traditional gowns for Scandinavian immigrants and their descendants. Words from Mormor's native language came up as she fingered the seams of the blue fabric. Through telephone calls and weekend visits, LaRae had picked up sentences and fragments.

"Lykke til, vennen min." Grandma's signature phrase of wishing her "good luck, my friend" before exams had settled the

butterflies in her stomach. Though several inches too tall for the gown, LaRae draped it against her body and stared at her long limbed, willowy arms and legs in the master bedroom mirror. *I'll modify it. Make a gown for my first child out of it.* Despite her singleness the thought made her smile.

When Dad returned, they loaded his truck with the clothes and she drove off but braked when remembering her mother's loathing of thrift stores.

"I'd rather be caught dead than shopping for used clothing." Her mom had expressed herself with unusual vehemence when Goodwill opened in Normal. "There is no telling what people did while wearing what you buy. For all we know someone cheated on their wife or committed murder and left dried blood stains on the clothes." Mother had shuddered at the thought. "We may be on a tight budget, but we are not poor church mice."

LaRae smiled at the memory. In order to honor her mother's strong feelings on the issue, she flipped the blinker and turned left to First Lutheran. Pastor Richter, whom her parents had recommended for counseling, would know where to send things. And maybe, if he proved a tad more amiable than he came across in the pulpit, she might also share the anguish about her upcoming decision. After knocking on his office door and being told to enter, she stepped inside.

"Well, hello Miss Gunther! I am relieved you decided to care for your father. I assured Norman you'd do right by your family. That boy sure is eager to settle down if you catch my drift."

LaRae eyed the minister with confusion.

"We are both members of the Elks Lodge. He confides in me. What do you need?" Pastor Richter spoke in low tones but his secretary craned her neck to listen through the open door.

"What do I need? I don't need a marriage broker!" She strode out and headed to the Women's Shelter to drop off the boxes, then aimed straight for the candy aisle at the grocery. Mortified about her outburst and dreading having to apologize to the meddling reverend, she grabbed a bag of dark chocolate truffles when a voice breathing down her neck caused her to jump.

"Girl, you are making me work harder than the FBI trying to track you. No response to texts or voicemails, are you ignoring me?"

LaRae turned and took in the subject of Richter's conversation. The beard had been traded in for sideburns but otherwise Norman was wearing his standard outfit: a Dresden Tiger's t-shirt and blue jeans. Her childhood friend was a hot catch in Dresden, but her heart skipped no beats at the sight of him.

"Delilah is raring to go. I'm all set except my date is missing." Norman flashed her a picture of his recently acquired Korean pot belly pig.

"The big sow? What possessed you to enter her into this year's pig race? I thought you were holding out for Rocket Boy? Think of the awards he has raked in at former fairs." She opened the bag and downed a truffle without chewing. Norman laughed.

"I am proving fat girls can win. Only I'm not doing it without you." It was the boyish beggar look that made her cave. She wasn't intrigued by the tractor pull competition nor dying to attend the rooster crowing contest, but the county fair had nevertheless been a childhood staple. Mrs. Cobb's blackberry cobbler was delicious and the two of them celebrated the wins by going up in the Ferris wheel.

When Saturday rolled around, she brewed a strong cup of tea to fortify herself for a day at the fair, then showered and put on the white t-shirt emblazoned with *Head over Heels for Delilah* that Norman had dropped off. After parking in a rutted field at the Agricultural Center, she joined Mr. and Mrs. Stubbs, who sported the same shirts and in addition carried pink and white pompons. Along with the rowdy crowd of onlookers, they cheered as General Snort, Lancer, Prancer and Delilah tore down the track, trotting towards the chocolate cookie prize. When the winner was announced, Norman swung LaRae in the air.

"We did it once again, girl. You're the best mascot," his mouth approached and smacked her on the lips.

"Norman! How dare you!" she wiped her face.

He chuckled and tickled her waist.

LaRae backed away. "I want to see the 4-H art and pottery now."

"Boring. We need a beer. Don't be a party pooper, Rae."

She sighed. "Okay, buddy. It's your win. The Ferris Wheel first. Let's go."

Two hours later, LaRae walked in the door and flung herself onto

the couch in the den. Dad looked away from the screen. Chuck Norris' gun was smoking as an episode of *Walker Texas Ranger* came to an end.

"I will pay you to come up with a reason for why I cannot attend the pig race next year." Her father laughed. "That bad, eh?"

"Worse than you think. As if the shirt is not bad enough, now I'm getting kissed."

"If you're not okay with that, there's a convenient word called *no*."

She emitted a heartfelt sigh. "I know. It just goes missing every time I need it."

A speck of a Midwestern town like Dresden did not boast an up-to-date medical facility. The 1960's vinyl chairs were permanent fixtures and so was the huge cactus in the window. LaRae thought it strange to put a prickly succulent in a roomful of sick and anguished people, especially children ready to touch anything in their path. She looked at the needles on the four-foot-tall plant and shivered.

Their portly family doctor looked up when the nurse ushered LaRae and her father into his office. An issue of *Outdoor Life* lay beneath a mug of coffee with Elvis's picture on it. A faded baby photo of his son stood next to the phone. LaRae felt gratitude seeing baby August sitting cross-legged on a blanket in white Stride Rites, fake clouds behind him. Now a Nashville resident and aspiring musician, she'd always be grateful to him for inviting her to prom. Though the event itself had been stressful and the dancing awkward, at least she had not stayed home like the loser she suspected she might be.

August's attempt at kissing her that night had been clumsy at best, but she'd appreciated the gesture. With light spilling from the porch lamp, she'd kept her eyes open in order to focus. That's how she'd noticed the living room curtains flutter. *Mom's eye is on the sparrow*—she'd reframed the hymn at the sight of the female outline against the flimsy curtains. Ever anxious about LaRae finding a career and a husband over the years, Mother had done so much more than peek through sheers to help secure her happiness. Even when quiet, she'd hovered on the periphery. But during her senior year of high school, her mother had resorted to prodding.

Dr. Wohler cleared his throat. LaRae jumped and turned to look at August's father. His double jaw jiggled at the effort of getting his words out. "I'm concerned about your insulin level, Mr. Gunther. I'm changing the blood pressure meds to a beta blocker, but you must abstain from sugar." LaRae took in the man's gut and thought of inviting him over for steamed vegetables.

In the car, Dad sat at the driver's wheel then turned and fixed his gaze on her, his mild eyes turning a steely grey. "You are still leaving."

"Yes, sir. But no returning to school before you promise to get with the program. I mean that literally, not figuratively."

The summer kept crawling along at a snail's pace. The daily routine that should have felt soothing had the opposite effect. While doing laundry she blocked the urge to draw, paint and ponder. In the afternoon, she cooked dinner, paid bills and did yard work while waiting for the night when she could finally unleash pent up creativity. But come 8 pm, she slouched on the couch instead, re-reading Jane Austin books and burying her inner artist.

This last day of July the heat index was climbing toward triple digits. LaRae wiped a spill on the counter and refilled her dad's coffee. He insisted on drinking it every morning even though it gave him massive heartburn.

"Come the second week of August, I expect you to hop on up to school. In a few months you'll be ready to apply for jobs. Do you think an artist career will work?" Dad's flaxseed pancake stood untouched, the grass-fed butter congealing at the center. In spite of her improved cooking skills, he barely touched food. "I need you to be able to support yourself."

She looked at him carefully, heart rate accelerating. "Is there something you are not telling me?"

He pored over the open King James Bible. It was weird to watch her father read and mark its pages, the ill-fitting reading glasses from the dollar store sliding down his big nose. The book had gathered dust on the living room bookshelf from as far back as she could remember. Perched over the "Dresden Sun" herself, today's headlines announced a stolen Tahoe had been found at the bottom of Spring Creek with two six packs of beer inside. The tame fox kept eating cat food out of a bowl at the nursing home. A picture of Frieda Stubbs's daughter with her newborn twins lit up the bottom of the page. Being born exactly at midnight was enough to make it to the paper's front page.

But reading did not make LaRae forget her father's words. *God. Is Dad okay?*

As if on cue, he looked up and grinned. "I'm just taking over your mother's harping." He winked. She smiled back.

While undressing that night, she thought of her father losing weight and caught a glimpse of her own skinny body. With its stick arms and legs, it wasn't exactly dating material. She brushed her thick mane, head upside down, and took comfort in the fact that the liquid B vitamins she'd been chugging added luster to her curls. She felt the soft swoosh of her cat against her bare legs.

"You are waiting to snuggle, aren't you?" She tucked herself in under the pale pink bed sheet and thought of her dad cracking an unprecedented joke about his wife. She commanded her taut muscles to relax because her father was just fine. Her cat settled on the chenille coverlet and purred. But instead of comforting her, tonight his steady purring felt more like an increasing rumble.

When waking the next day she put on shorts and a sleeveless shirt and undertook a morning walk around the lake while asking herself some hard questions. *Am I being morbid? Should the living aim to please the dead?* The answer would be no.

But in her head, Mother's voice was alive. Another deciding factor was Dad. The new house was finished and Amanda moving to Normal today. Dad would be alone.

Doing the right thing is the right thing to do. The familiar adage her mother must have translated from the Norwegian language she grew up with stuck with her. Her mother had also frequently said, "A bird in the hand is better than ten on the roof, Rae." That was code for "Settle for something practical within your grasp instead of chasing dreams." This new decision she was about to make met both expectations.

Her mind finally made up, LaRae hopped into the Corolla, glancing at her dingy clothes. Her sister's upscale subdivision sported a golf course and equestrian trail, a far cry from the bungalow Amanda and Christopher had owned in Dresden. Their new three-story brick home was in upheaval. A truck was backing out while a yard crew installed an automatic sprinkling system on a newly sodded lawn. A frail looking man tinkered with the heating and air unit, a walking cane by his side.

"Hi, Sis. You showed up in the nick of time! If I lift anything, I'll end up with a premature baby on this tile. Can you please move boxes?" Her highly pregnant sister, popping her head out of the kitchen, put a protective hand on her abdomen while curtailing Drew chasing Mickey.

"Sure." LaRae dropped the changing table she had picked up

from Toys "R" Us the day before on the floor, then wiped sweat from her brow. A faulty air conditioning unit would make it a long day.

"If one more thing goes wrong, I'm booking myself on the next flight to Cancun for an all-inclusive stay at the Grand Park Royal," Amanda took a sip from a Starbucks Frappuccino placed precariously on a box.

Christopher, who was hooking up a new espresso machine on the granite counter, laughed. "Lady, your man is maxed out because he upgraded every existent feature upon your insistence."

A wunderkind with computers, Christopher had been fortunate to land a great opportunity out of high school. After finding a niche as a software architect, his salary inched well into six figures. LaRae watched her sister waddle over and bump her belly into her husband's six-pack. Standing on tippy toes, she kissed him. "I love you for saying yes. The Miele appliances were a necessity. I need German reliability."

And a touch of luxury. LaRae reined in her attitude and eyed the downstairs chaos when her sister tugged at her sleeve.

"I swear the movers were high on Ecstasy. Look! They dumped my toiletries in the foyer. Why don't you bring the children's stuff upstairs? The majority of the boxes ended up in the library. After finishing, I need your opinion on the nursery."

LaRae started racing up the steps with a stack of children's books when her back spasmed. She groaned. But the thought of the master bath Jacuzzi perked her up. Before heading home for the night, she'd soak in the white marble and shiny brass wonder, buried in bubbles and drowning the sorrow of this morning's decision. It would also be payback for Amanda acting like a slave driver.

Upstairs, she balanced her body against the doorjamb of the nursery, in awe of the hand painted mural of Flopsy, Mopsy and Cotton-Tail when her sister joined in and pointed at a piece of half assembled furniture.

"Do you think it okay to ditch the dingy crib from Mother's attic for the Pottery Barn set? We argued over it. I got real aggravated looking for deals with her. Not to talk of the stores she insisted we visit." Amanda batted her lashes and fixed her with the practiced Bambi stare. "I need you, Rae. I persuaded Mom to let you go to college, but I've realized how indispensable you are. Please don't ditch us when you graduate."

After Dr. Wohler's latest health update, LaRae had waited for the conversation to turn this way. Jaw clenched, she looked out the window nook above a built-in seat that doubled as a toy box. "I'm coming back. I'm changing my major to Secondary Teaching Curriculum. I'll only minor in the arts."

Amanda emitted a scream then squeezed her in a hug that made her ribs hurt. "I am so relieved. You'll be a prim English teacher like Mrs. Meeks. Hopefully you won't end up an old spinster like her too!" Her sister laughed heartily.

LaRae wiggled out of the octopus embrace, tempted to look for a blunt tool. An invasive form of ivy was closing in on her, inching its way into every nook and cranny of her life and mind. *I need weed killer.* But deep down inside she knew no Roundup would eradicate its growth. Because she was its enabler.

Telling her father proved a different matter. The day before returning to the campus they pulled weeds and added mulch around the oak in the back yard. After crouching for a long time, LaRae stretched her lower back and touched a rung on the ladder hanging from the tree trunk, nodding at the structure above. "When you got the materials for this, I assumed you were building a vegetable garden, not a tree house."

"You were in such a state after scrubbing Mrs. Stein's picket fence clean of chalk." Dad shook his head while leaning against the shovel planted in the ground.

"I created art, - not graffiti like that old hag accused me of! I was ten and the Wisteria Lane sidewalk and the picket fence were ideal for a multi colored geometric design." She put a foot on the ladder and climbed.

Her father chuckled. "When Mother confiscated your allowance to pay for blueberry cobblers to appease the neighbors, I decided you needed a hiding place."

With a wave, she disappeared in the greenery. "I'm taking a break in my castle."

"Has the man lost his marbles? Bills to pay and he is building a frivolous fancy." LaRae crouched in the tree house while her mother's words played on rewind. The world map pinned to the coarse wall had the pins and red markings meant to lead her out of the dusty cornfields of Dresden. Pulled out of a National Geographic by the library lady, the woman had advised LaRae to come up with an escape plan from "the pits of civilization." The abode had been a hideaway where exotic and wildly dangerous journeys took place through jungles and tight mountain passes. Dragons got slain and evil got pushed back. While her body grew into puberty, she spent time lying on her back, nose in a book. She never dreamed of attending a prestigious university, yet this was where she had torn open the acceptance letter to Northwestern.

Wild with excitement, she'd sprinted to her mother who was ridding the attic of unwanted items. Grabbing the toaster that only worked on one side, LaRae also seized the opportunity to beg. "This is fabulous news! No offense Mom, but we can't turn this down."

When cajoling had no effect, Amanda responded to LaRae's begging and showed up with the closing argument. "The financial aid is free money for the taking. Plus, Rae has to learn to stand on her own two feet and not be constantly coddled."

LaRae sighed and descended the rickety ladder. The debt she owed her sister would soon be paid back.

That night she told Dad about her decision. He popped the recliner in the upright position and looked intently at her as if searching for signs of discontent.

LaRae activated dormant acting skills. "It's okay. I notified my academic counselor. I still get to do what I love, only on a smaller scale. Plus teaching Language Arts is inspiring," she lied glibly, glancing away from his probing stare. "It's risky to count on the arts only. Demand for art teachers is less."

"Well. Your mom would be happy if she knew this."

Please God in the heavenlies. I need her to know.

"Pleased and relieved," her father added a rare wink.

"I aim to make this house a home again. School will be busy. After graduation, I promise things will change."

Dad patted her hand. "Off you go. Pursue your dreams. I'm fine."

On August 10, she merged onto the Prairie State Highway towards Northwestern, the irony of Dad's words lingering. Determined to exhibit a good attitude for the upcoming semester, she gave herself a pep talk. *Kids will love you. You'll impact lives. Make a difference. Future generations will thank you.*

The campus simmered with high temperatures and activity. Shouts from a football practice and the hum of heavy machinery greeted her. Behind the soccer field a new dorm was materializing. When she walked into the air-conditioned suite of her dorm, Starr threw herself around LaRae's neck.

"I've had a fabulous summer! We sold jewelry in Ibiza. Greek guys are soooo sexy. Wait until I give you the scope on Parthenios." Starr rolled her eyes back dreamily, then frowned. "I hope the universe is on our side. I googled his name and it means virgin, which by the way he is so not!" She laughed, her voice throaty and sensual as usual. "Anyway, it concerns me because he might not be following his appointed trajectory."

LaRae wanted to ask what a girl named Starr's trajectory ought to look like and if her roommate herself was on track, but thought better of it. The question might open up a conversation that would last into the early morning hours. "Really? Sounds exciting. It's more than I can say about the regulars at the Elk Club and Sammy's Bar and Ribs. The barbecue makes up for it though."

Starr knitted her pierced eyebrows. "Gross! Next summer you are coming with me!"

LaRae made her feet find their way back into the classroom. First on the schedule was "Teach Ed 328: Dynamics of Middle

School Curriculum". Because her area of concentration was English, she scooted herself along to the Foundations of Reading and Language acquisition class.

After a couple of weeks of classes, LaRae was not sure whether she cared about making a difference. The required reading bounced off of her, the paragraphs void of meaning. The initial spark of her earlier freshman lectures snuffed, she pored over dry texts and downed chocolate squares while taking comfort in the upcoming student teaching. *Learn to shine. Unformed children's minds depend upon you for enlightenment.* The ridiculous pep talk made her want to both laugh and cry.

CHAPTER 5

On a hot September morning she climbed onto the city bus, armed with a newly purchased nylon briefcase. The air smelled of heated rubber, gum, sweat and liquor. She rode it to the south part of town, watching the surroundings change from department stores and pretty parks to pawn shops, a soup kitchen and a Salvation Army shelter. With a tight grip on her cell phone, ready to dial 911, she strode down a boulevard to the right address. A man in a Cadillac slowed the car next to her and whistled. Without paying him attention, she slipped through the school's metal detectors into a linoleum hallway where sixth graders flirted and listened to *Soldier Boy*. Today's task was part of her Student Teaching requirements and this round of Field Experience demanded she try her hand at presenting a new language arts concept.

A purple nailed secretary with a red wig peppered her with advice while showing her to the room. She took her place up front while the teacher sat in the back. When the students entered, LaRae grinned. Curious eyes checked her out before starting to text under their desks. She launched into the prepared grammar lesson on pronoun uses, trying not to stammer. One girl rocked to the beat of her headphones while another kid put his head on the desk. A couple of troublemakers must have wagered on who would break her first by asking questions not related to the subject matter. Mr. Nelson, the home room teacher, was not intervening but took occasional notes and picked his substantial nose. During recess she ran to the secretary, Elwina, who handed her a caramel with a sympathetic smile.

"Don't you pay them no mind, child. Just dig down deep to find the grit within." LaRae appreciated the advice yet wondered if that was an ingredient her life was short on. In the next class, she observed the teacher but walked the length of the room distributing work sheets to help out. When a boy snickered, she followed his gaze to the cell phone being passed around. Naked pictures. Mr. Nelson heaved his weight off the chair and lumbered down the row to confiscate the device.

When school ended she collapsed on the torn vinyl bench of the bus wondering about the disappearance of her laptop from the classroom during lunch break. Though assured by the principal they were doing anything in their power to find it, her hope remained slim.

"You look terrible." Starr handed her a kombucha. "Maybe it's the mole outfit. You have certainly found an efficient way to go unnoticed through life."

LaRae nodded in acknowledgment and stripped the brown suit off, then with a smoldering look tossed it in the clothes hamper. Grit. It was not something you just bought at the grocery store. That much she knew.

Google the term "grit". Figure out how to apply it. She added it to her mental checklist and flung herself on the bed, burying her head under grandma's carefully stitched quilt. With scraps ranging from velvet to wool and flannel, it was soft and a reminder of the dresses grandma had cut before arthritis set in. Over the next five minutes, three calls beeped in but she refused to pick up. Finally at the fourth call, LaRae forced herself out from the blanket.

"You have eclipsed yourself like that moon thing happening. First you missed the Lamaze birthing class, then the birth itself. My husband tried to breathe with me and passed out from lack of oxygen. My beautiful newborn is colicky. Mickey is hitting the terrible threes and Drew can't tell the letter 'b' from a 'p'. You will be here the week of Thanksgiving, right?"

"Hello to you too, Sis! It's a solar eclipse, not moon. I'm sorry about Wallie's tummy hurting, but I took on a job at Subway. Mom's funeral set Dad back. I will arrive Thanksgiving Day." LaRae listened to the screams in the background.

"Well, Rae. Enjoy your life while we struggle in the trenches." Her sister hung up.

LaRae clamped her jaw shut. Used to incurring the discontent of unhappy Gunther females, she would wait till the wrath blew over. She fumbled beneath the bed and grabbed her green apron and cap. The Subway station in the school cafeteria was awaiting her charismatic presence. As she ran across the square, a crazy thought crossed her mind. *I want a boyfriend.* The wish was so preposterous she told no one except Starr.

Three weeks later while seated at "Earthy Café" she wondered if enlisting Starr as wingman in the new endeavor proved a bad idea. Today's date was well built. Extremely large biceps flexed on and off as he explained in minute detail why anaerobic exercise was indispensable.

I wonder if he does it on purpose or whether it is unintentional. Curious, she made a mental note to Google this question too.

Two hours into the date, Ken had covered macrobiotic eating, slow and fast twitch muscles, as well as which brand of bicycle worked best for competitive races. LaRae sipped the green tea with hemp milk. The menu offered everything from alfalfa sprouts to kimchi. So far not one question was directed her way. The previous guy had been a worse flop. High on weed, he had taken her to a hookah lounge only to run into his ex-girlfriend, which in turn made him go outside to hyperventilate. LaRae had been resourceful, procuring a paper bag to help ease his discomfort. After calling a cab to get him back to the dorm, he cried on her shoulder, leaving a trail of snot on her silk shirt.

As Ken changed the subject to Fantasy Football, she thought

of her very first outing. Cute in a surfer type way, Bobby's eyes had hinted of the Adriatic Sea, his dreamy blond locks luscious. Unfortunately, a nervous tic showed up whenever talk of school came up. His mind had been made up to take off for the beaches of Bali. "Are you interested?" he had asked.

She decided he might shed the tic if his stress decreased. Besides, Bali sounded real nice with palm trees and lukewarm water. "In dropping out? Absolutely," she had quipped. *Let's see what happens now, buddy.*

"Cool." It was the first time she had seen a smile. Dimples in both cheeks added to the charm. "Do you have enough dough for two tickets?"

At that point she hit a dead end regardless of how badly she craved swimming in an endless turquoise ocean.

Tonight, she watched the clock tick above the bar while speculating how to wrap up her third and maybe final date. At least this one came with the bonus of a sprouted salad and vegan brownie. Ken wrapped up the monologue by admitting to winning substantial money for last year's Fantasy Football picks and agreed it was time to move on. He looked stricken when she turned down going to his apartment to do a round of ab crunches together.

"I've taught several fellow students these new techniques. One girl pays me. If you're uncomfortable in my room, we can meet at the recreation center."

She decided to bust his bubble by confessing how much she hated gyms. Shocked, he let her go, pumping her hand in farewell until it stopped her circulation.

On her way back to the dorm, she reflected on the silence on the home front. Her father had missed the weekly phone call. The next morning, she woke up to discover the reason why. Amanda's text lit up her phone during Pedagogy class. *At the clinic with Dad. Please call.*

"What is happening?" LaRae chewed her pinkie finger nail outside the class room door, while pasting her ear to the receiver.

"He keeps on fainting. They found him draped over the hood

of a car at the shop, head on the radiator. He could have cracked his skull!"

"Is the doctor running more tests?"

"He did last Wednesday. It's cancer."

LaRae groaned. Her father would not accept lying in bed. She checked the academic schedule on her phone. "I'm coming home."

The following day, LaRae raced to Dresden. Once inside the house, she sorted the vitamins and probiotics she'd picked up at Whole Foods into the compartments of a pill tray, then performed a quick inspection of the living room. Dust piled up on every horizontal surface. Norman was helping with handyman stuff, but housework obviously passed both men by. LaRae thought back to when the lace curtains adorning the windows were the prettiest snowy white. Today they hung limp and grey, barely disguising the dirt on the bay window. And instead of cheerful, purple and bronze pansies filling the patio pots, squirrels had turned the containers into storage for nuts. She scowled at the gnomes whose faces remained locked in mischievous smiles regardless of what miseries befell the Gunther household. "Ignorant and insensitive!" She berated the concrete figures while moving to the den.

"Dad? You're home? I'm so sorry about the news!" She watched him push up off the couch, a Cubs game was blaring on the television with the noise of the sixth inning. The dark wood paneling and the green carpet made the room feel unnaturally gloomy.

She leaned in, nestling her head on his chest.

"I don't want any drama, Rae. I'm starting chemo and if there are nasty side effects, Norman will drive me. In a few weeks, I'll be right as rain."

She stroked his grey, sparse hair. "You may go bald, but do whatever it takes. Do you want to watch a movie, Dad? I brought new DVDs."

"I'd rather watch a rerun of the Cubs. Norman is swinging by to do the yard. But I am glad to see you." Dad lay down again.

LaRae glanced at the microwave dinner on the coffee table. Judging by their moldy appearance, the enchiladas had been abandoned a long time ago.

"I am making scrambled eggs."

Dad straightened and gave a crooked smile. She picked up fast food wrappers and paper cups and cooked. When Dad sat down at the kitchen table, she noticed more weight loss. Her heart pinched in her chest. Fussing over him, she made him eat the eggs and swallow the supplements. They chatted until headlights pierced through the kitchen curtains and Norman's pickup rolled into the driveway. LaRae retreated down the hallway to her bedroom. This afternoon her white, girly furniture looked dated especially with the ancient Cinderella poster tacked to the wall. Why had it hung here all these years? It was as if the room and she herself were stuck in time.

She could have been a hip teen. If only she'd asked Amanda to teach her the ropes. The moment Amanda toddled into the world, she'd been the cool kid on the block. LaRae still remembered her mom's phone conversation with Mrs. Smith.

"You're asking Rae to babysit? I suggest Amanda. Rae is spaced out. Nothing that time and discipline won't fix, mind you. For now, our oldest daughter is what you need." And so it was that her sister started her career as babysitter supreme. Successful not only with the young, Amanda led Girl Scouts and organized yard sales and even took on auctions. Proud of her oldest offspring, her mother only worried about her sticking her naturally curious nose into other people's business. But on that front, Amanda heeded no motherly advice and instead became a prime source in feeding the local gossip mill. Ever informed on pregnancies, incidents of domestic abuse, and even the fact that Coach Parker secretly dyed his hair once a month at Rita's salon after dark, town folks quickly figured out who to approach for the latest news.

LaRae had been content for her sister to possess the limelight and no pangs of jealousy seized her. Life in the shadows was convenient. Like a snail, she'd grown comfortable inside her little shell. Sticking her head out from time to time, she invariably retreated when the outside climate got harsh.

"Don't be hating!" she admonished herself in the mirror while brushing her teeth. Lately she see-sawed between loving her secluded world and hating herself for hiding. Not well versed in psychology, she nevertheless thought it time to break out. One didn't have to be a shrink to figure that one out. But how did she break out when life's circumstances kept pulling her under? Her father's sickness added one more leaded weight, tugging and pulling her deeper. *I just need to keep my head above water. Forget breakouts.*

Hard rapping on the door shook her out of any introspection. "Rae! We haven't gone out since the 4th of July square dance." With tobacco breath, Norman kissed her cheek before his gaze travelled down her body and back up to her face. "Is this how kids dress in college? You scare me in all black."

"You thinking of getting me a pair of boots and a flannel shirt?"

"I already did." Norman rubbed his brown mustache and pulled off the John Deere cap to slick back his hair. Like his father, he used brut cologne. The smell wafted over and LaRae tried not to grimace.

"Come dancing; I bought you a pair of pink cowboy boots. It's been the hit since you left town."

"Right now my agenda is to get Dad better."

"He said to take you out. You've been cooped-up."

Grudgingly, she changed into a pair of jeans and put on the new boots before climbing into Norman's Chevy.

"We are headed to karaoke night at the Elks Club. Do you have lipstick? The other girls wear lipstick." LaRae shook her head. Since Mom passed, she hadn't bothered with makeup. "Never mind. Just make sure to order a beer. Do not ask for a sissy drink like mineral water or Sprite again."

She laughed. "No worries. I won't ruin your reputation."

Not every Friday, but once in a blue moon a night like this was fun, LaRae concluded while chauffeuring a drunk Norman to the

Stubbs' house. She parked on the street, then supported him to the front steps. He drooled and leaned in for a kiss when Mrs. Stubbs opened the door.

"Oh, the poor boy just works too hard. He needs a good wife to help make things easier on him." Mrs. Stubbs looked at her meaningfully while helping her son in the door.

Of course, Mrs. Stubbs. I can't wait to incorporate a weekly inebriated Norman into my already thrilling and eventful life!

Fortunately, the older woman smiled and waved goodbye, oblivious to the inner thoughts of her son's favorite woman.

That Sunday LaRae busied herself cooking rice and chicken, then noodles and ground beef. After many hours of cutting and stirring, she shut the door to the freezer with a satisfied clunk. Two weeks of simple but hearty meals were stowed away. The chicken was on the chewy side but beat Hardee's and McDonald's. On the way out the door to return to school she pecked her father's cheek.

"I'll be back for Thanksgiving. Obey the doctor's orders." In her rearview mirror she saw his form remain at the front door, his grease-stained right hand still waving as she rounded the bend.

CHAPTER 6

LaRae rushed to the Subway station in the school cafeteria, just missing the foreign student who was exiting the food court headed for the gym. Lars, the Scandinavian student, thought of how his workload had increased. *I need wilderness.* A scowl scrunched his pink cheeked face at the thought of being hemmed in by concrete and brick. He felt like a cold-blooded Atlantic cod dropped into Pacific waters.

Although fluent in English, he'd struggled since May to understand the local accent. The academic terms and trendy lingo of the university campus added another challenge. In the dorm and cafeteria, he listened in on students' interactions. Deciphering his professor's heavy Indian accent in the Engineering Aspects of Groundwater Flow class was easier than getting used to various American accents. Despite the privilege of attending the Environmental Geotechnics' program he wondered if coming to the Windy City was a mistake.

When he decided to study at Northwestern University, he'd felt ready to tackle another culture. Naturally curious and adventuresome, he didn't shun challenges, whether physical or intellectual. He could wield a snowboard expertly and rappel Galdhoypiggen. He navigated open oceans and hooked salmon in parts of the fjord where even his buddies had no luck. He read the Old Norwegian, remnants of Viking language fellow countrymen did not care to understand. During his volunteer stint in Africa he had felt socially adequate. But the campus world at Northwestern had caught him unprepared.

The students were not unfriendly but caught up in seemingly urgent causes. The latest agenda was trying to get disposable water bottles banned from campus. He learned that the hard way this morning when he got busted with an Aquafina bottle while walking to class. Rants and slogans reverberated against the concrete causeway as he humbly dumped his bottle in a nearby recycling can. Posters and banners announced grave concern for the environment. He didn't disagree. In favor of reusable containers and sustainable solutions to waste, it was the hostility accompanying the issues that got to him.

Greenpeace posters demanded an end to whale fishing in Northern Europe. "Should I tell them how delicious whale meat tastes?" he asked as he strode into the gym. Conscientious about nature's resources, and opposed to exploiting, he knew Nordic scientists and biologists worked hand in hand with the fishing industry to not deplete the marine population. It was strange seeing individuals far removed from this reality act hateful towards the industry. Whale meat had been a staple at his home. Accompanied by fried onions and boiled potatoes, for a single mother it was an economical choice.

His mom did not readily accept boxed foods, having more in common with modern "foodies". An eternal optimist, she coaxed the coastal soil to produce cabbages, carrots and beets.

As he lifted dead weights his mouth watered at the thought of Mom's organic strawberries. They would be worth their weight in gold in the school cafeteria. Each June when night remained as light as day, the berries hit their zenith in flavor. The warmth from sun filled days and light infused nights added sweetness to fruit. Served with yellow whipping cream, the berries made for a perfect dessert during the few weeks of summer his rugged country offered.

Lars finished the weights and hopped on the treadmill. Another eight months and he would return to Oslo to finish up the Master's degree. His dream of providing clean water to third world countries would finally come true. Lars smiled at the prospect of ending up in a tropical climate for parts of the year. Did gypsy blood run in his veins? Or perhaps the leftover genetic residue from his Viking roots made him share in their universal desire to explore and conquer foreign shores. Mom teasingly complimented him on coming up with a career that fed his wanderlust instinct. At least his adventurous spirit would serve the populace and not bring terror and harm like that of his Viking ancestors.

Thinking about the future sent his thoughts reeling towards Ania. They'd been inseparable in childhood. But he realized now how solid their friendship was. To be both fully known and loved was not something to be taken for granted but rather a rare and precious gift. His male buddies in their twenties hooked up with girlfriends and acquaintances. Stein, his class mate in high school, had ended up suicidal when a relationship did not turn out. After observing his peers at the university campus in Oslo, he noticed how sexual encounters appeared as normal as going for a jog or downing a beer. It was not lack of female attention but rather his traditional Christian upbringing that held him back.

But Lars preferred to liken his future plans to a well thought out game of chess. Only in this round he reserved the right to plan the moves on both sides of the board. He did so by not feeding into the superficial idea of romance, shunning sappy movies and hype from friends. He also refused the pursuit of skin thin happiness. While wiping sweat from his brow his mind crystallized and he made a decision to follow a safer path. He would choose Ania. A picture formed of how he'd court her while making every effort to remain pure until marriage.

He chuckled, wondering how he came across to others. He was a 25-year-old, male virgin totally inexperienced in the sexual realm. But it was no one else's business. Although abstinence was a tough road, Ania would shed tears when she realized his sacrifice for her. He thought of her spontaneity and mischief wrapped up in innocence. Through escapades and childhood pranks, she had remained his steadfast companion and best friend. The neighbors had learned to watch out for the two ragamuffins - Ania with her defiant smiles and Lars with his not-so-innocent blue eyes.

He thought of their small coastal town, hugging the rocky coast of the Atlantic like so many other towns and hamlets. Lars grinned when remembering how the neighbors rallied when the two of them had hijacked a row boat and attempted to cross the ocean to the neighboring country of Denmark. Since Denmark was five hours away by ferry, they had simply assumed it would take them the same amount of time to row the distance.

Ania had been responsible for provisions and blankets and brought whole-wheat sandwiches with brown goat cheese and Kwik-Lunch chocolate bars. As the man, he secured fishing gear in case they ran out of food. Using the prudence of a ten-year-old, he even brought a compass and "borrowed" an emergency flare. At the beginning it had been smooth sailing or rather smooth rowing. The little wooden boat danced perkily over the swells. But when the breakers of the open sea crashed in, their boat started taking in water. Ania scooped while Lars increased his grip on the oars. It was fortunate when the Coast Guard, put on full alert by his mother had rescued them. After that escapade his uncle Sven sat him down for a heart to heart.

He reminisced while stepping back outside but the breeze from the lake snapped him back to the present. He jogged to the dorm suite, dropped his sports bag and junk mail on the bed and crashed on the couch. With his feet up on the coffee table he relaxed. A gym was a poor substitute for the physical activities of back home. Chopping wood at his uncle's farm took care of the biceps and triceps. Rowing and reeling in mackerel further developed his chest. And scaling his favorite mountain beat the treadmill by far for his legs. He sighed.

Every hilltop surrounding his town had been explored including the remnants of the bunkers and tunnels, vestiges from the Second World War. When his class was allowed to camp out in a bunker he had lain under the Orion constellation, imagining what it was like to have armed German soldiers manning the lookout points. Their goal had not been to keep the local population safe, but to ward off the Allied forces. The occupying force had also put Grandfather in jail because he refused to give up his older brother's whereabouts. The Germans had incarcerated him in Oslo till the end of the war. Meanwhile, the oldest brother had hid in a white tent with other resistance fighters, receiving airdrops from England and instructions on sabotage actions against the Nazis. After hearing about his family's bravery, Lars became a zealous patriot.

And he still was a patriot.

Even though he yearned to travel the world and was doing everything in his power to accomplish that goal, his heart remained rooted in his hometown and country. Throughout Norway's history, the population paid a price for its freedom. Before Germany's invasion, both Denmark and Sweden ruled it. He would never take his country's independence for granted. He'd appreciate it and use it to enable future generations to thrive, continuing the legacy of all the brave males in his line. And Ania, his best friend, would admire him for it. After peeling off his shirt, he fired up the laptop and hammered out a long overdue email to her.

CHAPTER 7

Ania scanned the email from Lars twice then clicked the 'delete' button. Halfway dressed she turned on the swivel stool to study herself in the vanity mirror. Bored stiff in the bedroom of her parents' two-story white-paneled home, she planned on calling Karl, the guy she had met at the disco who told her she had allure. After looking the word up online, she agreed it probably described the traits that intrigued and drew males towards her—her high cheekbones and onyx eyes fringed with curved, silky lashes. Did her fellow countrymen tire of blue-eyed blondes, feeling drawn to her dusky complexion and starker features?

She knew how she had inherited the looks due to overhearing her elderly neighbor and self-appointed town's busybody chatting over the fence with the mailman. The open window had carried the conversation right into her room.

"'Tysker jente'—I knew it from the moment she went out with that soldier," Mrs. Smith's overbearing voice had drifted upwards. *German loving girl? What woman were they talking about?* Ania had been familiar with the term. During the Nazi occupation of Norway there had not only been traitors but local women who fell in love with German soldiers.

"Oh ja, the way she paraded about in nylon pantyhose when the rest of us wore knitted stockings. And her family ended up with double rations of eggs and butter, not to mention real coffee. And then all of a sudden she turns up pregnant and the cat was out of the bag! The doctor refused to see her during her pregnancy and the midwife didn't show up for the birth. And to think we are reminded of this every day now by who is living next door!" The mailman had mumbled a response and changed the topic to the weather.

Ania had sat on her bed while a weird numbness spread to her 12-year-old limbs. When her father got home, she had contrived a school project asking for family history that required specific dates, places and names. Dad had looked as trapped as a deer caught in a car's headlights but Mom had spoken up.

"Let's not dredge up the past. I'll give you birthdays but details will have to wait. I'm feeling sick." Mother had excused herself from the table. It had been hard work stitching the facts together: Grandmother had slept with the enemy but refused to talk about it and instead kept to herself.

Stunningly beautiful, with blond hair that didn't grey like other women's, Grandmother crocheted intricate doilies that covered every surface in her house. It was painstaking and slow work and lately when her eyesight was failing, she continued to work under a large magnifying glass. For a long time Ania had not realized her grannie was an outsider, living on the fringes. After reading history Ania suspected she'd been mistreated after the war. And Mother? As a child had she been harassed for being a product of a Nazi's liaison with one of their town's own daughters?

In Ania's research, accounts of cruelty and ostracism were common and stories of hazing recorded. In order to deal with the stigma, her mother seemed to have done the opposite of her grandmother. Instead of hiding, she had become a member of every civic organization, making herself indispensable to the community.

During her teen years, Ania realized that in tiny towns the past does not always get buried but often lurks underground. Secrets and cover-ups had "protected" her as a youngster. Yet Ania felt relief at knowing her origins. Unlike her closest female relatives,

Ania kept her head high and took pride in her unknown heritage. She refused to cower in shame or hide behind respectability.

She'd confided in Lars. "I already know. It does not change who you are," he had said while fixing her with his clear blue eyes.

But the truth had changed who she was. Ania stretched in front of the mirror. The long, slow, sensual stretch ended in a pose. Had Grandmother been seduced by the same kind of entrancing, dark eyes that stared back at her? Had the attraction been so strong that she had thrown all caution to the wind, including her reputation? Perhaps she believed the soldier would whisk her away to some Bavarian castle to live happily ever after.

When the German forces retreated and she found herself pregnant, what did she do?

In her research Ania had discovered that several thousand Norwegian women had become pregnant by German soldiers. Many had been put in Nazi institutions where they received obstetric care and their children were well nourished. The multiplication of Aryan offspring had been a project endorsed by the Nazi authorities where soldiers were encouraged to impregnate Nordic women. Shuddering with disgust, Ania felt relief that her grandmother had been rescued from this fate at least.

Studying her features, she wondered if generations of her own flesh and blood were still in Germany. When anyone brought up her looks or the past in high school, Lars had defended vigorously.

Today that thought was not appealing. Her childhood buddy spelled security. Stability. Solidity. But she didn't need rescuing. *I am strong. I'll show the world what I'm made of.* With that thought, a slow smile curled her heart-shaped lips.

Karl had a point—not only did she have allure, but she was definitely her own woman. Unlike the other females in her family, she wouldn't cower to anyone with a long memory. The new red dress set off her dusky skin tone. Why not accent and highlight the already existing allure?

Although the circumstances may have been sad, she had been

given assets that were the envy of her girlfriends. Wearing her new dress, paired with the right lipstick and new wedges, she was ready to take on anything. And anyone. A new text message from Karl lit up her phone: *Hola! It is salsa night at Bryggen. Coming? Forget hip hop, girl. What about trying out the new bar at the dockside?*

Ania giggled. Maybe with this undetermined, exotic blood running in her veins she'd be a natural at salsa moves. There would be no way of knowing unless she tried. Tossing her head back, she picked up her mobile phone from her vanity again and accepted.

Life was short and meant to be savored, moment-by-moment. She refused to pine away in this dreary town while Lars got to experience all kinds of excitement. *I need to create my own ticket out of this place*, she thought to herself as she headed for the shower.

And that ticket for sure would not lead her to some African mud hut or Asian village with indigenous people begging for help to drill for water and such. No, her idea of water was a steamy Vichy shower followed by a Swedish massage at the trendy new spa in the neighboring city. It was time to shake the dust off her feet and hop on new opportunities. With luck, she might just end up in a luxurious villa on the mountainside above that city. At night, the many lights below would twinkle with invitation and by day the sparkly view of the Atlantic Ocean could be enjoyed from a heated infinity pool.

Contrary to Lars' seriousness and rigid outlook on life Karl was eager to please and ready to have fun. The latest rumor had it that in addition to possessing a well-padded bank account he owned a villa high up on that exclusive mountainside. Anyone could find the energy to learn intricate salsa moves with that kind of motivation.

CHAPTER 8

"Dad is reacting to the chemo, but he has forbidden you coming home," Amanda reported. "You must keep your focus, he says."

LaRae obeyed and rushed to sell Subway sandwiches, garnishing them with an assortment of olives, onions, and tomatoes, topping them off with a fake smile before sleeping and rushing to class again.

While the lecture droned on, LaRae's mind clocked the hours till she could escape to the studio. When she finally sank onto the studio stool, the sensation was bittersweet. Sweet, because spurts of creative juices surged through her body. The surges enabled her hands to perform works that elicited compliments from her fellow students and even teachers. Bitter however, because it was too short a time, making her feel like a soaring bird let out on a tether only to be locked back up again. The sculpture assignment tickled her because it required longer periods of time in the studio.

"You will form your own head. Choose the clay—red earthenware or gray stoneware. Neck, shoulders and head only. I'll let you come and go for this project. The studio will be open," her ceramics instructor had specified at the start of the semester. As afternoon rays inched across the workbench, LaRae pulled out the partially shaped block of grey clay, exhilarated by the solitude of the place.

While working intensely, she pulled the stool closer. The project was due at the end of November. Soon, her face became muddied and stiff from the drying clay. Familiarizing herself with her own facial features, she kept on touching it while forming the mass in front of her. By casting frequent looks in the mirror and consulting the profile pic that was laid out on the worktable she corrected the emerging features.

Is the nose too narrow? No. The upper lip needs filling in. She grabbed a moist piece of clay and rolled it between her fingers while humming ethereal Enya-like tunes until her knotted shoulders relaxed. *The neck needs a more graceful curve.* She gripped the pottery knife and shaved layers of clay away. The next hour was spent nit-picking until she was finally ready to put the last touches to the bust. As she backed away to inspect her work, sudden giddiness filled her. Alone in the room, she talked to the head facing her with lifeless but open eyes.

"Live! Breathe!" She caressed the cool clay shoulders and stroked the curls she'd so painstakingly carved out. "Laugh! Dance! You can be magnificent," she whispered into the carefully crafted ear. "I am your creator and I give you permission."

Coaxing it to life, she threw her head back and laughed. But the sudden move caused the stool to slip out from under her. With a bang it crashed to the floor. She bent down to straighten it, but froze. Out of the periphery of her eye she noticed a tall male planted at the center of the room. A very blond haired, blue-eyed guy with broad shoulders and sturdy legs was looking at her. And by looking she meant not just casually looking, but intensely staring. Wide eyed, she stared back, feeling her pupils dilate and her heart hammer. It was as if he was plunging in deep, way below the places people were allowed to peek into. Then he shook his head.

"I, I am so sorry," he stuttered. "I did not mean to disturb you."

Mortified and feeling blood rushing to her head, she stood up on shaky legs. The back of her head felt close to exploding and she wanted to scream at him: How dare you!

Almost tripping over the stool, she ran past him into the hallway and took shelter in a doorway around the corner. Remaining concealed, she waited until he exited. Only then did she return to drape the sculpture. Out of all the rude things to do! Mortified, she swore to herself to avoid the guy at all cost in the future.

Over the next few days, her anger churned and she tried to forget about the incident. But the memory stuck with her and would not be forgotten. In the end the episode felt like a movie replay stuck on rewind. The great surprise she had felt was not only in being seen and heard by a total stranger but especially in a private and unguarded moment. The other surprising aspect had been the way she'd expressed such intense emotion. Emotions that apparently ran as deep as the hidden depths of the ocean. The passion that surfaced had felt like an irrepressible life force asserting its creative powers through her hands and lips. And weirdly, the budding recognition of this side of herself seemed intimately intertwined with the look that had been cast her way.

The awed stare that felt like unadulterated admiration had jolted her to the core. And had made her run. Run from herself and run from him. As the days passed and very much against her will she found herself drawn towards those blue eyes again. And the chiseled cheekbones and firm lips. And blond hair standing slightly on end, probably from him tousling it with his hands.

Much like a watchful scout, she started scanning her surroundings, telling herself that avoiding him at all cost was a necessary safety measure.

Then one day, while galloping down the hallway to the studio, she saw him. Peeking at him secretly, she watched his determined gait, his Fjallreven backpack slung nonchalantly over his broad, right shoulder. Before long she figured out which time of day he passed by. The peeking grew into a habit until one day she did the very thing she had promised herself not to do. Not prodded by anyone, LaRae took the initiative and walked right up to him.

"Hi!"

The young man in front of her looked up abruptly and seemed surprised.

"Oh hello. You are the girl from the studio."

"That I am," she looked him in the eye. "And who might you be? Someone with an appreciation for the arts?"

He nodded while his face turned a becoming shade of pink. She thought blushing males were passé, something that only took place in Victorian novels with namby-pamby, insecure men. On this particular specimen of a man though, she found it rather endearing.

"Lars from Norway," he said with a lilt to his voice, reaching out his hand for her to shake.

"And I am LaRae from America," she responded tongue in cheek. The pink shade deepened, but he smiled.

"Pettersen."

"Pardon?"

"My last name is Pettersen. It's kind of like having Smith for a last name in America. I am here to study this year."

She shook his hand, enjoying the firm, steadying grip. "You really caught me in the act the other day." She tried to appear casual.

"I know. I apologize." He lowered his backpack and stared at her face. "I think I know who you are."

Alarm filling her, she looked at him. "What do you mean?"

"I saw your work displayed in the art studio last summer. Only I didn't know it was you until now. I remember the name. The artist signature on the paintings." Shocked, she looked at him. "Your paintings stood out. I liked them. That's why I remembered. LaRae. Let me see; I know it is a German name. Gunther, right?"

Mutely, she nodded.

"Again, I'm sorry if I scared or embarrassed you the other day. I happened to see you working through the cracked door. Not thinking, I must have stepped inside. I was intrigued by your 'joie de vivre!', as the French call it. Your joy in living," he paraphrased for her.

Right there in the crowded hallway, LaRae surprised herself by laughing out loud. His words shocked her to that extent. This Nordic man had seen her as a joyful, creative and apparently attractive human being? Flabbergasted, she tried to recover.

"Well. It's nice to meet an admirer." She shot her hand out to him, thanking him. He grasped her hand and studied it carefully, turning it over slowly in his somewhat calloused hands. Then he proceeded to study the inside of her palm. LaRae felt her face heating and blood rushing slowly to her ears.

"Such gifted hands," he murmured. LaRae wondered briefly if he were going to lift her hand up to his lips and kiss it just like the gentlemen in her Victorian fiction. Instead he held her hand a little longer while squeezing her fingers. Looking down at her with his piercing blue eyes, he said in a penetrating voice: "Promise me you'll not let your talent go to waste?"

LaRae remained immobile. It took a while for the words to filter into the recesses of her mind and even longer to trickle down to the guarded places of her heart. They were unexpected, unfamiliar words. She felt embarrassed, yet strangely at peace. Something inside of her heaved a big sigh as if saying: I can rest now. That something kept on uncurling and unfurling. She smiled a tremulous smile. Lars smiled back.

Right then, she decided it should be illegal to own such a splendid display of even teeth. Fleetingly, she wondered what the Norwegian diet did for teeth. Was it the reindeer meat or the raw cabbage they ate for a snack? Musing and remembering snippets of conversation from her grandmother, she checked his teeth again.

"Do you really eat reindeer?" she blurted out.

"Pardon me?"

"Oh, sorry. My maternal grandmother grew up in your country and told me stories." She felt flustered and was definitely blabbering.

"Can I take you to the cafeteria so we can discuss the dietary customs of my people over a cup of coffee? Since coffee seems to be a universal beverage?"

LaRae chuckled and nodded her assent. Lars slung his backpack over his muscular shoulder and grinned while leading the way. She followed with trepidation, while two conflicting thoughts ran through her head: *Am I a naïve groupie joining his flock of admiring girlfriends or a desperate Goody Two Shoes forced to hunt down a man to get attention?*

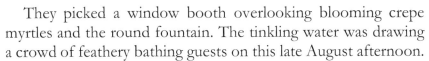

They picked a window booth overlooking blooming crepe myrtles and the round fountain. The tinkling water was drawing a crowd of feathery bathing guests on this late August afternoon.

"So tell me about your name. Is it French?" Lars bit into a sandwich.

Embarrassed, LaRae shook her head. "My grandmother insisted on naming me and my family let her." Sipping steaming tea, she continued. "Known for being a highly sensible woman she deviated from common sense when naming me."

"How so?"

"First of all, she didn't know any French. But watching her favorite movie, she got it into her head that LaRae was the main character's name. She insisted on spelling it in two words. It means absolutely nothing."

"I'd have to disagree with you on that. Since I know a little French, the La word is actually a definitive pronoun used to highlight a feminine noun. Just as if in saying 'the car' or 'the house'. In this case it would indicate a specific Rae as in The Rae."

She looked at him incredulously. "So you mean I have actually been The Rae all this time only I haven't known it?"

He smiled smugly at her and nodded. "Apparently so!"

After a moment of studying each other's faces with a serious mien, they burst into uproarious laughter.

"Wow! This is life changing. I've finally figured out who I am."

"The one and only. One of a kind. I'm surprised you never knew how special this is."

"It took your brilliant insight. I am inclined to feel gratitude towards my grandmother now."

"Me too," Lars concurred while his gaze swept over her. Before getting up and leaving, her new acquaintance looked at her uncertainly.

"I have a girlfriend in Norway," he confessed. "But I'd like to get to know you better. If that seems unfair to you I really understand."

LaRae sighed and teeter tottered. Friendship seemed safe and appealing. Could she bridle her heart?

"How about I show you Chicago?" she ventured. Standing up, his eyes crinkled at the corners. He squared his shoulders and straightened his back. "I brought my exploratory back pack from home: my Swiss army knife, compass and even emergency food rations. You are on, Miss LaRae!"

"I am so relieved you're equipped for the Urban Jungle. Do you happen to have a machete and battery-operated flashlight just in case?"

He smiled triumphantly and pumped his fists. "Better yet, I've got these and a solar light. You wear it strapped around your forehead and it lights up your night."

"Phew!" she sighed with exaggerated relief. "Then my simple contribution will be a tour guide book and American dollar bills. We use those instead of glass beads and such for bartering in this jungle. Before we take in culture let me show you the Magnificent Mile. For that expedition, it would be good to bring a square of plastic too," she added, waving her first ever credit card in the air.

CHAPTER 9

Saturday dawned, wrapped in a cloak of fuzzy fog.

"September can fool you. Deceptively warm one minute then switches to bone chilling cold." *I sound like a weather forecaster or an old worried maid. But what do I talk about when a super handsome guy accompanies me on North Michigan Avenue?* LaRae wondered.

They meandered down the sidewalk while she pointed out the Wrigley Building skyscraper and the neo-gothic Tribune Tower. Lars craned his neck. "Impressive. I'd like to rappel it."

LaRae giggled and kept on walking.

"Schwarz is one of the oldest toy stores in our country." LaRae stopped in front of Macy's department Store. "It's inside."

A tin soldier greeted them with a smile. "Are kids—how do you say it? Hula hooping?" Lars asked.

"Yes. Let's join in. I'm a rock star at it. Norway won't beat the United States in this game." After winning the competition, LaRae led Lars onto a piano laid out on the floor where the 24 keys were big enough for people to plant their feet on them.

"Play me a tune," she begged.

After a few missteps Lars caught the hang of it and an unknown melody filled the space, drawing toddlers and adults. "Our national anthem," Lars said and bowed to the applause.

When they exited the store, LaRae tried fitting a three-foot stuffed animal under her arm.

69

"Thank you for shelling out the bucks for this fierce creature! How come you knew I desperately need a lion in my life?"

"You look like that kind of girl."

"Ahem, someone in need of a strong defender?" She examined the lion mane and glass eyes.

Lars looked puzzled. "Is that what you think? On the contrary. I see you ready for adventure. Exploring the vast savannas of East Africa. Crossing the Amazon under duress. Climbing Mount Kilimanjaro. Or perhaps I should have picked a polar bear to spur you on towards our colder latitudes?"

She laughed, then sobered. "Truthfully, adventure is the last thing on my mind. But maybe you're able to peek in deeper and see things I can't. At any rate, I'm starving. How about a Reuben on rye?"

"Since my only notion of Ruben is the famous artist, please explain that suggestion."

"It is a sandwich they make at this traditional Jewish Delicatessen." They stepped into the 1950s-style diner. Loud customers relaxed in the heavily fish and meat scented air, seated on vinyl and chrome furniture eating out of plastic baskets lined with checkered blue and red paper. Beneath the glass-fronted Formica counter, smoked salmon, cabbage dishes and blintzes were on display.

Lars inhaled. "Ah. I dream of liver pate and pickled beets, but I will model adventure for you by getting the Reuben on one condition."

"Which is what?"

"You commit to trying a new dish, too." After selecting from the menu, Lars suggested seating by the window. They observed people passing by and invented stories based on their looks and behaviors till the food arrived.

"I beg your pardon but that woman is not rushing to give birth," LaRae chuckled. "She suffers from an acute donut addiction."

Lars wiggled his eyebrows and bit into the sandwich before taking a sip from the tall glass. "This is the strangest combination ever."

"You mean hot sauerkraut, corned beef and a chocolate milk shake?"

"Exactly. I'm eating dessert and dinner at the same time. No wonder they named this place the New World." He took another bite before looking over at her untouched basket; "How is 'gefilte fish' from the Old World?" She saw him wink before she shuddered.

"Awful."

"Here. Let's trade dishes." Unable to move, she watched him slide over half his Reuben and then devour her meal.

"So, Miss LaRae. Do you have a boyfriend?"

"I do."

"Oh. What's he like?"

"He is half-Persian."

"Really? And half what else? American?"

She nodded. "American alley cat."

Lars threw his head back and guffawed. "I see."

"My parents got him for my birthday from the local animal shelter. I miss him being with me, especially since Mom died."

"Then I hope he will be the most faithful of boyfriends and that you'll be reunited soon!" Lars squeezed her hand.

They lingered and chatted, arguing over whether cats or dogs make the best pets. When they hopped on the bus, Lars thanked her for the excursion.

"I have a surprise. Since you paid for our meal, I'm using my meager funds to introduce you to the Adler after Dark. Is tonight good?"

Lars nodded. "If it is about the universe, I'm a big fan."

They switched to the metro, then raced and arrived out of breath for a planetarium lecture on The Milky Way. A 3D panoramic show followed. It made LaRae deliciously dizzy and feeling as if she'd been airborne.

"Our tickets include hors d'hoevres and wine. Do you want a bite to eat?" LaRae offered.

"I am a man. I never turn down food." Lars seized her elbow

and gently steered her towards the buffet line.

After enjoying the refreshments, they headed to the ivy-covered Duane observatory built into a grassy slope overlooking the lake. "I dream of seeing the stars from the vantage point of Northern Africa," Lars confided. "The best night views are in the Sahara desert."

They ducked into the oval concrete structure.

"Wow. This is a 20-inch reflector, and picks up 5000 times more light than our eyes," Lars informed while continuing to describe the Sahara. "I'm considering a camel ride excursion guided by the Berbers. Participants camp in Bedouin tents. Surrounded by sand dunes, all you see at night is the campfire and incredibly bright stars. Sometimes an astronomer brings a telescope and accompanies the tour. At the right viewing time and with proper equipment, even craters and mountains on the crescent moon become visible. Go on up, LaRae," Lars nudged her.

Climbing the few steps, she looked up into the sky. The view was not spectacular and Lars's elaborate description was distracting her.

"On this particular excursion I read about, the instructor uses a powered laser to point out Orion and Gemini. Tourists even report seeing the rings of Saturn." As she ascended the last step, Lars steadied her, his eyes glittering with excitement. Then he climbed up and gazed into the lens. "Great idea to come here. This is a treat. Anyways, the Berbers play music using drums and a one string fiddle while the cook serves Tajin chicken."

They walked out into the night, and LaRae's stomach fluttered. Her mind had her dressed in Bedouin garb, leaning comfortably against someone's hard chest while mysterious constellations winked mischievously at her. A strong, familiar hand materialized out of the dark to feed her the ethnic chicken dish. Then it satisfied her thirst with a sip of tea from the kettle resting over the fire. For a treat, the hand proceeded to slip sun ripened, succulent dates between her lips. She sighed out loud and looked guiltily at her companion. But descending darkness encapsulated her, gently concealing her flushed cheeks and longing eyes.

Though she still rushed to attend classes and worked on Monday and Tuesday night, LaRae did not avoid her phone any more. She received health updates from Dad and after verifying the facts with Dr. Wohler and Amanda, joined in the cautious optimism. Another reason for keeping her phone nearby was so she could hightail it to the cafeteria in response to texted invitations to "catch up".

Today was an off-campus outing, and they sat on the train from Evanston discussing whether they should stick with the plan of going to the Lincoln Park Zoo. But a pesky Nor-easter made them opt for the snugness of the Sears Tower. They emerged from the station and marched at a brisk pace while Lars described his conquest of the Gladhoypiggen Mountain in detail. It had been an arduous task of rappelling and climbing. His group had traversed glaciers and climbed the northeastern ridge while struggling with shortness of breath and unexpected cuts and bruises.

"My Alpine climber friends and I chose to scale the most challenging side of the mountain. For other visitors there are easier ways to access the summit. A stone hut sits atop the ridge and they serve hot drinks. You could pick the easy road and still enjoy the sight and a cup of cocoa," he teased.

"I'll never be that desperate for a hot drink," LaRae sighed, then rallied. "In my neck of the woods we scale heights using something called elevators," she instructed, proving her point as they ascended to the 103rd floor of the Sears Tower in mere seconds. "Hope your stomach isn't too queasy with the rush of the speed? They say if you jump as the elevator reaches the top, you float for a second. My classmates grew up coming to Chicago for Cubs games and sightseeing."

Stepping out, she read from the open page in the guide book: "Opened in 1974, the Sky Deck attracts more than 1.7 million visitors annually who enjoy views up to fifty miles away and spanning out to four states."

Posing as Miss Know It All, she was showing off, not admitting that before meeting him she hadn't found the courage to explore the city. Behind Lars, Lake Michigan looked grey and stormy. But with excellent company even this bitter cold day sparkled.

"I dare you!" Lars displayed a mischievous grin and pointed his right index finger to the Ledge.

LaRae consulted with the book. "The Ledge consists of four glass boxes that extend 4.3 feet outside the tower, at 1353 feet above the ground. With reinforced glass on the floor, one is surrounded by an open view."

She looked at her companion, then over to the glass cubicles protruding out over the sharp edge of the building. "My knees are wobbly at the mere thought. But after you bragging of your feats, I'll prove I'm not a total wimp."

Gingerly, they both stepped onto the 1.5-inch thick, tempered glass floor. The view was mesmerizing. LaRae steadied herself against the transparent wall. After perusing the horizon she glanced up at her fellow adventurer and found his gaze riveted on her instead of the bird's eye perspective. Self-conscious, she laughed.

"Is there leftover spinach in my teeth from our salad?"

He shook his head. "Will you do me a favor?" he asked.

"Maybe. As long as it does not entail climbing that Norwegian mountaintop of yours," she cautioned. Visions of dangling over the sharp edges of Galdhoypiggen, Europe's tallest mountain, did not appeal. 8100 feet above sea level, compared to the mole hills of the Midwest, for the few brave souls who undertook the climb it was indeed a feat to boast of. Lightheaded and short of oxygen from listening to his story, The Ledge was doing nothing to improve her frame of mind. "What's the favor?"

"Please remove your glasses?"

She stared at him, dumbstruck. "Is there something in my eye?"

"Yes," he answered quickly. Resembling a gentle giant, Lars leaned over her and lifted off the gold-rimmed glasses. She stared into his blue irises, containing specks of grey and hints of ice. She thought of his forbears, crossing the Atlantic Ocean in their conquests of foreign shores. Leif Eriksen had made it to America a long time ago. This modern explorer in front of her seemed determined to plunge into the foreign shores of her soul.

"I just knew it."

"Knew what?" she asked, alarmed.

"Your eyes are a rare shade of emerald, with traces of warm amber."

"Upon lingering, are they full-bodied with hints of juniper and sage?" she quipped back, not knowing how to respond. "You sound like you're describing a vintage wine," she added weakly.

"Maybe I am? And wine deserves to be tasted, just not taken in visually." Lars wet his lips with his tongue. "It should be ingested, left to linger on the tongue with the senses of the palate given free rein to take in texture and flavor."

"That's excellent language for not expressing yourself in your native tongue." Her voice sounded shaky to her own ears.

He sighed. "If these eyes are the window to your soul, LaRae, then God help me!" He turned towards the city and she heard him mumble. "I may just have seen the most beautiful soul ever spotted. Right here in this place. The view surpasses what's in front of me. Even our national mountain." He leaned his forehead against the glass.

LaRae retreated and fingered her backpack with trembling hands when she realized her body was shaking. It must be true the tower moved on windy days.

"How about we top off today's exploration by hanging out at the zoo anyway? The primates and bird areas are indoors," she asked in as chipper a voice as she could muster.

"Yes, please distract me by showing me the apes and baboons. They may make me feel at home, familiar company and all that."

She laughed with relief. Another dangerous moment had passed. They were buddies again. She strapped on the rucksack and pushed the down button. Who did she think she was? Across the Atlantic, Lars' girlfriend was pining away for the delectable morsel rubbing shoulders with her in the descending elevator.

Tiny stick figures straggled and tumbled as they pushed against the Tuesday afternoon blizzard pounding Chicago. Students and professors exited the lecture halls and rushed down icy steps to cars buried in snow. With melting snow still trickling down her spine and a drippy nose needing attention, LaRae huddled in the school cafeteria while watching the fight against the elements outdoors. A fragrant mug of chai warmed her palms while she sorted through photos to pick a portrait subject. She fingered a candid where her mother's ironed shirt had been traded in for a yellow summer dress, and her stilted, stiff camera smile exchanged for one showing the crooked eye tooth she normally tried so hard to conceal. A noise made her jump as a laptop slammed to the table. "Lars!"

"You look like you need a treat. Did pedagogy class bring you to tears again?"

"Yes. Please engrave *killed by boredom* on the epitaph."

Lars smiled and studied her pictures. "It's terrible you lost your mother so abruptly. My mom is the most important person in my life."

"It was horrendous. But I am curious about your dad."

Lars raked his scalp, flipping snowflakes off his golden hair and pulled out a chair. "My father's ship went down at sea. He was a mechanical engineer employed by a shipping line and worked on different vessels. His ship got caught in a tropical storm. It was highly unusual, but they shipwrecked. My father was not among the survivors."

"How old were you?"

"Two. I don't even have a memory of him. The only thing I vaguely remember is him singing to me. Or maybe that is just my imagination. He had a beautiful baritone and sang solos in the community choir. My mother insists it's how she fell in love with him."

"Tell me the story, please?"

"Not without caffeine, woman." She watched him stride easily to the counter, shoulders squared and head held high. When he turned sideways and winked, a funny tingle rushed through her belly. She turned to the window, hiding any telling pink.

"Here. As Mother says: let's put some meat on those exquisite bones of yours."

"You asked them to heat the apple pie?"

"I also insisted on real whipped cream instead of Cold Vip."

She giggled. "It's called Cool Whip." He sat down and spoke.

"This is how the story goes. Every Christmas Eve the church choir performs Handel's "Messiah." In 1978 there was not a dry eye in the room after Dad sang. At the reception afterwards, my mother went straight up to him and introduced herself. He thanked her later because he was unbearably shy around women. And admitted he didn't possess the courage to speak to anyone as lively and pretty as her." Lars stretched kinks in his neck, then sat down at the other end of the booth.

"What a romantic story! Any recordings of his performances?"

"Sadly no. But Uncle Anders and Uncle Sven keep his memory alive. So anyway, my mother raised me and never remarried. I guess she made me her life project."

"I give her an A for her accomplishment! In my opinion, she was definitely successful." LaRae patted his hand. Her mind drifted off as she thought of how she'd been her mother's life project too. While all of mother's pies and breads took the shape of the forms and pans they got squeezed into, her daughter's genetic recipe had gotten mixed up. Despite her parent's Herculean efforts she'd remained a misfit.

"Sorry, I lost you. I did start to—how do you put it? 'Gab about child rearing do's and don'ts.' Another pet peeve of mine," Lars said.

"Wow, you have the gift of gab too? There is no end to your talents."

The man across the table threw a sugar packet at her. "My mother gave up her fast advancing career in the city, returned to my father's hometown and included my uncles in my upbringing. They were the ones who taught me how to fish and understand boat safety. I learned to sail. They also took me deer hunting and rock climbing."

"And encouraged you to become a hard-core daredevil. No wonder I can't impress you when exploring the humble state of Illinois."

"That's not to say I don't find other things impressive," he murmured while scrutinizing snow flurries performing a crazy whirlwind dance.

"Really? Such as?"

Lars kept glancing at the swirl, a faraway look in his eyes.

Snowdrifts were piling up the window by their seats, forming a dividing wall between them and the outside world. LaRae felt snug. The lights were dimmed and people's voices drifted lazily around them, weaving and enclosing them in their own little cocoon.

Lars redirected his focus to her. "You."

"As in me, LaRae?" she asked after a protracted silence.

His face opened slowly into a big grin. "Exactly and precisely. Very astute and observant. As in you, Miss LaRae."

They shared childhood stories. When they got up to leave Lars reminded her of his upcoming plan. "Be ready by 8 AM the first Sunday in December. No lounging in bed. Dress casual, but nice. And in the meantime: Happy Thanksgiving!"

"Happy Thanksgiving to you too!"

Lars leaned in and kissed her cheek, emitting a scent of cedar and apples and a strong dose of something she craved badly.

"Adventure," she trilled into the wind a few moments after they went their separate ways, raising her hands to embrace the storm.

She packed and grocery shopped for the Thanksgiving meal the next morning then headed down I-55 reminiscing about her and Lars' outing to the Botanical Garden's orchid room. All of a sudden a tractor trailer cut her off, she veered and screeched to a standstill on the shoulder.

"These bald tires are killing me! So much for being a mechanic's daughter," she pounded the steering wheel and decided that although unsexy she'd request new tires for Christmas. An hour later, she wound through their neighborhood's brightly lit homes with pumpkins scattered across front porches only to pull up to a deserted looking house.

Inside, the house was cold; she pushed up the thermostat and switched on every light before poring over her mother's hand scribbled recipes. By noon the kitchen had transformed into a steamy sauna and her father had arrived home and changed out of his overall. In the kitchen's mist, LaRae sucked blood from her cut thumb while surveying the battle field. The potato peeler lay buried beneath leftover root vegetables. A mound of empty cartons overflowed the trash can and dressing crumbs littered the fake brick linoleum. She pulled out the yeast rolls when an angry hiss from a boiling pot caused her to groan.

"Bummer Amanda and crew had to go to Christopher's folks. But at least they won't gag over my food," she grumbled to her father while placing the laden tray on the table between yellow and orange fall leaves and pinecones. As they ate she thought of going to the Swedish neighborhood in Chicago and Lars purchasing the candles burning in front of her. "Pure beeswax. I make them in the back," the fat little lady called Inga had held them up proudly in her yarn and décor shop. "Just like my family made them on our island outside Stockholm." They had smelled of hope and promise.

"Let me help light up this dark season for you," Lars had said as he asked for the candles to be wrapped up with a sachet of dried lavender. The clatter of a fork dropping brought her back.

"Sweetie, your dedication to cooking is impressive," her father said. She watched him saw through the turkey, his bald forehead reflecting the overhead light.

"I overcooked it. This bird is as dry as hardtack."

Dutifully chewing away, her father shrugged. "The mashed

potatoes are good."

"Glue consistency, but I drowned them in butter." She looked pointedly at his plate. "You should have taken us to your favorite haunt. Shoney's offers a holiday buffet." Compared to the lavish feasts in the past accompanied with a running female dialogue interspersed with screaming kids, today's celebration felt more like a chapter out of the book of Lamentations. She bemoaned the fact that the laundry lay piled up to unprecedented heights and the gutters were overflowing with debris.

"So how are you, daughter?" her father stopped chewing.

"I'm great, Dad. Everything's going fine."

"You look pretty today."

"Thanks, It's due to mascara and lipstick." *When you met Mom, did she make you come alive in places that you never even knew existed?* LaRae continued the conversation. "Art is taking up time right now. I am getting ready for an exhibit. I hope you will visit. I have new friends to introduce you to."

He patted her hand across the table. "I'm not up to it. Got a heavy repair load before Christmas. I suspect you are good though. Send me photos of what you're exhibiting? I'll share them with the guys at the garage and Norman when he comes to chop the fallen oak limbs."

LaRae hid a grimace. Not sure if her art would captivate the Gunther auto shop mechanics' attention, she nodded nevertheless.

She spent the weekend laundering and ironing, then pecked her dad on the cheek and returned up the interstate towards Northwestern. As a bleak November sun waned over the snow dusted, black fields, she thought about her father. Guilt ridden at the amount of time she was spending in Windy City, she decided to take him on the ridiculously expensive sleigh ride the Amish had started offering to tourists. She'd pay with the savings from her Subway job. Or better yet, she would get him to go to Florida with her over the New Year holiday! God knew they needed a break. If they experienced something new, Dad's lagging energy might come back. All of Lars' talk of distant places rubbed in the fact that she was living a sheltered life. Embarrassed to admit she had never even seen the ocean, she'd acted as if she could relate to Lars' fishing trips on the sea and the swims in the salty waters he described. But the truth was she had no idea. The two of them were definitely hopping on a plane for a week of fun in the sun. Forget bald tires! She'd request it and be adamant. Not a big spender, nor a believer in vacations, Dad's recreation was to fish.

"But I want to see starfish and seashells and white sand at a real beach," she'd uttered dreamily as they had gone swimming at the muddy shores of Emerald Lake ages ago.

"Think about sharks and stinging jellyfish and sunburns! There is nothing like a fried catfish straight out of this water," her dad had smiled contentedly. "As far as I see it, we have all of God's bounty right here at our fingertips." He had gestured over the sepia colored lake and pine covered countryside.

"I will prove to him that he was wrong!" she promised herself as she hit the urban sprawl. *And for once in a lifetime pitch a fit.*

The next Sunday she found herself on a public transportation bus with Lars at her side. "Today is an introduction to Scandinavia. Logan Square shares history with the Norwegian, Swedish and Danish immigrant community in Chicago," he instructed. Upon arrival Lars looked down at her with pride while motioning to the red brick church across the street sporting white trim and a gothic spire: "Minnekirken. Completed in 1912 and the only church remaining that offers a Norwegian speaking service in the city. Let's attend." As they slipped into a wooden pew, a gentle stream of organ music and spoken liturgy washed over LaRae.

While not understanding the words, the ebb and flow felt strangely soothing. With lids half closed, she registered the outline of the stained-glass windows. Peeking to the left, she noticed Lars reciting the hymns and prayers by heart, often with his eyes closed. He seemed at rest in a way most unusual for guys his age. A curious combination of drive and peace, she mused and redirected her gaze to the crucified form in the stained glass on the right. She startled when realizing how the person on the cross also incarnated both qualities. A man of action, not intimidated or deterred by demons or humans, he accomplished what he set out to do. Love drove him and cost him everything, yet he was named the Prince of Peace.

In a rare moment of soul searching, LaRae admitted she possessed neither. If any drive propelled her, it pushed her to please everyone besides herself. The urge tossed her, bouncing her from one person's opinion to the next until she felt like stopping up her ears and screaming: "Enough!"

She contemplated the agonizing human form on the cross above her, heart weeping in the multi-colored sunlight. Her mind knew the story depicted in the glass. But her spirit felt sterile. They left the service in silence and picked up hot dogs from a stand then walked along luxurious storefronts with elaborate Christmas displays.

"Do you have any purchases you want to make?" LaRae wondered.

"I need to get my mother a present that can fit in my hand luggage when I go home for the holidays."

"What do you think about something small but exquisite, like this?" LaRae came to a halt in front of a Swarovski display where one-inch crystal animals in various poses sparkled on a black velvet display. Lars stepped inside the boutique.

"May I have the miniature swan, please?" He pointed at the shelf and nodded to the attendant. "My mom loves to feed the swans. Even wastes homemade bread on them."

"You live near swans?" A bright flower caught her eye. "Oh look! My mother adored spring. Look! This is just beautiful. I'll give it to my sister in memory of her." The store clerk carefully lifted the Forget-Me-Not flower out of the glass case and wrapped both gifts in boxes and seasonal gold foil.

As they strolled towards the bus, Lars quickly squeezed her gloved hand. She saw him grin beneath the royal blue toboggan that did not compete with his eyes. "I so appreciate your company."

LaRae felt her cheeks blush. "You are not too bad yourself." She slipped out of the grip and chucked his steely biceps with a lightly formed fist, a voice on the inside begging him to lean down and enjoy the company even further.

CHAPTER 10

A tiny but bold stroke of red paint splashed onto the wintery Lake Michigan scene, adding a sharp contrast to the titanium white and slate blue hue. On a self-imposed break from cramming for midterms, LaRae flitted about the studio, checking the canvas from a distance only to step close and correct the tree line. When she stepped up to the palette, a text lit up her phone. *Call ASAP!!*

With paint-stained fingers sticking to the buttons, she dialed.

"Oh God, it's bad Rae! He is going!" Amanda screamed.

"Who? What?"

"He has eight to twelve weeks left to live!"

"Who?" *Denial.* Her heart knew, but her mind refused to get on board.

"No more chemo or radiation. The oncologist says to emphasize comfort and rest. I am devastated. What do we do? I cannot take care of a baby and two kids and stay at Dad's at the same time. Christopher won't tolerate it! My children will have no grandparents. I am simply beside myself!"

Through the phone, loud sobs pierced through the creative bubble in the studio. LaRae observed moisture dripping onto the sketch on the table, blurring the outline of the picture. *Tears. I am crying because Dad is dying.*

Forgetting to hang up, she sprinted to the dorm and curled up beneath Mormor's quilt, hiding in a world of the softest wool, with no plan of ever emerging. But the next morning, the Corolla, filled to the brim with books, clothing and other possessions, barreled towards Dresden.

"Watch out!" she caught her father stumbling out of the bathroom and steadied him. "I am moving home for now, but I promise to graduate." After situating him on the couch, she leaned in to kiss the hollowed, grizzled cheek.

"You quit school?"

"Requested a deferment. Let's have Norman over for supper. Deli chickens get marked down after five PM," she added, forcing a mischievous smile. "Since his domino game is improving I need to put him in his place. After napping, how about a shave?"

Dad lifted a tired eyebrow, but acquiesced.

She cleaned out the fridge, tossing out cream cheese with green fuzz and poured sour milk down the drain. The counselor promised summer classes would make up for lost time.

But I'll miss the most important thing. And that particular thing was a living, breathing person.

Steeling herself for the task at hand she installed her father in the threadbare, burgundy recliner. Reruns of past Kansas City Chiefs' games blared, while he and Norman argued over the referees' calls. In between games Norman chopped and carried armloads of wood to stave off an invasive December deep freeze causing sheets of ice to form inside their bedroom windows. Monday morning, LaRae grabbed her black down parka and stepped behind the patio hedge, secreted away from prying eyes and curious ears to dial a certain number.

"Prayers will go up for you every day," Lars told her after she shared her woes.

She sniffled at the timbre of his voice and kind words, then after chatting ended the conversation with a belly laugh as Lars explained how he'd ordered a breast at the cafeteria only to be accused of sexual harassment. As she broke through the bushes, a loud thud resounded.

"Why so happy all of a sudden? Who are you talking to?"

"Norman! You look terrifying with that hammer. Don't sneak up like this!" LaRae studied her childhood friend, knocking on a perfectly fine pergola, and decided to tell him about her new friendship. She watched a jaw muscle twitch and swallowed guiltily while embellishing the story, making things appear more romantic and intimate than what they really were.

Dear God, keep me from lying and fantasizing! And help Norman quit fixating on me!

But instead of backing off, the following week Norman showed up at 7 sharp every morning tending to a self-made "honey do list" he pinned to the pantry. In between fixing a sagging garage roof and leaky gutters, frequent trips to the kitchen were added for coffee refills and conversation.

"His workmanship is somewhat shoddy, but you could do worse than Norman," Dad commented as their friend left with another donut and a thermos refill. LaRae slammed a burnt pot of oatmeal into the stainless steel sink.

Do not leave any final death wishes with me! I dare you! "You may be right. But what if I appreciate other qualities in a man?" Her father folded the newspaper and shoved the chair away from a congealed bowl of porridge and a half-finished raw kale juice.

"Go pick up a McGriddle sandwich, Honey. This health food is killing me faster than the cancer."

"Ok, Dad." LaRae grabbed the truck keys and fled.

Later in the day, when she entered through the garage with bags of groceries, low voices, giggles and heaving sobs emanated from the den. She tiptoed to the open door. On the couch, Dad's eyes were glued to the screen where an old home movie played on the VCR. Consecutive images of Fourth of July picnics and family Christmases rolled across the screen. A faithful recorder of history, her father had toted the prehistoric RCA camera to functions since she was little. A picnic at the lake unfolded. Mom dished out fried chicken and German potato salad. LaRae counted the protruding ribs on her own 6-year-old, swimsuit-clad body. Next, Amanda dominated the church stage, announcing the tidings of great joy with a toothless grin when a glimpse of the braying donkey appeared by the manger. *Curse my excruciating shyness!* For years it prohibited a speaking part and after a mice infestation, the donkey costume had reeked so badly she had vomited. When she finally outgrew the suffocating head she progressed to whispering lines behind the curtain.

"Dad, that's me!" she exclaimed from the doorway then watched her father turn abruptly, face flushing from being caught displaying uncontrolled emotion.

"Oh, Rae. I'm sorry you got stuck in that stupid role," he choked.

"I know better now and am learning the word 'no,'" she reassured him then walked into the den and collapsed. "Thanks for the sympathy though. I did dream of being Mary for the longest time."

He drew her in for a hug. "You'd make an excellent Mary. You should've told us. The pastor's daughter monopolized that role way too long. I would've brought it up at the deacon's meeting."

She laughed. "I doubt it would be a deacon's matter. But I appreciate the thought."

They sat in silence. Her father pulled out his handkerchief. The blue cloth had come in handy for childhood scrapes, runny noses and unexpected sticky messes. Today the once starched linen got twisted between calloused, oil stained fingers. "Daughter, we don't speak of feelings in the Gunther family. Reserved and all, I guess it is awkward. But I want to tell you something."

"What, Dad?"

"I love you, Rae. And I am proud of you."

Like Tiffany ornaments on a Christmas tree the words hung suspended and sparkling and LaRae considered them with something akin to wonder. In a garbled and wobbly voice, she eventually turned to him. "I know I am not at all like Mom, Dad."

At that statement, her father looked at her for the longest time. LaRae sensed his scrutiny and had the odd thought he was taking a mental snapshot of her features. "Sweetie, that's just fine." He closed his eyes and drifted off.

LaRae continued sitting next to him, afraid to move, saturated with the goodness of the moment.

Water gushed into the kitchen sink stirring up detergent bubbles. The flow reminded her of Lars and his chemistry classes. They only spoke during brief phone calls because her friend was studying for exams in Global and Ecological Health Engineering. The curriculum was demanding, but his motivation to bring about change spurred him on. His dream was to offer what she was taking for granted right now by draining the dirty dish water and refilling the sink. Locating clean water sources and drilling wells was apparently what it took to enable others in more remote parts of the world to experience this. She shook out the dishrag while remembering his words: "Mine will be a migratory career, but with a home base in Norway. You are looking at a world traveling gypsy, LaRae."

The green-eyed monster of envy reared its head at the memory. *I hope your girlfriend Ania appreciates the adventurous life you'll provide.* She stopped midway in the dishes. While she was performing the most mundane tasks Lars was slipping away.

Though not a fiancée even friends said goodbye! He was homeward bound for the holidays and not returning till mid-January; the least she could do was offer a send-off in person. Quickly she took care of the necessary arrangements.

"Dad, I'll be back soon. Mrs. Stubbs is cooking a chicken tetrazzini casserole and has her phone nearby in case you need anything."

She zipped up I-55 and knocked on Lars' dorm room. While waiting, she resisted the urge to chew her fingernails and brushed snow off her hat instead. For all she knew, the separation was no big deal to Lars. Besides, his life was planned to the max.

Am I providing a pleasant interlude during a harsh Chicago winter, relieving the sting of being a foreigner and feeling out of place? Sticky thoughts piled on top of each other and she turned towards the stairs.

"Well, hello stranger, what a wonderful surprise!" Lars stepped into the hallway, his gaze traveling over her face. "I thought you'd forgotten this strapping Viking, trading me in for a corn-growing, tobacco-chewing farmer out there in that town of yours."

She felt her eyes widen. Although knowing he was joking, the image of Norman involuntarily flashed through her mind. LaRae winced and shook her head in order to relish the sight in the doorway. Mustering courage, she drank in the tousled hair and bare feet hidden in sheep skin slippers and his moose print t-shirt. She honed in on his face while carefully avoiding looking at the red pajama bottoms.

"I'm not sure what is running through your mind but you disappeared for a minute." Lars smiled, his eyes crinkling in all the right places.

"Oh sorry. I got distracted."

"You must be in town on business. But let me take you out for dinner tonight. After all, we will soon be oceans apart. Literally. The guys in our study module demanded a night off and the graphs on the laptop screen are dizzying. Geniuses need sustenance," he added with a crooked grin that showed off a left cheek dimple.

LaRae nodded then scurried down the steps to call her former suite mate. "Can I crash on the couch tonight?" She then rushed across the campus and waited till a squealing Starr opened the door.

"Stud boy is asking you out on an official date? Please wear your new creation!" They took the elevator to the dorm suite. The living room hung heavy with pot and cigarette smoke but the yucca palm shrouded in Christmas lights appeared unfazed and had grown an inch.

"The plum colored dress? I'm afraid it's too chic." LaRae thought back to when she'd picked up the velvet at an estate sale down the road and had enlisted the help of Grandma's Singer machine, appointing herself as head seamstress.

"How you stitched together that dress with ancient fabric, I have no clue. Especially in a city with designer and mock designer labels," her roommate commented. Confused, yet fascinated, Starr had followed the tediously long process of measuring, cutting, and sewing an empire waist fitted gown with gentle dips in the skirt and a neckline lower than anything LaRae had previously worn.

She slipped into the soft fabric.

"It needs something," Starr puffed smoke and lifted a pierced brow while motioning with her index finger for LaRae to rotate.

"Oh wait, I picked up the amethyst in the gold filigree at the jeweler's down the street." LaRae dug the necklace out of her purse. Her only family heirloom piece, the broken clasp had been replaced.

"Oh, it offsets your green eyes. You look *mamalicious*." Starr clapped her hands.

Locked in the bathroom, LaRae checked the unfamiliar reflection. The impulsive act of procuring contacts left her with mixed emotions tonight. Dark mascara and light eye shadow accentuated the almond shape of her eyes and Starr's lipstick highlighted her thin but curved lips. She washed the clamminess off her palms, then rubbed them vigorously on a towel. *Visible. What if I draw attention and stand out in the crowd? What if guys whistle or make comments; how do I tackle that?* She should have taken lessons from Amanda. *Who cares? I'll throw my head back and smile like her. With great enjoyment and no embarrassment.*

"Easy peasy," LaRae psyched herself into action. *But what if Lars thinks I'm showing off? Or trying to compete with his precious girlfriend?* At that thought, she cut a beeline to the bedroom and pulled out the jeans and Santa turtleneck she wore driving in.

But persistent knocking caused her to march into the hallway to crack the front door open. Lars's form filled the entry. A Norwegian looking black and white sweater with a complex star pattern complemented a pair of charcoal wool slacks and a fur hat. She checked behind him, expecting gnomes and elves from the Scandinavian Anderson and Moe fairy tales to trail in.

To her great chagrin, the man looked way too Nordic and

masculine for his own good. Exasperated, she blew a few hair strands off her face and resented him for not sporting a few pimples or speaking with a lisp. But something was clearly wrong because Lars stood stock still, his eyes fixed on her with an undefinable expression.

"Too formal? I sewed it but haven't taken time to check the seams thoroughly," she pointed to her dress. Prepared for him to point out stitches that had come undone, she searched for loose threads. Lars remained speechless while LaRae fumbled her neckline and sleeves. "I'll be back, let me change real fast."

Her comment injected movement into Lars' immobile body. In a swift moment he was at her side squeezing her shoulder. "Do not dare change," he said in a low, guttural voice. Grabbing her coat off the hook, he wrapped the down filled shell about her. Obediently, she zipped it, then put on a hat, scarf and mittens all the while puzzled at his behavior.

He spoke again. "I've called a cab. We have done enough walking to win an Olympic gold medal in the last three months."

It was true. They had trekked through the Swedish neighborhood, Miracle Mile and a dozen other places.

"I picked a place that seems like you but I may be wrong," he looked at her in the cab's dim light.

"Please assure me you didn't pick Midwestern fare," she asked pleadingly.

He shook his head, then winked but said nothing more.

As they entered through a golden Taj Mahal-looking portal and the pungent spices of Asia filled her nostrils, she felt reassured.

"Indian food! How could you tell?"

"I took a wild guess at what you might like. But judging by your dress this place does not do you justice. If I hadn't been on a student's budget, I would've taken you to the most excellent restaurant in town."

"Then you do not realize how seldom I have eaten Indian food. And I absolutely love it." Inspecting the other patrons' plates, she tried not to salivate. They were seated at a table sparsely decorated with a single carnation. The menu offered a variety of curries with basmati rice and lentils. The fragrance of fresh Naan bread wafted from a nearby booth. LaRae picked a goat dish then updated Lars on her father's wellbeing, as well as Mickey's milk allergy and Drew's upcoming Christmas play.

Lars ate but remained uncharacteristically quiet, yet his eyes stayed on her. "I cannot tell you how sorry I am about your father," he finally said. She watched his hand reach across the table and squeeze her fingers, the grip warm and comforting.

God. Suspend this moment in time.

They sat quietly, Lars' eyes searching hers. "Is this goodbye?" Was it her imagination or was his voice husky?

"I'm afraid so. I want to invite you to Dresden. But the circumstances are not right."

Lars looked at her pensively. "We are the most excellent of friends, aren't we?"

She used the napkin to wipe the treacherous tears, then stood and gathered her purse and jacket. "That we are," she croaked. They hailed a cab and when it came to a standstill at the campus, they huddled within layers of clothing and headed to the lake. Lars reached out and supported LaRae's back after a ferocious gust pushed her backwards.

"I'd like to show you Norway someday." They walked to the shoreline, feet crunching and breaking apart chunks of frozen sand then stood at the line where eager waves lapped at their boots.

She looked up at him. "And I have dreamt of seeing it." A sudden wind blast made their coats flap but neither one paid attention. Darkness concealed the blue in his eyes but LaRae watched Lars move so close that she inhaled his breath. It smelled of mints and promise. Her heart stuttered and performed an acrobatic flip.

Oh God, let him kiss me! She begged silently, then startled. *Did I say that out loud?* Her strong legs were spaghetti noodles and she pictured the next persistent gust tackling her to the ground.

Do not let him kiss me, it'll spell all kinds of trouble! She quickly remedied her request.

God granted her latter petition. Lars sucked in the crystal air sharply and turned towards the lake. "I hope you have the best Christmas ever," he whispered. Leaning in from above, he lifted a wayward curl out of her eye.

LaRae took in his features, the square chin and determined forehead that did not waver. His rosy cheeks showed stubbly growth from being too busy to shave. In her mind, she removed the mittens, stroking his gold hair, then playfully tugged the earlobes before cradling his face in her hands. In reality, she closed her eyes and committed the visual to memory.

"And a very Merry Christmas to you too," she uttered weakly, then sent a radiant smile his way.

Lars was surprised at the unexpected visit the morning of his departure. A burly looking man in blue jeans and cowboy boots stood outside his dorm, asking to speak to Lars Pettersen.

"I am here on behalf of Rae," he stated emphatically. "I don't know about your traditions where you're from." The bearded man put his hands in the pockets of a lumberman's jacket and rocked back and forth on scuffed boots.

"I want you to know Rae was promised to me a long time ago. In our neck of the woods some hold on to the idea of arranged marriages," he went on unperturbed. "Her father and I have squared away the details of the arrangement. We do not appreciate your interference."

Perplexed, Lars watched as the man pulled a clump of tobacco from a round tin box in his coat.

Deftly tucking the wad into the lower right side of the jaw it apparently needed to be rightly situated before he could continue his speech. "LaRae is in a fragile state with her dad dying. We ask you to kindly back off."

Dumbfounded, Lars thought of ways to respond but his mind was operating in slow motion. He nodded.

"I see we've come to an understanding." The bear sized man

grabbed his hand in a one-sided handshake, then rolled his shoulders backwards a couple of times before descending the steps to a waiting pickup. As if cheering for his master's performance, a coon hound barked excitedly from behind the window of the red Chevrolet truck. Lars saw the man raise a finger from the steering wheel in a farewell greeting, then nod briefly, before taking off.

The flight was crammed with luggage and passengers. Flight attendants scurried about, reassuring travelers worried about missing their connections. The plane took off late because the ground crew had needed to de-ice the wings. Babies fussed and a nearby mother complained that it was past dinner time and not even a snack had been served. Lars tuned out the sounds and ruminated over the day's happening. His first instinct was to fight back. Rent a car. Drive to the small town in the corn fields. Ask LaRae point blank if she had feelings for him. What if she laughed? Or worse, apologized and pitied him for having misread their relationship?

Filled with misgivings, he asked hard questions. Was LaRae's enjoyment of him a buddy thing? Did her friendship stem from innocent curiosity about someone from a different country? A desire for fun interaction in the midst of stressful circumstances? Had she mentioned him flirting with her to the fiancé? Besides Hollywood movies, what did he know about American girls anyway? Romance here and elsewhere remained an unsolvable riddle, growing more mysterious by the minute.

He must have committed a major cultural blunder. No wonder the girl hadn't brought him home! He'd thought it odd not to be introduced to her sister and father. Now, the conversation with her intended explained LaRae's reluctance. The potential awkwardness of defining their friendship to others had caused avoidance.

"Best friends" he'd described it. But the term was trite and unsatisfactory. *I want you.* Her freckles and the emerald twinkle in her eye rushed at him. The lips that had twitched when he ordered food and no one understood him, and then had stretched in a radiant smile and exploded in a giggle when he ended up with snails instead of the escarole and white bean salad in the French restaurant. How could he know that the French word for snails was "escargot"? He'd suffer looking the fool again for another impromptu moment of laughter. But instead, nobility called for him to retreat. To put the incident behind him. Focus on returning to what was familiar and dear. As the Boeing 747 shot across the Atlantic, he closed his eyes, falling into a dreamless slumber. Hours later and after changing planes, the whine of the engines woke him. Lars yawned but felt invigorated at the sight of the jagged coastline. Its many islands and inlets jogged his memory to get the fishing gear ready. Though many young folks preferred prime rib for Christmas, steamed cod and boiled potatoes was still considered royal fare with traditionalists.

In the small arrival hall, his mom ran towards him. He caught her by the waist and swung her in a circle.

"Silly boy, let me down. I'm a fragile, old woman."

He chuckled, noticing a new stripe of grey hair. But she carried herself with dignity and the same understated elegance. Her makeup-free face flushed with the excitement of seeing her son. The wolf fur draped her lean figure and he admired her trim look. Mamma swore it was due to the ice bathing, saying the freezing sea devoured every calorie. He hugged her fiercely and on the way out tried to explain it was considered politically incorrect to sport animal fur. She blew him off while handing him the keys.

The worn red leather seat in her car had cracked, but the engine hummed along and responded to his touch. His mother, in update mode, informed him of the latest happenings. Aunt Irene broke an ankle slipping on cake batter because the bowl tumbled off the counter while she fed a stray cat on the door step and she never noticed until stepping in it. His uncle obtained record price for the sheep. With Muslim immigrants arriving, the demand for lamb meat had increased. Lars drove through the city situated half an hour away from his hometown. With a renovated airport, a new hospital and a university it was benefiting from a population increase, the exact opposite of their sleepy hamlet where most of the residents were born and bred within four miles of each other. The exception was when occasional tourists who'd fallen in love with its summer charm decided to settle and brave its winters.

Lars thought of how the short summer months in all coastal towns in Norway made up for a miserable cold season. Flowers would cascade from wooden flower boxes and vacationers would travel up and down the coast by ferries, in RVs, buses, cars and personal yachts. The annual seafood festival would line the sidewalks of Main Street letting German, Dutch and French tourists gorge on crab, lobster and shrimp. The storefronts would exhibit traditional silver and pewter wares. The market would display sheepskins, local produce as well as heavy metal T- shirts and cheap watches from China. It was a nice reminder while he perused the dreary landscape. The snow was melting and dirty; he hated the slush filling the streets. The in-between weather kept him from skiing and no boating could happen before the annual overhaul. He craved the outdoors, if for no other reason but to formulate lucid thoughts.

"Is Ania coming over for rice pudding?"

At the mention of Ania, he watched his mother's eyes cloud over.

"She has not stopped in all fall. I left a voicemail for her but got no reply. Did she not *FaceTime*? I believe she's sick. Heard she is hospitalized in the city."

"I can't believe you didn't let me know!" Lars interrupted his mother's update indignantly. Already estranged by Ania's protracted silence, a feeling of foreboding now settled on him.

His mother looked at him with sympathy. "Actually, it's complicated."

"How so?"

"You'd better talk to Aunt Lisa."

They rode in silence and as he pulled up to the curb by their house, Lars sighed with relief. Individual candles lit up the windows and for as long as he could remember the illuminated paper advent star shone from the place of honor in the living room window.

A Norwegian spruce filled the corner of the den. "I'm glad artificial trees are still unpopular in this part of the world," he said and dumped the rucksack on the hardwood floor. The glamor of Chicago certainly had its appeal, yet as he inhaled the woodsy scent, Lars's insides unwound.

"Relax while I finish dinner," his mother said.

Lars nodded but needed to wrap presents and check on the wood supply for the tiered stove. He assumed his uncle had brought a new cord from his farm.

Nestled into a cove overlooking the ocean, the well-kept homestead had sheep roaming the hillsides while the spruce forest supplied extended family with Christmas trees and extra income. Lars decided he'd disappear the next morning in those very woods. When night fell, he ate stew with his mom then showered and dove beneath his goose down duvet.

Dawn appeared, offering a gift of cool sunshine that melted the leftover snow. He borrowed his mother's car and parked outside his uncle's barn before setting a grueling pace towards the summit of the Pettersen family land. Fir thickets closed in the overgrown path. A squirrel scampered by and hare tracks showed in patches of snow. His body brushed against bare branches and blackberry brambles as he climbed the trail to Lookout Point. Thorns stung and tore at his windbreaker. Not minding, Lars kept up a brisk run until collapsing belly down on the ground, sweat pungent and heaving for air. After a deep breath, he rolled over and out of habit scanned the copse of silver birch trees beneath for deer. But his mind was unintrigued by the surrounding splendor. Instead, it traveled back to the last months at Northwestern University.

Like wild mushrooms sprouting up overnight, unbidden images popped up: a girl in a burgundy velvet dress and green eyes with long, brown locks flying in the wind. The sight of her dressed up just for him had tripped him up more than he'd been willing to admit. She'd been gorgeous yet unassuming. Timid, yet bold. Modest, but enticing.

"Stop!" His right fist hit the ground in frustration. "This is what you get for playing the fool."

Disgusted, he heaved himself upright and started the trek down the mountain. There would be no dwelling on this tangled past. The message had been succinct; he had stepped onto forbidden territory.

He stopped by his aunt and uncle's gabled farmhouse, shoving his turmoil away. They were not just relatives but friends. Only a decade or so older than him he had sought their advice often. After devouring a stack of thin sour cream waffles and homemade raspberry jam, he told stories of what he'd seen in America. Uncle Sven, his father's youngest sibling updated him on timber prices and other relevant news.

Lars steered the topic of the conversation towards Ania but Lisa proved evasive. After cajoling and increasing the charm wattage, she finally relented.

"You know I am a nurse and I chat with my collegues," she spoke in a hushed voice. "This is strictly confidential." She poured a second cup of coffee. "Ania has been admitted for complications."

"Complications from what?"

"Well, a private abortion clinic has been constructed over there." She nodded towards the east.

Lars looked at her in shock, then flung the back door open and strode to the car. Not calling his mother, he sped to the hospital, parked and entered the gaily painted yellow facility. On the third floor he came to an abrupt halt in the doorway of room 251. There she was, his childhood friend, reclining against a white pillow, her usually animated face a pale moon. The normally sparkly eyes were a sunken purple but lit up as her head turned towards him.

"Oh! My very own "gull gutten"! The doctor removed a dreadful appendix!" Her hand clasped his and held on tight.

The nickname of *golden boy* made him swallow hard and block out the vision of an impish Ania romping in blueberry woods and jumping off timber floats.

She leaned in, the touch of her fingers on his forehead like icicles. "I've missed you terribly. I considered calling but didn't want to be a bother. Have you been dreadfully busy at the university? Come sit and talk about America." She motioned to the visitor's chair. "Did you experience the runway during Chicago fashion week? Remember I told you not to miss it and to send me pictures."

Lars sank onto the seat, tongue-tied.

Upon returning home, he stormed into the kitchen, slamming the back door for good measure. His mom was humming along to the piano strains of "Silent Night" while bending over a pot roast platter rearranging the carrots and caramelized onions.

"She obviously went out with other guys and ended up pregnant!" He moaned and fell into a pine chair. "Then she eliminated her own child?" His stomach revolted and he raced to void its contents in the toilet. Adding to the confusion was Ania's refusal to tell the truth. She'd kept up a nervous chatter, telling him of the latest hair styles from the continuing education classes. Red was out. But purple lowlights were the hot new thing in Paris. It would be a year before local salons caught on. Blah, blah, blah.

Too stunned to ask any questions he'd sat there like a boiled cod himself.

"Sit. Eat. It's your favorite." His mother's prodding made him pick at the spread to pacify her but she saw right through the charade. "Ok, son. You smell. How about a shower and bed? Sleep on it and by tomorrow things may look brighter."

He thanked her for the food and vanished upstairs. But his jet-lagged body did not allow for rest. After tossing and turning he slipped into a sweatsuit and boots and paced through the slush covered streets. Who had Ania seen? Was she in love with someone else, - one of their classmates? A neighbor? Or had some slime bag seduced her and she'd fallen for it? He kicked a chunk of ice and sent it flying against a metal pole where it splintered into pieces.

I have to get away! The idea crystallized his thinking and sprung him into action. He holed up in the study and made phone calls and typed emails. By Christmas Eve a new plan had taken shape. Lars rushed to make a few purchases and added them to the unpacked baggage, then double checked that the passport was in the carry-on. This time, his mother insisted on driving him.

"I cannot tell you how sorry I am to miss Christmas with you." Lars' gear disappeared on the roller behind the Scandinavian Airlines counter. "The Red Cross is asking for an immediate replacement. You do realize how hard I worked to obtain a position like this? The Red Cross hiring me without a finished master's degree is unheard of."

She smiled bravely and stood on tippy toes to kiss his forehead. "Let's pray before you take off."

They huddled, a faithful twosome, as had been their habit before games, exams and adventures.

"Father I commit my son to you for safekeeping. Restore Ania to yourself and to us."

"Lord, keep Mamma healthy and encouraged. Help me be successful."

His mother hugged him hard before swatting his backside. "Off you go. Remember to take the malaria pills," she hollered as he stepped through security.

Upon reentering the house, she removed her son's presents from under the tree. Then, as she stuffed them on the top shelf in the room she had commandeered into a walk-in closet, an idea crossed her mind. She flitted about, gathering the scattered frames. An hour later, she pinned the world map to the closet wall and added a pin to what she thought was the right place.

The photos documenting her son's journey into manhood lined the top shoe shelf. She undressed and pulled on her flannel gown, then lay face down on the oriental rug, an open journal and Bible next to her. "Son, you're not the only one going to work." While inhaling dust, her spirit interceded before the throne in the heavens.

Once up in the sky, Lars scrunched his body into the standard cabin seat and closed his eyes.

I am doing as the apostle, forgetting what is behind and straining towards what is ahead. He looked out the airplane window at the choppy waves below, mulling over the fact that even after applying the Scripture, he did not feel particularly spiritual. Instead, he had an odd notion that perhaps his actions were not spiritual at all. But Lars shoved the nagging thought aside, leaving all misgivings behind in the plane's wake.

CHAPTER 11

Ensconced in Dad's pickup, LaRae slowed at the light, leaving Normal's frantic mall and a too skinny Santa behind. The flat puzzle of brown and white fields lay before her naked and bereft, - not even a hint of yellow alfalfa lit up the monotonous prairie. Like a distant relative, the bleak winter sun paused for a perfunctory visit, but not enough to spread warmth or cheer. Nature lay dormant and LaRae felt trapped in a time warp, encapsulated.

She patted her jeans making sure her phone stayed put. Perhaps she was not entitled to special attention, but nevertheless the tiniest hope flickered of getting a call or an email. Or a card depicting horse-drawn sleds swooshing across a Norwegian winter landscape. Any little token acknowledging her continued existence would be welcome.

Torn by her father's diagnosis the painting intended for Lars leaned unfinished against the wall of the wardrobe closet. The winter scene was to be the first out of a series of four pieces, each illustrating a season of the year by Lake Michigan. She'd been adding two people in the foreground of the lake, the female in a signal red coat and a Prussian blue one on the man, when Amanda's call made her put down the brush for good. The same ringtone emanated from her pocket this moment.

"Yes?" LaRae picked up her cell phone.

"Don't forget the custard and prosciutto. Did I tell you Christopher gave the okay to go all out? Let's not wallow in gloom but make this Dad's best Christmas ever, I said. And guess what?"

"What?"

"Chris took off the hold on my Visa."

"Wow. Not sure we're up to anything big though. Just saying... Can we make it special without a fuss? Dad gets tuckered out. The Mexican crew hanging lights around the windows and roofline did a good job. With the inflatable Scooby Doo and Disney princesses, it's already quite a setup."

"Don't dampen my enthusiasm, Sis! Bring Mom's green Jell-O dessert and expect all kinds of surprises." LaRae swallowed a retort and returned home to continue her own preparations for the event.

As Christmas Eve rolled around, her father helped stuff presents in the car and she drove them to Amanda's house. By the driveway, a bar sporting an assortment of beverages was lined up next to a pot of steaming cider hung over a fire pit. A bartender in a snowsuit was mixing drinks.

"What in the world?" Her stoic father appeared flabbergasted.

Amanda waved from behind a tree lit up by flashing laser beams then danced her way to their car, dressed in a red outfit trimmed in ermine fur.

"Non-spiked apple cider for the two of us," Dad admonished while frowning at his oldest daughter's wine-filled glass. Despite his German heritage with its beer making traditions, he remained a teetotaler.

"Oh lighten up. Catch the Christmas cheer!" Amanda kissed his gaunt cheek and yelled for Drew and the neighborhood kids to stop the snowball war and welcome guests.

LaRae formed a snowball and tossed it towards her nephews when her glance landed on a familiar vehicle parked in the drive.

"Is that Norman's truck?"

Amanda giggled. "Part of the surprise. Wait and see!" Her sister handed over a steaming mug.

Like a soldier navigating a minefield in war times, LaRae entered the lit foyer to the shrill tune of Jingle Bells. *Get a grip, girl!* But the only grip she could muster was a frantic stranglehold on her father's arm.

"Boo!" The booming laugh sent shivers down her spine and a thump resounded as Norman jumped out of the wardrobe closet dressed as an oversized elf. Through the French doors, Mr. And Mrs. Stubbs, seated on the red micro fiber couch, waved.

Norman reached out and wrestled her away from Dad into a crushing hug, then whipped out a small box from the front pocket of the hoodie he wore.

"This is the first out of three. Open it."

His parents bobbed their heads with approval reminding her of the bobble-head dogs their neighbor kept in his Mustang. A spark went off in her brain and made her dizzy. She dropped the gift on the front hall table.

"I don't feel well, please excuse me." As she tore through the master bedroom to the bath, she grabbed a pillow from the bed and turned the faucets to full stream. Head buried in the pillow the rushing water muffled her screams.

"No! No! I am not doing this! I am putting my sister on that marshmallow skewer outside and roasting her slowly. And after I finish, I'm giving Norman the same treatment."

Tell Dad the truth!

No. He needs hope and reassurance, the ever-helpful inner guide restrained her.

At what cost? My own self?

"Auntie Rae? Mom says to help with the appetizer." Mickey's voice penetrated the mist and noise. LaRae splashed cold water on her face and rigidly straightened her vertebras. While deep breathing, she pictured herself putting on body armor, then opened the door and picked up her nephew, carrying him down the stairs. "Buddy, have you not taken the shrink hormones I gave you? Looks like you've done some more growing."

Mickey grinned, his summertime freckles now faded.

"You mean the candy you gave me? Mom said they were Tic-

Tacs. Also, she said it's not good to shrink me. I need to grow up and become a man."

"I know." LaRae stopped to breathe and rubbed his head. "I just want you to do it in slow motion, that's all."

Amanda inspected her from the bottom of the steps, but LaRae put a warning finger in the air. "Not one word. I don't want to talk."

Grabbing a platter of appetizers, she forced her lips in a rigid smile while she offered food around the cluttered great room. When another round of Jingle Bells resounded through the speakers she felt as if she were going berserk.

"Got you!" The tickle of a beard brushed against her right cheek. Like a store mannequin she froze when a wet slobber hit her lips. As laughter and clapping broke out, her grip on the platter faltered.

"Oh, blessed mistletoe!" Norman's arms locked around her trunk while blobs of stuffed mushrooms slid down her legs and feet. When the hold relaxed, she tore loose and ran outside.

The burly bartender was serving the next door neighbor but looked her way. "Ma'am, can I get you a Coke?"

"Yes. Add vodka," she shocked herself by saying.

He chuckled. "Lady of the house doesn't allow for that. How about mulled wine?"

Dad's pain meds! The alarm beeping in her pocket made her rush to the car and then back inside. Hovering, she made sure he swallowed the pills then exchanged her stained velvet pants for a pair of her sister's sweat pants before hiding in the play room with Drew and Mickey.

She was adding the last brick to the multi colored Lego skyscraper when Norman entered.

"Two can play this game!" Speechless, she watched him bound across the carpeted floor and playfully bump her. The skyscraper collapsed.

"Don't touch me or I'll smack you." Her threat made him roar with laughter. He picked up the nephews, tucked them under his arms and carried them downstairs. From the bottom of the steps, he hollered.

"Coming for you next!" LaRae stomped on the remaining Lego creations then bounced downstairs to Amanda who was cutting a coconut cake in the dining room and hissed.

"If you ever invite Norman over here again, I swear I'll tell Dad about you going to Cancun instead of your friend's Florida beach house for your senior trip in high school. And I still have the photo to prove how you behaved there. And I'll tell Christopher you lost the engagement ring in the move." Amanda's face blanched to match the color of the frosting.

"I hear you. But this might be your only chance." Fuming at the remark, the rest of the night she stayed glued to her father's side. When they said goodbye and she helped him into the car, she noticed three packages piled into the back seat. After reading the labels she huffed and drove to the back of Jewel Osco and stopped at the loading dock.

"Just a minute, Dad." She hauled the gifts out of the car and heaved them one by one into the store's dumpster.

Upon returning home, she helped her father get ready for bed while the adrenaline rush gave way to weariness.

The next day brought a quiet celebration with Reverend Richter stopping in for coffee.

The Yule days over with, she spent the next week on the lookout, ready to duck if Norman showed. The man finally cornered her in the frozen food aisle at the grocery.

"Are you avoiding me, Rae?" he asked, his Adam's apple bobbing up and down as he kept stroking his brown beard.

"It is not your imagination." *Something you're not largely imbued with.*

He continued to stroke his beard pensively. "Mother said I need to give you space. With your dad and all. I understand."

How about all the space between the Western and Eastern shores of the continent of America? "Your mother is right. I need a ton of space. Plus my very special friend will be back from Norway soon. I'll be heading up to see him and believe he is eager to see me too."

Norman's face clouded over and he strode to the tobacco

counter.

Two weeks into January, LaRae's insides started hopping with impatience. Despite her father's increasing weakness, she'd forced herself to finish the lake painting. Wrapped in glossy red paper and tied with a silver ribbon it rested in the back seat as she headed north to ask Lars to come visit. Sick or not her father needed to meet him. And after showing him her family's ordinary Dresden existence, she was going to spell out in words what her heart had concealed even to herself. And Lars could respond whichever way he wanted.

Watch out, girl! The cautious voice warned. *This type of initiative may lead to more heartache than you ever imagined.* But the Corolla plowed ahead and she with it. The thought of heartache led her to think of dad's frail body curled up on the couch as he had waived goodbye. In her mind she wanted to defy the approaching footsteps of death who was stealing her father. But neither threats nor cajoling would cause death to consider her heart. Onwards it marched and she, - a mere human, was forced to march along with it, regardless of whether she hated or resignedly accepted it.

She called to inform Lars of her trip only to discover his phone disconnected. Just a prepaid phone, used domestically while in the United States, he must have forgotten to reconnect it upon arrival. Pulse pounding at showing up unannounced, she knocked on the dorm room door once again.

"I'm sorry," Lars' roommate said as he stared at her. "He has not returned." The Asian grad student avoided meeting her eyes. "What is even stranger is that his stuff was moved out by the time I returned from the holidays."

Frantically, she approached his other classmates, but no one knew what had happened. In an attempt to find answers, she charged into the Dean's office.

"Sorry, but by law, I can't disclose any information," he told her.

She left, fuming at his lackadaisical attitude and the way he avoided her eyes by looking down and showing his bald, shiny pate.

Back at the apartment, Starr hugged her. "Hope he didn't dump you. I like his macho, athletic look. But perhaps he's not into your studious type. When girls act too serious, it scares fun loving guys away. The universe may be calling you to walk a different path."

Shut up! LaRae screamed silently.

Not even noticing the time spent on the road, she returned home. *I hope his plane didn't crash!* In horror, she researched the headlines around his travel dates. But there were no stories of hijacked planes or crashes. Only Lars himself had dropped off the grid. *Where are you? Come back to me.*

Even though she knew how Lars despised social media and had vowed never to create a profile, she checked *Facebook* repeatedly. "Is it left over paranoia from the Second World War? I read how the occupation affected people psychologically and in response, many learned to guard their privacy at all cost," she had asked him.

He had glared at her, indignantly. "And who is to say that that is not prudent?"

So here she sat, stranded, because of his stubbornness. Or perhaps he deliberately stayed hidden and Ania had proved so tempting he decided to forego the exchange program. For all she knew, his mother and Ania were busy preparing for a summer wedding right this moment.

Maybe Lars had proposed to Ania in the moonlight by some fjord on New Year's Eve? Meanwhile she'd sat in the recliner, watching the ball drop over Times Square with Dad curled up next to a vomit bucket. And here she was once more, languishing away during another January, with the endless, bare fields of Illinois encircling and besieging her.

How can I suffer claustrophobia in a wide-open country? The numbness started at the bottom of her spine and wound its way upwards until her throat was caught in a stranglehold. "Oh God, help me not to hate my life," she pleaded in bed listening to the rumbling of the snowplow preparing the roads for one more bleak day.

Fortunately, morning brought the gift of inspiration. Pulling her laptop onto the bed, she googled the White Pages for Norway. Bingo! There indeed was Lars Pettersen! Giddy with relief, she scrolled down the page, only to discover that the cherished name repeated itself 105 times, sometimes with different middle names. When peeking at their home addresses, she realized the names were spread out all over the small country. She shoved her covers off and grabbed Lorenzo.

"What unimaginative people." She raked his fur rather than stroking him while scolding the entire nation. "And Lars, - I thought you were one of a kind!"

In the vivid descriptions of his hometown, she did not recall Lars mentioning the town's name. If he had, the distraction of the "Nordic stare" had turned her brain to mush. LaRae padded down the hallway wearing yesterday's clothes when inspiration struck again; the country was tiny. How hard could it be to nail down the Lars Pettersen who lived on the coast compared to the others? In consulting the online map, it showed a thousand small dots along the peninsula shaped landmass. "Norway has the 7th longest coastline in the world," Wikipedia informed. Tempted to smash the new laptop she smacked it shut.

Weeks passed by, but she continued to stew. *Why did you let me meet him in the first place, God?* Wishing for an amnesia pill, she nevertheless dug in her heels and flat out refused her sister's suggestion of going on anti-depressants.

"All my girlfriends are on them," Amanda ventured. Her sister had dropped in to help set up a hospital bed in the den. "Christopher swears they saved our marriage."

Well, watch me grow into a depressed, old maid then, she almost retorted. If that was the price to pay for a "happy marriage" she instinctively knew she would rather opt out.

"I just know it's so hard for you to deal with Dad. Not to mention hospice coming in."

Together, they put their father in the rented bed in the den. His body was dwindling away and there was no map telling them how to navigate this unknown road they were on.

Like a ship whose moorings had come undone, he was gradually moving closer to the shores of heaven but further away from the rest of them. Lately there were times when his mind did not even seem to recognize her any more. The days were filled with an unusual stillness. Their pastor had started to drop by. Watching her father's contented expression when the man read the Bible out loud, she decided to take up the practice. When Amanda left, she sat down in the recliner and read from the book of Psalms out of her red communion Bible. Curled up in fetal position, his breathing shallow, her dad gave her a drowsy smile and looked like he was paying attention.

"If I take the wings of the morning, and dwell in the uttermost parts of the sea; Even there shall thy hand lead me, and thy right hand shall hold me." She stopped to blow her nose in a Kleenex then resumed.

"If I say, Surely the darkness shall cover me; even the night shall be light about me.

Yea, the darkness hideth not from thee; but the night shineth as the day: the darkness and the light are both alike to thee. For thou hast possessed my reins: thou hast covered me in my mother's womb."

I see you. Startled, she looked up from her reading to respond to her dad. But his eyes had closed and saliva dripped from his slack lips. *You are precious to me.* The words had bubbled up from inside. Her shoulders lowered and she leaned back in the chair drawing a long belly breath.

Precioussss? Another voice interjected, accusing. *If so, why is God stealing everything you hold dear, Rae Rae?*

She rose from the chair, the leather volume crashing to the floor. Forgetting to grab a coat, she strode down the lane, outpacing the conflicting voices. Lungs burning, fifteen minutes later she crashed through the library door and picked up a new release from the shelf by the counter. Who needed prescription anti-depressants with access to a room stocked with literature?

"Dawn's Promise". On the front cover, an Amish girl in a bonnet looked googly-eyed at the ripped biceps of jeans-clad man throwing hay bales on a truck bed. In disgust, she dropped the book and picked up "Wonders Above: Guide to the Constellations". With frozen fingers from traversing town in 35-degree weather, she carried the heavy volume to Dorothy, the librarian, saying she'd forgotten her library card.

Dorothy pushed back her bleached bangs, revealing grey roots, and checked the book out. "The first one you grabbed is better, Rae. But enjoy this one if you can."

With a "thank you" she sprinted home, ready to open the book and escape to a far galaxy.

One day at the end of February a letter showed up in the mailbox. Forwarded from her PO Box at the university, the address was penned in a familiar, slanted handwriting. Postmarked in Nairobi, it was addressed in a bold hand on a scuffed Manila envelope.

More nervous than a trapped feral cat, she slipped the letter into her pocket and hopped into her car.

"I'll be back in a few," she yelled to the home health nurse, then headed towards the lake. Heart pounding, she parked the vehicle and turned the heat up to full blast. With trembling fingers, she tore the envelope open. Handwritten, rumpled pages fell into her lap. With multiple creases, the paper must've been folded and unfolded repeatedly. Had the person who wrote it read and reread it multiple times before finally deciding to send it? The contents of the missive were direct and to the point.

Dear LaRae.

I hope this letter finds you in good health. I wish I could say likewise for your dad. But knowing the state of affairs, I can only say I have been praying faithfully for him. I know that miracles do happen and I'm asking for one for him. And if you don't get to experience one, then I pray that he will not experience much pain. I also ask that his time with you and your sister will be meaningful and sweet in spite of everything he is going through.

But before I go on, I am writing to you mainly to apologize for a few things. First of all please let me tell you how much it meant to have you as a friend during my stay in the States. I will always cherish the memories of our time together. I thank you for everything we got to do together.

You are unusually gifted. It has been a privilege to get to know you, both as a person and also every expression of the woman you are through your art. For that reason, I will never regret my overseas stay though for various reasons it has been cut short.

Salty tears started dripping down on the paper at this point, intermingling with the existing stains and blurring the writing. Pulling out a paper napkin from the car door, LaRae wiped her cheeks and blew her nose before continuing to read.

First, let me apologize if in any way I came across as more than a friend to you. I know I had stated that I had a girlfriend back home. It was never my intention to send you mixed signals. I am so sorry if I caused you pain or confusion. Know that my main concern is for your happiness and I would never willingly stand in the way of it.

LaRae frowned, mildly confused. How could Lars possibly stand in the way of her happiness? The statement was so ridiculous she laughed out loud. "Please come and stand in my way right now!" she pleaded to the page. It would *make* her happiness and definitely not obscure it.

I also am writing you to inform you that I am not coming back to the US. I ask your forgiveness for the suddenness of this decision. It caught me by surprise as well. But I have decided it is for the best. I have been offered a job with a development project in Africa. It is an unexpected but great opportunity for me. So that is where I am writing from.

The setting is actually idyllic, especially at night when the chaos of the day calms down. As I write tonight I sit by the fire in front of a mud hut on the high planes of Kenya. It has been a long day. We have been drilling for water with equipment that has been temperamental. Part of our job is to teach the local men how to operate the machinery involved. There have been many problems so far. But I think I was made for this. I love it in spite of the many frustrations and obstacles. I hope you can say the same about your life. Please promise me not to let go of your art! The world will be a richer place because of what you bring to it. I wish you much happiness. Say goodbye to the Windy City for me and stay safe. May God bless you and keep you!

Your Norwegian friend,
Lars Pettersen

LaRae looked at the envelope for the return address and realized there was none. Hammering her steering wheel in frustration she let out a loud scream. A rap on her window startled her.

"Ma'am, is everything alright?" A grizzled game warden examined her closely.

"No, sir. I am not all right and I can't really think of anything that is all right in my life right now." She stared him down.

"In that case, I'll be glad to assist you in any official capacity I can, ma'am."

Can you mutate and transform into a different man of my choice? After the outburst, it took a minute for her to reassure the warden she was not an imminent risk to herself or others. On her way home, she made a detour by Amanda's house.

"Is there something wrong with me?" she blurted out as she walked in through the garage door.

Amanda, who was seated on a bar stool nursing the baby while perusing a jewelry catalog, looked up at her quizzically. "Apart from the fact that you have become a hermit with antisocial tendencies?"

"Very funny. Taking care of Dad takes all my time and energy."

"Which is exactly why we hired hospice," Amanda interjected. "Your two nephews have forgotten what you look like. Plus I miss you babysitting so I can hit the gym." She pointed at her belly. The spandex outfit looked cute even with her leftover pregnancy bulge. But then again, it had also looked cute in her last trimester. Leave it to her sister to add pizazz to childbearing and make a neon yellow, clingy top look sexy. Even sack cloth would succumb to flattering her.

Wallie-boy sucked deeply, milk dripping down his fat cheeks. "Start shaving your legs again and join me in class tomorrow. I'll get a sitter. I bought you a purple Zumba skirt with the dangling gold coins!" Amanda gave her a once over and frowned at the grey sweatpants and green knitted sweater covered in fuzz balls. "Your wardrobe needs sprucing up. Add Lycra to accentuate your curves and Norman will go ring shopping in no time! When was the last time you got kissed anyway?"

LaRae grabbed her nephew from her sister's lap and marched to the nursery, but stopped halfway up the stairs and yelled: "I'm burping the only sane person in this place."

So much for a pity session. Maybe there is something wrong with me after all? Baby Wallie smiled as she patted his back in the rocking chair. Burying her nose in his downy head, she inhaled the scent of his shampoo and the milk. She crumpled the letter in her pocket into a ball and swore off all men except for her father to whom she would pledge her wholehearted devotion to the end.

CHAPTER 12

In his last moments, she held her father's hand. The clock ticked loudly in the quiet room. As he drew his final breaths, LaRae felt no brush of angels' wings. The only brush she felt was Lorenzo, rubbing his soft back against her calves. The nurse closed her father's eyes. "He was a sweet man. You are fortunate to have had such a good father."

Amanda arrived in a whirlwind of distress. "I was on the gynecologist's examining table with my phone on mute. I can't believe I wasn't here when he died!" The two sisters embraced, clinging tightly to each other.

Over the next few days, they implemented the arrangements prepared ahead of time.

Edmund Gunther's funeral was a weeping affair where even the heavens participated. The drenched attendants huddled under black umbrellas, listening to Psalm 23 being read by the graveside. Reverend Richter's voice rose above the patter of the rain; "Though I walk through the valley of the shadow of death I will fear no evil: for thou art with me; Thy rod and thy staff they comfort me. Thou preparea a table before me in the presence of mine enemies: thou anointest my head with oil; my cup runneth over. Surely goodness and mercy shall follow me all the days of my life. And I will dwell in the house of the Lord forever."

LaRae was grateful for Amanda's concession to a closed casket. Her father's emaciated, cancer-ravaged body was at least tucked away from sight. LaRae hoped the people assembled would remember him for his vigor and uprightness instead of his recent fragility. The sisters had arranged for refreshments to be served in the First Lutheran Fellowship Hall. Their parents' friends manned the table while Amanda and LaRae shook people's hands and received their condolences.

Uncle Walter showed up at the end of the line. Her father's brother and a widower, she realized with a shock he was the closest family they had left. His warm hands steadied her and under the bushy eyebrows his gray eyes scrutinized her face.

"I am taking LaRae home," he announced to Amanda in his usual gruff voice. Despite the stern façade he made sure she locked the door behind her and didn't drive off until she waved at him from the kitchen window.

The following morning, LaRae did not move from her bed but lay staring at the ceiling. By late afternoon she shuffled barefoot to the kitchen and poured a glass of milk, then gagged and spit the turned liquid in the kitchen sink while looking out the window. Her tree house in the oak stood out like a sore thumb against the pink sun, taunting her with its lost hopes and dreams.

LaRae forced herself to check voicemails. The first one informed that the utility bill was overdue. The second was the neighbor saying he'd had taken in her cat who seemed hungry. Her uncle's voice came on; "I desperately need someone to man the front desk at the business. Please call." Her barely veiled despair must not have gone unnoticed. In his unassuming way, Uncle Walter was tossing her a lifeline by creating a job at his dealership.

He must know I stink at organization.

Some secretary she'd make. Clerical skills were right beneath housework on her list of things to avoid in life. A week later, as she looked back, there was no clear memory of having actually started the proffered job. But as she took in her surroundings, LaRae found herself seated on a squeaky swivel chair behind a desk at her uncle's dealership, answering the phone and writing up bills of sale.

"Hop to it girl. Pull the Carfax for the white Escalade. We have a hot customer out there." Uncle Walter limped out to the lot and waved at an orange skinned man in a suit and sunglasses. The phone rang. Amanda was on the line, out of breath with excitement:

"Rae. Check out the customer I just sent over to buy a car. I gave him your number! He plans on starting a chain of tanning salons since *Tan Man* is so successful."

LaRae rolled her eyes and hung up. The prospects in Dresden were dizzying. Her uncle re-entered.

"Move it girl. Nice man. And an even nicer profit." Walter ran his hands through his thin hair before rubbing both hands together in satisfaction. Twenty minutes later as the Escalade left the lot, the new owner waved enthusiastically at both of them.

"Here Rae, he left a coupon for a free session. He'll take care of you personally when you drop in. Let's celebrate. Take this." Her uncle handed her a twenty-dollar bill. "Go get us some chicken salad sandwiches from the grocery. And a dozen chocolate chip cookies."

"Throw in another twenty and I'll buy a bag of organic Starbucks's coffee. And I'll deep clean your tar machine before I put those precious beans in it."

Uncle shook his head but forked over another bill.

"A small onetime bonus. But don't go all fancy on us, Rae. That stint in the big city messed you up some. Generic coffee keeps me going like the Energizer Bunny."

"That's because you triple the dose, Uncle." *And I have no wish to peer inside your gut.*

After finishing up work, she snuggled in bed with Lorenzo while devouring Lindt chocolate truffles. An indulgent habit, she needed to switch to Hershey's. *Uncle is right. I've adopted ways not compatible with my new budget.*

A multitude of scurrying feet above her ceiling made her hide under her covers. To avoid dwelling on a growing mice or rat infestation in the attic, her mind turned to the happenings of the last four months. She was *tired*. The next morning she managed to pry one leg off the mattress when her heart started thumping erratically. The clock ticking in the den fed its rising frenzy.

What have I ever done that's been truly significant? What if I live my entire life with nothing to show for it?

Seated on the edge of the bed, she grabbed two more truffles from her rapidly dwindling supply on the night table. The dark fruit of the cocoa tree had a calming effect. Who cared if it was 10 o'clock in the morning and that the formerly perfect ranch style home was still in disarray? Gone were the days when the washer hummed by seven AM while the silver lay immersed in a polishing agent in the kitchen sink and the scent of sausage and grits wafted into her room.

This poor house is crumbling under dust, dirt and neglect. Like a respectable middle class lady succumbing to a meager retirement without caretakers or rescue.

An accusing voice breathed down her neck, its breath familiar and pungent. "Pitiful creature! If you are going to be ordinary you'd better get this house under control," it wheezed. "And if you are going to be extraordinary then you'd better pop up right now and start producing."

LaRae mentally catalogued the secret wish list she hadn't shared with anyone. Carefully tucked away to the back regions of her mind, she rarely let herself dwell on it any more. A master painting, carefully and painstakingly depicted on canvas by LaRae herself. Or a brilliant, well-honed novel, conceived and written during the dark of winter. Or herself in a potter's studio producing and selling Florentine-inspired, elegant vessels, hand painted and glazed in untraditional colors out of a country estate in Provence, France. She imagined tourists and collectors dropping by to watch her work and purchase pieces.

Those were the real dreams. Except the word *dream* was so tainted with disillusionment that she shunned it like leprosy. She'd dabbled in the arts. Like a child frolicking in a mud puddle, her amateurish attempts had left her happy, yet muddied and frustrated in the end. She also had the weird sense of being a child trapped behind a wall, with no option except for staying in the mud puddle of mediocrity. What if on the other side of the wall there was actually a wide-open and limitless ocean? With the niggling thought of there being an unlimited sea, the puddle had lost its attraction. To her greatest consternation, the wall seemed insurmountable. Unscalable. Endless. And with no discernible door. She was trapped. So utterly and hopelessly trapped that her despair had become a cloak she wore day and night.

A crisp manuscript lay buried in the night table drawer of her dated, pink bedroom, the final chapter still missing. *You'll never finish it,* her inner accuser hissed. Incomplete oil paintings were stacked neatly in her closet behind piles of outdated shoes and clothing. Scenes of still lives, a portrait of Lorenzo and the abstract landscapes of Lake Michigan gathered dust without complaining. And the attempts at pottery were becoming a college memory by now. Had she been wrong in going? Had her ceramic bust found a resting place at the city dump? Or maybe— weirdly—it graced some stranger's mantelpiece after being sold at the school's *miscellaneous sale*. Her own head, painstakingly sculpted from clay and fired in a kiln with a natural bronze glaze added for the finish. The very project she'd been working on when Lars had walked into her life.

"This blasted head so full of ideas, yet disconnected from the rest of my body," she muttered to herself. "It is a most fitting image: a head full of great initiatives on a mantelpiece, yet lacking the body to get anything executed."

She was in awe of the ones who pulled the trigger, - in full blown admiration of those who lived out the Nike slogan: "Just do it!" The slogan sounded simple. Utterly doable. LaRae wiggled her toes to increase the circulation then padded to the freezing kitchen and made black tea. Seated at the table, she downed a bag of Cheetos with the hot beverage.

From a young age she'd observed the folks around her. Somehow, they seemed like little Play Mobile people who all got to wear different hats and accessories. Then you placed them just so. "Here is the guy in the hardhat. Let's put him next to the bulldozer. Here is the girl in the exercise outfit. Let her walk the dog. Here is the astronaut—for sure let's not place him in the zoo!" Life entailed so much hustle and bustle. From early childhood intense productivity had been the norm in the tiny geographical place in Illinois she called home.

Most people confidently slipped into their roles in this agricultural community. Not only did it seem a no-brainer to pick a career path, they also embraced it with vigor.

La Rae felt the inner paralysis sweep over her again. Hunched over the table, she counted the cracks in the linoleum of her parent's kitchen. Did other people ever feel this way? Caught up in indecision. Paralyzed by choices and possibilities. Yet all the while locked into realities so different from what had been hoped for. And then there was the occasional crazy thought that wormed its way into her consciousness: what if a trace of greatness resided within? And if so, was that minuscule possibility longing desperately to grow wings so tall and strong that one day she might soar?

A Holy Scripture from Sunday School floated up: "I said, oh that I had the wings of a dove! I would fly away and be at rest."

She vaguely remembered David the Psalmist longing for wings to fly away. It seemed that his wish to fly away was because he'd been hard pressed and persecuted. A bad king had been trying to kill him, causing him to hide in caves in the wilderness.

"Me? I'm in my own cave. Trapped in my own wilderness. Despair is so close on my heels that its putrid breath is filling my lungs every time I inhale."

LaRae picked at her arms where little sores had developed. When these thoughts haunted her, her hands would not be still but scratched at her own skin. As if every bother, disappointment and worry that clung to her could just be flicked off as easily as flies or mosquitos. *Maybe the stuff clinging to me is more like leeches? Slowly, but surely sucking the lifeblood out of me.* Picking at the outside didn't eradicate the problem. But unfortunately, that notion didn't keep her from trying.

"David, I wish for wings just like you. I need wings to fly into my destiny."

She pinched her forearms harder this time and wondered: "what do you do if you are wingless and your deepest longing is to fly?"

In all her schooling the most important things she'd been looking to learn had eluded her. Or had they simply not been taught? Mathematical formulas and spelling had come easily to her. Chemistry had required an extra effort. Biology had been interesting. In English she spun a good yarn for her creative essays. Pulling the trigger to get something published was a different story though. It would require being seen. Heard. On display. All impossibilities. Because just as her mother had perfected the art of keeping a spotless home, LaRae had perfected the art of hunkering down in inaccessible hiddenness.

She forced her feet to the bathroom to brush her very smelly teeth. The avocado green tiles had an even more nauseating effect on her today than usual. Studying her reflection in the square mirror, she felt no thrill at what met her eye. *Hiding,* she thought. "Wingless," she whispered.

Behind the gold rimmed glasses, green, almond shaped eyes stared back at her, scrutinizing the tiniest detail. Her oval face was lost in a sea of unruly waves of hair. The curls undulated over her shoulders, yet lacked in shine and luster. "Who froze you in time?" she asked her mirrored twin. "Did you arrive on earth in a warm-blooded body yet frozen on the inside?"

LaRae jumped when the alarm went off on her cell phone. Unfortunately even the frozen had places to be. Life was relentlessly pushing her along. Like a piece of flotsam caught in a whirlpool of activity she felt as if she was being sucked into circles, going round and round, deeper and deeper into the vortex. Yet, somehow, she was missing the very center of things. Shaking off her morbid thoughts, she threw on a pair of jeans and a sweatshirt and rushed to the driveway.

Thank God her Corolla started today! At least she wouldn't have to call Uncle Walter for assistance again. It was hard enough trying to slip unnoticed into his office without having to explain once again why she was late. Uncle
Walter's patience was wearing thin. Kind-hearted in giving her

the job, as much as she hated sitting at that desk, she owed it to him to perform and quit daydreaming.

"Walter Gunther Auto Sales, it's another great day in Dresden. What can I do for you?" LaRae quipped laconically while holding the receiver to her ear.

"Your enthusiasm is killing me, Sis," the voice at the other end piped. "What you need is to put some pep back into your step. I enrolled you at the YMCA."

LaRae sighed. Give her a climbing rope or a walking trail and she'd gladly expend calories. But working out in spandex fell into the same category as allergy shots. The local gym's air was saturated with sweat and other body odors and equally overcrowded. She avoided it all cost. And her sister insisted on her wearing the ridiculous belly dance scarf in class? When they'd met for coffee at *Miss Daisy's* to discuss the pile of medical bills her sister had drawn all kinds of attention wearing her hot pink Zumba scarf over her rounded hips. Mourning in black was not a thing anymore.

"Make sure you remember your promise to babysit tonight. In case you lost track again, today is Friday."

LaRae startled. The weekend loomed on the horizon.

"I bought your favorite pizza with the spinach and feta cheese."

"That's *your* favorite, Amanda. Remember I gave up gluten after Dad passed and the naturopath said I had developed allergies."

"Oh, I forgot. Don't dawdle. Chris and I are going to the movies. You can sleep on the couch. We'll be out late."

After wrapping up at the office, she stopped at the Dollar General and drove to her sister's. Her nephews were playing tag in the bushes of the front yard. "Come on, buddies! Strange things are going down in the woods out back. Let's paint your faces and head out." LaRae pulled her purchases from the back seat of her car.

"Wow! Bows and arrows!"

"And a feather headdress! Will you paint your face, too?" Drew asked pleadingly.

LaRae acquiesced. They finished the camouflage job and she put Baby Wallie in a sling across her belly. The next two hours they slinked behind trees and rocks, playing settlers and native Indians.

After cleaning up from the outdoor play Mickey beat them at Candyland. The nephews yawned.

"Aunt Rae-Rae, can we make a tent again? We brought down our sleeping bags early this morning," Drew asked.

"Yes. I'll read about Goldilocks after we settle into our indoor tent."

They went through the set-up drill, draping the dining room table in blankets and snuggled underneath it. With the baby monitor nearby because Wallie was asleep upstairs, LaRae read.

She woke up to a world of pink and red. Groggily she looked around and discovered the blankets and sheets of last night. She lay still on the hard floor, relishing Drew's steady breath on her face. Maybe kids were more therapeutic than ice cream?

When the clang of pots resounded from the kitchen, she got up and helped Amanda cook a country breakfast complete with hash browns, bacon and buttermilk biscuits. The boys inhaled the food, then told their mom about their exploits in the woods.

Later, Amanda followed her to the car. "Come back next weekend, Sis. The chaos lessens when you're here. You're also more fun to be with when you're around the boys."

LaRae shrugged and sped home. A steady curtain of rain clouded her visibility. With an armful of mail, she stepped into the kitchen and tore open an envelope from the Diagnostic Lab, when a drip caught her attention. Water was spilling from the ceiling over the stove. With her sneakers getting soaked from wading into the wet floor puddle, she placed a basin under the leak and threw bath towels on the floor, then tuned out the split splat of water by turning on a classic movie. She spent the night on the couch, then all of Sunday in the same spot, losing herself in Gone With The Wind, then Jane Eyre and the black and white rendition of Casablanca. The dry desert stole her mind away from the steadily increasing dam in the kitchen.

When Monday morning rolled around, she pulled her greasy hair in a bun and turned the key in the Corolla. While her car hobbled down the road, she wondered when she'd showered last. She slunk in the door to the showroom and hid behind the computer screen.

"You're late." Uncle Walter's gruff voice came through the crack in the door from his office. He walked to the counter and filled up his Elvis mug with coffee, then walked to her desk and sat down across from her. "I worry about you."

LaRae gave a feeble laugh. "Why?"

"Your house is falling apart and don't even try to tell me it isn't. I've seen the shape of the roof and the windows. Besides, when I mounted the new thermostat, I noticed the leak in the kitchen. You also keep on driving this disaster on four wheels. It isn't just a danger to yourself but the general population," he motioned to the sales lot out front.

He's on a rampage. And he was right. However, one thing her relative didn't know was that their parents' investments had gone down the drain in the nationwide economic downturn of 2008. What had been so painstakingly saved by their mother had vanished overnight. Fortunately, the sale of Dad's pickup and garage was enough to settle his astronomical medical bill. That her father had let his medical coverage lapse had been another shock. But he'd been distracted after Mother passed. *My fault.* The creaking sound of the swivel chair brought her back to the conversation at hand.

"At least park your car in the back from now on. It's bad publicity. Clients must think I'm selling ratty second-hand cars or that I pay you a pauper's pay."

LaRae followed his glance out the window. The blue Toyota Corolla's rust and dents stood out in the otherwise perky and balloon-filled car lot. Bought at auction for her sixteenth birthday, it had generously given her 219,000 miles. *I need a new car.* LaRae felt as if she'd been presented with an unsolvable math quiz. The missing factor in the equation was dollars. And how did she conjure such a thing up?

Uncle Walter pushed himself up from the seat and winced. His arthritic knees gave him fits, but instead of complaining he scowled at her. "You turn down my offer to give or lend you a vehicle. I call that false modesty."

He stomped into the parking lot. LaRae fingered the photo of a majestic Norwegian mountain she kept taped to her desk. *If only I had wings.*

CHAPTER 13

"Uncle Walter, you snitch!" LaRae winced at the pounding and hammering on her roof. Men were crawling everywhere, - in her attic, up against the gutters and around the AC unit. In the living room she marched to the window and yanked the curtains to block out their sight but yelped when a face popped up five inches away on the other of the glass.

"Sorry, ma'am. Just inspecting the window frame for rot," the man apologized. In an effort to avoid the frenzied invasion, she escaped to the mailbox and pulled out a wad of advertisements. A large envelope addressed to her fluttered to the lifeless lawn.

She retreated to the kitchen and brewed a cup of Ceylon tea, steeping it just right for three minutes when a knock sounded on the door. The foreman of the crew, wearing a blue hardhat and Poirot mustache, nodded. "We're taking off, I'll drop off an estimate directly."

"Do I need to brace myself for bad news?"

"The house requires extensive work." He lifted his hand in greeting, then strode to the company van.

LaRae made a beeline for the emergency chocolate supply tucked behind the chili cans in the pantry. She, like Mom had prepared wisely. After chewing a truffle, she tore open the large manila envelope and recognized the name of the lawyer who'd executed her parents' wills. Another smaller envelope fell out and as she picked it up she noticed red and green, foreign stamps. She delved into the contents, tripping on a few legal terms.

When done, she jumped up from the table and pulled down the folded attic ladder in the hallway. Bits of insulation hung from the rafters and a bird's nest clung to the eaves. She ignored any mice and opened a box neatly labeled "Family Correspondence". LaRae sat cross-legged on the bare plywood floor, sifting through birthday and Christmas cards before hitting upon a stack of yellowed letters in Norwegian, written in a neat, tidy script. With the box balanced on her hip, she descended the rickety stairs.

The shrill tone of her cell phone cut through the silence. "'A deceased family member by the name of Erna Halverson has bequeathed her estate in Norway to the closest living kin, Amanda McNeal and LaRae Gunther. House must be taken possession of within 180 days or the estate will be handed over to Miss Halverson's church. You read it, right? Aren't you wild with excitement, Rae?"

"I'm stunned. Wait, I recall now. Grandma's sister refused to accompany her to America. I'm trying to read her letters but they are in Norwegian."

"Oh, my gosh. This takes care of our problem, killing two birds with one stone. Christopher is delirious because this will afford us a condo in Florida."

Confused, LaRae listened while examining a faded sepia-toned photo of a birdlike woman dressed in a long skirt and fitted, buttoned up blouse.

"While you fly over to sell the property, we are renovating and selling Mom's and Dad's house. Afterwards you can rent an apartment or take us up on our offer to live in the basement. It's why we added a bath downstairs. Christopher is arranging the details with the lawyer."

"Hold your horses, Amanda! What are you talking about?"

"You flying over to meet the attorney. He'll hook you up with a builder to repair the siding. Then you'll find a local realtor and list it. The beauty is you get to live in the house for free while supervising the improvements. Chris and I will lend you money. You can reimburse us after the sale." Amanda rambled on when the doorbell drowned her out.

LaRae cracked the door open and faced Norman. Upon seeing her, his left hand shot out of his jean pocket, revealing two tickets to the Dresden High School baseball game.

"The Tigers will win tonight, Sweets!"

"You know I hate baseball."

"Well, it beats the funk you've been in." He wiggled his eyebrows. "Plus. I have a surprise afterwards." A peculiar glint lit his marsh-colored eyes. "The renovated Dairy Queen is reopening. A girl I knew a long time ago couldn't get enough of the banana split drenched in hot chocolate fudge. I wonder if she's still around." He winked while resituating a lump of chewing tobacco in his lower jaw.

"She graduated to Haagen-Dazs. I don't know, let me think about it. I have plans already." *Another night on the couch watching the Discovery Channel.*

Amanda's loud yell from the phone in her hand interrupted: "Sis? Are you even paying attention? If that's Norman, call me right back when he leaves."

LaRae sank into the avocado colored tub. Far from a spa, the steamy water still relaxed her knotted neck and shoulders. She submerged her body, enjoying the muted underwater environment but came up for air to the chime of her phone. A glance at the caller ID showed two missed calls.

"Yes."

"Girl, get your mojo on for tonight," Amanda squealed.

"Why?" LaRae's innate suspicion rose to new heights. News traveled fast in Dresden and her sister was the trunk of the proverbial grapevine. When locals asked LaRae "What's the news?" it had at last dawned on her they were not inquiring about the armed struggle in Somalia or the drought in Eritrea but were catching up on gossip. She ducked the question by referring them to Amanda who took great pride in sniffing out the secrets associated with small town living.

"Rumor has it Norman shopped at the mall in Bloomington."

"Who cares? Half of Dresden goes, acting as if the food court is French cuisine."

"Whoa! Are you snapping at me, girl? Wait till you hear the latest. They have a Kay Jewelers in there."

An alarm went off in LaRae's head. *Ding, ding, ding. Danger, danger, danger.* "Hmmm. For what date is Christopher wanting to book that flight?"

"Next Saturday. Imagine boarding the plane with a ring on your finger!" Amanda laughed. "I wonder if Norman splurged on a two-carat diamond. Then again, he is saving for a combine, so I doubt it. My girlfriend ran into a cousin who said Norman exited the store with a tiny bag."

LaRae hung up and toweled off before dressing and tacking a note to the front door. Then she sped off, ditching the date and the Tigers. She traversed the countryside, dusk obliterating barns and houses against the horizon.

After entering Bloomington, she passed a row of franchise restaurants and turned left into the mall parking. Funds or not, the momentous decision she'd made called for a shopping spree. *What do people wear on the streets of Norway in April?* In the mood for bohemian and frivolous, she thought of calling Starr for advice. As she entered a warmly lit department store, a sales rack beckoned, but she strode past it towards a deep green peasant blouse with lace trim. The red, embroidered roses around the neckline clinched the deal. She draped it over the cart when her eye caught sight of an ankle length batik skirt in brown and orange. An hour later, she paid for multiple purchases and decided to wear the new paper bead necklace imported from a Fair Trade organization. Next, she ditched "Payless" for a more upscale shoe store. She was trying on a pair of blue platform sandals when the clerk approached and shot her an admiring glance.

"I'd kill to have your slim ankles and calves."

"Oh, thank you! I'm too skinny but appreciate the compliment." The heels gave her model height. But who cared? Hopefully Norway's men were tall or wouldn't act insecure if she towered over them. *I know a tall man in Norway. But where are you?* LaRae paid for the shoes and a pair of cognac colored, fur lined leather boots then walked to the coffee shop and indulged in a Chai and an almond biscotti. Like trophies, her loot lay piled up on the empty chairs across the round bistro table where she sat. The spanking new wardrobe of light and heavy clothing had one common denominator: unique design and bold color. Her lips stretched in a smile when she pictured Mother's frown at her failure to check any price tags. As the chai spices titillated her tongue she thought of her mousy hair and wintery, oatmeal face staring back at her in the fitting room mirror. She gulped down the drink before hurrying to the opposite end of the mall. A girl with a nose piercing in the form of a crescent moon pointed to a red adjustable chair.

"Haircut or color?"

"Both, but nothing too drastic." LaRae's gaze rested on the turquoise tinged mane of her hairdresser. "Highlights might be nice."

The teen chewed gum but reached out her hand. "I'm Ima. We can leaf through examples for inspiration?"

LaRae nodded and decided on a look.

She relaxed as the girl shampooed her hair and threw in a peppermint scalp massage. Through the ensuing process, she learned that Ima had a six-month-old baby suffering from asthma and a boyfriend who'd taken off for California with her car and best friend.

"What do you think?" Ima swiveled the chair and LaRae stared at the unfamiliar sight. Only the high cheekbones and green eyes gave her away. "I like the rich chestnut base."

"And I adore your locks scintillating with golden highlights."

"My hair looks alive. The layering and feathery effects lighten its heaviness." She let out a giggle. "I'm going overseas. Thanks for helping me travel in style." After slipping Ima an extra twenty dollars, she chugged home not minding the rattling noises. With the newly acquired goodies her suitcases would be on the heavy side. But her heart would be traveling light and her ring finger bare.

"I disagree with your sister's hare-brained scheme. You've never been out of the state of Illinois. Now you insist on traipsing to places where young girls vanish and end up in sex rings?" Uncle Walter slammed the Elvis mug to the desk and spilled his coffee. "Ouch! I'm too old to drop everything to come rescue you."

LaRae grabbed a roll of paper towel and wiped his hand. "I'll be okay. I promise to stay in touch and return by mid-May. Sorry to leave you hanging as far as the job."

He harrumphed. "The job is the least of my worries. Take the key for the pickup to transport stuff to the dump and charity." She pecked him on the cheek and took off in his Chevy when Amanda called.

"I dropped off stickers and an iPad in the hallway. Pink is for keeping, blue for storage and yellow for trash. Take pics and list items for sale on the neighborhood app." LaRae agreed and turned on the radio to help develop a rhythm and got to work. They stored things of sentimental value in Amanda's attic and basement. Thursday, LaRae watched furniture being loaded into a thrift truck and braced herself for a wave of sadness. To her great surprise, both her mind and body felt as light as a helium balloon. The beds had served their purpose and so had the well-worn couch. Christopher swung by to pick up the antique Biedermeier sofa that was going into Amanda's library. The dining room table was going to the abused women's shelter. The linen armoire had been re-purposed into a toy closet by the Garcia family next door and the pots and pans so thoroughly scrubbed by her mother puttered with refried beans on their stove.

LaRae pictured herself tottering out of a long overdue childhood and embracing an adulthood of her own making. The thought made her stomach clench but her heart buzz. As large and unpredictable as the Western Frontier must have appeared to her forebears, the unknown stretched out in front of her.

"I bring witness to my family's ability to survive and create a life for themselves," she spoke out loud. "I'll follow in the steps of Grandmother." She thought of her "mormor" not knowing English yet not shying away from cultural obstacles but throwing herself fully into a new life.

With God's help Norway constituted the first step of her own journey. LaRae went inside to sort drawers, pulling out the tarnished heirloom silver and putting it on the counter. In a tribute to her mom, she polished and rubbed the forks, spoons and knives before delivering them to her sister's lockbox. A door slamming caused her to jump.

"What in the world? You look like a babe!" Amanda entered the kitchen with Wallie's chubby arms reaching out, begging to be held. With Cheerios glued to his chin and burp spots on his shirt, he gave her a toothless grin.

"What do you mean? It's just a bit of makeup." LaRae waved her hand dismissively in the air.

"You have a new 'do'. Blond! And dangling earrings. Contacts too?" Like a hawk, Amanda circled her, eyes narrowed. "You confuse me. Why now? After years of nagging? You didn't go to Sally, I would've known. Ah, I get it!" she exclaimed triumphantly. "You disappeared. Snuck off and got yourself a makeover in the city because you are secretly engaged. Congratulations!" Amanda caught her in a fierce hug. "No worries. I won't tell anyone."

"Have you lost your mind?" LaRae ground out the words succinctly into her sister's ear while locked in her arms. "It's a haircut. Stop acting ridiculous and let's discuss Mother's china."

"I don't care for it. You know I dislike old stuff." Amanda wrinkled her nose and tapped her manicured finger on the kitchen counter. "Store it in my attic till the wedding. Norman said anything'll be helpful to get you started."

LaRae flung the soup ladle she was clenching onto the linoleum floor and stomped her foot. "Stop it! I'm not marrying Norman!" She still fumed as the taillights from Amanda's car disappeared. With luck she'd be in the air above the Atlantic Ocean before the gossip mill fed on the latest. But knowing sister, rumors of her so-called engagement were spreading like measles this very minute. She dumped the silver forks in the sink, declining the incoming call from the subject of their conversation. Dodging her ardent pursuer had become a game requiring wits. *Sorry buddy. I'm just so busy preparing for my new life.* Once settled overseas, she'd write him, making it clear as rain that holy matrimony was not on her to-do list.

When Friday afternoon arrived, LaRae crammed herself and her luggage into the car. Her body was aching from having burned the midnight oil only to rise with Mr. Garcia's rooster. But "project move-out" had been accomplished and the ranch house was vacant. As a pink March sun had dropped below the tree line the night before, she climbed into her tree house to bid the beloved abode farewell. She sped to Normal and drove up the incline to Amanda's, then pulled the key out of the ignition just as smoke began rising from the hood. A sudden twinge of guilt jabbed her at donating the wreck to the Salvation Army.

Drew and Mickey knocked on the driver's window. "Norman has a surprise for you!"

"Caught you!" LaRae startled as her nemesis jumped out from the bushes, a big grin on his face. Dressed in Western boots and a checkered flannel shirt, he rolled back his shoulders and puffed out his broad chest. "I've been enjoying our game of cat and mouse," he said and wiggled his eyebrows as she unloaded a suitcase. "A girl playing hard to get whets my appetite." He removed his cap and wiped his forehead with a blue bandana. "But now the cat has a big surprise up its sleeve." *An awkward choice of words.* Norman took a step closer and motioned to the cab of his truck. "Hop in and grant your childhood sweetheart one single wish before take-off?"

"Please Auntie, Mom said we can come too!" Her two nephews shamelessly chimed in.

"Make it fast. I still have things to do." She softened her tone, reminded of her parent's devotion to the man in front of her.

"Climb in, Rae." When she mounted the step, he playfully slapped her hind quarters. She smacked his upper arm back, hitting a bulging bicep which made her hand sting. Norman chuckled.

"Oooh..." The nephews covered their open mouths with their hands.

"Guys, jump in next to Sweet Cakes." She scooted all the way to the passenger window, wedging the boys between them while wondering why she felt both powerless and dangerously furious at the same time.

Norman's truck spun out of the driveway while her sister waved excitedly from the kitchen window. The road took them to the south side of Dresden into Benton County. Hundreds of acres spread out on both sides, reminiscent of a quilt of black and brown with barns adding rectangular shapes of red. Norman turned right onto a narrow dirt track and his breathing increased.

"Can I blindfold you?"

"Absolutely not! Whatever your surprise is, I'll take it in with my eyes wide open, thank you. You know I dislike blindfolds." LaRae stepped out and squinted towards the end of the gravel path. A brand-new doublewide trailer loomed by the edge of the naked soybean field.

"Welcome to your future home," Norman whispered as he draped his arm around her shoulder. Speechless, she took in the grey vinyl siding and concrete steps leading up to a burgundy front door. "This is what I've saved for," Norman grabbed a handful of dirt and held it up to the boys' faces. "Smell it! Stubbs land. Best soil in the country." The dirt showed up wet and lumpy in his palm. "Delilah inspired me, Rae." He spun her sideways and looked at her. "Hogs. The price of pork is decent nowadays."

LaRae squeaked, frozen in place. "I'm so sorry Norman, I

don't have time to see the inside. I congratulate you on your perseverance. Your parents must be proud." *God? Help this man find a wife wanting to farm pigs and keep him warm in bed. In uttering the request, God: I am not a candidate.*

Once back in her sister's driveway, LaRae broke the news to him in the truck cab. "I may stay gone awhile, and am not ready to settle down. I don't even have romantic feelings for you." Drew stopped fiddling with the car radio, looking alarmed. Mickey unwrapped a stick of gum from a pack in the empty ash tray.

Norman seemed unfazed. "Wait till I tell Mother I showed you the property. She'll want to plan for a wedding." He grabbed her hands. "Take your time. No rush. I still need to put ten grand away for equipment. At least I have the tractor," he added encouragingly. "And Amanda offered to give a hand with planning once you're ready."

LaRae escaped to the guest bedroom and banged her head against the wall. Repeatedly.

"Auntie, will you travel with a big bruise on your forehead?" Mickey asked in a concerned voice. "Did you not like Uncle Norman's trailer?"

She grabbed Mickey by his spindly shoulders. "Don't you call him that again because he'll never be your uncle." Feeling badly about her outburst, LaRae enfolded him in a hug. "I'm sorry. Auntie will travel the world to find a great uncle. I have a passport and ticket. If you promise to do a real good job with Lorenzo, I'll look high and low for a boyfriend. Deal?"

He eyed her wonderingly. "Guess you don't like pigs. But okay. Deal."

Saturday appeared with a promise of spring. After weeks of intermittent rain and fog, blue sky greeted Normal. As they ate breakfast, Mickey fed their four-legged, furry houseguest a can of albacore tuna.

"This shows Lorenzo I'll take good care of him." He put the food on the floor by a new, velvet pet bed.

"If you ever doubted that I loved you, this ought to be proof,"

Amanda stated as LaRae hugged her cat goodbye. "You know I abhor animals. Yet here I am, putting a litter box in my spotless laundry room." Wrinkling her nose, she grabbed the baby and headed to the hallway. "Come on. Your two suitcases are bursting at the seams. One would think you were moving indefinitely! I hope you packed the Zumba outfit. I put it on your bed last night. Zumba originated with the Vikings, I heard."

"Latin America, Sis." LaRae hugged her and kissed her cheek. "Keep me in the loop. We can Skype. I don't want to miss Wallie's new teeth and Drew's next art work or Mickey's Lego accomplishments." She waved goodbye.

Her brother-in-law drove her to the airport and spoke at a red light. "My sweet wife may have a meltdown once you're far away. Thank God you got that passport last summer. I rushed into booking the ticket without thinking about whether you had one or not."

LaRae thought back to June last year. "The missions trip to Mexico got cancelled when our team leader suffered acute appendicitis. I'll miss it this year too." *So sorry team mates but I'm taking possession of my foreign property.*

With a strong urge to pinch herself they arrived at the O'Hare Airport. She pecked Christopher on the cheek and walked towards security. With a queenly wave directed at her brother-in-law, she hollered: "If I don't return, it means I'm staying forever. Come visit!"

Billboards announced the departures. She followed arrows until locating Gate A 13. Security was tight; she answered questions by two security agents before boarding, then buckled in tightly and studied the emergency evacuation directions. The plane picked up speed and swooshed up in the air. From her aisle seat, LaRae heard a couple of babies scream, their ears hurting from the ascent. She accepted the flight attendant's complimentary bottle of red wine and a bag of pretzels. At dinnertime pockets of turbulence sent cups and food trays reeling. Passengers apologized to one another for their scattered belongings. The flight attendants ran themselves ragged, picking up and cleaning spills. When the weather cleared, they sold tax-free goods and handed out extra bottles of water. Too wound up to sleep, LaRae observed a Muslim man reading the Koran in Arabic when a roll of Lifesavers appeared in front of her.

"Hi! I am Peggy. I nodded off during take-off and missed dinner." Her gray-haired neighbor motioned for her to take one. "I'm meeting my cousin in Amsterdam. She's a lab tech in the US military in Germany, bless her heart. No telling what nasty germs she deals with; the boys return from the Middle East riddled with PTSD and disease. We're going to see the tulips in bloom but are definitely avoiding the Red Light District. Then we take the train to Eastern Europe. I dread it already." Her voice dropped, and she leaned closer. LaRae didn't know much about Peggy except she must be on a raw garlic diet or suffering from halitosis.

"My colleague at the water filtration plant is Jewish. His father survived Auschwitz. I promised I'd go visit in his place." While getting ready to reveal one more piece of information above the droning noise of the jet engine, her new companion popped a Coke can open. "I just hope my corns won't act up. The podiatrist tried his best to remove them, but said they were in awkward places. I'll show you later." At the thought, her neighbor kicked off her leather shoes. "These are orthopedic. Cost me an arm and a leg. But Europeans walk everywhere."

LaRae sucked on a lifesaver, and Peggy spoke again.

"Mind you, my sister says that's why they're not obese. Of course, they don't have access to good food like we have either." Peggy rolled her eyes in pity. "I hope we'll be able to find a McDonald's or something else familiar to eat. They're nuts about cabbage dishes in Eastern Europe. Nothing gives me gas as much as cabbage. Mind you,I am adventurous. But I just can't handle that awful, heavy black bread they make in Germany. Creates a gridlock," she pointed at her rather visible belly. "Call me crazy," she whispered, "But I packed a loaf of Wonder Bread in the suitcase. And peanut butter crackers in my tote for when my blood sugar drops."

"Let's hope that doesn't happen." Her mind spinning with new impressions, LaRae sighed with deep contentment. She was a tamed bird out on a test run, temporarily untethered and cage free. She should be worried about traveling alone. Yet the only emotion she could muster was a sense of growing elation.

The seven hour difference in time zones made for a short night on board the Boeing. As the captain informed that they were descending, water canals and budding fields showed up on the ground and a windmill appeared in the distance. At 7:05 am, the landing gear hit the tarmac of Schiphol Airport outside Amsterdam. It was midnight at home but LaRae's legs bounced. While waiting to exit the plane, Peggy grabbed LaRae and hugged her tight. "You're a sweet thing. Don't let no boy fool you into running away with him."

"Yes, ma'am. I'll be careful," she promised and strode down the transit tunnel, turning left towards the main hub.

The clean, modern airport was teeming with movement, music and noise. A contingent of African women in colorful wraparound skirts and headscarves pushed recycled bags stuffed to bursting on trolleys while cutting up and laughing in what sounded like a tribal dialect. Like garments pegged to a clothes line, a string of toddlers hung on to their garb, fussing and crying while younger babies were wrapped onto their backs. LaRae checked the gates. The signs announced departures to Mombasa, Kenya, and Warsaw, Poland. Where was the gate to her scheduled flight? The billboard down the hallway fortunately announced upcoming departures. After doing the math, she realized she had a couple of hours before boarding and decided to check out the stores. The central hall boasted specialty shops. In the restaurants early morning travelers were sipping espressos and nibbling at croissants.

One shop had a fridge stocked with liver pate, pickled beets, and Gouda cheese while glass shelves displayed the famous blue and white Delft porcelain. She fingered the tiny porcelain clogs and windmills and examined the collectible pitchers and plates but made no purchase. The flower shop next door bulged with tulips, narcissus, daffodils, and hyacinths. Drawn, she stopped to inhale the fragrance and wondered if the little house waiting for her in Norway had a garden and whether it was the wrong time of the year to plant. Ignorance ruled because she'd turned a deaf ear to her mother's running commentary on every living thing in the yard. LaRae had learned to nod in the right places without paying attention to the details in the conversation. The thought delivered a pang of regret and her hand shot out and grabbed a bag of 25 multi-colored flower bulbs.

"My mother adored tulips; do you have any tips for me?" LaRae asked the apple-cheeked lady at the cash register who launched into a lecture in a chipper, Dutch accent. She paid and made her way to the other end of the complex, her ears attuned to the languages swirling about her, some guttural, others harsh, and then French syllables sounding soft as feathers. The sounds formed a veritable symphony where each instrument added to a whole. She thought how even smells vary in different geographic locations and as she approached the appointed gate, realized she was falling in love, - not with a man but with the world.

A tiny crowd of mostly blond and blue-eyed people waited at her gate, speaking in subdued tones. She had memorized enough of Mormor's language to understand bits and pieces.

"Ja takk, det er fint." *Yes, thank you. That is fine*, the woman next to her responded to her husband's question.

LaRae tapped her boot in excitement and decided to enroll in a language class. They boarded, and as the puddle jumper lifted above the North Sea, LaRae watched the stark blue of the ocean from a window seat. If her life was a book, the chapters of her Midwestern American saga so tainted with loss were closing. She sighed, wishing she could guarantee readers an improvement in the story line. At least the scene was changing and the predictability was gone. A bag of peanuts landed on the table in front of her and LaRae munched the snack. Upon arrival, she'd buy postcards for Uncle Walter and Amanda. If heaven had an address, she'd send one to Mom and Dad too. She hoped the town would be pretty and friendly yet knew it might be ugly with people not interested in making friends with outsiders. In an attempt to shake off any romantic notions from the novels she'd ingested she opened a book on Norwegian history when another pesky thought intruded. *One Norwegian I know lives up to all my romantic notions*...She squelched the thought by slapping the book shut and helping herself to a Belgian praline from the box intended for the lawyer meeting her upon arrival.

Less than two hours into the flight, a jagged coastline appeared and large swaths of emerald fir and pine forests rolled out. Interspersed with irregularly shaped fields, the landscape looked like a crazy quilt in plush shades of brown on a multi-hued, green background. As the plane descended, the rugged, mountainous landscape grew more distinct. In a land resembling one humongous mountain, how had its people existed before industrialization? History claimed the uneven terrain had not been a deterrent to cultivating the soil. For centuries steep hillsides had incorporated topsy-turvy potato and vegetable patches. Farms had been erected clinging precariously to the mountain sides, and footpaths had been the only way to access some of the farmsteads. Sheep and goats had grazed nimbly around cliffs and crags. Eking out a living had been challenging during the best of times. When scarcity abounded, many folks had immigrated to America. LaRae felt admiration for past generations' work ethic and ingenuity. The discovery of large reservoirs of natural oil and gas in the North Sea had turned Norway into a wealthy nation almost overnight. The per capita income had become one of the highest in the world. And here she was arriving, - a foreigner, yet sharing in the wealth. LaRae placed her hand on the seat belt, poised to unbuckle the moment the plane touched down on her partially native soil.

CHAPTER 14

A western wind buffeted the Fokker, and it landed with a screech. Passengers drew audible sighs of relief when the doors opened then unbuckled and shuffled down the stairs to the tarmac. LaRae stopped at the exit and stared in wonder at the sky. Like a huge azure shield it arched over the rural landscape.

"I know," a Polish woman behind her commented in a heavy accent. "The first thing I relish when landing in this country is the color of the sky."

Dazed by jet lag yet alert to new impressions, LaRae walked across the tarmac into the small airport where she gathered her now battered-looking suitcases and dragged them to the bus stop. To her great relief the local bus she'd been advised to take was on schedule. They headed towards 'The White Town' as her Great Aunt's town was nicknamed because of its white painted, quaint clapboard houses. Giddy with the strangeness of this new place, she reclined her head on the velvet headrest. Compared to public transportation in Chicago, the bus was clean and comfortable, and she'd snagged the best seat right behind the driver. After a few turns on narrow roads, she realized the ride was even more rewarding than the previous aerial view. Pristine lakes and snow-patched pastures unfolded. After passing through a tunnel they headed over a suspension bridge and rumbled through a city. Glimpses of the Atlantic appeared on the left and a humongous ferry loaded with cars and passengers pulled up at a dock. They entered more tunnels, then soared up hills and mountainsides. When she spotted a narrow body of water deep below that seemed to go on for miles, she gasped and pointed.

"Pardon me but is this a fjord?" She turned to the teenager on her right who took off his headphones and smiled shyly.

"Yes. Except you don't pronounce it like that. 'Fuirh.' That's the way we say it here."

"That's a real tongue twister. Do you feel like helping an ignorant American girl with your language?" she beamed at the tow-headed teen.

The next hour, LaRae repeated new words and phrases, all the while performing somersaults on the inside. *Me, the epitome of an introvert am interacting with a total stranger?* She pondered whether the image she'd painted of herself might be faulty. Was the inconspicuous, flopping sparrow changing colors and mutating into an adventurous, exotic species? Perhaps her latent genetic makeup would come to life when she set foot upon the soil of her forefathers.

Watch the Viking spirit rise within. She snickered at her ridiculous train of thought.

With a variety of Norwegian sentences tucked under her belt, La Rae and her mentor got off the bus at its final stop.

"It was nice meeting you," the guy blushed again. "'Ha det!' That means goodbye around here."

"Oh, okay. 'Ha det' back to you then. And thanks for your help." LaRae thanked the driver for pulling her suitcases out of the baggage compartment beneath the bus and looked around tentatively. To her left a modern, glass building with a grass-topped roof rose beside a river walk. Beyond it, a pedestrian bridge lead to the other side of a river where historic buildings were crammed alongside a busy street. Her stomach churned. What if no one showed up?

"'Hallo,' you must be my client from America? Miss Gunther, I presume?" An elderly pink-cheeked man reached out and shook her hand cordially.

"Indeed, I am. And you must be Mr. Hansen? Thank you so much for picking me up."

"Oh that's no bother at all. Sorry I'm late. A lady fell off her bike, and I stopped to assist her." Mr. Hansen sported a grey pinstripe suit and light blue tie with a silver clip; his feet were clad in immaculate and shiny wingtips. "I hope you had a good trip?"

"I did, thank you. But I can't wait to see the house and lay my head on a pillow. I assume you use such things here?" She smiled.

"Pillows? Indeed. Yes, we do. It will be a good goose down pillow if I knew Erna right." He loaded her suitcases in the trunk of an older model silver Mercedes. "The house is in disrepair but nothing a few crowns and skilled labor cannot fix."

"I only have a handful of your currency. But I'm sure we can exchange my dollars for 'crowns' in the local bank?"

"Of course, dear." Mr. Hansen opened the door to the passenger seat. "I can help. Just took stock of your great-aunt's little fortune. That Erna was good at scrimping and saving. Never wasted even a 'krone' or crown as you call it."

LaRae's eyed widened. "Must run in the family. My mother was big into saving too." As the shocking news sunk in, her midsection started unclenching. Apparently, she'd walked around with twisted insides, dreading borrowing money from Amanda. She shook her head, sending a heartfelt sigh of gratitude upwards, hoping it reached the inaccessible place called heaven.

Perhaps His eye is indeed on this sparrow. The well-known song was poetic but up until now she'd found it irrelevant. Ensconced in the pew of First Lutheran in Dresden she'd sung it in a low voice because her off-key voice embarrassed Mother. The stanza flitted through her mind now as they crossed the Mandal River. *Why should I worry? Why should I fear? His eye is on the sparrow. And I know he watches me.*

Worry had been her middle name for as long as she could

remember. If she wasn't worrying about other people's opinions, then she'd worried over Mother's unhappiness with her youngest offspring. After her mom died, worry over Dad took its place. In addition, when Lars disappeared she worried she'd done something to make him cut and run. Then she'd faced the worry over the funeral arrangements and medical bills, the neglect of the house paired with the knowledge of her anemic bank account.

If I carried around a worry bead bracelet, it'd fit on a giant's wrist.

The car was hot. She flipped her hair out of her knitted hat and grinned. "I'm sorry. I got lost in reverie. The news about the extra inheritance relieves me to no end."

"I'm deeply sorry for appearing misleading! Your aunt left her money to the Animal Shelter! A dog lover, she took in and fostered abused dogs during her retirement." He grimaced, and a gold molar flashed, mocking her.

She forced a laugh. "One can always dream, right?"

"Yes, dear. Feed the dream, keep it alive. In the meantime, our town will construct a five star facility for our four-legged friends."

Irrationally jealous of the town's stray cats and dogs, she eyed the clapboard homes lining the streets. The overall impression was one of traditional architecture and with a traditional white scheme. She understood why the town of Mandal had earned its nickname. The roads were narrow and the traffic lights virtually non-existent.

"We have a population of fifteen thousand today. In the 15th century this was a port with no road access." Mr. Hansen pointed to a fishing vessel at the river's edge. "Lumber and fishing were its main livelihood and drew traders who exported the goods. Dutch and English ships brought cloth, china, rugs, coffee and sugar among many things."

"I remember Mormor telling a story about her great-grandmother receiving an orange for Christmas. Her father was a sailor and brought this new delicacy home from Morocco."

Mr. Hansen chuckled. "Stories of piracy and shipwrecks

abound. If you like, we'll visit Mandal's nautical museum. Many artifacts have been preserved from the shipping days. I'm somewhat of a historian, you see, and would be delighted to show you our region."

"Yes, please!" LaRae clapped her hands. "But first I'm exploring the local beach!" Although patches of snow lay scattered on the ground, tomorrow she was walking to the beach regardless of weather and other impediments.

They crossed the main bridge connecting the two sides of town with the busiest half located to the west.

"Stay on the river boardwalk through downtown. The beach is only a good thirty minute walk away. I'll take you for a brief tour now," he pointed to a bronze statue of a short, round fisherman on a pedestal to the left.

"Our town's symbol. In the past salmon crowded this river. See how fish is stuffed into his pockets? You may still be lucky and catch something. But obtain a fishing permit. The fine will cost you more than a fish dinner at a restaurant."

At a roundabout Mr. Hansen aimed northwards again, and they passed a bike shop and grocery store on the left and a newer glass structure on the right. "Our commercial center all under one roof makes it easier to shop in bad weather." An appliance and fabric store swept by on the left and Mr. Hansen turned onto a narrow street behind the shop. "This neighborhood dates from the 18th century to the 1950s. Walk carefully because the cobblestones can be bumpy."

"And here we are," Mr. Hansen said as he pulled to the curb and parked in front of a low picket fence draped in bare branched forsythia bushes. "Watch your step. I had my secretary's son come over and spread sand on the walk, but it may still be slippery. Make sure to turn up the heat; it's been on a low setting since January. I'll show you how to switch on the hot water heater." He heaved for breath, her suitcases weighing him down.

LaRae slung the carry on over her shoulder and climbed three steps to a teal blue door. The hue added a touch of cheerfulness to the whiteness surrounding them. Two sets of six-paned windows framed the front door. LaRae imagined them watching her with a hopeful gleam asking if she had what it took to restore the dwelling.

Don't worry, she reassured the wooden structure. *I'll find your hidden beauty and once again display it to the world.*

Upon entering, she inhaled mustiness and a sharp odor. Mice again! In the tiny hallway, she noticed a cluster of portraits.

"This is your Great Aunt Erna when she received her seamstress award from the city. The former mayor is in it too." A smiling, petite woman in a 1960s style dress stood shaking the mayor's hand. LaRae's gaze shifted to the right and to her great amazement, discovered a photo of herself and Amanda with their parents. The picture had been snapped in her grandmother's rose garden in Minnesota when LaRae had been seven. With skinned knees and dressed in her signature pale pink dress, she pushed Amanda on the swing. Her sister was wearing a daisy print dress with freshly permed hair. *The swan and the ugly duckling.*

Mr. Hansen studied the photographs. "Oh that is adorable! You still have that brilliant smile!"

"Who? Me? No, that's my sister Amanda," LaRae corrected.

"No, young woman. I mean the younger girl missing her front teeth. Now that you're in possession of your permanent teeth that smile is even greater." Another and probably silly grin broke out on her face at his words.

There were more sepia-toned photos hanging on the wall of what must be her mom's mother and her sister Erna. A dated photo of a young couple with two daughters hung above the others. Mr. Hansen pointed to the daughters. "Your grandmother and her sister are wearing flour sack dresses. It was taken during the Second World War when fabric was not available. Enjoy your little house for now. I will leave you to rest. My phone number is on the kitchen counter. We'll settle affairs on Wednesday. In the meantime, I'll have the phone line reactivated so you can make local calls."

"That'll be perfect. Thank you so much for your help." LaRae squeezed his bony hand in gratitude and received the house key.

Too exhausted to take in more sights, she fumbled her way through the narrow hallway upstairs and happened upon a room with a bed covered in a white crocheted spread. While letting out a pent-up sigh, she tore off the new cognac-colored boots and pantyhose and collapsed onto the carved, pine bed fully dressed and slipped her body under the soft goose-down duvet. As a waning afternoon sun disappeared below the rooftops across the street, the slanted ceiling of the room faded and darkness fell along with straggling snowflakes that hadn't gotten the memo that spring had arrived.

CHAPTER 15

The dark beast with luminous eyes opened its mouth greedily. She tried to run, but her feet did not respond. She struggled to break free but the beast raged at her efforts, baring its fangs. Bent over her, its putrid breath soured her lungs. LaRae flailed, gasping for air and then realized the growling animal of her nightmare was the rumbling of an approaching snowplow. Its light beams pierced the window, illuminating a wallpaper of faded ivy and bluebells. Disoriented, she registered faint stars in what she assumed was a morning sky. A rocking chair with an embroidered cross stitch pillow stood in the left corner and a framed picture of a sailing ship hung above a pine dresser. The tumultuous events of the last days came back to her, and she checked her wristwatch. 1:07 PM. Her numbed brain computed the math and concluded it must be 8:07 AM in her host country.

She'd been asleep for sixteen hours.

With regret, she emerged from the warm duvet and tiptoed across the blue painted floor in search of a bathroom. "Just my luck, worse than what I left behind in Dresden," she said and stomped one foot on the cold linoleum. "So much for dreaming of a Jacuzzi." Bath fixtures resembling antiquated remnants from the Second World War met her eyes. Great Aunt had enjoyed a rustic life complete with a galvanized claw tub with no shower head and a porcelain sink with no cabinet. The toilet had a doll in a crocheted ball gown sitting on the tank lid. Curious, she checked out the doll and found an extra roll of toilet paper under her wide skirt. LaRae smiled, wondering if her aunt had made it.

Like a kid opening a box of candy, she explored the rooms. Homey, old lady touches abounded. A collection of silver teaspoons were mounted on the wall. Upon closer examination she found each one had the name of a city engraved on it. Teacups in different patterns lined a curio cabinet and crocheted doilies adorned every surface. The window sills showed dead begonias in porcelain flowerpots. "You poor darlings," she comforted before checking the pantry for anything edible.

A shelf revealed mouse droppings and a handful of labeled cans; a reindeer was depicted on a bigger can. "Seems like a good protein to start the day." LaRae gave herself a pep talk because her stomach demanded immediate food. When the bank opened, she'd go grocery shopping. The dated, electric stove proved to be in working order. As the sun rose over the neighborhood's snow-covered rooftops, LaRae leaned back in a wooden chair and sipped black tea with sugar while munching on reindeer meat balls and sweet tasting sauerkraut with cumin seeds. A crooked smile stretched her lips, as she pictured Amanda's abhorrence of her breakfast choice.

LaRae changed the thermostat to 25 degrees Celsius and grabbed a towel as thin and stiff as a square of sandpaper. Either Norwegians exfoliated this way or Mr. Hansen's assessment of Erna being overly frugal was accurate indeed.

After a hot bath, LaRae rubbed her skin to the hue of a new-born piglet then unpacked her cases. She put on pants, a sweater and the new boots and placed a red wool beret she'd picked up in Amsterdam at a jaunty angle on her head. In her newfound quest for confidence, LaRae had also acquired an electric blue, wool coat. For a second, she paused on the stoop, tempted to run back inside and put on something less conspicuous. But after looking around, she decided Norwegians were no prudes when it came to color. Across the street a woman in a lime green jacket pushed a stroller with a toddler in a banana colored suit. Down the road, flashes of kids building a snowman lit up the white yard. The front door to her right was a deep red, the next one royal blue. Shutters further down the road sported a mellow apple green.

Dorothy, her hometown librarian was wrong in her advice. "Europe is fashionable you know. Black is the raging color. You'll want to go darker and heavier on your makeup, too. My cousin toured Paris in pink shorts and neon T-shirt and drew ugly looks. The women wore black miniskirts and flirty little shirts that showed more than you'd care to see." She'd leaned in and whispered while her eyes darted around the library making sure no males were listening. "The idea of wearing a bra is passé even though they are the ones who invented it. Women wear sheer lace and flimsy fabrics. Oh dear. Blend in, but do not go all the way. Your poor mother should've been here to give advice. She always had you looking decent on a dime."

LaRae had tried to keep a straight face when the librarian pulled up a photo of her 240-pound cousin Shirley in hot pink shorts and a yellow neon shirt posing by the river Seine.

She walked southwards and was surprised at how several homes stood wall to wall on the street level. A newspaper boy stuck papers inside the slots in the doors and she hollered. "Excuse me, but is it nine o'clock in the morning?"

Surprised at hearing English, he stammered and his face reddened. "Ja, it is nine seventeen on Monday April two." In answer to her next question he pointed down the road in the same direction she'd arrived the day before. "The butikk and bank are on River Street."

"The grocery store is called 'butikk'?"

"Ja."

She thanked him and strolled towards the town center and found the bank on the corner of the main street and a pedestrian street. After exchanging money, she rushed to the grocery store. Upon entering, she checked the produce department. Cabbages, turnips, carrots, leeks and kohlrabi filled plastic bins. Mentally calculating, she discovered that fruit cost double the price. The dairy section tempted her more with its assortment of local cheeses, berry yogurts, kefir and quart size containers of milk in paper cartons. When she asked a clerk what was the most popular item, he pulled a rectangular, brown block of goat cheese off the shelf. LaRae accepted it and also loaded her cart with potato tortillas, pickled herring in three different flavors, and Norwegian chocolate and checked out.

Halfway through town her face broke into a full smile as her eyes landed on a bakery and cafe. Not even making a feeble effort at resisting, she entered. One look at the pastries displayed below the glass counter made her kiss any gluten-free diet goodbye. She ordered, then picked a table. Fresh from the oven, the almond filling of her Danish melted on her tongue while the flavor of real butter infused her taste buds. *Mom, what would I give to share this moment with you!* LaRae sighed heavenwards. *And don't worry! I am only splurging this once,* she added imagining her mother frowning at her frivolity.

"Oh, look who we have here!" Mr. Hansen's face lit up as he approached her table. "Let me introduce you to my friend."

LaRae assessed the sophisticated woman on his arm. In a down-to-earth manner, she reached out her hand and said, "Cora, my name is Cora Eknes and I am delighted to meet Erna's grandniece. For close to thirty years we were neighbors." In a face framed by speckled grey and dark curls, a brilliant smile lit up her dark eyes. "Welcome to our town and neighborhood!"

"Your English is impeccable," LaRae blurted.

Cora threw her head back and laughed. "That's because I haven't always been a country bumpkin like Toralf." She winked at Mr. Hansen.

"No, in fact Cora was once a famous artist in Oslo," he confided. "She also trained in Fine Art in London and picked up a crisp British. That she settled in humble, southern Mandal I've never understood why, but I appreciate it. Make sure not to miss her upcoming exhibit," Mr. Hansen beamed. "She has added culture to our provincial ways. Cora is displaying a new series of oil paintings. Each year she picks a local motif as her focal point," he explained while patting Cora's shoulder. "What's the theme again this year, dear?"

"Seagulls," Cora informed without further elaboration.

LaRae studied her features. Full lips revealed strong, healthy teeth and a firm chin jutted out above a pistachio Hermes silk scarf with a brown chain pattern. Her soft cashmere coat was in the shape of a black cape and she dumped a tote on the chair. LaRae spotted a drawing pad and upon closer scrutinizing, discovered paint specks and ink marks on the leather. *A woman after my own heart.* She smiled at Cora.

"Let's give you a lift when you finish. I noticed your heavy grocery bags," Mr. Hansen said and nodded to the floor as Cora ordered bread and raisin buns to go.

"Oh, please come by my house for dinner tonight?" Cora implored LaRae during the ride home. "A shame I didn't ask Toralf when you were coming! I would have cleaned Erna's house and stocked the fridge. What a poor first impression of Norwegian hospitality. Let me remedy that, do you like fish?"

"I've had catfish and an occasional rainbow trout but not many other kinds. I want to try new foods though. Just give me the house number and I'll be there."

"Number 15, two doors down on your right," Cora motioned to the biggest house on the block. Naked fruit trees stood guard in the front yard and the house was an impressive two-and-a-half stories tall with French doors and windows. "Come at 5:30 sharp. Don't be late, I hate over cooked salmon," she admonished and patted LaRae's hand goodbye.

LaRae sang while putting up the groceries then scrambled to locate furniture polish and rags. She dusted and cleaned the two-bedroom 1940s house. At first her voice sounded rusty and out of practice but as she kept singing, her vocal chords came back to life. Years ago, out of pure boredom and as a distraction, she'd made up silly songs while doing household chores. In this abode she chanted classic movie tunes.

Later, as LaRae dressed in her plum-colored velvet gown, her stomach quivered in front of Erna's mirror.

"Don't move. Let me see you," Lars had practically commanded as he walked into the dorm suite so long ago. Dumbfounded she'd watched him circling her, taking in the dress from different angles.

"You made this with your own hands?" he'd asked.

"Yes, silly. Who else's hands could I possibly have used besides my own?" she'd inquired.

He'd touched the fabric and goose bumps had formed under his touch, but she had concealed them by pulling away.

"I told you the fabric is vintage. I got a whole bolt of it at an estate sale."

"So soft," he'd murmured. "You are fantastic."

LaRae didn't feel fantastic now. She felt nauseated and chided herself for pulling out the gown. Clueless whether a Monday night dinner made up a formal or casual event, she hustled down the street wishing she'd bought a hostess gift.

"Oh dear, your dress is exquisite!" Cora took LaRae's coat and hung it in the front hall closet. "Is this in fashion in America? We hardly ever see real velvet anymore." She caressed the sleeve. "The quality outshines the newer, synthetic blends!"

LaRae launched into the explanation of finding the vintage fabric and sewing it herself, her face flushed from the unexpected compliment.

"Can I help with the meal? It smells good."

Cora passed her an orange and white checkered apron. "Do not spill on yourself! The salmon has been poached in saltwater and dill. Lift one slice at a time with the slotted spoon. Place it on the platter alongside the boiled potatoes and steamed carrots. I'll sprinkle fresh parsley over the potatoes. Let me melt the butter and then we'll sit down."

Cora busied herself at the stove while LaRae took in her surroundings. The kitchen was roomy with tall grey cabinets. Paintings leaned against the wall above the cupboards, canned lights highlighted an array of depicted wildlife. Lifelike foxes, hares and squirrels had been captured in their natural surroundings. Fresh herbs lined the windowsill over a deep porcelain sink. Gleaming copper pots hung alongside the wall and Persian tribal rugs in browns, purples and pink covered the hardwood floor.

"The floor is heated?"

"I splurged," Cora confessed. "I had heat cables installed on the ground floor last year. I was sick and tired of not being able to walk barefoot in my own home. My family and Toralf thought I was crazy, but now you should see how they enjoy it. I swear they come up with every excuse for why we should host at my house during the winter months."

"I never heard of such a thing. Would you mind if I try it out barefoot?"

"Not in the least. If you're accustomed to cold winters in Illinois, you must be ready for radiating heat."

"Last winter was especially cold and my utility budget limited. I must confess I brought long wool underwear."

Cora's full-throated laughter filled the kitchen. "Well, this must be the last of the snow, and I promise that although spring comes late to Norway, it makes up for it in beauty and freshness. I don't think you'll need long johns unless you decide to stay."

The farfetched possibility struck LaRae and her jaw went slack. What if she stayed a while? She could suggest Amanda and Chris keep the money from the upcoming sale of her parent's ranch home. And her own inheritance could be the house and half of Great Aunt's savings. "Perhaps somewhere over the rainbow skies really are blue."

"What dear?"

"Oh, I am sorry. I quoted a song from a movie out loud. When you mentioned remaining here, the idea sent me reeling. If I considered it, do you think I could learn the language?"

"Sweet Child, we have classes for immigrants. Not that you're an immigrant, but my friend Helen teaches the class. I'm sure you could join."

"I remember pronunciation and words from Mormor. A boy on the bus taught me some too; feel free to pitch in.

They sat down at a candle lit table and Cora prayed. She started the meal by pointing to a bowl. "Help yourself to the cucumber slices in vinegar. It offsets the richness of the fats."

"Delicious. This salmon tastes like it got pulled right out of the ocean, so clean and fresh."

"Well, that's because it was hauled out of the ocean this morning." Cora laughed and helped herself to seconds. "My brother-in-law fishes for a living and caught this one today while pulling in the nets. There's nothing like having your own direct line to the treasures of the North Sea," she said and winked at LaRae as she cleared the table and brought over a cake.

"Don't get the wrong idea. I don't always serve a dessert with dinner. But since it's your first meal in your grandmother and grandfather's country, I extend a warm welcome in the form of something sweet. This is a traditional 'bløt kake' a layered cream cake," she explained cutting a wedge of the sponge cake layered with strawberries and whipped yellow cream.

"This cream is extraordinary."

"I agree. I have travelled abroad and no other sources of cream rival what we produce here in my not so humble opinion." They giggled.

"You got me hooked. I'm afraid I'll be buying cream for my tea and coffee from now on," LaRae lamented.

"Who says that's not my goal?" Cora winked. "People of my generation prefer seeing more flesh on beautiful bones like yours."

"Ahem. I see how it is. Does that mean you have plans to fatten me up while introducing me to more culinary experiences? If that's the case, you have a willing guinea pig on your hands."

Cora stroked LaRae's hair in passing. "I thought you'd be good for me." She measured water and two scoops of coffee. "You have that special something, the French call it 'Je ne sais quoi.' Tell you what, how about I teach you traditional recipes?"

"Only if you let me do the clean-up in exchange for food," LaRae bartered.

"That's the best deal I've agreed to in ages! Let's do Mondays and Wednesdays."

Heat warmed LaRae's insides. How long had it been since anyone had stroked her hair in a caress? The touch felt deeply personal yet all right. Was Cora childless and appreciated the interaction? LaRae kept her eyes open for framed pictures giving away details of her neighbor's life. She seemed lively and happy, yet a few crinkles around her eyes indicated either loneliness or sadness.

"Dear heavens, what happened in here?" Cora exclaimed from the sunroom, a modern addition to the house. "I'm helping Helen by taking another stray she insisted on me adopting. This is how he repays my kindness." Cora lifted a striped cat from a mess of paint tubes spread out on the floor and threw it out the French doors.

LaRae entered the room and peeked out on a frozen garden with a rose arbor and a pedestal birdbath.

"This cat can't coexist with my artistic endeavors. It's the second time he has toppled over my canvas."

"You are speaking to an experienced caretaker of the feline sort," LaRae ventured. "If this remains a problem, I can try boarding him till your exhibit is over. That way you'll have peace of mind while painting and keep your friendship with Helen intact."

Cora looked relieved. "It was the best of luck meeting you today, LaRae. And the answer is yes! I'll pack up the cat food and guess what?"

"What?"

"You may name him. He is nameless."

"I'll sleep on that one." LaRae yawned. Before long she nestled underneath the covers in Great Aunt's bed again, only this time a black and grey furry companion perched proprietarily at the end of the bed. "Fast way to grow a family," she said with a chuckle and drifted off.

CHAPTER 16

The next morning LaRae awoke in jitters, realizing Amanda must be worried sick about her. In all the bustle of meeting new people, it had slipped her mind to call. The sidewalk was slick with melting ice. Rivulets of water dripped off the gutters as she traipsed over to Cora's in Great Aunt's one-size-too-small rubber boots.

"I am sorry to disturb you but my laptop does not have Wi-Fi and my cell phone's not working here. Do you have a computer so I can email or message my sister in America?"

"Of course. I'll show you its whereabouts and then I need to get right back to work."

A bandana was wrapped around Cora's grey curls and she had a paint stain on her chin. Her apron was heavy with dried paint layers. LaRae glanced towards the sunroom and noted the palette of grays and blues. Drawn, her feet moved until she was poring over the canvas.

"Titanium White, Payne's grey, and Indigo. I love cerulean blue the most. It has such a translucent quality about it. Probably captures the skies here pretty well," LaRae commented.

"Oh my goodness! You're familiar with the paint process. What have you not told me?" Cora scrutinized her, peering over pink reading glasses.

She felt her face flush. "Sorry. I didn't mean to barge into your studio without permission. I took art classes in college but didn't graduate. Things got complicated; my plans did not pan out." LaRae choked on the last few words and to her consternation felt her eyes water.

Cora motioned to the comfortable daybed in the sunroom, piled high with velvet pillows in jewel tones. "Sit. Or lie down. I'm making tea. Your sister can wait. Did you eat breakfast this morning?"

LaRae shook her head.

"I thought not." Cora disappeared and LaRae leaned back on the daybed, listening to pots clanging while inhaling the aroma of bacon and eggs permeating the sunroom.

"Reassure me you have no food allergies? Because I'm offering real treats here." Cora plopped a lacquered tray down on the round pine table and poured two cups of strong, black tea. "This is the cream you committed to last night." She lifted a ceramic pitcher in the shape of a cow glazed in blue and white. The cream poured out of its mouth into the cup. "This is honey from our bluebell and daisy flowers. My brother-in-law keeps bees," she motioned to a jar in the shape of a yellow bee hive. On the domed lid a honeybee served as a handle.

La Rae swiped her eyes. "Do you know the potter? These are fun pieces."

"Don't tell me you know about pottery too? You're looking at the potter. My parents set up a workshop for me when I was in high school. They had an outbuilding with a fireplace. My dad converted it into a kiln and shop so I could sell my pieces to locals."

Mouth agape, LaRae took in the facts her new friend divulged to her. "What a stunning act of love. Your father appreciated your artistic ability?"

Cora laughed. "Over time both my parents did. They first had to get over dirty dresses as I stayed 'stuck in the mud' in our backyard, crafting items out of dirt and offering them as gifts. When they recognized it as talent and encouraged it, I achieved a measure of success." Cora rose and pulled an album with faded newspaper clippings off a nearby shelf. Together they pored over the articles.

LaRae thought back to her own mother's reaction to her own pottery stint. "Playing with dirt? While the institution charges you fifty grand a year in tuition? This is why I suggested the dental hygienist training. How will this establish an income, Rae? Remember, I warned you about this high falutin' college. It's not only liberal but filled with dreamers. These are activities for kindergarteners, not adults!" Mom had shaken her head in disbelief almost rubbing through the glass while cleaning the kitchen windows.

Since then LaRae had kept creative projects under wraps while highlighting her math and science achievements. As she looked at the pictures of a young Cora wedged between a beaming bespectacled couple, LaRae pushed back the annoying torrent inside. But a batch of fresh tears hit the album, and the floodgates burst open. Moments later she doubled over, her body heaving. She cried wrenching sobs and wished for Lorenzo or even better for Lars. At the thought of that remote possibility her sobbing increased.

"Come here." She felt Cora's warm hand pull her in and LaRae let herself get wrapped up in the woman's embrace. That action released another cascade of tears. She cried again but this time the tears didn't feel laden with despair, but more like an endless string of sadness being pulled out of her. After a long while, her breathing calmed, and she rested, leaning her head on Cora's chest.

Her neighbor was stroking her hair in a soothing, rhythmic motion. "There now. As surely as the Lord lives, all will be right as rain. Come into his shelter. Let him comfort you."

LaRae's labored breathing stilled even more. She drew a shuddering breath.

Cora stroked her back rubbing circles around her shoulder blades. The Gustavian clock in the living room ticked loudly. A dog barked outside. "I'm ready to listen," Cora stated emphatically.

LaRae pulled her feet up and tucked them under a paisley wool blanket draped over the daybed. A box of tissues got dropped in her lap and she blew her nose, then faced her elderly friend. "It's a long story. Your paint may dry out," she smiled tremulously.

"Easily fixed." Cora got up and wrapped her palette in plastic wrap, then pulled her legs up under the blanket. Stray curls escaped her pink bandana and paint specks looked like white freckles on the tanned complexion. But her deep blue eyes stayed focused on LaRae. "Confession is good for the soul. I am all ears."

Two hours and three cups of tea later, LaRae found herself out of breath. She had shared pertinent memories of her mother all the way from early toddlerhood. The morning sun had traversed the tribal Persian rug. At this instant, the rays strafed the easel and the canvas depicting a seagull in flight above a steel colored ocean. Its wing tips spanned from one side of the canvas to the other.

"One thing is for sure. Your mother loved you. Of that I am convinced." Cora leaned over and patted LaRae's hand. "I identify with her because after the Second World War so many people developed a deep seated fear of how to make ends meet. Even before the war, times were hard. Many of our men left for America to help provide for their families, even the married ones. Their wives tended the farms and gardens and raised the children. I learned to work hard and embrace duty from that generation, no matter how dull it seemed. I was an exception when my family let me go to Oslo to pursue a career in the arts. Didn't your grandmother follow her fiancé over to America, but he still sent money back home?"

LaRae nodded. "They scrambled to buy land in Minnesota, all the while trying to support my grandfather's family here in Mandal. My grandmother was a workhorse. Raised chickens and knitted for people. Took in sewing. You're right. She never relaxed, not even when we came to visit. I loved her baking, but she never sat down with us."

"How do you think your grandfather's abrupt death affected your mother?"

LaRae sighed. "Probably made her anxious. I guess Dad was raised the same way with his German background. He backed her up."

"It seems to me your parents did their best. I agree it may not always have felt like love. But I'm sure you mother tried to watch out for your happiness in ways familiar to her. I'm sorry for how it came across and how they did not understand your temperament and makeup." Cora rubbed her own neck. "I get so sore from painting. But contrary to your Mama, I value creativity enough to put up with the aches and pains. And the poverty it may entail." She flashed a sudden smile. "I was fortunate though. Even though I lost my husband, his life insurance policy enabled me to continue painting. Now I have wealthy patrons and clients backing me. Don't despair, little one. The Father has gifted you differently from your Mama. Will you be obedient to the calling he has put within you?"

The clock chimed again in the other room but neither paid it any attention. Was the maternal woman in front of her insinuating the Maker himself would be pleased at such a prospect? LaRae felt sweaty. She tossed off the blanket and stood up on wobbly feet. "Do you mean to say God desires me to paint? Or do pottery or write a book? Because that's in my heart, too." She gritted her teeth. "Do you think my desires could be important to God?"

"Why not? Do you believe he only gives bad desires? Or that his desires for you are only things you dislike?"

"Yes." LaRae shrugged. "Maybe I am wrong. I will rethink things."

"In the meantime, will you do me a favor?" Cora asked, eyes alight with merriment.

"More cats?"

"Heaven forbid! I wouldn't wish more than one stray cat even on my worst enemy!" she exclaimed.

LaRae grabbed a raisin bun off the porcelain tray and waited.

"I'm in a time crunch. My exhibit is mid-August. Do you know how to prime canvases?"

LaRae nodded. "But I am very busy."

Cora stared at her.

She swallowed hard; "That's not true. I am afraid of stirring it all up again. Terrified actually. I know it's silly. Something happened, and I shut down that part of me."

"Well, this is priming pure and simple. If you can force yourself, please do as many as possible from the stack over there. I'd be grateful. And if you can find it in your heart to mix up more Titanium White with Ultramarine in five different shades that would help me greatly, too."

"I might mess up." LaRae sounded tentative, her voice a little shaky. "After all, you're the renowned artist and I'm just a lowly student."

"Student or not, have you finished any paintings?"

"I did an impressionist rendering of Lake Michigan in the winter in similar hues to the ones you're using. Except I included people in colorful clothing." *Like Lars and me.* LaRae gestured with her hands. "My idea was to paint the lake in a series, depicting it in spring, summer and fall, accentuating the difference in the seasons." LaRae looked out the window and lost herself in the past.

"Whenever I picture something as clearly as you're describing, I take it as a sign from heaven to flesh it out in real life," Cora stared at her with challenge in her eyes.

"Oh. I attributed the scenes to my lively imagination."

"And who might we say gave you an imagination?"

"Are you implying it was given to us for a reason?"

"I am absolutely implying that."

"Oh."

"What's the silence about, dear?"

LaRae shrugged her shoulders. "You have no idea how my imagination got me into scrapes."

"Let me guess? With your mother? And sister, Amanda?"

"How did you know?"

"That, my darling, is no mystery. People who lack imagination are the same around the world. They either act dumbfounded with admiration for the ones who have a healthy dose of it, or they do the opposite."

"Which is what?" LaRae inquired.

"They despise it. It's so foreign it seems like a waste of time and energy to them. They might pity or despise you for running down endless rabbit trails of creativity. Fruitless activities having nothing to do with 'real life,' as they put it. Why, I was most fortunate to have my husband fall in love with me. The artistic mind fascinates certain men but they would never marry it." Cora shook her head. "Mark my words, the man who values imagination is a real treasure."

LaRae remained speechless for a long while. But on the inside it felt as if missing puzzle pieces were being fitted into the formerly chaotic inner picture. She drew a deep, shaky breath. "Thank you Cora. I needed to hear every word you said."

"Good! Now make yourself useful." Cora untied her navy-blue apron. "Finish the eggs and bacon from my brother-in-law's farm, I'm running errands. I'll be back in the afternoon."

As the front door slammed, LaRae turned on the computer and let Vivaldi's Four Seasons fill the house. Then she pushed up her sleeves and went to work. Six canvases later, LaRae stretched her achy body but relished the burn.

After locking Cora's house, she headed straight for the ocean, following Mr. Hansen's directions till she arrived at the pier. It jutted out into the sea, flanked by the Mandal River on the left and a shallower ocean alongside a mile long beach to the right. She strode towards the end of the concrete structure when sea spray hit her right in the face. Her left foot slipped. LaRae yelped and scurried back to the steps, descending onto the wet, packed sand. In an act of reverence, she crouched down and lifted a handful of Sjosanden, the "Sea Sand Beach", kissing its coarse, yellow grains.

"I've waited a long time for this moment," she whispered to

the waves and wind. "But believe me, it was worth the wait!" She'd pictured her first walk on a balmy beach in Gulf Shores. Never in her wildest imagination had she envisioned it in a tiny coastal town in Norway, a buffeting wind scouring her cheeks. She wiped her eyes, unsure if the wetness stemmed from the cold or gratitude.

"Thank you. I like it!" LaRae yelled to the grey sky.

CHAPTER 17

"I'm nine pounds and two ounces heavier and blame it on the Hardee's bacon burger! The strawberry shake tastes divine with it. I tried to break the habit, but it wiggled its way into my carpool routine. Then the Zumba teacher got pregnant and had to be on bed rest, abandoning us just like you abandoned me. I attended cycling class, but the instructor is a sadistic maniac. Wallie has the flu so we haven't slept in a week." Amanda smacked her chewing gum in indignation. "And you're over there making reindeer hats while my life is coming apart at the seams!"

Laughter trilled from the sunroom. LaRae motioned for Cora to hush through the glass doors.

"It's not reindeer, silly. I am learning to knit. Cora helped. She created the moose pattern."

"You modeled it on *Facebook*! Mauve and pink! Who are you nowadays?"

"I posted online because it's an easy way to keep Starr, my former roommate, updated on my whereabouts. I can knit you one too."

"Hilarious. Christopher booked your return ticket for June 10. Did the lawyer recommend a realtor? When the repairs are finished, list it right away. Stop posting scenic pictures on *Facebook*, and report daily about the chores you're knocking out."

"I am too busy to *Skype* daily." *Because I attend language class and sightsee.*

"Christopher is ruining us by paying for a maid. The boys act rambunctious and complain about how Chiquita doesn't know how to build tents or play hide and seek in the woods. Chiquita had the guts to tell me it's not part of her job description! In broken Spanish. You just can't find good help nowadays. It's true as they say. Get that place fixed up so life can return to normal! Did the contractor finish the roof?"

"You mean Consuela?"

"Whatever. Quit stalling, Sis. Is the roofing finished or not?"

I want a summer abroad. "I'm comparing quotes. And I have sorted Great Aunt's clothes, linens and china collection and put things up for sale in an antique booth."

"Forget sorting! Dump it and come home."

"I love you too, Mandy." LaRae blew Wallie kisses before hanging up.

"So sorry, honey. Did Amanda hear me snickering?" Cora busted in from the kitchen with a plate of steaming heart-shaped waffles. "Sounds like your sister missed her calling. She'd be great onstage!"

"You think she's a drama queen?"

"If ever I heard one."

"You're right. If we had had a professional theatre, she'd request the prima donna role."

"She has worked you over, hasn't she?"

"Maybe... I guess? Now Christopher gets to be her primary audience."

"I hope he can handle it," Cora commented.

"He finds it adorable. Most of the time." They ate and knitted some more.

When April eased into May, blue and white anemones peeked

through the dead leaves in the woods and daffodils shot up in LaRae's back yard. Outside, workers ripped old siding off the house façade. LaRae put on a windbreaker and hiking boots. Deprived of an ocean view until the ripe old age of 23, she was making up for it by roaming Mandal's shores daily. At the start of the routine, she'd been giddy with excitement, then sore and ready to swear it off until her complaining caught Cora's attention.

"Here. Take the spare key to the bike lock and cycle to the beach. Do your loop. Then pedal back home. This is the way we do it. We don't kill ourselves experiencing nature." Her neighbor's olive-green bike came in handy for going to the library, shopping and running errands as well. With a basket up front and two saddle bags at the rear it held a week's groceries. A primary means of transportation, kids bicycled to school, parents to work and little old ladies to the cafes. A grid of bike paths enabled citizens to get business done and even ride on paths through the woods. This afternoon she pedaled through town to the pier, then walked the length of Sjosanden. Though "The Sea Sand" was the main tourist attraction, today the dunes and pinewoods cradling it looked deserted. LaRae perused the surf for driftwood. One fact she omitted telling Amanda was that she was amassing piles of driftwood, sea glass and birds' nests while she rid the house of Great Aunt's possessions.

"So sorry Dad but you were wrong." She talked out loud, scuttling sideways from the incoming wave. "Pine Lake does not compare." The saltiness in the air cleared her sinuses and the ever-changing rhythms of the sea and winds settled scattered thoughts. With nature as her classroom, she learned hues by studying shifting light on the water.

My grandparents were blessed to live here. Did they walk the same beach? She'd yet to figure where they had lived. Mr. Hansen, a walking encyclopedia on local lore and history, was performing research on her behalf.

She picked sea shells, thinking of how Cora's friend Helen, had been sworn to secrecy about LaRae attending language class. Seated alongside Somali and Iraqi women in headscarves, LaRae performed oral and mental contortions, pronouncing syllables foreign to the American tongue and learned the masculine, feminine and neutral pronouns of nouns.

When practicing at home, her cat remained a passive listener, purring at her progress. Then again, sharing a goose-down comforter probably made any feline purr. LaRae imagined Lorenzo pitching a fit upon discovering his competition. American boyfriend cat pitted against Norwegian boyfriend cat. She chuckled. Such was the extent of her romantic love life. It was time to work on the "uncle deal" for nephew Mickey. After all she'd shown a proclivity for Nordic men; last fall had proven that fact. An internal door snapped shut at the thought. Aware of Mickey's affinity for animals, bringing back a second cat might just seal the deal while sparing her heart turmoil. LaRae left the sand, trudging up the boardwalk protecting the marram grass. At the campground vacancy signs showed on the cabin doors but two RVs were stationed in a copse of birch trees. She pushed herself up the hidden, rocky trail of a steep cliff, inserting her body between narrow boulders and reached a lookout point in the form a precipice. Wind sent her loose locks flying. Below, a fishing vessel was thrumming its way to port and the light house on the deserted rock island lay veiled in a low-lying cloud.

Where are you, Lars? She scolded the inner voice and sprinted down a slippery trail to the former Lord Manor House then on to the adjoining Cardamom beach named after the spice because of its dark reddish-brown sand. Sweat made her forehead slick, but she ran a full circle covering three more beaches hidden in coves before crashing by her bike. Legs shaking, she stretched her glutes by bending forward at the waist, taking deep gulps of the briny air. Her gaze raked across the pink cotton candy sky and a seagull swooped down eying her water bottle. "Sorry, no crusts today." She savored the moment, knowing she was living on borrowed time. The money part of Great Aunt's inheritance had gotten tied up in the repairs of both her parent's ranch house and her present abode.

"I told the realtor to hold out for an American couple," Amanda had confided during the *Skype*. "Immigrants and illegals are invading the neighborhood."

"I find different cultures and languages enriching," LaRae had blurted.

"Why learn a new language when the world speaks ours? The History channel shows Chinese kids learning English at the opposite side of the globe. I bet people understand you but just play hard to get. Candy told me how a snotty waiter in Paris forced her to order in French. She picked *foie gras*, assuming it meant grass fed beef, then freaked when they explained she'd ingested a fat goose liver. He mocked her French too. A mean trick it was. I demand people speak English. There's no telling what you've been eating either," Amanda had added.

LaRae wheeled through town. As she rolled onto their cobblestone street, she caught sight of Cora unloading her car. Sealed cartons and virgin canvases filled the trunk. Her foot clamped down on the bicycle brake while she gaped at the goods.

"Wow, new art supplies!" Cora approached and cradled LaRae's face between her palms.

"The pink flush in these cheeks is lovely. Can we skip history with Toralf tonight? I need your help. I'll make meatballs if you say yes."

"No-brainer. Yes. Does everything go into your work room?"

"Please. It needs unpacking and sorting. Would you do it while I cook?"

An hour later, they sat down for the meal. While gobbling down potatoes, homemade gravy and meatballs, LaRae kept peeking into the sunroom. The built-in cupboards housed oil paint in Ochre, Cadmium Red, Payne's Grey, Ultra Violet, Emerald Green and Lemon Yellow. Vertical shelves contained neatly stored canvases and sketching pads. Drawers concealed an assortment of pastel crayons and charcoal sticks. There was also a carousel for paintbrushes where she had organized brushes by size.

"What an ingenious way to store supplies!" LaRae forgot to chew and nodded toward the studio. "Everything at your fingertips and you seem to have enough to last you for a decade. Are you sure the paint won't spoil before you get to it?"

"I'm pretty sure, but it depends on circumstances outside my control."

"Such as your health? But you're in great shape, aren't you?"

"That I am, thank you, Jesus." Cora's special, radiant smile reserved for when she spoke about God lit up her face. She lifted a speared meatball using her left hand, knife poised in her right hand.

LaRae frowned. "I know this is off subject. But humor me. You are right handed. Why, may I ask, do you eat food with the left one?"

Cora giggled. "Here, we cut the food with the right hand while feeding ourselves with the left. Look how the table setting has a fork on the left and knife on the right," she nodded to the table.

"Oh. I see." They both giggled. "I guess you'll be painting up a storm?" LaRae commented.

"A storm? No, I'm not painting bad weather!"

"Oh sorry! It is an expression. An idiom. It means a lot and fast."

"Um. That's not my plan." Cora patted her full lips with an embroidered linen napkin. "Now that we've had your birthday dinner, it's time to open the present."

LaRae's eyes widened. "My own sister forgot. How did you know?"

"A little bird called Toralf gave me a heads up. He has access to that information, darling. Come see what I have. The gift comes with strings attached."

"All the new supplies are for me?" LaRae asked in shock.

"Yes. But there's a catch."

"What? I need lessons first?"

"No, silly. You have to start using the supplies tonight and a minimum of three canvases must be completed before month's end."

LaRae ran her fingers over fat tubes, caressing their metal surface. "I am overwhelmed."

"And a little scared, I know. Let's leave the kitchen a mess and paint together, shall we?" Cora tossed her a brand-new apron and watched her tie it around the waist.

LaRae turned to her neighbor, looking her deep in the eyes. "You believe I can do this?"

Cora moved closer and LaRae felt her palm land on the left side of her chest. "Paint with this. Your most important piece of equipment."

CHAPTER 18

Lars counted the money and growled. Swindled again. He hit the top of the jeep roof with his fist. "I swear these guys do it to me every time!"

Hans laughed a deep belly rumble. "It's those innocent blue eyes. The vendors fool you because you're not suspicious nor driving a hard bargain. I agree the bangle is plastic, not bone. Go find something else while I load the potatoes and rice."

The open-air market in Nairobi teemed with produce, chickens and wares. Sunburned tourists plucked at leather purses, handmade jewelry, and traditional tribal masks. Ensuing haggling turned into a game of indignant, raised voices expressing occasional outrage mingled with pleading and flattery, only to end with a handshake and friendly banter. The biggest laughter was reserved for when the pink tourist wandered on, clueless to how he or she got taken advantage of. To the observant eye, vendors slapped each other's backs after a profitable sale.

Lars crouched by a geometric design cloth on the ground displaying carved animals and an array of jewelry. "May I?" He picked up a silver ring one quarter inch wide and asked about the engraving.

"Swahili names for love and friendship," the older African grinned a toothless smile and put the band on Lars' little finger.

"Make Sweetheart happy."

"It's for my mother's upcoming wedding anniversary. My father is long gone, but she celebrates the date of their sacred vows."

"You honor tradition?"

Lars nodded, examining a carved piece of mahogany until realizing it was a phallic symbol.

"I'd like to buy her a tree but customs don't allow shipping plants." He thought of how she'd dropped a hint in the last letter, saying a banana tree would complement her collection. With a reputation for rescuing dying plants, the local nursery set aside wilting plants for her visit. In return, the staff enjoyed free access to the pavilion and bench in her garden. The gate leading into the yard let in all nature lovers. People's enjoyment of the garden made his mother endure the strenuous weeding and care. Lars felt bad missing another event after his abrupt departure.

"I give you good deal because you honor parent."

Lars shook his head and examined a woven basket.

Utterly focused on escaping the pain of recent events he'd been blind to his mother's needs and expectations. A picture of her seated alone by the Christmas tree made his stomach churn. Why was it such a challenge to prioritize others? Hopefully she enjoyed his vivid descriptions of life in the bush.

"The ring." Lars stared at the merchant, then negotiated and put on a show, shaking his fist, then pretended to walk away. When he finally left with the newly acquired purchase in his cargo shorts pocket, a group of sellers patted him on the back, applauding the performance.

Hans waited at the wheel, ready to escape the smog and chaos. Charged with replenishing dwindling supplies and picking up spare parts for the drill, they'd spent the day in the city. Lars thought of how the initial geological survey had suggested boring in a particular grid in the foothills. But the site required heavier equipment than calculated, and the bore hole needed to go two hundred feet deeper than estimated. Then the rig had broken.

Hans patted Lars on the back and yelled above the blaring horns and crazy maneuvers. "Next time you shop, I'm going with you. I speak Swahili. I have a feeling the inscription on the ring has nothing to do with love."

"What? Did you read it?"

"Yes, it promotes fertility and great sex." They guffawed.

"Keep that secret. My mother would never let me forget about it."

"How about I help offset your financial loss by treating you to a real dinner? I'd appreciate a change from goat meat and maize. They serve spicy samosas and chai right down the road. And curry." Hans rubbed his firm belly and grinned. "The only thing missing are our female companions. That Liv livens up any party."

"And that Ella girl drives you to distraction with her hips and legs." Lars smiled back at his colleague. "At least I don't worry about you going native on me. I heard of a guy working for an NGO here that married into the local tribe."

Hans laughed. "I love skiing and winter too much."

"And air conditioning," Lars added, using the edge of his t-shirt to wipe a trail of sweat off his neck.

"That too. Speaking of snow, are you flying home for Christmas this year?"

"No." Lars shook his head. "The Tanzanian mail service will send 'mamma' her gift. An explorer at heart, I'm fulfilling my two-year term before returning. It took me nearly three decades to get to this destination. Next thing on my list is a four-day safari at the Masai Mara Wildlife Reserve. Are you interested?"

"Absolutely! Give me time to put aside funds." Hans scratched his sunburned nose. "Any chance we could invite the girls?"

"To sleep in tents with an outhouse for a bathroom and lions loitering nearby? Sure thing. I think they'd be delighted." Lars wiggled his eyebrows.

Hans honked at a car running the red light. "I need a cold

beer before tomorrow's rig repairs."

"And I can't wait to see what difference having accessible water will mean to this community. The drip irrigation system should increase the maize crop yield," Lars commented.

"Women'll get a break from carrying water six miles a day."

"When everything goes wrong, the stories villagers tell of being wiped out because of bacteria infested water motivate me. Makes the crazy hassle worthwhile. Surface water accumulated during the rainy season definitely requires purifying when stored for long periods."

Hans nodded. "What kills me is seeing the kid who contracted polio drag his weight about with no wheelchair. Access to clean water should decrease dysentery, typhoid and cholera outbreaks."

Lars agreed and pondered the new deadline for the current site. The NGO they contracted for had added an extra month to complete the project.

They pulled into a crowded parking lot, then stepped out into the moist heat and chose the restaurant patio. Lars pulled out a chair by a rattan table while Hans went to the rest room.

After ordering, he pondered the mechanical problems still left to solve with the rig. But his mind strayed to the new team members. From a professional viewpoint, the Swedish nurses proved a great addition, training in hygiene, de-worming and performing vaccinations. So far Liv and Ella had put up with the primitive living conditions of bunking in a concrete structure with no utilities. Their next venture would take place in Tanzania with its beautiful beaches. He'd have to deal with the girls in bikinis. Lars watched a woman balancing a tray on her head while soliciting patrons seated on the terrace to buy pineapples. He nodded, offering fifty cents while she lowered the platter and pulled a gleaming machete from a fold in her skirt. She sliced the fruit into bite size chunks. Lars closed his mouth around the lukewarm sweetness and thought of growing up on the coast in Norway where he'd witnessed everything from string bikinis to topless ladies.

He remembered the attempt to set aside a nudist beach in his home town. Unfortunately for the small number of liberated folks who frequented the beach, they caught townspeople spying on them from rock crags above the secluded area. Bummed at the lack of sophistication of the locals as well as the gossip, the nudists dropped their agenda and put their swimsuits back on.

Lars turned his focus upwards, chuckling: "Lord. You have helped me this far. I ask for strength for this new season." His mind switched to the project. If successful, 2000 Masais would benefit. But obtaining results in the bush-bush of Africa could be relative, because certainties turned into uncertainties with hurdles aplenty. A wildfire, broken equipment, theft, and sickness were just a small part of what had happened so far. At times, living in the Third World had been maddening, yet despite the frustrations, his bones had settled in as if he were home. The years of training had not been a waste and his childhood dreams not empty fantasies.

When Hans returned, they bit into crispy, deep fried samosas, the traditional potato and pea filling fragrant with coriander and cardamom, then dug into heaps of basmati rice and chicken Masala. With an Asian population close to 80,000, Kenyans had learned to like curry and chai and Lars heartily shared in the appreciation. When the Indian cook emerged, Lars shook his hand, and over the din of the Samba music voiced enthusiasm for the garlic and butter Naan bread. Despite his boots being stolen from the camp and having to endure occasional runs to the outhouse, Lars smiled, fine with the heat and pungent smells, at peace with his mission. They finished the meal and crashed at a ramshackle motel outside the city.

The next morning, they gobbled rolls with orange marmalade, washed down with local coffee, before heading to Mkungo in the Great Rift Valley.

Approximately half a million Masais lived around the valley's 160,000-square kilometers of land. A tall race of people, the mostly nomad population still dressed in traditional red shukka cloth and wore elaborate beaded neck jewelry. Known for their athletic prowess and hunting skills, Lars thought of how much he enjoyed evenings around the campfire with the indigenous crew. "Let's compete tonight, seeing who can jump the highest and furthest and who runs the fastest. I'm sick of getting beat by our tribal competitors. After last week's practice, we have an edge," he suggested.

Hans shook his head. "You're dreaming."

They passed a herd of gazelles, souvenir stands and vendors of rhubarb, carrots, and potatoes.

Dust kicked up as they entered the village but willing hands appeared, helping them unload. As the sun set, the team gathered by the fire for a briefing and dinner. After finishing, Lars asked about local legends and tried to imitate the language. Soon, their hosts rolled with laughter as he massacred their native tongue. "Teach me a song instead," he asked.

Under a star-studded sky, they chanted, then launched into stories of lion hunts and initiation rituals. The next morning, a group of young hunters showed up at breakfast to teach tracking and hunting skills. That afternoon, they set up a target range made of withered, compressed grass in animal shapes, and practiced spear throwing.

Before dawn one Saturday morning they tiptoed into the dark with the tribal hunters. Squawking and buzzing noises filled the air and Lars swatted at invisible mosquitoes while attempting to keep up with the hunters who headed up an escarpment. A thorn ripped his right ear and blood trickled down his neck when a growl moved the foliage to his left. Lars froze, realizing he might be the hunted. As the moment hung suspended, rapid movement and a crashing thud followed. A weight dropped at his feet. In the dawn light, a 120-pound wild cat lay prostrate, pierced by the fifteen-year-old chief's son.

As they limped into camp an hour later, Ella approached.

"I need to take the mobile health clinic to the most outlying village and check on the WASH team. Liv is sick. They also want to thank you for the water filtration system you installed and asked that you show them how to maintain it."

Lars gulped down a cup of coffee, loaded the medical equipment and took the wheel of the Jeep. After a rugged ride up a dirt trail, they lurched to a standstill. Eager little hands and faces plastered themselves to the windows. Lars jumped out and taught the kids to perform high fives. But the squealing crowd preferred touching their blond hair and white skin. Like a bee swarm, the fan club followed them each step as they demonstrated to the team of village elders and women how to cleanse wounds with sterilized water and helped establish a hand washing station. Lars appointed a young guy to do maintenance on the hydraulic water filter made with sand that filtered the rainwater. As the sun set, the villagers insisted on throwing a party. Lars radioed the camp to say they'd stay the night. Ugali, the maize staple and collard greens puttered in big pots while the chief served them fermented cow's milk. Later, red dust rose in clouds as bare feet trampled and jumped to the drum beat. Lars knew better than to resist the prodding to join the pulsating throng. Wrapped in an honorary cloth, he flapped his arms and hopped up and down till his toes blistered.

Ella collapsed in a heap of sweat and grime, laughing. "I never received this kind of attention before. Works wonders for my low self-esteem. How about you, Lars? Should we move into the hut and celebrate our new hero status?" she motioned to the painted wood and mud structure prepared for the guests. With the backdrop of the fire, Ella's blond hair appeared a burning halo, her blue eyes hinting at more than camaraderie.

Lars shrugged, forcing a laugh. A natural extrovert, Ella brought zest to mundane activities and disarmed suspicious villagers with her jokes. Tonight, a clingy native wrap accentuated her well-shaped body.

"I've got business with the chief. Get some rest." He pecked her on the cheek and turned towards the gathered elders.

When Ella disappeared through the small opening of the hut, he drew a deep breath. An oval face with high cheekbones and almond-shaped green eyes, surrounded by hazel curls, paraded through his mind. Slender shoulders supported an elegant neck. Below the neckline there were curves in the right places though carefully tucked away from sight. Lars forced the memory to a standstill.

The particular woman he was daydreaming about was most likely married while teaching children in the fair state of Illinois, a world away.

Remembering Norman's visit to his dorm room at Northwestern, Lars still cringed at the guy's dismissive tone. Another part fumed at LaRae for succumbing to tradition. Had she submitted to her parents' wishes without consulting her own heart? Early in their friendship he had detected her penchant for seeking security and acceptance from people. He wondered if she sacrificed her own desires in the process.

LaRae's weakness had stirred up an instinct inside of him. A wish to be a knight in shining armor instead of a simple university student. An urge to snatch her up on his horse and ride off into the sunset had prodded him. His heart dared her to join him on adventures around the world and to discover the land of her forefathers.

But he'd done no such thing. A perfect gentleman, he'd respected her boundaries as she respected his.

Oblivious to her own subtle but real beauty, he had curbed the urge to convince the girl of her greatness. An invisible fist hit his gut. He hoped her talent did not go to waste and that her partner appreciated her worth. But his midsection quivered. Despite appearances, he believed LaRae was fragile. Smooth as glass on the outside but with a brittle inside. He rubbed the knots at the back of his neck and rubbed tension from his scalp.

Could she crumble from too many blows? Was her father buried by now? Lars looked up at the Big Dipper and wondered what constellations shone over Dresden. Eyelids lowered, he prayed for her comfort and help. For himself neither comfort, nor help showed. As he'd flown away to exotic lands, the place she'd filled with delight had turned into a gaping hole.

CHAPTER 19

LaRae pressed the delete button. The third email from her academic advisor vanished without a response, the request to finish her degree in Education ignored. "Rumors abound of someone keeping their artistic ability under wraps?" LaRae's head snapped upwards. She shut the laptop and scooted her chair away from the bistro table.

"Mr. Hansen!"

"Let me guess: you'll have a Napoleon cake?" Her lawyer straightened his bowtie before pulling out his calf leather wallet.

"So will you! I already ordered for us." LaRae's eyes crinkled.

Her pink-cheeked friend laughed. "Oh, that there was more mystery to me. Men versed in the law tend to be terribly predictable, myself included. What do you have to say in your defense? Artists live on whims, driven by impulse, no?"

LaRae sighed. "Once you've discovered the best, why settle for less? I prefer its custard to my feather duvet, which is saying a lot."

A waitress with an elaborate hair bun slid a tray down onto the table. "Two coffees, two pastries."

"I wish my sister hadn't taught me how to count calories," LaRae bemoaned her plight while balancing a forkful of the crisp, multi-layered pastry before her mouth.

Mr. Hansen chuckled. "I was a married man once. Heard all about those pesky things. Do not enlighten me further. Besides, don't wiggle off the hook. Instead show me what you have produced? My curiosity keeps building."

LaRae's cheeks heated. "Cora exaggerates. For the life of me I can't figure how she did it."

"Did what, dear?"

"Jumpstarted my dead battery. Is she a secret psychologist? Because I had foresworn the arts."

Mr. Hansen appeared astonished. "I understood it was your true love in college?"

La Rae gazed out the window where townspeople strolled by. Chubby, blue-eyed babies gawked from strollers and children, backpacks strapped to their shoulders, skipped down the cobblestones after school. Older ladies pushed bikes, their saddlebags loaded with produce from the local market. The sound of French horns and trumpets echoed from the buildings and paved street. A marching band was practicing in the plaza.

She turned to her gentleman friend. "Painting was considered a frivolous pastime by my family members. Each time I grabbed a brush, guilt bled into the strokes. A guy I met at the university helped me overcome the barrier. When I lost him, all creative urges vanished. Now I throw myself into a world of color, void of thought, then stand back and see painted canvases. Does that sound crazy?"

Mr. Hansen's blue-veined hand reached out and patted her across the table. He smiled. "I know grief. Recognize it when I see it. My Solveig lived up to her name: 'sun's path'." He excused himself and walked to the counter for a refill.

LaRae watched him polish his lenses with a linen handkerchief, then surreptitiously wipe his eyes.

"But I've been gifted with the friendship of a famous artist and another up and coming one. If I were smart, I'd snatch up the novice's works before she becomes known and unaffordable!" Mr. Hansen sat down and poured extra cream into his coffee.

"Enough flattery! I'll let you judge my work. It's okay to not find it appealing. How about dropping in after the genealogy update?" Mr. Hansen nodded and opened his briefcase, shuffled some papers and placed a family tree in front of her.

"Traced us back to the Vikings?"

"Not that far, but I found someone called the Herring King." LaRae laughed.

After learning about her ancestors, she climbed into Mr. Hansen's car. "How about a detour pointing out the Norwegian Rococo architectural features of Town Hall?"

"Only if you enlighten me on our own neighborhood, especially the homes that appear a cross between a Swiss chalet and Victorian?"

They rode and talked until her friend pulled up to the curb outside her picket fence. LaRae admired the new coat of white paint on Great Aunt's house.

Mr. Hansen pointed to the windows. "Those red geraniums perk up the flower boxes."

"Cora keeps them indoors through the winter. This year, she insisted on planting them here. Carried away, she also splurged on the ceramic pots with crimson roses. Called it an additional birthday present. Said she couldn't stop herself, the doorstep was crying out for help."

"Our Cora in a nut shell. Hears atmospheric cries other mortals miss. I returned from vacation to a bonsai tree in the office and pink cushions on the tweed sofa."

They stood at the curb, surveying the property. Yellow flowers bloomed on the forsythia hedge, former snow shapes had transformed into fruit trees with a cuckoo bird taking up residence in a hollow stump. LaRae had given her cat strict orders to keep away from its nest.

She unlocked the door, stomach churning. The dessert did not sit well today. A glance inside the living room revealed the afternoon sun highlighting the canvases. With Aunt Erna's knickknacks donated to the thrift store along with the lace curtains, the new look was clean and simple. Or more like simple but neither polished nor scrubbed.

In the corners of the room, dust bunnies danced in the sunlight. LaRae contemplated them lovingly. "As if you would ever do anyone any harm," she murmured. "Cats and bunnies and cuckoo birds make life more fun."

"Erna's place has a new lease on life." Mr. Hansen walked in. "You could go into restoration!" He wandered into the sunlit space and grew silent. LaRae watched as his white hair formed a luminous crown against the afternoon rays and he ambled, taking in one painting at a time.

"Flott. Absolutt flott."

"A strong expression! Do you really find them interesting?"

"Young lady, I may have resorted to flattery in youth, but with old age such habits get trivial. I take pride in recognizing quality. You have not had the privilege of seeing my rather extensive art collection. Extensive for a small-town solicitor, that is." He smiled, showing a gold molar. "'Flott' means excellent, not interesting."

At his words, something wound up tight inside LaRae relaxed. She sank onto the emerald green chaise lounge while watching her internal world unfold. Her soul was laying down on sun-kissed rock, letting its granite heat penetrate the frostbitten places. *Please God, let my soul camp here forever.*

"I am your rock. Let my love radiate into you".

LaRae started. "I think God spoke to me!"

Mr. Hansen turned, looking nonplussed, as if she'd made a comment about the weather.

"I'm serious! It wasn't audible or you would've heard it," she rambled. "The words were quiet but distinct. I didn't imagine it." Exasperated and exhilarated at once, she threw her arms up in the air.

"My dear Miss Gunther. What wonderful news! I am happy for you. It is my greatest joy to hear His voice."

"Please have a seat. No one ever told me it's normal or possible for God speak to people."

"How else can one explain the words of Jesus, the Good Shepherd? Remember the Scripture?"

LaRae shook her head.

"My sheep hear my voice and they follow me. Hearing precedes following. Jesus said his sheep heed his voice but tune out that of a stranger. Unfortunately, in my experience we tend to do the opposite."

"As in tuning out Jesus' voice and heeding the false shepherd or stranger?"

"Exactly. We pay attention to the voice of the enemy whose sole goal is to inflict harm, to steal, kill and destroy."

"I'm not following. How can he inflict harm by talking?"

"By telling lies, dear." Her elderly friend eased down beside her, pulling out his signature handkerchief with embroidered navy-blue initials. "By offering lies that match our experience so closely that they feel true. We swallow the bait, hook, line and sinker, as you say in English. As you look back, can you not think of a lie you fell for?"

LaRae's forehead creased, trying to grasp the concept. "You mean Satan dishes up lies on a silver platter and I gobble them up?"

"Yes. Let me give you an example. Do you assume I was born into a wealthy family who supported my scholastic achievements and encouraged a worthwhile career?"

"Yes. You are poised and self-confident. Sophisticated."

Mr. Hansen laughed. "It might surprise you to learn I grew up a bastard in this small town. Not a big deal today. But half a century ago it limited one's opportunities and blocked entry into social circles. Besides, I suffered what we now call dyslexia. At the time I was considered thick in the head. My mother did her best to help me. 'Never give up, son. Bravery means pushing through obstacles till you come out on the other side.' But other voices contradicted her advice. 'You are a stupid son of a bitch, Toralf. A born loser. A pitiful excuse for a human being. No matter how hard you try you'll never get ahead.' Sorry for the bad language but inside, demonic voices are not kind! If they seem kind, it is only to suck you in. To set you up for future torment." Mr. Larsen wiped sweat beads off his forehead. "Such was the state of affairs while I was a teen. Would you like to know how things changed?"

LaRae nodded. The cat leapt to her knees and she made room on her lap.

"Home alone one night, I was sneaking vodka from a bottle tucked inside a rubber boot when God spoke. Not audibly, but in my spirit, much the same as what you just experienced. I'll never forget standing over the kitchen sink, bottle hidden beneath a bowl in case Mother walked in. I was gutting a mackerel I'd caught off the pier that morning. Despondent and hopeless, the alcohol numbed me when this voice spoke out of the blue saying: 'There is no condemnation for those who are in Christ.' I argued out loud: 'All I have known is condemnation. And I agree with it. I am a bastard. And an idiot. Can't even read. I have no future. Failure is my middle name. Thief has become my last name.' I peddled stolen goods. Do you know how the voice responded to my arguing?"

La Rae shook her head.

"The strangest thing happened. I expected silence or taunting voices to jump in. But not this: 'Child, my son took the chastisement in your place. He was considered unworthy, impure and filthy. To make you worthy, pure and clean.' I was astounded. Yes, I'd been to church. But this was different. For the first time in my life I believed it possible to step out from self-condemnation. From people's judgment. But also from deserved condemnation for my contempt towards the accusers."

"Wait a minute!" LaRae interrupted. "You hated yourself?"

"Yes. I hadn't supported my mother but acted like a nuisance. Skipped school. Gave up trying. Ate myself fat to dull the pain."

"Then you stepped out of the whole condemnation mess?"

"I decided that God was right, and I wrong. I came out of agreement with the lies I believed. Over the fish guts in that sink. I accepted the truth that Jesus bore my shame and inadequacies. And hatred. He carried it in his own body on the cross. Do you see how it became real to me, Miss Gunther?"

"Did things change?"

"Certainly! I worked day and night to graduate from high school and later university. I decided law was the path. Never looked back. It wasn't easy, mind you. God became a father, teaching me perseverance and patience. So, if you heard his voice today, I shall bug off as they say in Britain. It might be good to take time pondering what was communicated to you."

Mr. Hansen stood up. "Please promise me first dibs on this one?" He pointed to the canvas in the far left corner, the abstract, stormy seascape she had painted on her birthday.

"My debut painting? Only if no money passes from your hands to mine. Accept it as a thank you for what you've done for our family." LaRae unhooked the canvas from the wall and wrapped it in an old linen sheet, then walked him to the car before leaning in through the window, kissing his cheek. "Thank you," she whispered.

He patted her arm. "'Tusen takk'. Rest assured this will get a place of honor."

CHAPTER 20

Constitution Day was a big deal in Norway. Told to dress nice and be ready at 9:30 AM, LaRae straightened the black, woven wool skirt reaching to her ankles and cinched the laces in the red corset over the starched linen blouse. To shut out the morning mist she draped an accompanying black shawl, embroidered with a floral garland in shades of crimson, blues and greens over her shoulders when Cora traipsed in.

"Lovely! I wish I could still squeeze into that gown. But seeing you in it helps me live vicariously. Let's go. The first parade starts at 10 from 'Pine Forest' Elementary." They rushed downtown and elbowed their way to the front of the sidewalk. As the marching bands and hundreds of kids approached, onlookers cheered and shouted "hip, hip hurray". Like LaRae, many women and kids wore traditional gowns, each county displaying its own unique colors and embroidery. Men sported knickers and knitted socks. Handcrafted silver brooches and silver buckles on the shoes completed the outfits.

LaRae marveled as the normally sedate and introverted locals celebrated. Under Danish and Swedish rule long ago and occupied by Germany during the world war, Norwegians cherished their freedom more than anyone else she'd known. Parents beamed at their kids filing by, carrying flags and shouting loud hurrahs.

The parade snaked its way up to the Lutheran church, a white painted wooden structure with simple lines and a tower with chiming bells at its center. Perched on a hill it overlooked the town and ocean.

"Let's go in." Cora draped an arm about her shoulders. Together they mounted the worn stone steps and entered the two hundred-year-old building. Inside, the décor in shades of grey created a neutral back drop for the gleaming brass chandeliers, candlesticks and big organ. Simple and serene, it reminded LaRae of the church Lars had taken her to in Chicago. Once again, she found herself seated in a pew while majestic music filled the vaulted space. Surrounded by children's voices she contemplated the stained-glass windows depicting the crucified Christ. To her surprise, the scene no longer made her feel ill at ease. On the contrary, a brook of gratitude gurgled. After the service, she raced home to make preparations. By dusk, Great Aunt Erna's house beckoned like a lighthouse, with every lamp turned on inside and strings of patio lights illuminating the backyard and front stoop. Streamers and Norwegian flags flapped on the porch. Inside, she'd pushed the furniture to the edges of the living room. Tea candles flickered from the windowsills and lanterns burned out back. Mr. Hansen oversaw the cooking on her new grill where hot dogs and hamburgers sizzled. LaRae poured homebrewed iced tea into cups.

"What a great idea! You were serious about hosting the party for Cora! And to add dancing to our Constitution Day party? That was a stroke of genius!" Gunhild, her sixty two year old neighbor and new friend, gushed and peeled off her high heels, revealing swollen ankles.

"I hope no one minds me dancing barefoot. Did you invite the mailman like I asked? Fortunately he has seen me in slippers and curlers and in worse shape than this over the years." She stroked her newly permed hair and fluffed the size 18 dress. "He was married then. We chat over the mailbox most days. The whole town has me pegged for a confirmed old maid. If he asks me to dance, I will act real casual. There's no need to impress."

LaRae squeezed her arm. "He's coming. And you're impressive without trying. Be yourself."

Gunhild giggled. "My sixteen-year-old self was hotter than what you see today." She studied her ample bosom and varicose legs.

"Don't be too hard on yourself. Your chocolate cake is to die for and holds the place of honor on the dessert table."

Gunhild grabbed her arm. "Serve mailman Trond a piece. Though the 'kringle' recipe is his favorite. He hand-delivers mail on baking days."

LaRae wiggled her eyebrows. "I'm hitting the dance floor. Join in for the 30-minute instruction time before we let loose."

"You ain't nothing but a hound dog," Elvis' voice blared over the speakers. Cora's two brothers-in-law and their wives lined up on the make shift dance floor. Gerda, another neighbor and a speed knitter had left her knitting needles at home and clapped to the beat. Helen, whom LaRae had gotten to know through attending language class was taking on the role of rock and roll instructor. Tonight Helen flitted through the room, meeting and greeting, dressed in a flared skirt with white Keds and ankle socks.

"Hi Sweetie! Did you know I ran a dance hall in Brooklyn in the late 1960s? I memorized the hits while there. Now let's get organized," Helen spun in a circle and LaRae responded.

"Is your polka dot shirt vintage? Your matching lipstick cinches the deal."

"I'm the sentimental sort. I keep this outfit in a trunk and wear it every May 17th!" She clapped her hands and rallied everyone.

Cora shuffled her way over to LaRae's side. "There's only one thing missing," she yelled over the music.

"What?"

"You of all people should notice," Cora scolded. "Look around: there isn't one eligible male in this bunch. My brother-in-law Sven is 39 years old and sexy, but married. And he is the only male under 60 in attendance. I've decided you require help in this department!"

LaRae bowed. "You have proved a good neighbor so far. Why not?"

Cora saluted her. "At your service. Expect a phone call without further delay."

LaRae laughed. "I can't wait. But contrary to Gunhild, I'm not ready for a widower."

"I made a list. You need someone young, single and with an appreciation for the arts. God fearing. Not too short. Smart. Organized."

"I am scared to add to it. It might already be too tall of an order to fill!"

"Oh but nothing is impossible." Cora flashed her signature megawatt smile before snagging her beekeeping brother-in-law Anders for a dance.

As the party wound down the mailman, a short, skinny man with a lisp brought Helen to translate to LaRae. "That was a nice time."

"I'm glad. Sorry you didn't dance."

Mailman Trond shook his head. "I never had quick feet but I don't complain. They get the job done," he looked down at his sturdy black lace ups. "I walk seven miles a day."

LaRae picked up a paper plate covered in foil. "Gunhild's chocolate cake. She said for you to take home the leftovers."

"'Takk'. That woman can cook. And bake." The mailman blushed. "She's good to think of me. I will thank her tomorrow."

LaRae shook his hand.

"Happy seventeenth of May!" she called out as her guests gathered up belongings and slipped out the door. Each one expressed appreciation for the festivities and American food.

At midnight, LaRae sighed and put her feet up on the veranda railing. The night was cool and the house a wreck, but she didn't care. When Cora had confided she was stressed about putting on her annual national holiday party, LaRae had volunteered to host it. "Focus on the collection," she'd ventured, then she had panicked at being a hostess for the first time. She stretched her long limbs, picturing the *Facebook* posts she'd put up the next day. What would Starr say about her old geezers get-together? LaRae smiled at the ridiculousness of her situation. Perhaps she'd missed her calling. If all other plans failed, she could start a retirement community. In bed, she laughed thinking of Gunhild dancing to the rock-and-roll music. A lot of extra stuff bounced with her vigorous moves.

The following morning her favorite grey-headed person called as soon as the cock crowed.

"This is it," Cora's voice was firm over the phone. "We're going to Oslo. I have business there and you have not seen our capitol. Plus we'll take the train and the ride itself is priceless and an easy way to sightsee. You can't tell people you've seen Norway if you stay stuck in this little town. Granted it's picturesque, but tiny. We have culture to show!"

LaRae was slow to catch on because all she wanted was to sleep in.

"One more thing. Bring three of your latest paintings. I know it's a hassle, but it'll be worth it, I assure you."

"Cora. Is there something you're not telling me?" LaRae rallied and sat up in bed.

Her neighbor tittered. "Possibly. Do me a favor, will you? Trust me."

That afternoon, the two women plopped down on the velvet seats in a train compartment and after the whistle sounded, they blazed through forests and hamlets. Lakes glided by, reflecting a cerulean blue sky. LaRae thought of the roof replacement happening on Erna's house and how she was escaping the clatter of ceramic roof tiles being placed in rows, one at a time.

In rare form, her older companion shared the plan. "We'll see the palace this afternoon. Tonight we're having dinner with a friend of mine at the hotel." Cora looked pleased with herself.

LaRae admired her neighbor. Dressed in a wine-colored linen

dress, which offset her silver curls and elegant neck, Cora looked chic, yet relaxed. Matching lipstick highlighted her pearly white teeth and a pair of comfortable, grey pumps completed her outfit. Trips to the big city brought out her neighbor's refined taste.

"I see you left the pink bandana and blue paint apron at home. You look fabulous. Do I look ok?" LaRae straightened her fuchsia hippie skirt and bolero blouse.

"Adorable," Cora responded in a matter-of-fact tone as she turned to the conductor. "Careful with those, mister. They are valuable pieces of art!"

"I'm sorry, ma'am, but they blocked the walk. They're okay now."

"They'd better be," she chided the man as she turned back to her young protégé: "I'm so glad you brought your paintings. Bring them along for dinner."

"Okay, boss. Will do. And I won't even ask you why. I hope you are proud of me."

"Very." Cora patted her shoulder.

The Norwegian King and Queen lived in a palace. LaRae pondered this piece of information as she took in the Neo-Classical stucco building on the hill. It overlooked Karl Johan Street, Oslo's main thoroughfare. During the walking tour, the guide pointed out the recent renovations. "The residence was renovated. It went back to the original wall paper patterns and textile colors of wallpapers and textiles. Though not an ornate style, it's an interesting mix of understated elegance paired with vibrant color. This is the Bird Room, also called the Royal waiting room," the enthusiastic guide informed them. "The mural is original and boasts 14 species of birds. The scenes depicted in detail are well-known waterfalls and mountains, meant to welcome both the lowly and powerful for audiences with the king."

"Impressive paint job," a nearby tourist commented.

But Cora's favorite was the ballroom. Its white and gold theme was enhanced by the sky-blue coffered ceiling and pink walls. "I came here for a ball once," Cora admitted.

"Seriously? Please do tell!" LaRae exclaimed.

Cora laughed. "Well, it was not with the love of my life," she ran her hand over one of the gold chairs. "I was a young, aspiring artist and ran in Bohemian circles. A famous poet invited me to accompany him. He was in acute distress because his fiancée had broken up with him. I stressed over what to wear for weeks. My girlfriend and I pored over back issues of *Vogue* magazines until we were cross-eyed."

"Then what?"

Cora was taking in the Pompeian dining room as their guide moved them along. "In talking about *Vogue*, this Pompeian theme was the vogue in the 1850s. Several countries in Europe went gaga over this style. And yes, we actually copied a dress pattern based on a photo from the magazine. And we fabricated it."

"No kidding? What did it look like?"

"We picked red chiffon and sewed princess sleeves with a tapered waist and an ankle-length, full-bodied skirt. I have a photo of the event at home. The ball made it to the magazine covers."

"Did you get to shake the King's hand?"

"Yes. King Olav ruled then. Today it's his son, King Harald, who is the monarch. He is folksy and amiable. You know, he married a commoner. Queen Sonja was a regular girl."

"Wow! Is there an eligible prince around? All of a sudden I feel hopeful," LaRae interjected.

Cora laughed. "I'm afraid he is already taken. Check out the china collection in this dining room, it's Royal Copenhagen and contains two hundred different pieces hand stamped from copper engravings. They depict Scandinavian and German flora and fauna."

"I love it. I wish my mom were here to see this. She loved flowers." They took in the careful shading of the delicate, hand-painted pieces and after wrapping up the tour, walked to the Grand Hotel.

"Wow," LaRae admired the hotel's white granite façade and clock tower. "Thank you for picking such a nice place for us to stay. The huge flowerpots filled with orchids in the foyer are real; I pinched the leaves to make sure when we checked in."

Cora laughed. "It is a treat to myself as well. I'm glad you like it. The Grand Hotel is historic. Situated below the Royal Palace on the Main Street, it has been a landmark for the last hundred and fifty years. Did you know the Nobel Peace prize ceremony is held there each year?"

"I had no idea." They took the elevator to their shared room and changed before descending to the dining room.

CHAPTER 21

LaRae stopped inside the entrance to the restaurant. The smell of clams, browned butter, and garlic wafted from a nearby bar. Situated on the main floor of the Grand Hotel the restaurant had at one point been an open-air garden but had been encased in a Victorian glass dome. A twelve-foot fountain tinkled at its hub. Wing-shaped green velvet banquettes surrounded the waterfall which was held up by female bronze statues. Upholstered modern chairs looked dwarfed beneath the tall glass cupola. The place oozed old glamour. Another steaming dish paraded in on a plate etched with the Grand Hotel logo.

Her fingers bearing down on her companion's arm, LaRae stopped Cora's forward stride. "I don't feel comfortable about you paying for our food and stay. This must cost a fortune. After Tokyo, Oslo's considered the second most expensive city in the world. A simple hamburger costs twice as much here as in the USA."

Cora shrugged. "These are legitimate business expenses. You'll soon understand why I can include you in those."

"Okay—if you're sure. I'll take your word for it." A couple passed them and were led to a candle lit table in the corner. A male in his thirties with black, wavy hair combed off a high brow sauntered in and halted next to them, pecking Cora's cheek before turning towards LaRae.

"Hello. I am Matthias. I'm enchanted to meet you."

"This is my agent who helps maintain my fame," Cora said.

LaRae smiled and the man's deep set brown eyes swept over her. From Cora's description, she'd envisioned a grey, wizened gentleman. But clad in a navy cashmere coat with white pants and a paisley foulard neatly tucked into his shirt neckline, this male was anything but old and stodgy. He leaned in to kiss her on the cheek, then led them to a table by a wall of orchids, pulling their chairs out and seeing them comfortably seated. Leather bound menus dropped into their laps. "If you're adventurous, I recommend the reindeer medallions," Matthias said and eyed her above tortoise shell reading glasses.

LaRae accepted the challenge. Upon her first bite into the meat, she discovered it was tender, and roasted carrots and fingerling potatoes offset the earthy flavor. The creamy gravy had traces of brown goat cheese and a hint of juniper berries. A tart lingonberry relish accompanied the dish. LaRae shut out the conversation and moaned when chewing a forkful of chanterelle mushrooms. The hum of patrons' subdued conversations lulled her and flickering candlelight cast a romantic glow inside the glass dome. LaRae startled when a hand landed on hers. "I'm sorry, did I miss something?"

"I hope you do visit the Munch museum. *The Scream* is exhibited there. It's part of an autobiographic collection called *Frieze* by Edvard Munch. Our famous painter spent time in Paris and Germany but was a citizen of Oslo. Sadly he only attained local fame later in life. It took decades for the general populace to accept his unorthodox style."

"As gifted as he was, he was a soul in torment." Cora sighed.

"He came from much dysfunction. His family suffered mental problems and premature death," their host described.

"Like many of the great painters of that era. Consider Picasso with his sexual addictions and Van Gogh's bouts with depression and despair. Much of it rooted in an unhappy love life," Cora added.

"There was Matisse. A one-woman man despite his sensual

depictions of women," Matthias offered.

"Yes. But he too went through periods of protracted anguish, recurring panic and mental breakdowns. I think it reflects in his painting style." Cora narrowed her eyes. "In this last century the artistic expression of the dark side of our nature got elevated. Meaninglessness and absurdity got embraced more readily than works based upon truth and light."

Matthias raised a hand, his ring finger sporting a cut ruby in a gold setting. "You may be right but *The Scream* feels true to my own experience. I identify with the angst. I can say the same about the work of Picasso, Van Gogh and others."

"We all do at times. None of us are exempt from the negative spectrum of emotion. It plays an intricate part in human experience. Who among us has not encountered abandonment or grief? Or betrayal and other tumultuous emotions and states of mind?" Cora leaned over the grey linen cloth and straightened a tilted rose in the round crystal vase. "But my objection is that we glorify the negative aspects and wallow in these emotions and remain stuck! Absurdity and futility have become deities. What if there is a way out of torment? Much as the sun rides in after devastating storms, health rebuilds after disease, and spring follows winter."

"Do you imply that we prefer dwelling in ruins and devastation? Instead of rebuilding? Or remain frozen in a harsh landscape, resisting the offer of something better?" LaRae asked.

"Yes. I have staked my whole existence on the fact that rescue is available. That hope, forgiveness and soul restoration call out to us in the direst of circumstance. Even if outward situations don't change, internally, the entire landscape can transform. And transformation affects one's art."

Matthias laughed and sipped his glass of Chardonnay. "I adore her preaching on her soapbox. She has made it a habit to exhort me every time we visit. Have you noticed how her eyes blaze when she gets passionate? Sparks are flying." Matthias fanned himself with the linen napkin.

LaRae nodded and smiled. "I love her zeal and intellect. I have craved this kind of interaction for a long time. She has a valid point."

"I'm zipping it. Matthias, tell our guest about contemporary Oslo and the new opera complex that looks as if it's tilting right into the fjord." Cora resumed eating and let her agent launch into titbits about metropolitan life and politics and ending it with a historical synopsis of the region.

LaRae relished the story of Max Manus in the resistance movement during the Second World War. "He helped sink German ships and blow up their planes which rallied our spirit." Cora interjected. "But something you don't know about my fabulous agent is that he owns a successful art gallery!"

"And I have a talent for spotting up-and-coming artists," Matthias added. "I'm too young to take credit for the discovery of Cora but am honored to represent her works of realism."

The waitress cleared their plates and rolled in a dessert cart. LaRae picked from the selection when she heard her name mentioned. "Sorry. Did I miss something?"

"Mathias just mentioned he'd love to see your paintings after we order dessert and coffee. That's all."

"That's all?" Suddenly queasy, LaRae excused herself and ran to the ladies' room.

In the beveled mirror, her green eyes pinned the recoiling little girl on the inside. She admonished: "In two weeks, you'll be sleeping in your sister's basement, wiping noses and scrubbing her floors. Who cares if a foreign art critic tears your work to pieces? Get yourself together. I'll get Cora back before leaving." She slapped cold water on her flushed face, then took a deep breath. After squaring her shoulders, she sashayed into the dimly lit dining room, head held high. "Perhaps it's more advantageous to see the paintings upstairs than in the lobby? We'd have fewer distractions."

"You're right! Why don't we finish up, then you can lead the way?" Matthias handed her a fork for the waiting dessert. But the chocolate ganache cake stuck to her esophagus like wet clay. Hot coffee did not flush it down but only seared her tongue. LaRae contemplated a distraction maneuver of dropping to the ground and counting on Cora to call in the paramedics. She tried transmitting her thoughts to her friend, but Cora was either immune to telepathy or chose to ignore her plea.

"This has been charming." Matthias insisted on picking up the tab. "What luck to be surrounded by such genius."

LaRae coughed. After discussing the grand impressionist masters, she admitted that it was much easier to criticize others' work than to be brave enough to produce and display one's own!

In the elevator she discovered a newfound admiration for the aforementioned artists' resolve to keep painting despite massive public criticism. In her case, a connoisseur's constructive criticism would be helpful. *Baloney! Your spun sugar confidence will collapse,* her self- appointed inner guardian warned. After opening the door to their room, LaRae's trembling hands tugged at the wrapped canvases until Cora lent her a hand and propped them up against the beds. Matthias took a few steps back, then switched on the bedside lamps.

"The lighting is all wrong." A furrow creased his elegant forehead. His dark eyes roved over the details of her paintings.

"Oh, sorry! I'm just a beginner, you see. Basically, I splatter paint on the frame for fun. And therapy," she sent arrows in Cora's direction. "I had to quit class before they taught about lighting."

"Oh no, I'm talking about the glare from the lamps. And the fluorescent ceiling fixture. That's all. These paintings require specific lighting because of the glazes you use."

"Oh. I see."

"You are right once again, my dear Mrs. Eknes. I should employ you as a scout."

Cora wiggled her eyebrows. "So what do you suggest?"

"Hm. How about including LaRae in your own exhibit in Mandal in August? That way a small town discovers her and its paper provides press coverage. If it goes well, and she's willing, I'll seize the momentum and spin it further."

LaRae grabbed the door handle for support. "Do you guys

happen to be talking about me or am I suffering hallucinations from the mushrooms?"

"You, my chérie, are my next protégé!" Matthias lifted her hand to his lips.

Cora laughed. "Don't let the gallantry scare you. My friend's charm extends beyond our borders. I'm sorry for setting you up but I worried you'd refuse to come if you knew what I was up to!" She motioned for LaRae to come sit by her on the bed. When she did, Cora put her arm around her shoulders. "I believe you're talented. There's an edge to your landscapes. They tug at one's heart. The color mix is unconventional, but it works somehow. I confess to bringing you here intentionally." She motioned to the artwork. "I needed a second opinion to confirm my hunch."

"What do you say? Will you exhibit in August?" Matthias examined brush strokes up close.

LaRae fell back on the bed. "My visa expires at the end of June. I promised Amanda I'd put the house on the market next Monday. Money's tied up in it."

Except for traffic noises and laughter drifting from the open window, the room fell silent. Warm enough for people to shed coats and stroll, the night had attracted a crowd below who enjoyed drinks beneath gas heaters in the outdoor café.

"I believe a more appropriate question is: what does LaRae want?" Matthias turned and stared her down, a vertical wrinkle forming between his wing-shaped eyebrows.

Cora sank backwards on the bed. "I know you're afraid to believe in yourself. Let me do it in your place."

LaRae closed her eyes and Lars' words floated up from her memory. "Promise not to neglect your gift." Sobered, she sat up and gazed at the two people awaiting an answer. In a determined voice with not so much as a quiver she spoke: "Yes. I will. If Matthias can help with extending the visa?"

Cora dragged her off the mattress into a jig. "It's settled. Matthias, explain to the gallery owner in Mandal about the change in plans. And please work out the legal stuff with the proper authorities."

"Consider it done. And you my chérie," he clasped LaRae's fingers. "I pray this is only the beginning of things to come."

In bed that night it all seemed like a dream.

But the next morning, the snoring that rattled the bed across from LaRae confirmed that recent events were for real. It felt strange to wake up in a room with a woman who'd been a total stranger two months ago. She'd never slept in the same room as her mother. A memory surfaced of her childhood where bacon sizzled to the music of the washer spinning and the iron hissing before 7 AM. Even on her 41'st birthday Mother had bustled about till LaRae made her sit down. She'd been so excited about the gift she'd saved for and with a flourish presented the wrapped box. Once her mother removed the tissue she'd stared.

"A lavender silk robe! Do you see me as a diva lounging on the couch watching soap opera? Did you get me a box of chocolates too?" Picturing her mother in front of "Lifetime Movies" had been a far stretch even for LaRae's imagination.

"Fancy frilly clothing. Thanks, but don't try pushing a new lifestyle on me. If you saved the receipt I'll put the amount towards a new vacuum. And Rae? This gesture concerns me. God knows I've done my best to teach you how to avoid laziness." Mom had folded the bathrobe and boxed it then stuffed the hand-painted birthday card in the kindling basket. Afterwards LaRae had slipped out the back door and isolated herself by the lake, little waves lapping at her feet. With her freckled nose buried in the pages of a book she'd read until forgetting who and where she was.

LaRae stretched in the hotel bed, shaking off the memory by letting her imagination toy with a picture of Mother floating around heaven in the lavender robe with a flower wreath around her head. With her long legs aimed towards the ceiling she inspected the increased muscle of her thighs and calves, then put her feet on the carpeted floor to check the weather. The fourth-floor window revealed modern buildings side by side with older brownstones and traditional store fronts. Below, restaurant staff draped sheep skins over the cafe rattan chairs, an ingenious way to keep the patrons' bottoms warm. Pigeons picked at the previous day's leftovers and a red tram rattled by.

"Good morning, Sweets! I'm bad company before drinking coffee in the morning. Would you mind getting me a cup? And please tell me I didn't snore. My adult child says it's more like an airplane drone. Did I keep you up?" Cora rubbed her eyes, her hair coming unpinned from the foam rollers.

LaRae laughed. "I've slept through tornadoes and blizzards on the plains of Illinois. Not to worry."

"Good! I didn't have you pegged as a finicky type but one never knows." Cora winked and pulled her worn red Bible off the nightstand. "I'll be ready in 30 minutes but need a bite of daily bread first." She patted the gilded edges on her lap. "If you like, I can share a chunk with you?"

"All right, but let me get our caffeine first." LaRae descended to the foyer and filled two ceramic mugs with coffee then stuck a copy of the international *Herald Tribune* under her arm.

"Thank you! Today's reading is in Luke 14. Come to me all who are tired and carry heavy burdens and I will give you rest." Cora read out loud,

Like a yellow sticky note the verse stuck in LaRae's mind. She spoke out loud. "I wonder if I am so used to dragging around my heavy burdens that I don't notice their weight anymore? Also, I always assumed there wasn't an alternative to doing it myself."

"The alternative is a willingness to relinquish the burdens." Cora squinted above purple reading glasses. "The offer's on the table. But it can be challenging to give them up. Do you feel more in control if you carry your own burdens?"

"Oddly enough, that appears true."

"Well. It's an illusion. Our backs are not made for carrying worry, concerns and every problem we face. When I finally allowed myself to be like a little girl, something shifted. I envisioned myself with a backpack full of concerns. I shrugged it off daily and deposited the burdens at the feet of Jesus. Do you know what happened after a while?"

LaRae shook her head. There was no telling.

"One day when I stood before him, Jesus asked me to climb up on his lap. I snuggled with him! Crazy, right? But remember he said: 'Come to me all who carry heavy burdens and I will give you rest.' That's the Word right here. Nowadays, I rest on his lap, knowing he's at work on my behalf." Cora clapped her hands. "Hallelujah. I'm so excited to belong to Jesus and God! And to Holy Spirit of course. Now let's pray and then hop to it. We have things to do!" She lifted her hands in the air. "Father, this is another fabulous day. We love you so much! Please help us as we go exploring. Bless our family. And bring back our prodigals; we are expectant!"

Upon pronouncing the last words, Cora jumped out of bed, her legs showing at the knee-length hem of the pink flannel gown.

"How do you stay so tanned?" LaRae admired her friend's color.

"It's called doing yard work in a halter top and shorts," her friend replied impishly. "The hawthorn hedge grows high enough to conceal this fifty-five-year-old, half-naked body from public view." She pulled up her gown to show her belly. "See. I even have a tanned midsection. Because of eating blueberries, I don't worry about the sun's rays. The flavonoids our Father put in them help prevent nasty skin cancers." She sighed with contentment. "It's almost time for a new crop."

"Oh, do you grow them?"

Cora laughed. "No need. They grow by themselves in our mountains. And they're free for the picking. Do you have a hankering to help? If so I'll share my homemade blueberry drink concentrate with you."

"Is that what we've been drinking? The burgundy Kool Aid drink?"

"What an insult. Kool Aid has nothing to do with 'saft'! What I offer is raw, concentrated berry with a little sugar, the way we've made 'saft' for generations." Cora stared at her indignantly.

LaRae raised her hands in self-defense. "Sorry. Of course, it's all natural. And I'll pick berries in order to obtain a few precious bottles. Tell me where and when and I'll show."

"Good girl, that's music to my ears. My back appreciates the help." Cora pulled on jeans and a turquoise top. "Our first stop are the two Viking ships. They were unearthed in bogs and pieced back together. There are also ancient weapons, tools and clothing and the museum is close to the king's country estate."

"Will I have to look at shriveled bog men? The one discovered in Denmark looked like a prune."

"Courage, girl! And, no you won't. Bring your camera, I'm ready to hit town."

A short while later, they boarded a city tram and a bus. After paying the museum admission fee, LaRae snapped a picture of the elongated boat. Built around 830 A.D. the oak vessel measured 70 feet and had been rigged with 15 pairs of oars and a square sail. The bow soared upwards in the shape of a coiled serpent. She had to rush to keep up with her travel companion who sputtered facts at the speed of light along with impromptu instructions and juicy tales. After leaving the museum, they headed to a fortress where cannons had fired at the German invaders in 1940 but had been unable to stop the advancing force. Next they entered the new Opera House where the angled, architectural metal and glass feat did indeed appear to be rising out of the depths of the blue fjord.

"Whew! May I sit on this bench for a minute?" LaRae pleaded a few hours later. They had knocked out the Fram Museum where a polar ship was on display. She had learned that Norwegians had undertaken other ship expeditions after the Viking era and an explorer named Amundsen had been the first to reach the South Pole and the first to navigate the Northwest Passage. A daring spirit and a thirst for knowledge had propelled his endeavors. It reminded her of a certain somebody. *I understand Lars better now.* And weirdly his unquenchable thirst for exploration echoed within her as she ventured out of her own comfort zone.

"My artistic eye is overwhelmed. These sculptures are exquisite." LaRae gestured to the left. The famous Vigeland Park surrounding their bench was green, peaceful and filled with families and individuals out for a walk. But the main attraction was the sculpted human forms, all naked yet gloriously rendered in their various stages of development and aging. LaRae noticed the crowd massing towards a certain area.

"They are flocking to the statue of the little boy known as 'Sinnataggen'. It means 'The furious little tag along'," Cora explained. "He has become the icon of this park. Notice the stomping foot?"

"His left hand is shiny?"

"Yes. People grab the hand when posing for photos. The rest of the statue is dark because the copper oxidized."

Japanese tourists were swarming, taking turns holding the statue's left hand. LaRae rose and followed Cora up the steps towards an ascending monument called the Monolith totem. At 46-feet-tall, it spiraled upwards, depicting an intertwined humanity, starting on the bottom but straining towards the top. Men and women carved in stone climbed over each other, heedless of who they were crushing. Struck by its depiction of ambition and greed, LaRae found it both abhorrent and truthful. As she rested on the bench, she realized the man who created these works had deep insights into the human psyche. Strategically placed in a circle around the tall pillar was a depiction of the human life cycle from cradle to grave. A nude mother lifted her baby exuberantly with outstretched arms. And at the end of the cycle a heap of entangled, dead bodies rested. In between the two extremes, a young couple was depicted embracing, their naked forms pressed against one another.

Instead of feeling embarrassment, LaRae felt deeply touched. Raw and vulnerable, the statues represented mankind without its cultural trappings.

Cora interrupted her philosophical thoughts, reading aloud from the guide book. "The site draws one to two million tourists a year. The artist, Gustav Vigeland, must've had no idea how famous his works would become a century later. From the small town of Mandal, the sculptor spent a lifetime perfecting his craft."

"I'm not sure my parents would've been comfortable here. Yet the statues are poignant." LaRae gestured towards the bronze and granite forms immortalized before them.

Cora nodded. "Most Scandinavians are at ease with nudity. It's good and bad if you ask me. Good because we have an easier time accepting our different shapes and figures." She laughed. "That comes in handy when you've lived over half a century," she pointed at her hips. "Some wear and tear and a few new bulges don't stop this woman from going to the beach. I decided to wait till the water heats up to 18 degrees though."

"68 degrees Fahrenheit? Wow. I must steel myself. And about the bad part concerning nudity—do you care to elaborate?"

"Well, naked ten-year-olds on the beach, in our internet society does not seem wise. It's time for our kids to suit up. Secondly, if you're trying to live a sexually pure life, just navigating public parks and beaches can be tricky. I pray for my son in this area." They descended the steps.

"I am so curious to learn more about your son. He's your only child, right?"

"Yes. And dear to my heart. His name is Gunnar. He's working hard and I am proud of him. One day when we Skype I'll introduce you."

"Am I detecting a matchmaking aspect?" LaRae shook out her ponytail and closed her eyes letting the sun caress her freckled face.

"I wish!" Cora stopped to pet a panting Labrador who brought her a stick. "This could make a great impressionist painting." She pointed to the activities taking place on the lawn. Picnic blankets dotted the ground. Kids were chasing soccer balls and kites. A standard poodle stood erect at the center of a formal garden. "My son has his mind made up about his future spouse. One day I'll introduce you to the girl, —which brings me to the topic of Matthias. Do you wonder why he is still single?"

"None of my business but the thought did cross my mind."

"He is a good man. Married a flight attendant he met in Brazil. It was a stormy romance. Esmeralda swore the cold of a

Norwegian winter was worse than the flames of hell. Flew back to Rio without telling him."

"What did Matthias do?"

"He moved to Rio. Things were all right for a while. Then she took up flying again. Met a wealthy Libyan oil magnate. That was the end of their marriage."

"I feel so sorry for him!"

"I do, too. But he is not lacking for attention from the opposite sex! Though he has become—what do you call it in America? Shy of the gun?"

"Oh! Gun shy. That's understandable. Maybe someone solid and responsible will come along and win his heart."

"I am holding out for that! Besides, you fall into that category." Her friend placed her hands on her hips. "Selfishly I'm trying to keep you in this country. I've always wanted a daughter as well as a son."

"And getting me married here would accomplish that? Well, you win the prize for scheming and innovative! I'm flattered. But there are only 37 days left on my visa. If you miss me, you can always visit Dresden, Illinois. I'll take you sightseeing!"

"From the double wide on your hog farm if your friend gets his way," Cora quipped. The two women laughed uproariously and made their way back to the hotel.

A sobering shiver streaked down LaRae's spine. *Send me to China or Timbuktu, dear God! Anywhere but back home!* But a moment later the prayer itself appeared dumb. Because after the ranch house on Wisteria Lane sold, she would not have a place called "home".

CHAPTER 22

It was Wednesday and the Crochet Club had gathered. A regular attendee now, LaRae opened Cora's mint green door and stepped inside to greet her three neighbors. "Come sit. We are discussing Gunhild's crush on the postman. She is too bashful to let him know." Cora waved and pointed to the sofa.

Gunhild's double chin quivered while she flattened the wrinkles of her massive house coat. LaRae jumped in: "Trond is nice. He rings my doorbell daily with a new vocabulary word to help my Norwegian."

"The poor soul lost his spouse to cancer last year and according to Ellen at the grocery, all he eats is deli roasted chicken and instant mashed potatoes! For anything else that can be said about his wife, let's agree she knew how to cook, eh?" Gerda, who was bony and gaunt winked. "Though it must be refreshing to enjoy silence. Something I doubt he experienced in 42 years of marriage."

"Dripping faucets. I think there's a verse in Proverbs about us nagging." Cora's eyes twinkled.

Gunhild came to the mailman's defense. "You never know. He probably misses it by now."

"Like I'd be missing that woodpecker on my roof." Gerda scowled and the group once again howled with laughter.

"I am ashamed of our gossiping selves. We need you to moderate, LaRae. Guard our wagging tongues! But that may be a task too great even for you. Help us, Holy Spirit." Cora glanced towards heaven.

"Amen!" Gunhild added emphatically. "And help these women respect my love life!"

"Oh honey, we can do better!"

"What?" Gunhild looked at Gerda with suspicion.

"We go back a long way. How long would you say?"

"Mm… I knew you in the first grade when you traded caramels for kisses."

Gerda chuckled. "That proves my point. Cora and I are the romance experts; heed our advice."

The conversation flowed in Norwegian with Cora too enthralled to translate. "Oh, my goodness! Listen everyone: I understand you! I never thought this would happen, not with your broad local accent!" LaRae rose and exclaimed.

"Mamma mia! I need to watch my words now," Gunhild slapped her hand over her mouth.

"Goodness! This is huge, let's celebrate!" Cora jumped out of her chair and grabbed LaRae for a waltz around the room, then disappeared down the steps to the basement. A moment later she reappeared with a bottle of black currant wine. "This was saved for a special occasion and we have witnessed one this morning. LaRae, please get the sherry glasses out of the china cabinet." Cora brought a damp rag and wiped the dust off the bottle.

The four women clinked their glasses together in a toast.

"To the newest resident in the neigborhood!" Gerda announced.

"To health and happiness. And thanks for saving me from my cat!" Cora grinned.

"Cheers to her for befriending the mailman in his time of need," Gunhild added. LaRae's laugh tinkled and the threesome looked at her.

"Like silver bells. Such infectious, wonderful laughter. How can we get you to do this more often?" Cora questioned.

"By having get-togethers Monday through Friday." LaRae kept a straight face. "I love how you meet at each other's house for coffee and that outside of sickness and holidays, no other circumstance interferes with the routine. The knitted teapot warmers, mittens, socks and crocheted bedspreads are beautiful. And the blankets in colorful yarn donated to the foster care system for kids who find themselves evacuated overnight? Imagine the children huddling beneath their very own coverlet that you have prayed over."

"Well, thanks. The Christmas bazaar at the Lutheran Church is fast approaching. The proceeds will go to orphans on the island of Madagascar," Gerda fixed everyone sternly.

"Oh. All I know about the island is that the cute lemurs from the Disney movie are native to it," LaRae quipped. She leaned back and thought that even if the handiwork hadn't contributed to a good cause she would've fallen head over heels for the spunky women. The first month she'd remained mystified, trying to understand their prattle in Norwegian. Cora had done her best to translate but sometimes got too engrossed in conversation to remember LaRae's limited linguistic knowledge.

Luckily, the language classes had paid off. She thought of the interactive computer program she did at Cora's house so that her friend could correct any mispronounciation. She chuckled while thinking back to when she'd learned the word "drive" in Norwegian.

"No, no. You're saying that all wrong." On that particular occasion Cora had held out a wedge of her half-eaten apple.

"Stick this in the back of your mouth as if you're about to choke. Make the noise you would to get it out."

LaRae had endeavored to form the guttural "kj" sound, pushing out the harsh syllable much like trying to spit out food stuck in her craw. When her eager efforts caused her to swallow the apple instead, Cora had had to slap her back multiple times to get her breathing again. Her friend had ended up sweaty from the effort.

"Now you'll be truthful if you ever declare that learning Norwegian almost killed you," she'd blurted while wiping LaRae's eyes. The two had fallen out with mirth.

"Your help just about did me in. We need to stay away from apples as an educational tool. Funerals abroad are expensive. As much as I appreciate your input, I beg you to focus on keeping me alive from now on."

LaRae had turned her nose up only to have Cora slap her behind. "You naughty girl, this is the gratitude I get? Maybe I should leave you to your own devices."

Still smiling at the memory she sighed and closed her eyes. The bantering wrapped around her, a soft security blanket, as crochet needles dipped to hook the thread and knitting needles clicked. Porcelain cups clinked as her friends plotted how to make Trond pursue Gunhild. LaRae emptied the liqueur from her glass, its subtle fire and warmth permeating her to the point she thought it might just spill over.

It was a dreary day. From the kitchen window LaRae watched fog inch in from the ocean and wrap familiar surroundings in a ghostly costume. She sorted through the mail on the counter but the visa extension was not in the stack. If the authorities didn't grant the renewal she'd be heading back to Dresden in 18 days. Eternal optimists, Matthias and Cora urged her to keep on painting towards the exhibit regardless.

Beneath an advertisement a hand written letter peeked out. *Lars found me!* As she sat down and tore the envelope a photo fell out. She leaned in, stomach flopping and studied the glossy picture and groaned. The scrawl on the page read:

Dear sweetheart,

Your silence has been disheartening. But as you can see, I kept my promise to give you space. I hope by now you've had time to realize how well we fit together. Much has happened since you left. This spring I hired my cousins and between the three of us we built the pens. I bought 100 pigs at auction. Pork prices are on the rise so we are set for success. A cash crop of corn is sprouting; we are moving closer to our dream!

I know your father would be proud of the way the farm is advancing. Amanda said for the trailer to appear homey I have to paint our bedroom pink! My buddies hang out over here but I told them to bring their own beer to cut down on expenses. They crash in the living room. The bedroom is off limits. I hope you appreciate how considerate I can be!

Amanda gave me your address since you do not answer my Facebook messages. If I don't hear from you after this letter I'll come myself to check on you. Amanda told me you refuse to return home. I said maybe you are being held under duress against your will. All kinds of shenanigans happen across the Atlantic.

My gut says you're scared, abroad all by yourself. I should not have let your family pressure you to go. Just know I'll make it up to you when you get back. Also, Amanda and I checked out the new bridal shop in Normal. We found a gown with luxurious ruffles, ribbons and bows. You'll look like a real Barbie doll in it. Sorry. I'm getting ahead of myself. (I can picture you saying that right now.)

I admit to swinging by the shop and asking the owner to put it in layaway. Since you've been strapped for cash, I don't mind helping. Mom says hello. We are all waiting to hear from you.

Love you so much, Rae Rae.

Yours forever, Norman

LaRae pushed away the letter. The movement made her mug tilt and crash onto the floor. Hot tea burned her toes. In one leap, she barged out onto the veranda, her mouth opening in a scream. The shrill sound ricocheted off nearby walls and fences.

"Goodness child! Is that you acting like a wild banshee? I thought it was crazy Mr. Lund, two doors down." Gunhild leaned over the neighboring fence, clippers in her right hand. "Did a mouse make you scream bloody murder? I am great at killing varmints. Those beasts don't scare me. Should I come over?"

"Yes! I need rescuing. From something bigger and scarier

than a mouse. Please jump the fence. I'll make coffee and you can try my spice cake. Who is Loon?"

"Lund. But he is looney, ok. The poor man took a bullet to the head during the war. It deranged him. As for me, I'm too old for jumping fences even for spice cake. I'm coming through the front door and may stop to catch a word with Trond. I've been lurking in the bushes trying to think up an excuse to chat with him."

"Tell him I'm indisposed and you need to bring my mail. It's close to the truth."

"Great reason. Thanks! See you soon."

LaRae poured loose Earl Grey into the teapot for herself and poured water into the coffee maker for her neighbor who despised tea, calling it a poor British substitute for coffee.

"Tell Gunhild all about it," her large bosomed neighbor busted through the door, cheeks flushed but stopped abruptly. "Man trouble. I know it when I see it. That's why I never tied the knot. Look at me now, losing my head." She lumbered towards the window with a doleful stare at the receding mailman's figure.

LaRae smiled despite erratic heart beats. "He is a sweet man. I'd love to see you married but suck at romance."

"That makes two of us. Now tell me about your troubles."

LaRae shoved the letter and photos across the table.

"Hmmm. Those will make good pork chops. I prefer them with sour cream and mustard. Who is the smiling man in overalls? Looks like he ate the canary. Is he the proud farmer?"

"That he is," LaRae admitted. "He has picked out a wedding gown for me back in our hometown."

"What in the world. Why didn't you tell us you're engaged? Congratulations! My father farmed sheep. He made a good living. When hard times hit, your larder will be full!" At the mention of food, her friend helped herself to cake, while continuing her economic dissertation. "During the war people who lived on farms stayed well fed. They were about the only ones. With crazy terrorists bombing your cities, there's no telling how things will turn out in America. Add cows for milk. If the grocery stores run out, you'll still feed the young ones. And you could use bacon." Gunhild scowled and nodded towards LaRae's gangly legs exposed below her nightgown.

"I am not engaged! And for your information I'll starve to death before marrying a hog farmer!" She leapt out of her seat.

"Hold your horses. Don't marry the man unless you want to. Why are you twisted up like a pretzel?"

LaRae collapsed on a chair burying her head in her hands. "I'm sick of having everyone else run my life! My mother did, even from the grave. Then I did what Dad wanted even after he passed! Now my sister and Norman dictate to me. Only the cat leaves me be."

"Of course! Cats do their own thing and let you do yours. They're not like dogs, begging, slobbering and whining. I'm a cat person myself. And as for people, why do you let them do it?"

"Do what?"

"Run your life. The living ones and the dead?"

LaRae sank back into the pine chair and rubbed her forehead. "That's a very good question. I need to think about it. Unfortunately after my visa expires, Norman will pursue me once again. I need to learn to say 'no'. And back the word up with action." The kitchen clock ticked off a minute, then two. Gunhild added a spoonful of sugar to her cup and ate more cake.

"Take your time thinking. I'll just sit here and daydream. The mailman sure appreciates my cooking. The poor thing has lost even more weight marching like a soldier every day with no one to feed him. Maybe I'll invite him to check out my prime rib. I have an heirloom recipe."

"As long as that's all you let him check out."

"Oh, miss Smarty Pants, I can show you some prime rib right here." Gunhild motioned down her heaving chest and well-padded torso. Except this will be off limits till after we cut the wedding cake," she roared with laughter.

LaRae couldn't help but join in.

"What? Am I missing out on all the fun?" Cora stood in the kitchen door, brandishing a new swimsuit. "I've been shopping and need your opinion on lime green. Is it too trendy for someone my age?"

"Model it for us. We're already discussing body parts. And wedding gowns," Gunhild added motioning toward LaRae.

"Goodness! Did you have a revelation you truly love what's his name?"

"No! He picked a wedding gown for me without my consent." LaRae gesticulated. "And to answer the question, I know the reason why I feel trapped. I try to please everyone."

Applause erupted in the tiny kitchen.

"Well done! I'm so proud of you." Cora grabbed her in an embrace.

"She figured out she's a cat girl! About time. Now write that boy and tell him to leave you alone. It's simple. Let him pant and wag his tail and bark all he wants." Gunhild heaved her body off the chair. "Come on, child. I'll help with the letter. An old maid can straighten this out in no time."

"I'll go change into the swimsuit. But no flattery. Give me your honest opinion."

Gunhild rolled her eyes. "Sometimes that woman is just too much," she whispered as Cora disappeared to the bathroom. "These artists with their sensitive temperaments! And lime green. Help me break this to her!"

LaRae giggled. "I'm a sensitive artist too. I love lime green."

Gunhild harrumphed. "I'm dictating. Write. Ready? 'Hello Norman. I received the letter. Things are going great here. However, I will not be marrying you. I wish you the best. Hope the hogs get fattened up and you get a good price for them. I hate pastel pink. As for the wedding gown, - another girl will like it and wear it for you. It will not be me. Do not write anymore or try to come to Norway. I won't let my deceased father's wishes influence my decisions any more. I honor his memory but will decide for myself who to marry. Good luck to you and goodbye. LaRae Gunther.' Was that terrible?" Gunhild finished the dregs of another cup of coffee.

"No. Freeing. Now you can add moral support to your mice exterminator resume. I thank you." LaRae smiled and stuck the letter inside an envelope.

Cora appeared in the kitchen and pulled a stamp out from her wallet and licked it. "How about I take this baby and mail it right away?"

LaRae shrugged. "Are you afraid I'll change my mind? Don't worry. I'm proud of this milestone. But please send it. Only you might not want to wear your new swimsuit to the post office."

Cora came to an abrupt halt on the threshold, inspecting herself. "Oh, thanks! Hope the mailman didn't see me walk out the door like this."

Gunhild heaved an exasperated sigh. "He has other things on his mind, I assure you. Ditch the lime green for red. Do you think prime rib is my best dinner?"

"Yes," Cora nodded. "Especially to a starving man. He might ignore every swimsuit in sight for a bite of that succulent dish. Make sure to drizzle it with love."

LaRae raised her eyes to heaven as her neighbors left. "Lord God. Your mercies must indeed be new each morning. Thank you for sending them in female form." Still dressed in Great Aunt's flannel, she peeled it off and filled up the bath tub. Steeped in hot sudsy water, she used a loofah sponge to exfoliate. On top of life again, she performed a routine breast exam and came to an abrupt halt. Her left index finger ran across a pea sized, hard knot. *A benign cyst.* Starr complained of them during her period. With practiced moves, she continued the exam, forcing her mind to dwell on the upcoming weeks where the primary goal was to meet her painting deadline. She had fought Amanda to have this summer in Norway, butting against the resistance. Her sister's eventual approval had come with a warning: at the slightest hint of sickness or distress, Amanda would personally drag LaRae back home.

"I refuse to send more money. If you demand independence,

you must learn what it takes to support yourself." Amanda's voice had climbed to the stringent timbre of their mom's when the grocery budget exceeded her limit. LaRae had smiled.

"I'll be fine." She would live off of Cora's produce with rice and beans, take cold baths and illuminate her home with candles. With an opportunity of a lifetime, who cared? Her fingers traversed the foreign lump in otherwise soft tissue. *The annual check-up in September will cover this detail.*

With skin scrubbed pink, she sank beneath the water line, relishing the new feel of freedom. In this light-infused country, a grace had appeared. It was a grace enabling her to live not elsewhere or deep inside but in the moment.

CHAPTER 23

Heathrow Airport welcomed another batch of humans into its bosom. Fellow female travelers cast envious glances at Ania's figure and lustrous hair glimmering with violet highlights. Designer jeans hugged her hips and a black top revealed the curves of her torso; four-inch heels completed the outfit. She applied a coat of lipstick in the airport's bathroom mirror, gold jewelry flashing, competing with her bronzed skin. Ania rearranged the chain around her neck. A gift from an ex, it belonged in the collection of admirer jewelry.

No exterior marks displayed what had happened six months ago. Her recent boyfriend had admired her physique too, the body betraying none of its secrets. On a warm day in May they'd taken advantage of the privacy offered by a secluded inlet close to his summer house. Stretched out on the deck of his sailboat she had lounged in the sun.

"A pity you grew up in such a backwards place," he'd sighed after throwing the anchor overboard. "You are model material. You'd make a great living from it."

She had looked at him in wonder, admitting the instructor job at the beauty school was a dead-end position. After pondering the model idea, she decided to put her assets to better use. Lars' venturing into the world boosted her confidence; she now followed in his footsteps. Ever since her friend's vanishing act, she'd been besieged by a restlessness no casual male could tamp down.

A professional photographer had put together her portfolio. She marveled at the results. With her head tilted back and the fan aimed towards her face, it seemed as if the wind was caressing her face.

Responses from different agencies popped up in her email account. One led to today's adventure. She strode out of the restroom, cradling the passport with both hands before handing it to the customs officer. After reclaiming the red booklet, she said "good riddance" to small-minded people and small-town thinking. London waited, inhabited by trendsetters who made things happen. Electric jolts coursed through her. *I'll be discovered.* She'd prove she had what it took to climb to the top!

A man in his early thirties waved a sign with her name scrawled in permanent marker. After introducing himself as her agent Minny, he helped her to his car. They passed double decker tour buses and Big Ben but veered off into a part of town where graffiti-stained brick buildings towered above immigrant grocery stores and fast food stands. The agent paid the driver, then motioned for her to climb rickety steps to a flat on the fourth floor. Upstairs, he threw the suitcase on a bottom bunk in a room stacked with eight beds, then introduced the flat mates before pointing to her luggage. "Let's do the triage, luv."

Minutes later, half of her new wardrobe lay discarded in a heap on the faded carpet. "Wear the rest to castings." His steely eyes roamed her body. "Two egg-whites for breakfast and a dressing free salad for lunch during the week," he quipped before leaving.

"A small price to pay for glamour," she told an Asian-looking roommate named Lotus. South African Claire with ebony colored skin nodded. Mia from Slovakia warned, "No snacking; we weigh-in daily. And on Mondays, Minny assesses us."

"Juice fast," Minny, dressed in black jeans and a singlet, said and nodded towards Ania. She soon discovered that intense coaching and hard physical workouts accompanied the fast. Not having been forewarned, Ania had assumed she'd go straight to work but Minny said her current weight did not qualify her for the labels the agency planned on casting her in. So instead of being light-headed from excitement her head started spinning from the new starvation routine.

A hectic month followed. Ania learned to walk, stand and sit like a model. Over time the days filled with shoots and castings. On a wet afternoon, she paraded in a skimpy bikini in front of studio cameras while trying to stop shivering. After finishing, she cinched the belt of a yellow rain slicker before running through a deluge to the next destination. There, she stripped and put on new clothing. When done, she rushed out again to the next appointment while clutching a can of Red Bull. The dream of being shuttled from castings to fittings in a luxury car had evaporated; instead she turned into a sprinter, long legs hammering sidewalks to catch the next bus or tube.

As weeks passed, work fell into a routine, and Ania accepted the merry-go-round. At the beck and call of a slew of casting directors, photographers and designers, she pasted on a mannequin smile and tossed her hair in sexy sulkiness. But her real self surfaced after sundown, the buzz of the urban, cosmopolitan nightlife waking her senses. The attention the girls garnered at night became an adrenaline shot to her body.

On a dull Friday where a steady drizzle had soaked Ania to the skin Mia exclaimed while Ania dried her hair: "Giovanni just texted!" They dressed up in time for the white limo to drop them at the trendiest club in London with an offer of immediate cash pay and red-carpet treatment by the club manager. They were hailed as VIPs by the crowd. Ania seized a glass of gratuitous champagne, feeling bubbly herself.

"I don't know about you," she confided to Mia over a new cocktail, lights creating pink patterns on the girl's Slavic cheekbones. "I feel as if people finally see me for who I am."

Mia bit her lip. "I can't decide if that's true or if all they see is my body."

Ania sent her a long look.

"Darlings, let's take your photo for the *Examiner*. Show us what you've got!" They rose and dangled on the club promoter's arm while the press snapped pictures to catcalls and advances. Ania flashed her trademark smile.

"Mia Cara, when can I introduce you to my favorite bar? I'm off tomorrow." The Italian accent of Giovanni, the club promoter, tickled her ear. Ania thought of Lars' golden hair and honest eyes and shook her head. But as another month progressed, she discovered Italians were persistent. A stream of flowers and jewelry started showing up at the flat, causing the other girls to cast her ugly looks.

One Thursday night she fled the girl drama and took Giovanni up on the drink offer at the Piccolo. Dressed in an Armani suit, Giovanni handed her a rose as she slipped into his silver Porsche. Her agent didn't like her going out alone. With a promise to return by midnight, she'd reiterated she was no one's prisoner. With sleep an unwritten, but required part of her contract with the agency, the early morning commitment would serve as an excuse to take it easy on the first date.

They danced and sipped vodka. Ania floated on a cloud of compliments before falling into the Giovanni's muscular arms. When their lips met she thought Italian kisses beat all others! She kicked off her heels and hiked up her skirt and as the night wore on she kept complying with her date's suggestions.

Ania pried her eyes open hours later. Gold satin sheets caressed her legs and sunshine scintillated off the linens. Disoriented, she examined the opulent surroundings and floor-to-ceiling windows.

"Come work for me, Cara."

She turned to see Giovanni's naked body bend over to nuzzle

her neck.

"You are fabulous. I can set you up in style. Forget bitchy girls and arrogant agents." He stroked her bare shoulder.

Dazed, she looked at the man.

"I have contacts. Important, powerful men who'll pay a lot to be with you. I run a high-end service." She watched him reach for a cocaine bag on the night table. "I'll take care of you. You have developed a taste for the finer things in life in the last 24 hours." Giovanni stretched and rose to make espresso.

On unsteady legs, Ania grabbed her black dress off a gilded chair and forced herself through the doorway and down an elevator. After hailing a cab, she dragged herself up to the apartment only to run into Minny.

"You missed the morning casting. I'm annulling the contract." Frantic, she apologized and promised to never screw up again.

Upon entering her room she found Mia throwing clothes in a backpack. "My mother was right. If I stay, I will sell my soul."

Ania burst into laughter at her melodramatic statement. "Sorry. I hope the chicken factory takes you back."

Mia turned. "Take care." With a squeak, the door shut.

The following morning a Polish girl who had no scruples about her soul moved in. She and Ania checked each other out and entered a silent competition over who could maintain the lowest body weight. The tricks of the trade—drugs, diet pills and laxatives—became ways to deal with the weight and constant pressure. Though she'd been slow to embrace the lifestyle at first, Ania discovered they helped get the job done. As the stress increased, the highs from the cocaine balanced her, only she made it a rule not to accept it from strange men.

One day a letter from her mother showed up, expressing worry over a magazine picture she'd seen. "You look emaciated. I'm worried."

Ania shook her mother's concern off while entering into another whirlwind of events with new designers.

Several harrowing days followed until one steamy night, Ania took a lukewarm bath then checked her reflection in the mirror. A sudden realization struck like a lightning bolt. July 21. If nature had been allowed to run its course, her child would be pressing, forcing its entry into the world this day. A flash of breasts engorged with milk ran through her mind, but the mirror mocked her with a shrunken chest and desolate belly. The internal landscape concealed from others had been denied its cultivation of life. Instead, she'd allowed a bomb to obliterate and devastate. Ania forced herself to look at her reflection. No dark pupils sparkled; two burned lumps of charcoal had taken over the orbits of her cranium. Makeup hid the circles beneath her eyes. But what of the festering inside? Perhaps Mia had been right. What if she was selling her soul? As she had her child's... Ania paced the floor, forcing her mind back into denial. But like Chinese water torture, truth drops bombarded her. She smacked a hair brush into the mirror, cursing its honesty then dove headlong into work and night binges. Increasing heart palpitations made her head feel close to exploding. As she stared into her future, Ania no longer saw herself at the pinnacle of fame with a top model salary. The long-awaited hefty pay was not materializing. Instead, an abyss of despair was cracking open.

One Saturday morning, as the railcar rattled to a stop, she pushed her quivering stick legs up the stairs and emerged at Piccadilly Circus. The fog lay thick. Dressed in a short leather skirt she tugged at her torn shirt, wondering what had happened and why she'd woken in a strange hotel room. A group of cheerful Brits greeted passer-byes. Stationed by a trolley, they doled out sandwiches and paper mugs of tea. She grabbed a proffered sandwich letting her mouth explode with the flavor of mayonnaise and egg while her mind dredged up picnic lunches with Lars.

A bespectacled girl handed over a card. "Here luv. When you're ready to get out, these folks will help you detox. The Teen Challenge program has been around since the seventies; it's Christian run. It saved my brother. This is why I bother coming here."

A month earlier Ania would've scoffed at the proposition and given the plain teen a piece of her mind. Today, she slipped the card into her bra, then stumbled home. She vomited the mayonnaise then called the phone number. An interview was set up and while she waited during the next two days, she bit her finger nails to the quick. Tuesday, after catching two buses, she perched on a vinyl chair, sucking droplets of blood from her fingertips.

A thin man with gold-rimmed glasses and bony hands brought her into an office and seated himself at a glass topped desk. Behind him a poster portrayed Jesus pulling a drowning Peter out of the lake.

"Program requirements are strict. Uneducated as well as professional women attend side-by-side. Everyone gets treated the same with no exceptions. One cannot miss functions or activities. Are you ready to make this kind of commitment?" the man prompted.

Ania rubbed her bloodshot eyes then straightened her sagging posture. "Please take me! I cannot do this by myself. I need help."

The man nodded somberly. "You'll be in for a rude awakening." His gaze brushed her designer clothing and makeup. "We are not the Ritz. Our women's premises are rather austere, set in the countryside. Can you can handle that?"

Ania smiled. "I'm not a big city girl. In Norway I used to roam the countryside."

The man shuffled papers and offered a ballpoint pen for her to sign the admittance. She signed and took the tube home.

At the flat, Minny slammed the door and handed her the agency's bill. "Pay your debts or we'll sue. We furnished your habit, rent, transportation and meals."

With her salary already spent on other things, Ania agreed to reimburse him with interest as soon as she got cleaned up.

"You'll beg to have your job back within a week," her agent warned. "But don't fool yourself. If you walk away, it'll be for forever."

Ania nodded.

The next day she boarded a train headed for Southwest Wales. Upon her arrival in a small village she walked to the large Victorian structure the address indicated. A typical formal British sunroom had been added to the east wing. Ania drew a sigh of relief. Her mind had conjured up something akin to a penitentiary but the faded elegance soothed her.

During the next few days she discovered the program was indeed demanding. And her body fought a war of its own. As the glitz of her former life got exchanged for a motley bunch of women in various stages of addiction, she felt contempt towards both herself and the other participants. Up at 7:15 AM, the residents attended chapel and three classes daily. Ania longed for solitude but performed manual labor instead. After detoxing, mealtimes became the highlight. Steak and kidney pie, mashed potatoes, bangers, pasta and rice—as her stomach re-learned to digest fats, like a long-starved prisoner she devoured food. And as the nutrients entered and the toxins departed, her head cleared.

Unexpectedly, the new sobriety also caused old emotions to surface. Why had she spurned Lars, her best friend and the most reliable person she'd ever know? Instead of valuing his desire to deepen their relationship she'd hopped on a frantic dating carousel, turning her body into a commodity. The next four weeks she adhered to the program's requirements but her insides churned like The North Sea in a hurricane.

If she came clean with Lars would he consider taking her back? One Thursday during their free hour she snuck into the garden and hunkered down behind a hedge. Sitting cross legged on the damp lawn she pulled out paper and a pen and wrote, mascara and snot streaking her face. After finishing and before she could change her mind she sprinted to the office and mailed the missive to Lars' mother's address.

Would Cora forward it? If so, Ania chewed her fingernails trying to imagine the outcome. Nightmares started intruding upon her sleep with Lars' face contorting and his mouth screaming at her, calling her names. Both bothersome and pesky they nevertheless confirmed what she knew to be true: this time she'd gone too far and Lars would turn his back on her once and for all.

CHAPTER 24

A lizard streaked across Lars' arm and a monkey squabbled above in the mango tree. The Indian Ocean glittered below the motel terrace on the Tanzanian coast. With the Masai project complete Lars sat on a folding chair and watched his colleagues sprint towards the surf. Though the work had been strenuous, they'd succeeded. The Red Cross field supervisor had expressed appreciation for a job well done.

Lars fingered the forwarded letter from Ania, then scanned the last lines again.

Please pray. I may have to travel to hell and back but I need to break free. Last December when you visited at the clinic I had had an abortion. After making that choice I tried running away from myself in every possible way and ended up addicted to drugs.

I remember us running away years ago in the row boat, crossing the sea to Denmark and so excited at the prospect! As the waves crashed in on us, reality came crashing in too. We realized we might end up on the ocean bottom instead. I feel the same way now. My Denmark never appeared. The ride has almost drowned me. Just as the rescue vessel saved us, I'm hoping Teen Challenge will do the same. I understand if you hate me and join you in the feeling. Selfishness led me to this place. I love you and admire you for making good choices. Hope you are doing fine. Mom says you're in Africa.

P.S: Do not feel obliged to write me back.

Goodbye for now, Golden Boy.
Kisses and greetings from your childhood friend, Ania.

Lars tossed the page on the table, rose and paced the length of the weathered concrete patio, then slammed his fist against the stucco wall. Eyes smarting, he threw a pebble at the monkey to make it shut up. If anyone were to blame, he himself played a part. Wrapped tight in his own pain, he'd not considered the fact that Ania would need help after the abortion. What if he'd stayed home, determined to wear down her defensive posture? Why had he not asked his mother and other women who loved her to help?

"Some friend you are." He kicked off the flip flops and strode towards the turquoise, undulating waves. A sunset of purple and orange clouds competed with a scintillating pink sea. Oblivious, Lars broke into a run, bare feet pounding the hard-packed sand, his mind pedaling backwards to the previous summer. His plans had been neatly tied up, sealed and stamped. With Northwestern completed, he'd finish the Master's degree in Oslo while celebrating a spring engagement to Ania. After obtaining financial security he'd take on the marital commitment, then head abroad, his own special girl by his side.

What arrogance! Coupled with pure fear, he realized how the two masters had driven him. What he'd considered wisdom now appeared a need to exercise caution and control. Had he been undergirded by a belief that life worked like a computer program, simply responding to the keys he touched? A belief that because *he* had a plan, circumstances would bend and usher it into place.

Though his head understood marriage to be a two-way relationship, by assuming Ania's feelings were as solid as his, he'd left her heart out of the equation. As if her emotions could be machinated and folded into his own plan.

Then in the fall at Northwestern his feelings had proved themselves anything but "solid". Introduced to a certain American girl, the long-term infatuation with Ania had faded almost overnight. Against his will, he'd fallen victim to a roller coaster of feelings, and had been forced to question his assumptions. As the green-eyed girl's grin hit his chest like electric shock paddles, he suspected he'd erred in what he considered sound judgment. Nonchalantly they called it "sightseeing". But the most eye-opening sight became peeking into his own soul where desire warred with common sense, the word "desire" becoming a rich, multi-hued animal. There'd been physical sparks too, intense ones. But also an insatiable curiosity to get inside LaRae's head. To make her giggle. Shocked at the pleasure of hearing her tinkling laugh, he'd bent over backwards to make it happen. With newfound creativity, he'd invented excuses for why he "needed" her assistance. Had she seen through him? Perhaps laughing secretly at his pitiful attempts to spend time with her?

Somehow he didn't believe it was true. With a smile curling his lips, Lars slowed the pace, reliving the conversation by the telescope. As he'd described sleeping under the stars in the Sahara, LaRae's eyes had sparkled, her face flushed. That night he had dreamt of them riding camels over moonlit dunes, LaRae a veiled Bedouin but her emerald eyes seeking his. "Stay with me," she'd implored. Once awake, he'd shaken off the dream, attributing it to having inherited his mother's lively imagination.

Then he had tucked tail and run at the first sign of adversity. He who had mounted Galdhoypiggen against all the odds and under horrific conditions. He who had won the triathlon championship in Oslo. Although he'd been called a few names in his life, "quitter" hadn't been one. But he **had** quit. Twice. On top of that, he'd done it to the two women he cared for most in the whole world.

As the bloody sun dipped below the horizon, Lars returned to the motel, locking the door to his room and sinking to the concrete floor. Prostrate, he took inventory. While a giant cockroach scurried to safety under a backpack, his tears dripped and mingled with the dirt. Outside noises of people chattering, glasses clinking and music sifted in through the screened window. But Lars' gaze stayed directed inwards.

The following morning, he woke to a loud rap and cast a glance at the alarm clock. 6:11 AM.

"Hurry up, lazy bones! The ladies are waiting," Hans hollered from outside the door.

Lars rubbed his eyes, peeled himself off the cement floor, and crawled stiffly to the door. He cracked it open and squinted against the fluorescent light. "Sorry, I'm not coming. Changed my mind."

"Are you nuts? The weather's superb for surfing! Plus we have the hottest babes around here." Hans winked, pulling the waistband of a neon yellow swimsuit that glowed against his tanned skin.

Lars smiled. "Yes partner. It's killing me. But something came up. I'll take a rain check though."

"Okay." His friend looked at him. "Are both girls open hunting territory or have you staked a claim? Just asking, that's all." Hans flushed under his tan.

Lars couldn't help but snicker. "Moving on rather quickly, aren't you? Thought you and Liv were a number? Never mind. I'm not throwing my hat into this one but keeping it strictly professional. Less complicated with wells to dig and villagers to educate."

"Come on, party pooper! I'm trying to do better. But I swear if Ella wears that pink bikini again, my better judgment will go out the window! The least you can do is watch over me."

Lars slapped his back. "I have great confidence in you. Prove yourself worthy of it!"

He watched Hans roll his shoulders back and strut down the hall before re-entering the room and digging through the meager belongings of his back pack. With his father's name scrawled on the front page, the black leather Bible had been a gift from his mother for his 18th birthday. His father had underlined passages in red ink. Over the years Lars had marked others in blue. Today his gaze fell on a verse spoken by Jesus in the gospel of Matthew.

"He that finds his life shall lose it and he that loses his life for my sake shall find it."

While chickens scratched in the dirt outside his window, the words found new meaning. Strange that his father underlined the verse before dying. "My dad didn't find life by trusting you. That's why I always thought it a risky business to trust you God. Believing in you, yes! But reserving the right to plan my future."

Was he basing his choices on a lie?

Lars grabbed his laptop, testing to see if the sporadic Wi-Fi worked. A different version of the text appeared online and the phrasing hit him.

"Then Jesus said to his disciples: if anyone desires to be my disciple, let him deny himself, disregard, lose sight of, and forget himself and his own interests and take up his cross and follow me, cleave steadfastly to me, conform wholly to my example in living and, if need be, in dying also. For whoever is bent on saving his temporal life, his comfort and security here, shall lose it. And whoever loses his life, comfort and security here for my sake shall find life everlasting."

He moved out to the patio and his eyes took in a choppier sea. "I wanted things my way. I believed a secure and well laid-out plan would protect me from danger. I judged you for what you allowed to happen to my father, resenting you for taking him from me. Accused you of not being trustworthy. I tried to save my own life by safeguarding it from people and even from you."

The swooshing sound of women's brooms sweeping the nearby courtyards filtered through a bamboo partition by the terrace. A rooster crowed, reminding him of Peter's betrayal in the gospels. "Like Peter I wimped out, scared of negative consequences. But today I yield to you, allowing you to stake out my course. Please show me your way."

An argument broke out behind the bamboo enclosure. Two voices rose and a wood splintering crash followed. A teen tumbled through the fence, picked himself up and ran. An older man chased him. The youth reminded Lars of himself. "No more scuffles. No more running. Thank you for your forgiveness instead of chastisement."

The invisible weight pressing down on his chest lifted. He relished the inner stillness. He'd write Ania. And fly to England to see her after his next project was completed.

"Sorry God. I just made plans without you again. What do you think?" he quickly remedied and laughed. *If it takes 21 days to break a habit, then this is day one. Let me leave Africa a new man.*

The next few days, the girls romped while the men bought fresh supplies. On Wednesday morning the team regrouped and started the journey to the interior. At the wheel, Lars navigated pot holes, but when a thumping noise persisted, he stopped to inspect the tires. With the help of Hans and a jack, he repaired a flat. As they climbed higher and rounded hairpin curves, a dial on the dash showed the needle on the temperature gauge moving into the red zone.

"The radiator's overheating." Lars eased the Jeep to a standstill near a precipice. Despite the hassle, a canopy of peace stretched over him. They let the radiator cool off, then plugged the leak with Ella's chewing gum. Going slowly they arrived at the new site past sundown, too weary to build a fire but huddled inside their mosquito netting on mats instead. The next day after setting up camp, Lars rested his legs on a wooden crate and composed a letter.

> *Dear Ania, I'm honored you wrote me. Though blindsided and shocked to learn the news, thank you for confiding in me. I've been a poor friend to you! Will you please forgive me for not taking an interest in your heart the last two years? I loved you but didn't communicate. I also assumed our friendship was evolving into a mature relationship ideal to found a marriage upon. But I never asked your opinion. As far as the abortion, I actually knew about it. After seeing you at the clinic I was furious with you for hiding what you'd done. But I acted like a coward and took off. You deserved for us to have an honest conversation. I forgive you for*

what you did and don't hold it against you. Will you please forgive me for not being there for you? As for the modeling and ensuing addiction, I am sorry too! Are you enjoying food now? Remember the girl who stole her mother's anise cookies to eat in our cave? A true cookie lover like you can't just ditch the habit. Anyway, I am so proud you are sticking to this program and will visit once our project is over. Attached is a copy of the airline ticket I purchased. I'm ready to cross oceans to ascertain you're okay.

Lars paused, pen in the air. With his support hopefully his childhood friend could start over. His gaze fixed on Ella sorting through a supply of vaccines. Ania would make a good nurse. Besides, LaRae wore a ring on her finger. Whether she wore it happily or not was none of his business. In America, citizens took pride in exercising their right to choose. A bird swooped in and snagged the crust off his metal plate. He smacked at it, then scribbled.

Secrets fester; open up about your struggles. I learned this the hard way. It's better to trust. I'm tired of being a loner; are you, too? Please forgive me for the ways I hurt you. Much love from your friend, Gull gutten. Or as they say in Britain, Golden boy.

A week later in England, Ania laughed, then cried after reading the missive. That night, as she stepped in the shower, the water gushing down on her felt like a waterfall of hope.

Amanda's voice crescendoed. "What do you mean, Rae? You're painting but not Great Aunt Erna's house? I thought we sent you over to supervise and pick the colors. What exactly are you up to?"

LaRae wanted to cower but straightened her back and stared into Amanda's blurry face over the computer screen. The cable installed at last, her laptop sat on a desk below the window overlooking the street. In a white, billowing rain coat, Gunhild bobbed down the sidewalk, a ship whose sails were driven by a gale. With canning season upon them, the rhubarb LaRae had picked in the yard was ready for peeling, chopping and being turned into jam at Cora's canning party and the Crochet Club was showing up.

"Look." LaRae aimed the laptop camera towards the living room wall.

"White walls, I know. You told me."

"What else?"

"Oh, paintings. Are they worth anything? Can we auction them?"

LaRae sighed. "The art will be exhibited. And perhaps sold."

"You bought those? How could you? We have limited funds until the houses sell! Christopher will have to explain this to you again."

"Don't need an explanation. I have full knowledge of the finances and have not purchased anything. *Except the coffee table I crushed on.* The paintings are my work."

"It's your work?"

For once her big sister seemed dumbfounded. LaRae wished she had a tail to wag. "My new friends insist that I am gifted. They have begged me to exhibit and I accepted. If my visa expires, the agent will exhibit them without me."

Amanda lifted Wallie onto her lap and changed the topic. "Things are not the same without you. This baby clings to my breast like a leech. Drew and Mickey are bottomless pits of energy and food consumption. I spend two hours every morning at the gym trying to work off extra pounds and even added Pilates to my routine. And I'm only eating salads and veggies. Well, maybe some bacon bits, dressing and croutons. Healthy fats calm my nerves. The new gluten-free cookies at Walmart are to die for. No nasty wheat, just chocolate, nuts, sugar, eggs, butter, and no artificial flavors. Christopher picks up a pack on his way home from the office every day. Is that man sweet or what? Especially since you're not here to run errands."

Amanda smiled accusingly before continuing. "We encouraged you to stretch your wings. Next thing we know you're taking off in every sense of the word! What is happening; is this a manic episode?"

LaRae rolled her eyes. "The flight was overdue. Thanks for kicking me out of the nest. I like using my wings so much I'm considering not returning!"

Excited yelling interrupted as the nephews crowded the computer screen. "Aunt Rae Rae! You must come back. Mom set up your bed downstairs."

"I have a better idea! Why don't you come see me and attend the exhibit? If the visa gets extended I'll book a cottage for all of you. Amanda, your roots are here as well."

Her sister's jaw dropped. Then she threw her head back and guffawed. "Why not? We need change, too. Despite complaining I am relieved. I feared you were becoming an old spinster because of the way you always act. Like a porcupine in menopause. This is sexier. Finally, you've got fun news to share! We can help you set up a Web site. Pink background, perhaps a gold unicorn logo? If you become famous, make sure to introduce me to people."

LaRae shook her head. "Wait till you see the gorgeous sunsets and tan in the warm sand. While here, we'll decide on the price for Aunt Erna's house and check out the ancestral homestead."

"We're visiting the Vikings! I'm bringing my sword." Mickey jumped up and down.

"I'll bring my axe," Drew chimed in.

LaRae wrapped up the conversation. Christopher would have to sign off on the idea. And foot the bill. But knowing the height and breath of Amanda's charm, if only LaRae got her visa the family would pack their bags and come.

She tied on Erna's yellow apron and rushed off to can produce and returned home that afternoon tired but ready to pluck Mr. Hansen's brain about the family history. She placed a call to his office.

"Hi! I'm cramming in important things in case I must leave soon. Did you figure out the location of my great-grandparents' farm?"

Mr. Hansen responded. "Yes. I can bring you to the area this weekend. I'm not certain if the structure still stands, but I uncovered an address."

After agreeing to his suggestion, she hung up and took a long overdue bath.

When Saturday rolled around, the sun shone bright and the trees in the back yard sported green acorn-sized buds. Whether they were apples, pears or prunes she couldn't tell. The June nights were chilly but noon time was balmy. School kids were hankering to get out for summer vacation next week and excitement was building for Saint Hans Eve.

On the Manor Beach, a pile of driftwood, grass clippings, twigs and leaves was growing into a mountain under the supervision of the city clean-up crew. On June 23'rd, bonfires would roar into the wee hours with people celebrating the longest day of the year. It was hard to imagine nights getting any lighter because the sun already stayed up till eleven. The light made LaRae feel like she was plugged into a high voltage outlet. She stepped outside to the curb and thought of how she was painting in Cora's rose garden these days, a floodlight illuminating her easel till midnight. She worked quietly. Sometimes using a brush and sometimes a palette knife she added layer upon layer of textures. Cora watched, refusing to paint at night but bringing out fresh squeezed lemonade, strawberries and grilled cheese sandwiches with sliced tomatoes.

A honk penetrated her thoughts. She eased into Mr. Hansen's Volvo and put on the newly acquired Ray Bans.

"Did you bring a swimsuit?"

"Yes. But the water is freezing. You won't persuade me!"

Mr. Hansen smiled. "Then watch me dive in. The winter's

over. I've waited a long time for warmer temperatures."

The day was close to perfect. A light breeze pushed puffy cotton ball clouds along, and daisies and bluebells nodded. No crews groomed the roadsides here. Instead, weeds and wild flowers intermingled happily, making it hard to tell one from the other. As they left Mandal behind, red barns and white homes dotted the landscape. Holstein cows and sheep were grazing on zig-zag patches of verdant land.

"We're headed south."

"South? Aren't we living in the southernmost town in Norway?"

Mr. Hansen chuckled. "I see you're not familiar with the region. Lindesnes, - the southernmost point of our country, has a light house on its very tip and is a tourist attraction."

He left the highway and followed a local narrow road with hairpin turns. When they arrived in a small hamlet by the ocean, Mr. Hansen slowed. A campground and a handful of houses lined the road. "Fishermen live here. And a few farmers and locals who commute to nearby towns. The farm on your right offers self-serve strawberry picking." Little tow-headed kids and parents crawled on all fours gathering berries in green paper cartons. "There's the weigh station. They pay per kilo. A good way to stock the freezer."

The older gentleman checked his note and nodded. "As I thought. The property is coming up on your right."

LaRae clapped her hand over her mouth. Two houses stood side by side, a stone's throw from the river and just up above the road. One appeared simple but the neighboring house was a frilly Victorian.

"They're pink!"

"Unusual, I know. The only pink houses I've ever seen in the county. But they've been this way since I was a child. Never realized Erna grew up in that fancy delight," he motioned to the left.

"Oh please, can we knock on the door? Or is that rude?"

"Worst case scenario? They may shoot us."

LaRae gasped.

"That was a bad joke. So sorry. Considering the crime rate in the U.S. I should not banter like this. Not to worry. Here, guns get used for hunting and that's about it."

Mr. Hansen eased the car into a tiny spot on the dock by a red boathouse. A barn further up the slope was also part of the property. They climbed to the doorstep. LaRae stopped briefly and took in the vista. The house overlooked a river turning into a fjord that merged with the ocean. Wild Rose of Sharon bushes framed their path adding a sweet scent. Mr. Hansen knocked. No footsteps sounded.

"Let me take pictures. Hard to believe my great-grandparents lived here, I always thought they were poor. We assumed my grandmother came to America because they couldn't make it in their own country. Can you dig up more facts for me?"

"Absolutely. I'll find out who lives in the home and see if they'll let you visit."

LaRae leaned over and hugged her friend. He was sporting stockinged feet in sandals and white knees protruded below the hem of his khaki shorts. A straw hat and a blue Lacoste shirt completed the outfit.

As they descended the path to the car, Mr. Hansen stopped at the mail box. "Uh, oh."

"What's the matter?"

Her driver scratched his head and double checked the paper. "Do you notice how the number 9 fell over? Looks like a 6 on the mailbox?"

"Oh my goodness! I'm strolling around some stranger's yard snapping photos that have nothing to do with my family?" LaRae looked wistfully back at the pink beauty. "I got fresh inspiration for my art though," she comforted herself.

They stopped at the grocery and asked an ancient-looking, weather-bitten man for information. He pointed them to a simple gravel driveway ending in a field.

"No buildings left on the land? Just pasture owned by the neighbor?"

The store owner nodded. "I remember young Erna." His mustache opened in a crooked, lemon-yellow smile. "Loved her cats. Never saw a need for a man though. I would know."

LaRae and Mr. Hansen exchanged knowing glances and thanked him.

"The lighthouse is another forty minutes further south. Are you up for it?"

"More scenic experiences and fodder for my paintings? You bet!"

The winding, hilly drive took them to windblown cliffs covered in heather and rough sea grass. At the seeming edge of civilization a white lighthouse towered atop of a tall, rounded rock. Mr. Hansen wiped his forehead. "Be my guest if you want to climb to the platform." He pulled the local paper from the car door and eased onto a granite bench next to a picnic table in the parking lot.

LaRae climbed the steep cement steps set in the rocky hillside. To her right chains barred the public from a set of concrete tunnels. A stone wall had rectangular openings and peep holes. Curious, she read the sign that explained these were barricades and strategic defense posts employed by German forces during the Second World War. Chills went down her spine as LaRae mounted the spiral staircase in the lighthouse. It was weird to think of her family suffering with enforced blackouts and food ration cards during the occupation. She wondered if they'd taken part in the resistance. A family member of Lars had been accused of sympathizing with the resistance and it had led to imprisonment, he'd said. She emerged onto a circular red deck with an open diamond pattern. A deep ultramarine blue stretched out as far as the eye could see. But looking down through the metal grid made her head swim.

The last time she hovered up so high had been in Chicago in the Sears Tower. She'd been giddy and faint but due to the company, not the height. When Lars had leaned in to inspect her face she'd felt as if the world's clock arms came to a standstill and the earth stopped rotating. Two pairs of eyes had sunk into each other's soul. *Soul fusion.*

An ache crested, she shook her head, clamoring to the rail.

"I don't know how to do this, God. Give me hope." Because God felt more real, the overwhelming loneliness was loosening its hold. Would the toxic residue from losing Lars clear too? The railing slick beneath her fingers, she leaned on her elbows and stared towards the west.

"I want to trust you." Like a child to her daddy, she spoke simply. The sun burst from behind a steel cloud. LaRae took a picture, commemorating the moment then undertook the descent, thigh muscles protesting.

"I'm starving! I must have burned a thousand calories and will settle for a Kit Kat bar or a hot dog, anything edible. Oh, look. They sell waffles at the souvenir shop." She pointed to the kiosk offering sea shells and post cards.

Mr. Hansen laughed. "Cora warned this would happen and packed us a surprise. Her friend popped the trunk and pulled out a basket and a checkered table cloth with matching napkins. LaRae lifted the lid of the wicker container and sighed contentedly at the sight of a bottle of blueberry juice and egg salad sandwiches, apples and chocolate cake.

"Ah, a good substitute for my nap." Mr. Hansen opened a thermos and poured two cups of coffee. They people-watched as German and Belgian tourists parked RVs and entered the souvenir shop. Kids licked ice cream cones and adults munched on warm waffles with raspberry jelly. While wrapping up the leftovers, LaRae turned to her friend.

"Aren't you too full to swim?"

"You sound hopeful. I hate to disappoint you. The lake is a mile away. It'll be just enough time for our food to settle." Mr. Hansen coasted down the narrow lane and forced his vehicle off the road into a hollow. They walked through thigh-high grass to the edge of a cerulean blue body of water. LaRae stuck one foot in the shallow end, then squealed as Mr. Hansen sprinted and showered her with his belly splash.

"Come on, young woman. Prove your Viking genes didn't wash out."

"Give me time. Some things can't be rushed." Twenty minutes later and after inching her way limb by limb into the pristine lake, cool water submerged her body. She attempted a few vigorous strokes. "Weird. I'm not numb."

After they toweled off, the unlikely pair laid down side-by-side on the sun warmed rock. Before long, snores rose from underneath Mr. Hansen's hat.

So much for caffeine. LaRae listened to the buzzing of bees and flies and flicked off ants marching across her belly. Blueberry bushes and birch trees stood guard as they lay supine. When a fly landed on her chest, she swatted at it, then ran her fingers across her chest. The lump was still there. *Go away.* As soon as she arrived in Dresden she'd get an X-ray. Her thoughts turned to home.

If only Norman could see me. She giggled at the sight she and her companion made. *He might surmise I got myself a sugar daddy.* Exhaling, she soaked in the sun's rays pondering how she'd lost common sense. In her right mind, she'd be ridding Grand Aunt's house of its possessions and sticking a "For Sale" sign next to the plum tree by the picket fence. With no visa extension every tick of the clock gobbled up her seven remaining days in Norway. Come next Sunday, like a homing pigeon whose wings had carried her out into the world, it'd now take her back home. Except home had become a relative word where place of origin no longer spelled belonging.

CHAPTER 25

Nocturnal animals crawled, stalked and shrieked. While locals rested, weary from labor under the African sun, life in the bush and savannah thrummed. At the campsite beneath the radiant stars of the Tanzanian highlands, Lars was not enjoying the night's respite. A tree frog croaked and he jerked off the blanket, accidentally ripping the mosquito net surrounding his bed in the process. Parched, he reached for the water bottle from the nearby folding table and shakily raised it towards his lips, but the liquid spilled down his chest. He winced, as if blasted by ice water. His mouth opened to plead for help but a hyena barking and the cicadas' frantic concert drowned out the cry. He regretted not charging the walkie talkie connecting him to the girls across the compound. With Hans gone and the local hires asleep in the village, he was alone. A night guard patrolled the work site and periodically the camp. Lars strained to hear footsteps. But except for a bush baby crying, the generator drowned out most sounds. *I need to crawl out and find people.* He willed his body to respond but it remained still no matter how much his brain prodded the limbs to move. A raging fire had hit his bones and the chills that had caused him to put on a hoodie and pants had passed. Unable to tear off the clothing, his mind drifted into feverish sleep, and he picked up the chase. But the shifting shape eluded him at every turn.

"Wait for me," he begged. A green snake slid from a branch, fixing him with beaded eyes, hissing.

"You destroyed the women you loved. Some protector you are!" The reptile dropped and slithered close. Lars bolted but to no avail. The serpent caught up and wrapped around his legs, then waist, an ever-tightening spiral compressing him. He fought with all his strength, but the creature was suffocating him. As abysmal blackness seeped in, his body went rigid.

"Lars! What's going on? Are you feeling worse?" Liv pulled at the sheet entangling his body. Trapped like a mummy, he wrestled against her grip.

"Want to live. Please don't!"

"You're burning up! Let me get Ella again. Here. Sit up. Sip the bottle."

Discombobulated, Lars let himself be pulled to a sitting position. After a thorough check up, Ella shook her head. "If he doesn't respond to the medicine, we'll have to transport him to the closest clinic. His temperature is too high. I've sponged him down but with no success. I told him yesterday afternoon we needed to head to a clinic. He refused, digging in like kookaburra."

"Could it be dengue fever or malaria? Please radio Hal." Behind blurry eyes, he watched Liv pack essentials in a backpack while asking Ella.

"Yes. Hal is an experienced supervisor and knows the doctors in town."

Later in the day and with the help of local men the girls loaded Lars into the back seat of the Jeep. Accustomed to death and nasty diseases, the crew wished them good luck and waved goodbye.

The rains had hit and potholes the size of kiddie pools riddled the mud road. They should make the nearest town within a couple of hours. Liv pressed on the accelerator, eager to make good time. But ten kilometers down the path they skidded on the slippery rust-colored mess, skirting a palm tree. Liv tried to straighten the vehicle but the wheels didn't cooperate. With a thump, they landed sideways. The engine stalled.

"Hold on." Ella jumped out and gathered twigs and branches to create traction. The red dirt splattered her as the tires caught the grip. They continued at a snail's pace for another thirty minutes. But when they rounded a sharp curve, a goat stood in the middle of the road. Out of reflex, Liv hugged the brakes and the Jeep went airborne. With a thud and giant splash they landed at the bottom of a mud hole stretching across the road. Ella wrenched the passenger door opened and hollered.

"Quick! Get Lars. In his state he can't lift his head above the incoming water." The two teammates dragged the sturdy but limp body out of the car. Thigh deep in mud, they half-carried and half-dragged their patient to the side of the road.

Ella punched a number on her cell phone. "Still no service," she exclaimed in disgust. "I don't know what to do."

"We must find the closest village. Ask for help to pull us out." Liv looked around for signs of life. Lars's inertia was disturbing.

Ella's fingers fumbled inside her backpack, searching for supplies. "I'm starting a general spectrum antibiotics treatment." She pulled out a syringe, then stuck it inside the glass bottle from the kit.

"Auntie, you need help?" At the voice, they jumped, then turned. A face beamed from the bushes.

"Yes! Please!" The boy disappeared but before long returned with reinforcements. Wiry, young men in tribal garb flocked around the car, eager to lend a hand. Loud jabbering, then arguing filled the clearing. Some spoke in English and others in their tribal tongue.

"Brothers say bring sick Mzungu to village. We help carry him. Others say push car but we need to cut trees first to put wood under car. If not, you will—how do you say? Slip?"

"Yes," Ella responded. "The car will slip. Plus, the engine won't start while submerged. Tow. We need to be towed." She gesticulated, asking if the village had a truck.

255

"One truck. Gone to market."

Ella looked up at the pink sky, knowing how fast it turned to inky blackness. The men were right. With the steep angle of the mud pit, it would take time to get the Jeep out. "We need buckets to get rid of the water." Her new helpers nodded. The men formed a chain but water kept seeping in, refilling the hole. Furious with herself for having miscalculated the road conditions and the time it would take to get to the nearest town, Ella swiped a tear. "We can't drive in the dark with these dangerous potholes."

Her friend nodded in agreement and pointed in the direction from where the villagers had come. "Village? Please take us? Let us spend the night?"

An older teenager nodded in affirmation. They fabricated a stretcher out of branches and vines. As the men carried Lars, they shook their heads and smacked their tongues against the roof of their mouth, pitying the white man. Limbs dangling, Lars himself remained unaware of his surroundings and the attention he garnered. They scurried through the darkening forest stumbling over tree roots and arrived at a circle of huts. Acrid smoke stung their nostrils. Tribal women watched from a distance while kids rushed towards them, touching the stretcher.

"No!" Ella swatted at the children.

A woman as wrinkled as a walnut emerged from a hut. As she hobbled closer, Ella noticed amulets tied to leather thongs hanging from the neck. She lifted a wizened arm halfway, pointing to the prostrate form. Ella protested, not ready to hand her colleague over to a witch doctor, even if the woman had good intentions. Stories abounded of witch doctors using plants and potions to treat locals, but she believed the custom leaned more on superstition than herbal medicine. The last thing they needed was a ceremony consulting with spirits.

"Me Doctor," she pointed to herself assuming an air of authority. Though a far stretch from the truth, they recognized the term better than nurse. "I heal him."

Ella smiled at the wizened face and seized Lars' floppy hand.

"I stay with him."

The woman's caved in chest heaved in merriment. "He be your man. But no make babies tonight."

Ella already caught a guy's hand movement illustrating Lars' lack of virility. The crowd howled with laughter.

"You sit with him. We feed you. Tomorrow we help with car," the woman said.

The two expatriate girls looked at each other, then nodded in agreement. Moments later, a simple meal of maize and an undefinable green sauce appeared, wrapped in banana leaves. They accepted gratefully.

"Never leave home without extra food supplies and extra batteries for the flashlight; please remind me," Ella said glumly. "I swear we're eating monkey." Seated on straw mats, they took turns cooling Lars with wet rags while forcing drops of water down his throat. He seemed delirious, his body thrashing. He vomited repeatedly and finally started retching on an empty stomach. With dehydration a threat, Ella kicked herself for not bringing the intravenous feeding tube and bag. If this was dengue fever, it could turn into dengue hemorrhagic fever which could cause serious side effects—death being the worst case scenario.

As the night wore on, Liv slept and Ella fought exhaustion. She thought of how Hal had radioed back yesterday saying a doctor would be waiting at the clinic. It had been a rare challenge to set up camp in an area with no electricity. Even the well the men were working on would be solar powered. The generator provided power to their laptops but without Wi-Fi. Regular visits from Hal plus newspapers, and a solar radio kept them in the loop about the outside world.

Ella chewed her lip. They would have to make it tomorrow. She had dealt with tropical diseases before, even nasty ones like malaria. But this one was a whopper. Exhausted, she stretched next to her girlfriend. As she dozed off, neither she nor Liv noticed Lars' grimacing face or stiff body three feet away.

He tried to scream, but no sound came. The snake was back.

"You thought you'd be the one who got away?" The slick scales squeezed around his chest then up his neck. He felt his breathing grow shallow, his lungs clamoring for air.

A continent away, the rounded shape remained motionless under the covers. Only crickets chirped and a few moths circled the front porchlight of the house. Dew forming on the grass glistened like tear drops. The moon was fading but left a silvery sheen on the flowery bed covers and made the grey head on the pillow sparkle. Were it not for the regular breathing, the form could be mistaken for lifeless. But right before the crack of dawn a pair of feet absorbed the chill before slipping into the sheepskin slippers by the bed. A slight grunt ensued.

"Lord, did you wake me? Another one in distress?" The woman wrapped a velvet bathrobe around her shoulders and padded into the den. "You know I enjoy sleep. Please help. How do I pray?" Looking out at the dim light suffusing the tree line, she listened. "I see." She grabbed her sword, the well-worn Holy Scriptures, brandishing it in the air.

"Father I beseech you. Rescue this one. I don't know what the trouble is. But I plead for his soul. And safety. Jesus, your blood is sufficient. You get the final word. Rebuke the hand of the enemy! Lord we declare your light scatters the darkness." Her knees creaked, but she rose, pacing the worn path over the rug through the kitchen and dining room before making it back to the den. A soldier at war, she pushed ahead on the front line.

"Father, I declare your purposes will prevail." She switched into a different language and something akin to Native American syllables rolled off her tongue increasing in speed and volume. Then as the new day dawned, a mantle of peace settled. Back in the rocking chair, she started singing.

"All hail the power of Jesus' name. Let angels prostrate fall. Bring forth the royal diadem and crown him, crown him, yes crown, oh crown him Lord of All." The Bible back on the table she spoke, head high.

"That includes ALL angels, fallen and unfallen."

As she shuffled to the kitchen to make a cup of expresso-strength coffee, back in Africa Lars opened his eyes in a smoky cave, head throbbing.

"Where am I?" His voice nothing more than a croak, it still woke the slumbering nurses.

"Oh! So glad to hear you talk. We are safe. On the way to see a doctor. Please sip this and rest. You've been very sick," Liv said.

As chickens scratched the dirt and women relit their fires, the handful of men in the settlement used a truck to pull the car out of the pit. The juju lady brought tea in tin mugs.

Ella sipped the hot brew. Fortified by the beverage, the duo rose as runners sprinted into the village with good news. The Jeep had been extracted and the engine started.

"Miracles *do* happen," Ella twisted from the front seat and touched Lars in the back of the car. "You'll make me a believer yet," she winked at his strained face.

Hours later, muddied and weary to the bone, the girls dropped Lars off at a small and somewhat underequipped clinic in the nearest town. An angry rash had spread across his body during the journey. A nurse drew blood and attached an IV. The next day, the test came back positive for dengue fever, the mosquito-borne viral disease so common to African countries.

The doctor addressed Ella. "We must wait and see if his condition improves or if it takes a turn for the worse. The next few days will be touch-and-go. If hemorrhagic fever occurs, a blood transfusion is required. I am working with a private clinic in the capital; the medical staff is trying to rush a matching blood type to our facility."

In the ward, Lars' stared at his reflection in a cracked mirror he lifted from a night stand shoved in between him and his neighbor. His eyes lay sunken in a pallid face. Curled up on a flimsy mattress on a metal bed, he scoured the bedroom where illness surrounded him. To his left a young child lay unconscious while a nurse explained the symptoms of cerebral malaria to family members. Visitors crowded the room, crying and arguing over pots of food. A single light bulb cast shadows on people's faces at the outskirts of the room. With the man to his right in the throes of diarrhea the fetid odor was overwhelming. Lars caught sight of Hal, his supervisor, only to have the man tell him to wait before he disappeared.

Minutes later, an orderly appeared. "You are being transferred to air conditioning and quiet. Your boss is insisting." The orderly placed Lars on a gurney, then wheeled him to a rickety ambulance that delivered him to a local hotel.

Here, the girls waited and when his legs buckled, they supported him into a room.

"You're not out of hot water yet. The girls are monitoring you. We are keeping our fingers crossed." Hal scooted out of a vinyl chair by the bed and pulled out a portable chessboard and placed it on the night table. "I'm hoping to win a match at last. This time, if you lose you can salvage your pride by blaming it on brain fog and the meds. How about getting our boy situated then fetching us two Cokes, ladies?"

Ella sighed. "I know soft drinks are sold out of ramshackle sheds by the roadside all over Africa and that honored guests, even in the smallest villages, get offered a bottle of Fanta or Coke. It's been a safe way to avoid contaminated water in the past, and even now, with water bottles available, people are in the habit of quenching their thirst this way." Hal wiggled his eye brows.

"Please?"

Lars moved chess pieces while slouching in a chair yet his eyes got drawn to the window. From a makeshift stand on the street corner, Liv picked up the drinks and a whisky bottle filled with roasted peanuts. The shanty shop offered cigarettes, lighters, matches and cooking oil along with snacks. The girls stopped again and bought meat kebabs on tiny sticks. A boy picked them off an oil barrel-turned-roasting pit. Tarabu music rose from a cellphone vendor's stand. A boom box strapped to a teen's back blared out Swahili pop music, each tune competing for attention, creating a cacophony of sounds. A setting sun was casting an orange glow on the faces of passersby, bathing the dust and litter in gold, and for the tiniest moment it even made the trash look pretty.

This is Africa, Lars mused. Africa, so complicated yet simple. An amalgam of violence and danger, yet light-heartedness in the midst of daily life. Poverty and ingenuity existed side-by-side. Disasters were commonplace but often followed by optimism. He removed Hal's queen while concluding his train of thought. Despite his present circumstance he realized something right there and then: Africa's heartbeat was infectious. As he wiped sweat from his brow, his heart joined in with the upbeat feel on the street.

You have brought me this far. And delivered me. I trust you, God.

He stroked his stubbled chin and sent Hal half a smile. "Watch. I'm making my last move."

His boss groaned.

CHAPTER 26

LaRae tore open the envelope and stared at the new visa before breaking into a celebratory dance by her mailbox. She called Cora, Matthias and Gunhild to share the news that she'd be present at the art show. The thought made her dizzy with anticipation and shaky with nerves. To work off the jitters, she biked to the beach, walked 3 miles and purchased an ice cream cone. Licking the cool cream while riding her bicycle she greeted the mailman on her street but braked at the puzzling sight ahead. A sporty two-seater was parked outside Great Aunt's house. This was definitely not one of her elderly friends dropping in. Sweaty from the workout, she used her bandana to mop her shorts clad legs and bare arms. The stronger sun had painted her body a honey hue this week and new freckles surfaced like measles. She pushed back her hair which had become a mixture of salon color and sun streaked gold.

A flash of blue by the porch caused her to open the garden gate. A man rose from the front step.

"Hello! I'm checking on my new protégé." Matthias leaned in and kissed her salty cheek. "Mm, you taste fresh, a nice change from exhaust odors and turpentine. Your rather wordy and large neighbor said you'd arrive within the hour. I decided to wait."

"I had no idea you were coming! Are you wanting to see the

collection?"

"Yes, ma chère. This is a business trip where I offer input and recommendations plus advice on placement and lighting."

"Give me a moment to freshen up and I'll show you my work. I'm still adding the last touches to a piece. I'm afraid I have been too prolific and may need to pare down the selection."

Matthias, ever the gallant gentleman, held the door while she entered. "Great. But let's discuss the details over dinner. A seafood restaurant nearby is referenced in the Michelin guide. I enjoy their menu when down south."

"Oh! Well, thank you. Outside of Cora's cooking lessons I mostly eat snacks. A meal out is a real treat!"

"The grilled halibut is presented on a bed of wilted, mixed greens with a dash of garlic and parsley. For the appetizer I recommend their seafood consommé. It's low calorie, yet flavorful with a tad of sherry and scallops added to the mussels, shrimp and cod."

LaRae laughed. "You could write for a gourmet magazine. Only describe food when I get to eat afterwards. If not, it's cruel."

The refined man in front of her grinned. "I'll keep that in mind."

A couple of hours later, they delved into a shared gastronomic experience. "Cora couldn't come?" LaRae looked up from the steaming bowl of soup.

Her host blinked. "Sorry. We need time to discuss your own part in detail. Let's talk about ways to handle the public's questions and compliments. And how to tackle critics. But try the margarita first."

As the steaming main course appeared, Matthias told her about the chain of art galleries he had bought into, regaling her with stories of meeting celebrities and famous artists.

"The chain has storefronts in Hamburg, Germany, as well as London, England and Stockholm in Sweden. If a painter becomes popular, we move the work from one metropolis to the next until it travels full circle. Sometimes the artist joins the circuit for the premiere in each new location." Their margaritas finished, Matthias eyed her over a glass of Chardonnay. "There are no guarantees. But if you become a hot item," he winked at her, "imagine the places and people I can introduce you to."

A server whisked away their dinner plates and planted a dish of crème brûlée on the table. Matthias smiled at the server before winking at LaRae. "Think of the cuisine I could initiate you into as well."

Lightheaded from the drinks and male attention, she pondered how to respond. Used to whiling away hours alone, lost in a world of shapes, forms and color, it would be a different story being wined and dined, introduced to strangers and receiving possible recognition around Europe. An unaccustomed rush galloped up her spine. She squelched it. Her paintings might flop. Cora's part would be a hit. Mr. Hansen explained that fans showed up from afar for her neighbor's work, the exhibit having become an annual pilgrimage for collectors. Matthias interrupted her musings.

"It's such a charming evening. The local night club beckons us."

LaRae pointed to her peasant blouse and long, ruffled skirt. "This outfit does not allow for it."

"Do the garments allow for a moonlit stroll in the formal garden at the Lord's Manor House?"

"If I kick off the wedge sandals. And Matthias?"

"Yes?"

"Thank you for helping me obtain the visa extension. If not for you, I'd be airborne."

"Happy to assist, dear. When I heard the news this morning, I decided to come celebrate with you. If you truly love living here though, matrimony may be the way to go."

LaRae's cheeks flamed. "I'm pretty intent on marrying for love only."

"Sometimes the fair bloom of love springs from unlikely soil. I for one am delighted your feet get to stay on our solid, fertile soil." They walked gravel paths between flower beds, chatting about his travels and places worth seeing. "Look at these photos on my cellphone. This is a sunrise over the colosseum in Rome," Matthias said.

"Beautiful! Do I recognize the acropolis ruins in Athens in this one?"LaRae pointed.

"Yes, but only go in the fall. Temperatures rise to 43 degrees Celsius during summer."

Back in the car, the leather seat molded itself to LaRae's body. As Matthias sped down the highway a piano overture by Chopin trilled from the speakers. With the rooftop lowered, she stuck her arms in the air, wind rushing through her fingers.

Residents of Dresden, take this in! She imagined heads turning at the two of them cruising Main Street in the Alfa Romeo. The ride beat Norman's bumpy pickup and the smelly minivans of her childhood carpools. She chuckled, thinking how the sight would send former classmates' tongues wagging. The uncool Gunther girl was making her way up in the world. To complete the picture, all she needed was a fancy silk scarf wrapped around her head like the women in a James Bond movie.

Matthias swooshed down her street then came to a standstill. "You are excellent company, Miss Gunther." He leaned over the gear stick and kissed her cheek smelling of expensive cologne and high-end cigars.

Before he had time to get out, LaRae pushed the door open, thanked him and disappeared inside. Her most ardent admirer greeted her with a purr. "What do you think? Are we cut out for glamour and traveling in style?" Her tiger-striped buddy jumped on the bed. "Would you go for calf liver or fresh tuna?" After pawing the feather duvet the cat laid down. "Champagne or aged scotch?" He licked a paw.

"I know, so stressful having to make decisions. Perhaps we should stick with cans for now. I'm still partial to canned reindeer meatballs."

The next morning Cora marched in the door before LaRae had fully awakened.

"I hear you went on a date last night?"

"Kind of. I thought you'd be there, too."

"Nope. I did not get invited. Not that I care for the overpriced menu at the Boathouse. Last time the arugula was slimy and the asparagus were limp noodles. However, my good friend and agent is showing himself quite solicitous of you." She slapped the newspaper she'd brought down on the foyer table and pulled down a shirttail caught in the woven belt on her jeans.

"I'm keeping my interest in Matthias strictly at a professional level. That is, in case you want to ask but are worried you'd come across as rude or nosy," LaRae said.

Cora laughed and walked to the living room to give her a hug. "I'm sorry. This is none of my business. I know." She crossed her arms and huffed. "But I can't help make you my business. You've grown on me ever since that first day I had you over for cod." Her friend looked her deep in the eye, then glanced away, a wrinkle forming between her eyebrows. "I've always been big on Matthias. He is such a great guy. Smart and successful. Savvy. But he keeps butting his head against the brick wall of spiritual unbelief." She stroked LaRae's curls. "You are an attractive girl. It's hard for an intelligent man not to appreciate your unique qualities."

"And?" LaRae headed to the kitchen to brew a pot of tea. Dressed in Erna's flowery bathrobe, she got a kick out of the attractive comment.

"Be picky about who you choose for a life mate."

LaRae unwrapped the block of sweet goat cheese and opened the jelly jar. "Have a piece of toast." As she bit into the bread, she chewed thoughtfully. "Picky, you say? No one ever said that before. You think I can afford to be?"

Cora fixed her with a no-nonsense stare. "Absolutely."

"Ok. Thank you. I will bear that in mind."

The doorbell rang. LaRae streaked to the bathroom. "If it's Matthias, I'm not coming out until dressed."

"Scaredy cat!" Voices drifted up, then familiar laughter boomed.

Cora spoke again: "Gunhild brought over tomatoes. They give her gas. I called Matthias. I'm borrowing a neighbor's van for us to haul the paintings to the downtown storefront."

They met at noon and examined the building on the street corner between the pedestrian commercial street and Main River Street. Large windows faced both streets with the main entrance on the corner. The room was spacious with wall partitions to create more hanging space and divide the art into separate themes. After much discussion and shuffling of canvases, everyone expressed satisfaction with the layout. Matthias created a template of the floor plan on his laptop, then helped put the works back into the van.

"Whew! That made me thirsty! Lunch is on me. Homemade bread and soup. Let's regroup at my house," Cora ventured.

In agreement, LaRae hopped into the Alfa Romeo passenger seat.

"Here." Matthias handed her the car key.

"You trust me behind the wheel?"

"No. But we only live once. Why not live dangerously?" The man winked and hopped out, gesturing for her to slide over. After doing so, LaRae adjusted the side and rearview mirrors.

Matthias crawled into the passenger seat, put his arm around her shoulders and squeezed her left bicep.

"Hm. You may have to withdraw that hand. I need to concentrate on the task," LaRae suggested.

"Oh, sorry. I can be a real distraction. At least that's what women tell me."

LaRae couldn't help but giggle. After leaving behind the city center, a flat stretch opened, and she pressed the accelerator. From the corner of her eye she observed her passenger white knuckling the door handle for the two mile drive home.

"Not sure if that was as exciting to you as it was to me,"

Matthias wiped sweat beads off his high, elegant brow. "I hope a cold beer awaits me!"

"I'm so glad all is set for our big event," Cora exhaled as they'd wrapped up their meal on the deck. Surrounded by roses in bloom, the fragrance permeated the balmy July air.

"I am so nervous, I'll look anorexic by the time we get around to it." LaRae shoved the untouched soup bowl away.

Matthias stroked her bare forearm. "It's normal to be apprehensive." He reached across the wooden railing, snagged a pink rose and handed it to her. "I'm not one bit concerned. Attendees will love your work. And eat out of your hand. Can I show you Oslo this weekend?"

Cora clicked her tongue. "Oh Matthias. Are you headed back tomorrow? It's too early for your gallantry and for distractions. We are working women with paintings to frame and catalogs to put together before we can allow ourselves to enjoy such attentions."

"Point taken, dear. Thank you for a lovely luncheon in exquisite company." Matthias kissed both of their cheeks. They followed him to his car.

Cora waved goodbye, then sighed. "As much as I love the man, I can't decide if I like the attention he showers on you or whether I feel like a growling mama bear."

"I'd go with the latter." LaRae hid a smile, went to the porch and stacked the bowls, then made her way to the kitchen to run hot water.

Cora put away the food. "I'm going out to pick the latest produce."

Through the kitchen window, LaRae admired her friend's spry body bending over a row in the vegetable patch. When Cora walked in the door with an armful of lettuce, LaRae turned to her. "I'm in the mood to perform a mundane, mindless task. Can we spend the rest of the day down on our knees getting dirty?"

"Weeding? That's the best offer I've had in ages. Not even in my wildest dreams did I imagine anyone begging to weed my garden. You are one of a kind. I'll start the coffee while you run home to change. Dress grubby!"

LaRae reappeared wearing cut-off jeans and with her bare feet in rain boots. She borrowed one of Cora's floppy hats to keep the hair out of her eyes. The dark loamy soil was warm to the touch. Weeds sprouted, wrapping themselves around strawberry plants and the tops of carrots and cabbages. They used their fists to pull out small weeds and a big, pointed shovel to dig up stubborn roots and hack vines. The wheelbarrow filled with dandelions, thistles and morning glory as they worked in silence.

"You know," Cora said and sighed as she sat down on her bottom, wiping her face with her trademark pink bandana. "This reminds me of what God does inside of us."

"How so?" LaRae joined her on the ground and lay down on her back. She stretched while guessing the shapes of the fluffy clouds against the azure sky.

"The Enemy loves to implant lies in the soil of our heart. I am convinced his shenanigans start when we are young and naïve."

"Um huh," LaRae studied the outline of a flying dragon cloud.

"What was meant to be the Garden of Eden gets infested. Deception vines entangle and choke off truth and light."

"Do we give permission for it to happen?" LaRae wondered studying her dirty nails, then sucking a cut on her little finger. In the eagerness to burn off nervous energy, she'd forgotten to put on gloves.

"Unwittingly. Unexpected, bad things catch us by surprise, overwhelming our senses. Flooded with negative emotions, we accept seeds of doubt and unbelief and switch to self-protection using control and hatred."

LaRae thought about Mr. Hansen's words in one of their earlier conversations. "I chose to agree with the lie that I was worthless and powerless," he had said.

"I have felt all alone," LaRae confessed. "Abandoned. A

voice insists I'll never belong anywhere, but always be out of place. A square peg in a round hole if you've ever heard the saying?"

"No. I haven't." Cora lay down next to her and rolled over on her side. "I know where you belong." Her older friend smiled mischievously.

"Well, if you do, don't keep it from me?" LaRae flicked away a grasshopper.

Cora laid her hand over her own chest and patted it. "In God the Father's heart."

"Me? Belonging inside God the Father's heart?"

"Yes, darling. A perfect fit." Cora kicked off her wooden clogs and wiggled her toes; lavender nail polish lit up against her tanned skin. "In Christ we are presented before God without specks or flaws, cleaned up and flawless. It's the best news ever. Because of his hard work and not our own feeble efforts. You'll get me excited if you let me go on preaching!"

LaRae giggled. "Have at it preacher woman!"

Her neighbor straightened. "You girl, have become perfectly acceptable and lovable to the Father. Because you are in Christ, aren't you?"

LaRae sat up too. "I think so. Are you asking if I believe he is the world's Savior?"

"Hm. Is he your Savior right now?"

"I can't say there has been a transaction." LaRae flushed. "I grew up in church. I pray."

"My darling child! This is a personal decision we are all asked to make. Do you want to say 'yes'?"

LaRae nodded. "I do. But how?"

"Keep it simple."

LaRae's heart hammered to the point she thought it might jump out of her tank top. As clouds drifted above, she spoke out loud. "Jesus, I am tired of sitting on the sidelines. Alone. Sad. Frustrated. But I come to you now. I ask you to forgive me for not running into your arms a long time ago. I am sorry for pulling away from you. For not believing what you promised about rest. I need your cleansing. Your forgiveness. I accept it is true that you died for me. You paid the price for all my sin. For my resentment. My self-hatred. My self-pity." Her gaze still fixed on the sky, wetness trickled down her cheeks, slipping inside her mouth. Tears intermingled with snot. She took the bandana offered by Cora and wiped her face. "In my mind's eye I see a picture of Jesus. He is coming towards me. I think he wants me to run into his arms. Would that be okay?"

Cora laughed and cried at the same time. "Okay, child? You're killing me, it is more than okay. It is the most sensible thing I've seen you do so far. Run!"

With new dirt smudges covering up the freckles on her sunburned face, LaRae walked into the arms of Jesus. As she inhaled and then slowly exhaled, the taut muscles in her body began to loosen up.

"Beloved child. I have longed for you! Stay with me."

After hearing Jesus speak, LaRae opened her eyes. Cora was sitting cross legged in front of her and beaming: "This is the greatest moment I've ever had in the potato patch!"

Laughing, they pushed themselves into a standing position. "I planned on weeding the yard and here God goes and pulls out the biggest weed of all." Cora shook her head and climbed the steps to the back porch then stopped in mid-stride. "He never ceases to amaze me. That's one of the reasons I'm so crazy about him."

LaRae used a twig to pull her hair into a bun. "I can relate to your way of speaking about God now. Before I considered you a Martian when it came to spirituality. You use such intimate terms. I felt embarrassed when you talked of Jesus." While kicking off her boots, she faced her friend again. "But now I'm psyched! I want to learn everything about how to maintain this connection!"

Cora laughed. "Holy Spirit now lives inside you so you are connected. I am a happy woman but also a tired one. I need to top this fabulous milestone off with a catnap."

LaRae nodded but stretched out her arms. "Come here first."

LaRae wrapped her friend in a tight hug. "I love you so much! Thank you for helping me reach this tipping point!"

CHAPTER 27

After his discharge from the clinic, Lars returned to the settlement in the hill country. In the rain forest, wild orchids bloomed and the scent of eucalyptus trees cleared his sinuses. The drilling started, and the next two weeks filled with training and problem solving. The team even tapped into sporadic WiFi. It worked best in early morning, which explained why today he was still sitting in front of the fire. Lars scrolled down the page on his laptop, reading the email while Hal, his boss, hovered nearby.

> *Golden Boy, I've got great news! Mother has worried herself sick about my bad choices and has lobbied the center nonstop. After she promised to pick me up at the airport and put me safely back on the returning flight four days later, the leadership granted permission for me to spend a weekend in Norway. I'm going home to reassure her I am on the mend.*
>
> *I'm so sorry to hear about your sickness and complications from fever. Get back to your strong, macho self as soon as possible. LOL. I'm so excited about you coming to England. It's the highlight I look forward to the most. Keep me in the loop. I love you, Ania.*

He sighed, happy for her. Besides bouts of sudden weakness

and a runny stomach everything was going well. As if reading his mind, his supervisor sipped his coffee before speaking.

"I think you suffer from amoeba and parasites." Hal broke into his reflections. "The girls told on you. Although you insist you've recovered, no one believes it. Symptoms worsen when the immune system is weakened."

Lars smiled. "I'm toughing it out. This well will improve the locals' lives. Can't believe they've been carrying buckets three miles each way for years now! If I were chief, I'd have relocated the tribe!"

"Places near water sources get overcrowded. And people are attached to their ancestral land. I appreciate your hard work though." The supervisor crouched on the three-legged stool by Lars.

Dawn was the best time of day in the mountains, the air crisp and mountain mist shrouding the ground. Today birds chirped, and the sun was piercing through the dense foliage. Embers from the campfire still glowed. Through the open doorway, Lars watched Liv and Ella scrape off the remnants from their dishes and wash them in a blue plastic basin.

"I'm making an executive decision." Hal fingered a file and handed over a document.

"About the recent robberies? Increased security?" Rumors circulated that it was wildlife poachers who had attempted to break into the Red Cross camp. But since digital devices fetched a good price on the black market theft happened often. "It was probably someone desperate to make ends meet. Don't think we're in danger otherwise," Lars said.

The director responded in the affirmative. "I agree. Besides checking on you guys, that's very much the reason for my visit. An armed guard will show up tonight to watch over the equipment and vehicles. His supervisor took another sip from his steaming mug. "But the decision I mentioned concerns your health."

Lars looked up. "I'm on the mend. I haven't missed any duties since my return."

"I have no complaints about your work ethic or knowledge of geology. But your new symptoms indicate you suffer from a parasite and possibly amoebas. I want you thoroughly tested and to get adequate nutrition and meds. I printed out the details on this paper."

"Are you wanting me to go to Zanzibar City?"

"No, I am ordering you to take a month off. Check in for follow-up at a regional hospital in Norway that specializes in tropical medicine. Before you protest, let me add: we consider you an asset and lean towards promoting you. On a personal level I see colleagues fizzle out like shooting stars because they refuse to take their health seriously. Recover, then get back into the game."

Lars rose and paced, feet pinched in the leather boots. "I am impressed by the integrity and expertise of the International Red Cross organization in Sub Sahara. My passion is to supervise projects and I love the mobility and interaction with ethnic groups. Even challenges motivate me."

The director stood up and headed to his dusty Land Rover. "We are in agreement then? Sometimes being a hero means submitting to good advice." He winked. "I'm attending the village elders' council. Be packed by tomorrow. I'm taking you to the airport in Dar El Salam."

Lars threw up his hands in surrender. "Okay, boss. You win. My backpack and I will be ready. I will put together a detailed job description for whoever is taking my place."

"Great." Hal responded and drove off in a red cloud. Lars explained to his colleagues about the new arrangement. Ella hugged him and Liv volunteered to do his laundry. Hans slapped his back.

The morning journey was uneventful, except for frequent stops with Lars sprinting into the pine woods or crouching behind outcroppings when there were no nearby latrines. To avoid dehydration, a mixture of water with traces of salt and sugar rested in his lap. At the airport, Hal wished him luck.

Lars boarded, cringing at the possibility of having to race

repeatedly to the restroom. In an effort to show goodwill, the airline rearranged his seating to an aisle seat by the bulkhead. He sank into the chair, greeting the thirty-something bespectacled woman next to him. "Lars Pettersen, returning from humanitarian work. How are you?"

The girl scowled. "Netta. I'm running from a possessive, jealous, Arab boyfriend recruiting me into his harem."

Lars' eyes widened. "Can I help?"

"Be my body guard if he follows me on the flight!"

Lars scanned the rows. "If I doze off and you need me, squeeze my arm. If there's a marshal on board, notify him too."

The girl blanched. "Don't get the authorities involved."

"Okay, no worries." Lars sent up a prayer for his fellow passenger, then thought about Ania's email, realizing the dates he'd be home with his mother coincided with her trip. He felt like a schoolboy needing to be put in time-out at the way he'd abandoned both in dashing off to Africa. But instead, their faces would probably light up in surprise at him appearing on their doorsteps. *What are you up to, God?* In his pitiful shape it would be good to crash in familiar surroundings. The females would fuss over him. His Adam's apple bobbed in indignation. *I'm an invalid.* No, he'd sit on the diagnosis. August was a good month to get out in the boat. Memories of reeling in mackerel by the hundreds with his uncles popped into his memory. Lars reclined, letting his mind roam. With all the hustle, he had neglected his inner world – had even ignored it. The wagging finger appeared: *You're avoiding the shame.* The memory of the feverish nightmare in the jungle returned, and he shifted in his seat, knee bouncing. The snake pursuing him had hissed accusations. *I acted the gentleman with LaRae. I withdrew so as not to confuse or hurt her. Baloney,* a more honest voice interjected. *You dug your own grave by playing it safe.* A wave of regret crashed in. Lars staggered to the bathroom, pressed the faucet, and slapped cold water on his face.

Father God. Is self-protection my default button? And denial? A stab through his liver made him wince. *Why did I let her go?*

"Coward!" He hammered the sink, then grabbed the tiny counter and pushed his upper body towards the square mirror. Rippled muscles still bulged in the right places. He flexed his biceps.

"You call yourself a warrior. Adventurer. Explorer. But you didn't fight for her! The adventure seemed so risky you willingly forfeited the price!" While turbulence rocked him, Lars splashed his face again, then tore out paper towels and scrubbed his skin.

"Was she not worth it?" he stomped out of the bathroom into a flight attendant hammering on the door. The uniformed lady hissed at him with bits of spittle hitting him.

"You are endangering both of us, go to your seat."

He stumbled back, and clenched his teeth at a shooting pain. The pilot's Dutch-accented voice crackled over the speakers. "Please remain buckled. More turbulence ahead."

Father, I surrender my weakness to you. And shame. Guide me. Make me willing to do your will. The plane shuddered and jerked. A laptop flew by and peanuts rained on his lap.

Netta looked up, clutching People Magazine. "I'm feeling sick," she said.

Lars leaned towards the pocket in front of her, trying to locate the paper bag for motion sickness. As he did, he saw her body convulse. Before he could move, she hunched forward and a spray of vomit hit him. Looking down at the half-digested airline food on his t-shirt, he jerked back in disgust, then laughed uncontrollably.

CHAPTER 28

Amanda waved at Christopher and ducked behind the store shelf. The sales sign outside the duty-free boutique did not apply to the Gucci drawstring purse. After casting another glance over her shoulder, she pulled out the credit card. If her baby sister was turning into a celebrity, her older sibling needed to look the part. Just because they grew up between corn and soybean fields didn't mean it had to show in her wardrobe. She added a scarf to the purchase and used it to disguise the handbag while thinking of her conversation with Norman.

"You can take a girl out of the country, but you can't take the country out of the girl," he'd confided while handing her a package meant for LaRae.

"As far as my sister goes, that saying may prove false. She has fallen head over heels for her new country and is not pining away for you or anyone else here. Doesn't even cry about her cat any more. I'm telling you: Rae worries me!"

"Me too. This is my final attempt at getting her back." He'd pointed at the package. "She ain't the only candy in the store, if you catch my drift. Got women standing in line to help with the hogs and the rabbit breeding."

"Well, congratulations! I hate to break it to you but I'm not in the market for rabbit fur but am holding out for mink."

The man had scoffed and launched into a lecture on the

delicacy of rabbit meat. For a moment she had contemplated throwing the gift back at him. Amanda straightened and huffed at the memory, then headed to the gate where Christopher was rallying the troops and folding the stroller.

"Thanks Chris. Drew, don't pick your nose. Both of you boys go with Dad. Time to board." She bent down and sniffed Wallie's diaper. "Find our seats, I'll change him."

After the clean-up, she balanced down the narrow aisle of the plane, glancing at their boys. Enthused by the movie choices, they fingered the screens. Amanda buckled in and downed a bottle of white wine while watching the kids eat the foil wrapped meal as if they were gourmet fare.

"Christopher, hold Wallie, please. Let's buy tax free perfume for that Cora woman and cologne for the cute, little lawyer. I couldn't bear to bring them cabbage relish and T-shirts from home."

"Honey. I trust your choice but not your spending." He grabbed the baby and leaned in close. "You broke the bank persuading me to take this trip. Keep the gifts below fifty a piece."

Amanda put on a fresh coat of lipstick, sucking her lips into a pout.

Christopher laughed. "Don't try that on me, woman. It's why we've had three kids in seven years. Do you really want a repeat?

She squinted her eyes. "Light summer nights in Scandinavia are the most romantic of all."

"Let me guess: the Dresden librarian who reads every Harlequin romance novel the library acquires told you this?"

She nodded demurely.

"Did she happen tell you the same Scandinavian Vikings brought female captives from the countries they marauded? I'm not sure those women found the summer nights romantic!"

"Party pooper." Amanda turned her head the other way, studying the glossy airline magazine offerings while blowing a bubble with her gum.

LaRae cut another length of packing tape and yelped. "Ouch, I nicked my finger. It's worth it to avoid any last-minute nicks or scratches on our masterpieces though." She surveyed the room. Canvases leaned against furniture, wrapped in sheets, secured by tape.

Gunhild bent over, wiping away a paint spot on the hardwood floor. "What are you going to wear to the opening? I suggest something flowy and bohemian. Perhaps a wide brimmed hat with roses. You want to add an air of mystery. But nothing too sexual."

Cora erupted in laughter. "Gunhild! Have you been reading the latest fashion column?"

The big-chested woman's face deepened a shade. "I may be well over sixty but thought it useful to get some advice. I bought an issue of *Vague*."

"*Vogue!* Does that explain your outfit?" Cora looked pointedly at the mauve velour jump suit with jewel decor.

"Doesn't it just say sporty but not straight out fitness enthusiast?" Gunhild made a little circle, trotting heavily around the room, showing off her outfit from various angles. Each angle looked even scarier than the last.

The two friends tried hard but couldn't help but explode with laughter. "Not sure anyone would worry about the fitness enthusiast part. People know you're a great sport when it comes to cooking though. If I made a wild guess, I'd say the mailman is crazy about you in a house apron," LaRae comforted.

"Really? You wouldn't just flatter me, would you now?"

LaRae shook her head. "I love your flowered dresses and aprons. You have established your very own brand of trendy."

Gunhild looked relieved. "You know what? I'm burning up. This suit gives me hot flashes. I'll run home and change. Be right back."

Cora leaned against the wall, her shoulders still shaking with laughter. "Remind me to ask what she's wearing for the reception. Visions of Gunhild as a sugar plum fairy or in a strapless mini dress are dancing in my head. Neither is comforting. It's time for the Crochet Club to help reel this man in before she loses all common sense."

"That's a conspiracy I'm glad to be part of." LaRae's stomach turned into a rubber ball whenever the exhibit was mentioned but laughing eased it.

The next day they hung the art, then headed to the airport in a borrowed van. "Sure hope my sister enjoys my paintings and the improvements of Erna's house." In the passenger seat, LaRae snapped pictures of the passing landscape. *Mom and Dad! Please peek down from heaven.*

Cora glanced sideways. "Even if Amanda hates your art and the house isn't to her taste, you can both still have a great time."

"Oh." LaRae's jaw dropped.

Cora giggled. "Is that a new revelation?"

"Yes, ma'am."

With eight suitcases, back packs and totes, the American family stood out in the tiny airport. Amanda squealed and ran to hug her. The nephews flocked in, joining the group hug.

"Aunt Rae Rae, where are the Vikings?" Mickey brandished a plastic sword, frowning at the new surroundings.

His brother shushed him. "They're dead, dummy! But the ships got dug up. We're going to check out their loot."

Christopher and Wallie joined the circle and LaRae reached for Wallie. Chubby and blue eyed, he nuzzled her neck. She inhaled his scent. "I missed you," she cooed. "Be a good man like your namesake."

"Uncle Walter took the godfather calling to heart. I overheard him promising this kid a Cadillac for his eighteenth birthday," Christopher said and winked at her.

Amanda tossed her platinum mane. "I think he plans for the baby to take over the dealership."

"Let's hope he'll like cars then." LaRae sat him on her left hip and introduced Cora.

"Welcome! I'm so excited to meet you! But let's ride to the campground. You must be exhausted." Cora put her arm around

Amanda's shoulders. "You're a brave woman, crossing the Atlantic with young ones."

Amanda looked up. "I had to change clothes three times. A Kool-Aid spill and spit-ups killed my wardrobe. Excuse me for wearing my husband's t-shirt."

"You're as cute as a button. Here." Cora handed her a bouquet of roses. "From my yard."

"No wonder Rae talks about you like a mother figure."

Cora shook her head and helped the kids climb in. "I wouldn't dare try to take a mother's place. My son Gunnar, lives elsewhere. Thanks for letting your sister ease my loneliness. Besides, I find LaRae adorable."

Amanda stared. "LaRae seems so different. Vibrant and talkative. And self-assured. I don't know what to say except you must be rubbing off on her."

As Cora stuck the key in the ignition, she told the newcomers, "Buckle up. Traffic fines are steep in Norway and no one talks the police out of a ticket! I try my best to obey the rules."

"Let's count sheep and cows as we go, boys." LaRae, sat in the back, pointing out landmarks until they arrived in Mandal. They rode through town to the campsite by the Sea Sand Beach. Nestled against the backdrop of the pine woods stood a handful of brown stained wood cabins.

Amanda's gaze raked the cottage's exterior. "How rustic."

"It has air conditioning and hot water. Where's your sense of adventure, Honey?" Christopher chucked his wife's chin playfully.

"It'll reappear when I locate the closest mall. In the meantime, I am first in line for a hazmat shower." Amanda rolled her eyes at her stained shirt.

"That's my girl." He unbuckled the baby.

"Can I take you to the local seafood tavern tonight? You must be starving," LaRae interjected.

"Yeah. I want whale meat!" Mickey exclaimed.

Cora picked up the little boy. "No whale meat on the menu but we have scary looking crabs."

"Cool. I will eat one all by myself."

"I'll teach you to crack it open and pick it. But first let's wash your hands."

LaRae watched her neighbor. *Hope you get a batch of grandchildren soon.* She indulged in wishful thinking on her newfound friend and mentor's behalf.

They spent the following day at the beach recovering from jet lag while tanning, playing and catching up on the latest news. "I could get used to this." Amanda dug her painted toes into the warm sand.

"It was not as charming in April when everything was covered with snow. A rubber boot, plastic bottles, and even a car tire drifted in on the tide." LaRae sifted the rough, yellow grains through her fingers. The sun heated her emerald one-piece suit, making it stick to her torso. She relished the heat but applied one more layer of sunscreen to her chest. Her fingers strayed to the lump lurking beneath the Lycra. The UFO. She'd avoided the offensive knot in her breast as if it were an unidentified flying object invading from outer space. *No breast cancer history in our family. I'll deal with it after the exhibit.* She rose and shook out the towel while shaking off the intruding thought.

Amanda was wrinkling her nose. "Oh hush. No more talk about winter and pollution. Let's pretend we're in paradise! How about fetching this nursing mom a Diet Coke?"

LaRae leaned in and kissed Baby Wallie's toes one by one on her sister's lap. "Is it okay to treat the boys to popsicles?"

"Of course! Keep them away as much as you like. Don't worry about me. I'm fine right here." Amanda put lotion on the baby and waved goodbye.

The boys kicked pebbles as they headed towards the snack stand. "Aunt Rae, do you miss Mr. Norman?"

"Drew, Sweetie, why do you ask?"

Because Mr. Norman told me to. Said he'll still marry you but you must decide real fast."

"Oh? And if I don't?"

"Then I won't have an uncle." Mickey jumped in.

LaRae laughed. "How about a cat for an uncle instead? I have someone special waiting for you."

"Really? Another man-cat? Can we meet him now?"

"When we go to my house. And you can name him!"

The day passed quickly. As the clock neared dinner time, sunburned tourists and locals packed up their belongings and headed home. LaRae bathed the kids in the cottage bath tub, then changed into a sun dress.

"Cora insists on feeding you a traditional stew called 'lapskaus'. Everything is ready and we can go straight from seeing my house to hers. She lives two doors down."

Amanda put on diamond earrings. "I decided to be jealous of this fabulous woman. But after meeting her I kind of like her."

LaRae laughed. "I've got more people to introduce you to. Hope you'll decide to like them too."

Christopher pulled up to the bungalow in an enormous, rented Volkswagen. "Your chauffeur has arrived. Please step into your carriage."

The ride to the opposite side of town elicited comments. Amanda loved the robust geraniums and begonias in people's window boxes. Christopher wondered about fishing in the river. The boys wanted to check out the fishing vessels and sailboats crowding the dockside. Belgian, French and Dutch flags whipped from the masts of small and big sail boats. Tourists reclined on the boat decks, sipping drinks while watching the traffic and people wandering up and down the waterfront.

LaRae pointed to the dock. "Look. To your right is the local fresh market; the day's catch is on display." Hungry customers were flocking to the establishment. "See how the top floor is an outdoor cafe overlooking the river? The downstairs shop offers raw and prepared seafood. You must try the fish burger."

They turned on to the cobblestone street north of town. LaRae smiled. The white houses lining the sidewalk reminded her of genteel ladies standing guard, preservers of history and ready to ward off the contemporary architecture on the hill.

"Oh cute! Great Aunt's place looks like a doll house!" Amanda exclaimed as they parked on the street. Upon entering, the family applauded the simplicity of the space.

"I was worried you'd go crazy on this house and turn it into an eyesore," Amanda sighed with relief.

LaRae chuckled. "I let myself go wild with color while painting the canvases and kept a neutral palette for the decor."

"Good for you! I can't wait to see your art." Christopher patted her back. "I might even purchase a piece for my office."

She felt a blush creep up her neck. "People's taste is an individual thing. It's okay if my work does not appeal to you."

"Oh hush, Rae. We're here to promote you, not the opposite. Right darling?" Christopher shot a glance at his tanned wife in her red halter sundress.

"Sure. But introduce us to your manager; what's his name again? He sounds suave as they say in France."

"Quoting your librarian's massacred French?" her husband said, winking at LaRae who turned to her sister and spoke.

"You mean Matthias? I'm so glad you're visiting Oslo afterwards and I am certain he'll invite you to his gallery. He may even introduce you to other artists and celebrities."

"I can't wait." Amanda clapped her hands in excitement. They sauntered over to Cora's house and LaRae gave them a garden tour before stepping into the dining room.

Cora dished up the stew on her "Blue Willow china" and said the blessing before explaining the recipe. "This is a simple meal of potatoes, carrots and cubed beef with parsnips and parsley, but it is traditional and filling."

"My favorite is the kohlrabi. I'm mashing it in with potatoes these days." LaRae held up her fork with the orange root vegetable on it.

After they finished and cleared the table Cora carried a layered cream cake into the dining room. "We serve this festive cake for birthdays. I know you missed LaRae's big day so here we go. Come on boys;" she handed over pink birthday candles. Mickey stuck them in the whipped cream topping and Drew lit them. LaRae listened while everyone sang happy birthday then blew out the candles. "I didn't make a wish."

"Why not Auntie? I could have helped you." Drew looked concerned at the lost opportunity.

LaRae smiled. "Everything I wish for is right here. Friends. Family. Food. Lovely surroundings." Baby Wallie picked at her sleeve, eyes fixed on the strawberries. She kissed his forehead. "Thank you so much—for the cake, for flying all the way to see me, for everything. I am very touched."

"I almost forgot! I've got presents in my purse." Amanda dug through her new bag and and handed the first one to Cora.

"Ah, how wonderful. Jasmin fragrance. I'll wear it during winter when everything looks dead outside. Thank you so much!" Cora squeezed Amanda's hand across the table. Amanda handed LaRae two gifts.

"Do you need help?" Drew sat down on LaRae's lap.

"Not with this one. Opium perfume, wow. Thanks."

She let Drew open the other package only to throw her head back and laugh, then held up a framed photo of a wedding gown with row upon row of ruffles and gigantic, puffy sleeves.

"Do you see me in this Amanda?" Flustered, her sister's gaze wandered, a childhood gesture indicating she had something to hide.

"It's extravagant. Norman said just because he farms doesn't mean he can't get you married in style."

Cora studied the picture. "Honey, no need for a cake in this dress. You'd be the scrumptious confection. A decked out creampuff! Oh, there's writing on the back. Do you want me to read it aloud?" LaRae nodded. "It says, 'Last chance.'"

"I guess I'm headed towards spinsterhood." LaRae smiled at everyone around the table then tore the photo into pieces and handed the frame to her friend. "Thanks for dinner, it was delicious as always. I need to iron my dress for tomorrow."

"Matthias arrives in the morning to do our walk-through. The reception starts at 6 PM. There will be red and white wine and appetizers. The mayor will open the exhibit. I'd love to introduce you to him," Cora offered the American guests.

"I can't wait! I hope a TV crew shows up." Amanda gathered the boys and got everyone to the van. Christopher helped his wife climb into the front seat. After waving goodbye, LaRae turned to Cora.

"I'm wearing the plum colored dress tomorrow night. Do you think it is appropriate?"

"Honey, please wear it. Do you know I am proud of you?"

"No, why?"

"For many reasons. You are choosing to step out of your comfort zone. You're not letting your sister boss you as much." The older woman embraced her. "Go make yourself even prettier and sweet dreams. Remember to rest in the Father's love."

She tried resting in God's love. But through the night she kept on waking up, her emotions swinging like a pendulum from excitement to panic.

At noon Matthias showed up at the art gallery. He double checked the lighting and placement of the paintings then touched base with the caterer to make certain everything was on track. After hanging up his phone, he turned to LaRae whose head was swimming for lack of sleep.

"Young lady, I am treating you to smoked salmon canapes accompanied with a light Chardonnay tonight. That is unless you become so wildly popular you don't have time to eat. I am delighted your family will be present. The local paper asked to do an interview with you and for permission to use your background bio. 'American artist in residence in Mandal'. Not bad?"

"Excellent. That's good work Matthias. I'm assuming you put them up to this?" Cora stepped close.

"Part of the job my dearest."

LaRae tried to control her trembling hands. "I won't be able to eat. My tummy feels like a washer going through the last spin cycle."

Her friends laughed and patted her back. Through the window the sun reflected off sail boat masts and a breeze ruffled the blue ribbon river. Kids biked from the beach, sandy and wet haired while tourists took in store fronts. *Relax. Life goes on whether your work gets celebrated or massacred.*

She went home to change and returned when the afternoon turned into evening. The art gallery was lit up with halogen spotlights and exterior lighting. A string quartet played in the corner. When the mayor arrived, he introduced Cora and LaRae to the building crowd. A camera flashed and LaRae blinked. Local reporters recorded the speech. Standing to her left Cora looked glamorous in a long silver gown that blended with her silver-streaked hair. Ruby lipstick added a dash of color. Older, distinguished looking gentlemen, middle-aged couples and younger wildlife enthusiasts lined up to greet Cora.

Matthias took LaRae's arm and introduced her to acquaintances and strangers. As the night wore on, her calves ached from wearing heels. She seated herself on a stool while answering questions and responding to compliments. After finishing legal business with Amanda during the day, Mr. Hansen had taken her visiting family under his wing. She saw him introducing them to a local rock-and-roll singer across the room.

Close to nine o'clock, LaRae excused herself and took refuge in the restroom. The reflection in the mirror showed curly hair piled in a loose bun on her head with a few locks dangling by her ears. Gold hoop earrings matched the amethyst necklace. She reapplied the raspberry hued lipstick, a daring choice, but with tanned skin she decided she could pull it off. She thought about how much her life had changed since a year ago and how the twelve months had been a rollercoaster journey without time to catch her breath. The highest point had a name. She relegated the forbidden thought of Lars to the locked vault in the back of her mind. Tonight was another high. Determined not to miss out on its enchantment she offered a brilliant smile to the mirror then made her stilettos do an about-turn and headed back out to the waiting crowd.

CHAPTER 29

After enduring the brunt of his fellow passenger's air sickness, Lars reeked. And in Copenhagen The Fokker 87 developed technical problems. Upon arriving on Norway's beloved soil he ran, checking his wristwatch. The last bus was turning out of the parking lot. He sprinted faster, yelling and waving until the bus came to a halt.

"Takk."

The driver nodded before turning back to the wheel. Lars flung his military-style carryon onto the vacant seat next to him, glad that he didn't have to call his mother and blow the surprise. Reclined against the headrest, he took in the limpid lakes and fir woods at dusk. The sun sank behind the purple tree line, and a hush descended over the pastoral scenes of sheep and cows. He recognized every single barn, hill and clearing. Last time he was home everything had been covered in snow and he'd also been too distressed to appreciate any beauty. Tonight however, he soaked it in and in the process forgot about changing his shirt.

A good hour later, he descended from the bus. His stomach had settled down enough to walk. Alert, he checked out any changes to town. His feet carried him past the new civic center and on to the controversial pedestrian bridge. Some residents abhorred it, resenting the intrusion. More progressive citizens embraced it as a modern architectural asset. Lars took in the Saturday night lights and sounds from the main thoroughfare.

People partied on the weekend. Music from a live band on a floating dock by the outdoor restaurant hit his ears. Inebriated couples swayed, and he thought of how the nearby lifesaver might come in handy. The storefronts' illuminated windows reflected yellow and orange in the lapping water. The shoe shop displayed rubber boots and fall footwear, and the gallery was milling with people. Drawn to the poster in the window, he studied the artist's painting style and smacked his forehead.

Cora Eknes. The red letters stood out. Lars scanned the throng, trying to locate her inside the brightly lit room. When someone moved, he caught a glimpse of her and he could tell she was in her element, chatting and patting children's heads. He stepped over the threshold, eager to see her reaction at greeting this unexpected visitor straight out of Africa. After a moment of stunned silence, not one but two distinctly female squeals rendered the air.

"Gunnar! What in the world are you doing here?"

"Oh my God, it is Lars Gunnar!" Before he had time to assess the situation, Lars found himself engulfed in two embraces at once. Giggling and stroking his cheeks, the women kissed him, then proceeded to wipe away tears.

LaRae took in the dramatic scene unfolding at the front entrance, clinging to the door jamb of the hallway. Her head turned icy hot but her limbs were overcooked noodles void of strength. The commotion stilled other conversations.

"Son, I can't believe you surprised me like this! Out of all the mean things to do. You couldn't let me go crazy looking forward to you coming?" Cora pinched his cheek. "I'll forgive you but don't do this to me again." She wagged her finger in front of his tanned face then hurled herself at his neck again.

"Golden Boy!" A young, gorgeous girl leaned into his chest. "I had no idea you planned to surprise me after emailing you the dates! I can't believe you came for me!"

Cora took a long look at the girl. "Ania-sweetheart! It looks like God has brought you both back from abroad. I've missed the two of you terribly. How is England?"

The woman displayed immaculate teeth in a wide smile. "It's a long story. But I am so happy to be reunited! Your work is excellent as always, Cora."

"Oh, thank you. We need to catch up after this show. Will you come for coffee tomorrow afternoon?"

"Sure. Would you mind if I bring Mother? I'm here for a few more days and would like to include her."

"Of course, dear. If you'll excuse us for now, I am grabbing my boy. He needs to see the rest of his family. Are the two of you getting together tomorrow?" Cora seized both of their hands.

LaRae emitted an audible gasp and recoiled. Lars reached for Glamor Woman's hand. "How about breakfast?"

"Sure. I'll make your favorite blueberry pancakes. See you around ten?"

"Good. See you then." After hugging one more time, Lars was steered towards the red leather couches in the center of the room. Pandemonium broke out as friends and family welcomed him.

LaRae tried to move too. *Get away. Run!* But her heels stayed glued to the floor. The walls tilted and the bolt on the door hinge grazed her forehead. She sucked air into her constricted lungs. *I'm fainting.*

What was that advice about preventing a fainting spell? Pinch both earlobes while bending over?

Intent on putting the thought into action, she attempted a forward move but with no result.

Help me, dear God. I don't know what to do.

She watched Lars sit down with Cora. Could he be Cora's son? Her mind raced to previous conversations. "My son works away from home. He has a girlfriend, and it is fairly serious." LaRae thought back to the faded photos of the tow-headed young boy on the mantelpiece at Cora's house. One photo showed a boy and a dark-haired girl in pig tails, a snowman standing between them. Her son's name was different though. Transfixed, LaRae's gaze honed in on Mr. Hansen introducing

Amanda and Christopher to Lars. Cora's brothers-in-law approached and shouts reverberated in the building along with back slaps.

LaRae's eyes darted to Matthias. Unfazed, he discussed business with dealers and collectors while sipping wine and adding new contacts to his cell phone.

She tried desperately to catch Matthias' attention to come and save her. But the concerted effort at telepathy produced no result. Or if it did, the signal crossed the room to a totally different person. She felt her pupils dilate. Was Lars staring at her from the sofa? Abruptly, she jerked her body further into the hallway. She decided to sneak out the back door but remembered there wasn't one. The corridor only led into a labyrinth of locked offices.

I may be desperate. But I'm not willing to spend the night on this floor. She looked at the grey and white linoleum squares.

Besides, she'd be missed and panic might ensue. Teeth gritted, LaRae squared her shoulders and forced her feet to move toward the closest couple. A mindless chat followed about how she'd found inspiration during a storm on the beach. The couple expressed awe that she'd withstood the blast, fingers and toes frozen, all in order to capture the grey blue hues and foam-capped waves. *I'll take a tornado now, please God. Suck me out of here.*

At the opposite end of the room, Lars stood stock still, afraid to draw another breath and lose sight of the shape. A woman in a doorway had reminded him of LaRae, but her hair was lighter and her body fuller. For an instant he swore it was her, then shook his head and blinked twice adding it up to sheer exhaustion. His mother prattled on but he lost the thread and let her voice lull him.

"So anyway, remember I told you. The most shy and insecure thing. But when I discovered she'd done some painting, I was all over it. Mind you, I had to use reverse psychology to get her to pick up a paint brush."

"Mom, so sorry. I lost you for a minute. Who exactly are we

talking about?"

"Never mind, gull gutten, I know you're tired." His mother patted his arm. "I'll just introduce you. She can tell you the rest herself."

His mom stood up and tugged at his shirt. "You stink, but come on. Don't scare her by saying anything smart-alecky. She's already on edge about this whole thing."

Tugged by the shirt hem he crossed the floor to the large, rectangular canvases so different from his mother's style. The abstract landscapes were full of contrasts and vivid color. Bold, sweeping strokes gave the impression of nature bursting with life. One was an ocean scene. He let his gaze wander to the next; it looked like a combined mountain and pinewood setting where light purple and emerald green faded into various shades of blue. A wheat field bathed in sun glowed a bright yellow. Stepping closer, Lars scrutinized the signature painted in green block letters. As it imprinted itself on his mind, he turned towards his mother.

In a voice barely recognizable even to his own ears he asked: "What exactly is the name of the artist you have helped?"

Exasperated, his mother frowned. "I just told you. It's kind of unusual. When I first heard it, I was puzzled. Now I've come to love it because the girl is so adorable. I'm telling you, Matthias has never been this attentive towards any female artist. He flirts with her right under my nose and is even contemplating moving her into his apartment so she can establish herself in Oslo."

Lars' brain did a double flip. Exhilaration rushed through him. The most unbelievable thing was happening and he had done nothing to create this whole scenario. Dumbfounded, he started to scan the room. Out of the corner of his eye he spotted the plum colored, velvet gown. Golden ringlets spilled down the elegant neck as she turned sideways to Mr. Hansen.

"Oh my God, I was right! I really did see her!" Lars took in the soft female form. Her hips had fleshed out. The familiar face was glowing and her cheeks were flushed. He watched her gesturing animatedly, and registered the hand motions with a knowing smile, remembering how she needed her hands to help express things when emotional.

LaRae repositioned herself. Their gazes interlocked, and her green eyes widened, reminding him of a doe caught in the crosshairs. Currents of adrenaline surged through his chest and he wanted to run across the room, throw her over his shoulder and carry her away from the noise, people and Matthias! He reined himself in, but his feet propelled themselves towards her.

Their eyes locked as they kept advancing until they were mere centimeters from each other. "LaRae Gunther! I can't believe it!" He watched her lips tremble and grow into a radiant smile that made his belly tingle. Lars grinned back. Time slowed while wordless language flowed from one pair of eyes to the other. Then he opened his arms and drew her in.

LaRae closed her eyes, searching for his heart beat. *Don't let me go.*

Mr. Hansen cleared his throat. "Ahem, am I mistaken or have the two of you met before?"

"I have the same question? What is going on right now?" Cora put one arm around her son and the other around LaRae.

"We know each other, Mamma. We became friends at school in America. LaRae and I both studied at Northwestern University in Chicago."

"But you were at the Mc Cormick's School of Engineering?"

"It's under the same university."

"My goodness! God's ways blow me away. He managed to surprise me greatly this time!" Cora laughed uninhibitedly. "And you girl—why did you not tell me you had a Norwegian friend named Gunnar?"

"You mean Lars?" LaRae looked questioningly at her older friend and mentor.

"English speakers don't pronounce my second name well. So I call myself Lars Pettersen when I go overseas. Mom called my father "Lars". So it made sense for her to call me Gunnar to separate the two of us."

"Lars Gunnar! See how you complicated things by being finicky? Take pride in your whole name," Cora scolded him gently. "And you girl, not telling me about hanging out with my only child. So secretive. My, my, my! Oh, well. I'll focus on God's marvelous ways for now."

It hurt too badly to tell you about him. "But your last name is Eknes?" LaRae felt confused still.

"My husband insisted on me keeping my maiden name. It's not unusual in Norway."

"What Mom isn't saying is that my father took such pride in her artist name, he insisted she keep it."

"One more reason why I loved my spouse. But, oh! It's time to wrap up the exhibit. Sorry to interrupt your reunion, but we need to shake the guests' hands and tell them goodbye." Cora motioned towards the exit where Matthias was seeing people off by himself.

As they joined him, Matthias greeted LaRae. "Where have you been? I searched, but couldn't find you. Here." He opened a mini iPad, showing a row of figures. "The paintings will remain exhibited through the week before shipping. But the transactions took place." Matthias leaned in and kissed both cheeks. "Congratulations." His breath tickled her ear. "I told you you'd be a success!"

From the sofa, Lars observed the Armani clad art dealer and his intimate conversation with LaRae. He'd met the man before, and they were on civil terms. With a sophisticated air, his mother's agent was generous and ethical. As the lights switched off, Lars shook the man's hand. Matthias asked LaRae to wait for him while he pulled up his car.

"We'll take her home. We are exhausted and need our beauty sleep, right Rae?" Cora picked up a used paper napkin and tossed it in the trash can. LaRae nodded, but an awkward ride ensued. Lars drove, his mother by his side. Through the rearview mirror he saw LaRae examine the back of his matted, bleached hair.

"My heart is full to bursting! Let's regroup in the morning. Get some rest, my love." His mother squeezed LaRae's hand and sent a smile to the back seat.

Lars opened her door and LaRae stepped out under the street lamp outside Erna Gundersen's house. The church bells started ringing, adding to the surreal feeling.

"I'll see you in the morning. Sweet dreams." He looked at her probingly, then watched as she climbed the narrow porch steps.

"Good night, Lars Gunnar," she called softly before closing the blue front door.

As he climbed back into the car, he sent his mom a warning look. "I don't want to talk about it. I need to sleep."

Cora let out a long sigh. "Son, I am old and tired myself. Let's solve the world's problems tomorrow, shall we?"

The smell of honeysuckle wafted in from the open bedroom window and a breeze played in the sheer curtains. LaRae undressed in semi-darkness then shuffled over to pull the curtains shut. A light turned on in the formerly dark upstairs bedroom at Cora's house. "Aha. Your room! I can't believe I ate, painted and cried under your roof."

The male silhouette moved.

"Dream about me," LaRae pleaded as she climbed into the antique pine bed and stroked her cat's fur.

Surely you are not cruel God? You wouldn't lead him here only to let me lose him again? Help me to trust you!

The moon cast cool rays over the snowflake patterned crocheted bedspread. Her eyelids sagged when a voice older than time whispered in her spirit. *Child, enjoy my gifts.* She drifted into a deep and dreamless slumber.

A massage performed by the paws of her cat on her belly woke her. "Oh shoot! I forgot to let you out last night." LaRae flipped off the duvet, sat up straight and squinted at her alarm clock. 10:33. With a start, she flew out of bed, the wheels of her mind clicking into gear while the previous day's happenings came back. She called Amanda. "I must cancel seeing our family land and the light house with Mr. Hansen. I'm not sure about going to Oslo either. But Matthias will take care of you."

Her sister demanded an explanation. When LaRae didn't have one they said good bye on strained terms.

LaRae relived the moment of sheer discombobulation when Lars appeared in the gallery. Her stomach jolted when thinking about the familiar contours of his body and the white hair illuminated by the spotlights. His jeans had looked loose however and his stubble unkempt.

His arms and face were tanned the color of pecans and his shirt stank, but she had honed in on the essential. His eyes. And thank goodness, the unwavering blue had stared back. When probing their depths, relief and giddiness had washed over her. That was, until she remembered the other woman's welcome.

Ania. As beautiful as a midsummer night's dream, the girl's skin-tight, black dress revealed shapely legs while raven hair glided over bare shoulders. And during Lars' embrace, her eyes had shone like onyx.

Yes, you're fabulous, though definitely on the worrisome side of skinny.

Even so, why had Lars vanished from Chicago without saying goodbye? She thought about his Christmas gift relegated to Amanda's attic along with the other tattered and shelved dreams. In a flutter she dumped two cups of Epsom salt into the antiquated bathtub and climbed in. The salts fizzled and dissolved; she begged them to loosen her wound up muscles.

"In fight or flight response mode," she diagnosed herself while forcing her body to stay put. "An acute stress response is a physiological reaction that occurs in response to a perceived harmful event, attack or threat." The textbook definition came back while her head hovered above the steamy water. "The chemicals discharged prime the person to fight, flight or freeze." Ducking beneath the water, she admitted that after freezing most of her life, fleeing might become her new default button.

After toweling off, LaRae put on a pair of cut-off jeans shorts and an old shirt, determined not to try to impress her long-lost friend. After all, Lars had known her during her worst moments and she was not in any beauty competition.

"I'll see you in the morning," he had said.

Clock is inching towards noon, buddy.

She shrugged. Her house was a study in neglect. Armed with a broom and mop she charged from room to room, bashing furniture and slapping rugs against the porch. An hour later, she finally threw the dust rag at the wall in disgust. "You can lead a horse to water but you can't make it drink". The adage came to mind, but she changed it to fit the situation. "If the horse won't come to the water, the water will go to the horse," she slammed her front door shut.

"Good morning, love! Come check out these yellow roses. I'd given up hope, but they are blooming. You won't believe the pests I fought off. First a nasty fungus appeared. Then aphids sucked the life out of the foliage." Cora tossed a weed in the full wheelbarrow while wearing her red and green silk kimono. A gift from her husband's sea voyage to Japan, it was threadbare from decades of wear. "Then a red beetle army attacked and my conventional weapons couldn't match them. Am I boring you?"

LaRae opened the garden gate and walked in to pore over the specimen.

"No. I'm admiring your passion and perseverance. Sounds like things got personal."

Cora nodded her head fiercely. "I'm into humane and organic forms of pest control. But this time I brought out the big guns." She plucked off a yellow bud, then handed it over. "Take this home. Watch it open up. Gunnar gave me this bush for my birthday five years ago. That's why I was upset about losing it." Cora pointed around the yard, highlighting bushes and trees her son had given her over the years. "I expected a banana tree from Africa, but customs are too strict about importing plants."

"Africa? Well that explains the gorgeous, um, I mean dark

tan. Has he worked there all this time?"

"Yes, dear. I thought I told you about the email updates."

"I misunderstood. I thought he was with his girlfriend in Asia doing humanitarian work."

Cora clipped a diseased branch. "If you and Gunnar were good friends, why have you not stayed in touch?"

LaRae ducked the question. "Have you made coffee?"

"Help yourself. Gunnar slept in, poor thing and now he's gone. Got a feeling he's hiding something. I've never seen him so peaked. The Lord had me up praying through the night recently. Now I think he was the one I battled for."

"What do you mean by 'gone'?"

"Oh, it's exciting." Cora peeled off her gloves and patted the seat next to her on the garden bench. "Get us a coffee and I'll catch you up. Bring the homemade rolls from the bread drawer," she hollered.

LaRae returned, balancing the lacquered tray onto the wooden bench.

"Thanks, honey. What a great show last night. I was so proud of you! Can you believe you sold three paintings right off the bat? The City Council purchased one for the Civic Center. The mayor said you capturing the Sjosanden Beach in a gale is more authentic than portraying a summer day. Plus, he didn't want it painted with a bunch of tourists in it. He said locals enjoy it the most outside of tourist season and in all kinds of weather. Just like you! Funny you're not a local; you have taken to our ways so quickly. It must be a sign your ancestors' blood is still running through your veins."

LaRae couldn't care less about the blood in her veins since whatever blood she had was draining from her face. "Lars Gunnar left?"

"Probably to propose! My son came home for Ania. She has been abroad, too. They've been apart for so long and Ania has gone through some rough times. That part is personal, and I cannot share except to say I've spent hours on my knees for that girl!" Cora sipped her coffee and grabbed half a roll with butter and homemade strawberry jam. "I am working off the excitement in the yard but a blood sugar slump made me faint. There is so much happening, I barely know what to do with myself."

LaRae's eyes stung. She dropped to her knees, crushing a weed between her fingers. "What is happening?"

"Well, it is their story to tell. They'll probably get everything squared away today. Ania and her mother are visiting this afternoon. Her mother and I always thought the kids would become a pair." Cora grabbed another half roll, this time with brown goat cheese. "They were something else growing up. Trouble and adventure tied up in one. When Lars wrote from America about proposing to Ania, I was delighted." Cora took another bite.

"He mentioned a girlfriend. I didn't know she is his fiancée."

"Not yet. Ania has needed to grow up and get her head on straight. I'm afraid there's more hard work ahead. But I'll be a supportive mother-in-law. I owe my son that."

LaRae stabbed a plant with murderous jabs.

"Careful! You are chopping my geranium!"

"Oh, I'm sorry. I've got to go." Pesky, obnoxious tears blinded her. LaRae stumbled, then found the garden gate and ran. Nonplussed, her neighbor watched her run. "You'd think demons were chasing her. Was it something I said?"

CHAPTER 30

LaRae threw herself onto the bike, heedless of the semi-flat tire and zoomed through town to the beach. Ominous clouds gathered above her but she parked the bicycle and traipsed up slick cliff paths and down hills. A downpour hit. Arms in the air, she welcomed the icy torrent and increased her pace. Out of breath at last, her muscles screaming for relief, she crashed against a sturdy pine. Stitches jabbed her left side.

Good! My body's catching up with my heart. While wiping her face with the sleeve, she looked at her wrist watch. She yelped, scrambled to the bike, and raced to the cottage at the campsite.

"Oh my God! Did you fall into the ocean? You're drenched. We called you five times!" Amanda rose in alarm.

LaRae's red rimmed eyes gave her away.

"You've been crying!" Amanda rushed across the bungalow living room and swooped her up. "You regret turning down Norman. Shush. It'll be okay. I'll patch it up for you. I *Facetimed*, telling him you said 'no'. But we can make him believe I misunderstood you. Don't worry. This one is on me."

LaRae looked her sister in the eye. "I appreciate it, but I am a big girl now. Please sit tight while I take care of things."

Amanda squeezed her tighter. "Baby Sis, go for it."

"Mandy, I am coming with you. Forget my backing out; I'll be your tour guide in Oslo."

The boys overheard the latest comment and jumped on her. "Yeah! We told Mom Aunt Rae Rae doesn't lie! She is taking us to the Vikings!"

LaRae laughed a brittle laugh.

"Great, because I have a perfect spot for her in my car." Matthias popped his head in the door of the wood paneled cottage.

"Hi! What are you doing here?" LaRae took in his pressed linen suit and loafers.

"I answered your sister's distress signal, dear. So happy you were located. Let's depart at 3:30 and have you ride in my car so that we can discuss business. That way your brother-in-law will be able to fit the baggage in the rented van. What do you say we caravan to the big city?"

Christopher stacked another suitcase by the door. "Perfect. Can we stop for a decent meal though?"

"No worries, I have a most spectacular location in mind. A surprise!" Matthias said.

By late afternoon, everyone was buckled in and the two vehicles headed out. LaRae tied the silk scarf Amanda handed over beneath her chin. With the top of the convertible down it only made sense to contain her hair. A shower and a fresh change of clothing had helped her step out of the swamp of despair.

Matthias' head swiveled from the highway. "Looks like I am taking Audrey Hepburn for a ride. I am privileged. Once your brood returns to America I have an offer you might consider."

"What? Producing more paintings is not a chore. I'm eager to dive back in!" *And lose myself.*

"That is part of it. The other suggestion is for you to leave this provincial town. Although charming in the summer, the action and stimulation in our metropolis is invaluable for your artistic temperament. I'll introduce you to the vibrant theatre and opera culture. And *avant- garde* scene. Networking and strategic connections will propel you forward." Matthias lifted her hand to his lips. "You are unspoiled yet so intriguing. A rare treasure. My apartment is spacious and I enjoy extending hospitality to my closest friends."

She smiled, then closed her eyes, pretending to doze. Matthias' idea made her feel off- kilter. She adored taking in culture. But to become a part of it? She pictured herself in Oslo, but it seemed a far stretch of the imagination. But what was the other alternative? As of this morning, Mandal was out of the picture and not for reasons her manager suggested. Dresden held no appeal. *Chicago? Completing school to teach?* LaRae retrieved her cellphone and dialed the well-known number.

"Hello!" Mr. Hansen answered. "I missed a chance to tell you how proud I was of you last night. You displayed such poise."

"Oh, Mr. Hansen. You were instrumental in spurring me on. I can't wait to see where you hung my painting. I'm calling because I want to move up the selling schedule. Will you give the spare key to the realtor so that she can list the house tomorrow? Gunhild is keeping the cat."

Mr. Hansen assured her he'd fulfill her request and offered her a guest room in his home should the sale take place quickly.

"That's so sweet of you. I'll be back to sign the legal documents and say goodbye. I'm not sure what's next."

"I will pray for you. Remember Proverbs 16. 'Commit your works to the Lord and your plans will be established'."

LaRae finished another business call while taking in the rugged coast to her right.

Matthias slowed and turned into a small rest area. Both vehicles spilled their passengers out onto a precarious looking spot by a guard rail. A massive fjord spread out below them. A group of Japanese tourists were snapping pictures and LaRae joined them at the lookout point. The boys sprinted to her but Christopher issued strict orders not to climb the railing. Fir topped mountains dropped into an escarpment descending several hundred feet to ocean level. The panorama was both dizzying and gorgeous. LaRae grabbed her nephews' hands, squeezing them tight.

"Let's enjoy the view from inside the restaurant." Matthias

gestured to a glass structure up the hillside. They rode up, parked and found a table with an expansive view.

"I'll order fish. Set an example for the kids." Amanda wrinkled her nose. Matthias pointed to the menu.

"I recommend the halibut, sautéed in parsley and butter with toasted almond flakes. And new potatoes."

"Chicken fingers and fries for me." Drew grimaced as the waiter placed a trout on the nearby table. "They eat fish eyes here? I am an American. We don't do that." His voice was tinged with borderline panic. Everyone laughed.

"Children in Norway often order hot dogs and *pommes frites*. Does your mother think that's okay?"

Amanda nodded.

Wallie's diaper smelled and LaRae took him to the restroom. When she returned, Matthias beamed.

"Such a domestic scene. I must say I am enjoying myself."

"Poor guy, I'm sorry you've been deprived of such elemental pleasures," LaRae quipped.

Matthias's gaze brushed hers, then fixed on the floor. Remembering the betrayal he had endured and how it caused him to miss out on fatherhood, she rushed to apologize. He avoided her glance and cracked a joke about life as a single man.

"I myself am envying your elegant linen suit," Amanda chimed in. "I can't wear white. The baby burps, making sour milk my go-to perfume. Plus, I no longer have a mind. Last week I rushed to the kids' school before the Garden Club. In a linen dress, hair done up nicely, I crouch to grab their forgotten lunches from a tote, but what do I see? Bunny slippers peeking up at me, ears flopping on the office floor. Then I caught the secretary rolling her eyes at the principal. Should I continue? Are you still eager for domestic life?"

Matthias laughed. "Stop before you scare me away from matrimony for good!"

After dinner, they split two enormous slices of marzipan-covered cream cake, then got back on the road. As night fell, they arrived in Oslo and entered the Grand Hotel. After seeing them ensconced in their rooms, Matthias offered to assist with the sightseeing expedition the next day then said goodbye.

LaRae stretched out on the bed. Two freshly bathed nephews crawled in with her, eyes glued to Bugs Bunny on the screen.

That's me. Tweety Bird on the run.

Only her pursuer was the pungent breath of despair. She breathed in the boys' shampoo scented hair.

These people love me. I need to appreciate the good things. I am successful. Daring. Unperturbed.

The pep talk unraveled. Resignedly, she sank into the down pillow and reveled in the memory of a haggard face with a stubbled chin and eyes as profound as the Atlantic. She sighed at her own pitiful self and wondered if she'd still be replaying the same reel fifty years from now. Alone and curled up in bed.

CHAPTER 31

"What do you mean? She ran away?" Cora stepped away from the ironing board and took in her son's indignant face framed by the blue doorway. The iron positioned on the embroidered tablecloth hissed. She righted it and cast an eye to the bone china plates and cups on the counter. Too tired to bake, she'd gone to the bakery to pick up Danish pastries and had run into an old acquaintance. They'd visited over tea.

"I knocked repeatedly on the front and back door of her house. Then I biked to the campground to see if she was at her sister's. But the office said her family had just checked out. By the time I turned onto our street, two cars took off from her house."

"No reason to panic, son. She has not vanished into empty air. LaRae checks in daily. If we don't see her by tomorrow morning, I'll call. Though I must admit it was out of character for her to leave so abruptly."

Cora carried the starched cloth to the coffee table and hollered. "Your fiancée is arriving any moment. Bring the silverware and china. Is this visit not more important than catching up with LaRae? Ania only has two more days before going back to England. Don't you want to spend every waking minute with her?"

Instead of minding her, Lars sank onto a kitchen chair. Cora re-entered the kitchen and got side-tracked by a vein throbbing in Gunnar's temple. His face was turning lavender, his eyes boring into her own. She winced. Her son reminded her of a rabid animal. She sat down across from him, smoothing the wax cloth on the table, willing the wrinkles to disappear from the confusing conversation.

"Did I say something wrong?"

Her son's jaw clenched, his Adam's apple spasming. He shoved the chair backwards and sprinted to the bathroom. Returning, he righted the fallen chair and slung himself into it. "I am sick." He spat out the words with gritted teeth.

"I knew it! You've never been able to hide illness. Do you have malaria? I'm calling Doctor Stensen. He does house calls on Sundays."

Lars' fist banged the kitchen table and Cora jumped. "Enough! Let me talk woman!"

His mother sharpened her glance and leaned back, arms crossed at her midsection. "Have at it, Gunnar. Spill the beans."

Leaning his elbows on the sturdy pine boards, Lars fixed her with frosted eyes. "I am sick and tired! That's what I was going to tell you. Sick and tired of misunderstandings. My body's crumbling too, but that does not concern me. Hear me out before you speak."

Cora remained immobile. Her boy had turned into a man. Asserting himself had not come easily, but right now he was the epitome of an Alpha male. Although strange to be put in place by her offspring, if she'd been wrong, she wanted to make amends. *Oh Lord. Something is evading me. Did I mess up? Please help me fix things.*

Lars Gunnar stared her down.

"I do not love Ania. I like, enjoy, and appreciate her. A year ago, I was an arrogant young man feeling lonely and out of place. I thought getting a life companion might fix it. Naturally I gravitated towards my childhood friend. She was a safe bet. Many marriages fail. The solid ones seem to have common denominators. One is respect and honor. The other is friendship. I omitted romantic feelings from the list, judging them as flighty and unreliable."

Cora bit her tongue and clenched her arms.

"I sent an email to Ania indicating I wanted to pursue her towards marriage. But she blew me off. Said we'd get together upon my return from America. My focus shifted to the master's degree." Lars rose and tore off his sweater. "Then I met LaRae."

Watching her son's eyes go dreamy, Cora jerked but reined her body back in. The clock chimed four but louder bells gonged inside her head. *Dear Lord, stitches are coming undone! Keep me from bursting at the seams.*

Lars paced, sweat beads trickling down his temples, a crimson flush creeping into his cheek bones. "Her art was displayed at the students' Fine Art Show. The pottery and paintings intrigued me and the uncommon name stood out. When a chemistry class took place near the pottery studio, I formed a habit of peeking inside. The scene reminded me of home. But this particular day when I glanced through the crack, curiosity got the best of me and I snuck inside. Seated on a stool, a girl was chatting to a head she was forming on the wheel. With the help of a tool, she shaved off excess clay, reworking an ear. Then she touched the shape of her nose before straightening the plane of the sculpture's nose. Engrossed, she never noticed me. When finished she threw her arms in the air and laughed. I shared in the exhilaration. The head was a true replica of the girl herself, except it didn't have glasses."

Cora watched her son's limbs loosen. She thought of his enthrallment with her own creative process. "Mom, can you make a container for my arrows? With a lid and leather strap like the ancient Israelites?" Her ten-year-old boy had studied archaeological artifacts in history books and his hopeful face had seemed confident his mother could reproduce the items of interest. She had indulged him. Armed with photocopies and drawings of antique pottery, they had experimented. Over the next three weeks she'd furnished him with oil lamps, pots, jars and even tools and weapons. The collection was becoming a relic itself, drowning in dust on a built-in shelf in his bedroom.

Unaware of her mental rambling, Lars Gunnar proceeded. "When the girl discovered me, she freaked out. Rushed out of the studio. I gave up on seeing her. Figured she was furious." He leaned his back against the kitchen sink. "Then the strangest thing happened. She reappeared, blocking my path to class two weeks later. I expressed how much I appreciated her art and came up with excuses to get together with her. We explored Chicago. Excited to the point of nausea, I told myself the new experiences caused the jitters. But it was the company I craved."

Cora's heart double thumped.

"But life was becoming difficult for LaRae. Diagnosed with stage four cancer, her father required assistance. She bent over backwards to help ease his pain, even dropped her studies. I wanted to visit and introduce myself. But she never invited me. I wondered if we might have a future together. I thought of discussing this with you and asking for advice. I also decided to wrap up loose ends with Ania at Christmas before telling LaRae about my emotions. In the meantime I bought her a pendant of a swan in flight, intending to mail it with a poem for New Year's."

Gunnar wiped his forehead. His face took on a green tinge. He rose and scrambled to the restroom. When she heard him retching her mother's instinct screamed to pack him in the Volvo and shuttle him to the emergency room in Kristiansand.

He returned and took up the story where he'd left off. "Then something weird happened. A guy showed up out of the blue, claiming he was engaged to LaRae. He ordered me to bug off or there would be trouble. He mentioned being a sharp shooter. I'm embarrassed to say I never doubled-checked those facts with LaRae. It was dumb of me. I got stuck on feeling hurt and deceived and decided to regroup over the holiday. But after learning what Ania had done, I ran away instead." Her son crossed the room on unsteady legs and rummaged through his jean pockets, then pulled out a printed itinerary.

She skimmed the print-out. "You're flying to Illinois?"

"I was. To find her and apologize. I booked it in flight on the way home. I was going to see if she actually married Norman. If not, I was going to propose."

Cora's heart stopped. "Propose? To who? LaRae?"

"Yes, Mother. Call me crazy but that was the plan."

She excused herself from the conversation and stepped outside to the patio. A hawk circled the rabbit den in the corner of her yard. *Dear Lord, I am confused and elated.* Out of her son's eyesight she shed her shoes, jumping up and down, emitting a scream.

Back inside, she stopped at the sink and drank a glass of cold water. "Son, do you love her? I mean you only spent what, three or four months together? And never dated?"

Lars Gunnar nodded. "I do."

"I am breathless. And speechless."

"Imagine that." He grabbed the car keys off the hook. "I need to find her. I'm not waiting another day."

"I'm afraid you must. I just checked my phone. LaRae texted to say she's gone."

"Gone? How can she vanish? I just found her!"

"She went to Oslo with Matthias. Her family is sightseeing there. Erna's house is going up for sale. LaRae said she'll be away during the listing process."

Lars turned a deeper shade of eggplant. "I knew I should have spoken to her first thing this morning! You should have woken me! And I should have ignored the promise to Ania." He bumped into the ironing table striding to the door. The iron parked precariously towards the edge dropped to the floor with a crash. "Sorry. Last night I told myself she needed to get over the shock of seeing me. So I gave her time to process. I am a fool!" Lars catapulted towards the back door. "Now it's too late. She's crushing on your agent and coasting along in that Alfa Romeo. I saw the guy smiling like a fox in a hen house."

Cora jumped as the door slammed behind her son. The front

doorbell broke the ensuing silence. Weak kneed, she walked to the foyer. "Goodness, it is nice to see you Ania. And you too Mrs. Skog. Please come on in. Make yourselves comfortable."

"Where is Lars Gunnar? If he is making the coffee, it'll be as black and gooey as asphalt." Ania giggled.

"So sorry. He won't be here. But we girls know how to have a good time, don't we?" The women nodded in the affirmative but Mrs. Skog put her hand on Cora's forearm and leaned in.

"My heart is relieved at these two getting together." Cora forced a smile and used heating the pastries as an excuse to flee to the kitchen.

Gravel scattered. Lars Gunnar screeched to a halt behind the barn at the sheep farm, hopped out and headed for the woods. Familiar with the area he'd be okay even if dusk fell. The highest peak was a challenge, but he could use his cellphone's flashlight to bring him back after dark. The formerly well-trodden path had turned into a tangled mess. Fir branches slapped his face and brambles snagged his clothing, one ripping his shirt and skin. It felt good. At the crest of the mountain, he slowed the pace, panting. A fierce sting started jabbing his abdomen forcing him to his knees.

"I lost her!" He smacked the ground with a bloodied palm, yelling to the dark woods below. Silence enveloped him, the wind carried no answer only a cold sting.

Matthias had seen LaRae's potential. Brains and beauty. Matthias, not him, had enabled her to become a success. Matthias had believed in her, encouraging her to take risks. Not only promoting her but using his extensive connections to ensure fame. He'd suggested LaRae move in with him. Shocked at his mom's disclosure, he assumed LaRae's morals did not allow for such a thing. But had he misjudged her?

Lars groaned and forced himself to sit up. Thinking of his own life, what could he offer? An unfinished degree. Student loans. A gypsy existence. Moderate pay. From draught-ravaged villages to malaria-infested jungles, they'd camp in harsh conditions, risking bandit attacks and sickness. He crawled to a fir and leaned his weary spine against its solid trunk when another cramp seized his intestines. He slumped forward. The pine trees blurred and faded. Blackness engulfed him.

Cora wrung out the dishrag and cracked the kitchen window open. Knockout roses had climbed all the way up to the window sill and their fragrance wafted in. The visit with Ania had gone better than anticipated. On her way out Ania confessed she hoped for more than friendship from Lars Gunnar. A new softness made the girl appear less high-strung. Dark circles peered through makeup beneath her mother's eyes, however. Sleepless nights and worrying had been her constant companion since Ania flew abroad, she confided after the daughter left.

"I hope the ghosts from our past have been dealt with. I blame myself for hiding our history. You may know that my grandfather was a Nazi soldier?" Mrs. Skog blew her nose. "Denial is how we coped, clueless to how it affected our child. Disconnected and estranged during her teen years, I labeled Ania as arrogant and headstrong. She acted that way. But with good reason due to our family history, I now realize."

"Rest assured of our continued friendship and support. I have buried all bitterness from the War. How about inviting your mother to our Thursday Crochet Club? She is so gifted with her hands."

"She's a hermit but we'll pry her out. It's painful to watch her isolate herself. Although I've been an accomplice to her hiding."

Cora had sent her off with left over pastries and a hug. Now she realized she'd offered to broaden the Crochet Circle before checking in with Gunhild and Gerda to get their vote. She called Toralf for advice.

"Why don't you drop in? LaRae's painting hangs behind the desk in the library. I need your input on the Fang Choy," her friend asked.

"Feng Shui. You must pick me up; Gunnar took my car."

"I bought a bottle of Pinot Noir. You prefer the French one still?"

She sighed. "You know me too well. Please tell me there's leftover blue Stilton?"

Toralf chuckled. "I wouldn't dare finish it alone and risk the lady's wrath. I also acquired a Camembert and a wedge of Gruyere."

The understated elegance of her friend's home assuaged her raw nerves. A fire roared in the slate fireplace, the flames casting shadows on the mahogany walls and burgundy carpet. They reclined on the Chesterfield sofa and chatted about the latest events until the evening news came on. After the news they washed the dishes. Cora checked her watch. "It's past eleven. Lars Gunnar must have blown off enough steam. Will you reason with him? I've messed up royally and need a diplomat to run interference."

Toralf wiped a lipstick smudge from the rim of a crystal glass. "Your wish is my command. I'll try my best to navigate these danger fraught waters."

But her driveway was empty. "Strange. My car is not back. I'll call his cellphone. Oh, wait a minute! He has no service. I suspended the line since he lives in Africa." Cora entered the house and called his name. "I'll call the farm, Toralf. When upset, he retreats to nature and ends up confiding in his uncle. They top off the conversation by smoking cigars. Lord knows how hateful that odor is to me."

Minutes later she hung up and turned towards her friend. "The Volvo is behind the barn. They never saw Lars Gunnar. My guess is he went hiking and something happened. Carl is organizing a search party. I'll be back in a jiffy; I just need to change. Get the engine running." Cora put on a sweatsuit and rain boots and fished a flashlight out of her dresser.

Upon arrival at the farm, several cars converged and neighbors spilled out of the vehicles. The sheriff rolled in with flashing lights and barked instructions.

The night seemed endless. Dogs sniffed and followed various trails but got confused and ran in circles by creeks and swamps. Women gathered in the living room where her sister-in-law Lisa organized a prayer vigil. Cora filled thermoses with coffee, stuffing her frustration at being denied participation in climbing the mountain side. Close to 2 AM, fatigued and out of sorts, she stumbled into the circle of women. "Ramp it up, sisters. Do not allow the enemy an upper hand. Father God, direct angels to lead the men!"

A cellphone broke into the intercession. "Good news! They found Lars Gunnar but they need an ambulance." Lisa announced the news.

"Okay, people. Let's increase our prayers! Lord we declare he will make it off the mountain. Thank you Father for steadying everyone transporting him. And bless my son's spirit to come out of torment. Jesus, still the inside storm!" Cora asked out loud while leaving the room with blankets packed in the crook of her arm.

As morning dawned, a dense fog rolled in from the ocean. Men emerged from the mist balancing the stretcher. Only the white face of Lars Gunnar showed, the rest of his body was wrapped in Mylar foil. Unconscious, her boy was oblivious to the ruckus he was causing.

"I'm riding in the ambulance," Cora said and leaned over his still form.

The medic pulled her aside. "No ma'am, I'm sorry. We need to administer first aid. Please meet us at the ER."

"I'll take you," her sister-in-law Lisa patted her hand. "I had a late afternoon nap. You close your eyes in the passenger seat."

Cora did not shut an eyelid but performed deep breathing exercises instead.

A similar fog had descended upon her when news of her husband's drowning reached her twenty-nine years ago. Lost in that fog she had become a ship adrift with no mooring. This morning had better not bring tragedy to his namesake. She balled her hands into fists praying and her right foot tapped the floorboard in staccato rhythm. *Restore him. Life, life, life.*

CHAPTER 32

"Bad cat!" Gunhild scolded as she scoured the neighborhood, looking for her temporary charge. The furry feline had disappeared the previous day and she'd drunk honey and milk at midnight to calm down. "Once again I let my soft heart run away with me. I hate cats!"

And why hadn't the girl named her cat? Who was she supposed to call for if the animal didn't have a name? "Cat! Come home! I've got fish for you," she yelled. "More like a spanking," she muttered. Now she wouldn't have time to change before mailman Trond showed.

With her hair in curlers, the timing couldn't be worse. "And for it to happen this morning!"

Today she was going to wear the Opium perfume LaRae had bribed her with. The incentive for the pet sitting had sent her better judgment out the window. Mortified, she looked down the street. All was lost. Trond was whistling and ambling up the sidewalk. She ducked beneath a bush, then opened the closest garden gate and crouched by a wooden terrace. Knees creaking and thighs trembling from the strain, she wondered how long she'd have to sit like this when her eye caught sight of a tool shed only a few yards away. To make herself comfortable while Trond finished his rounds, she pulled the rickety door open.

A voice pierced through the quiet. "Thief! Stop the thief. She is going for the lawn mower. Get my gun, Alice!"

Gunhild threw her hands in the air and did an about face. "Don't shoot, Lund. I am innocent," she yelled back at the irate man on the terrace.

"Innocent? I'll show you innocent!" Her half-crazy neighbor barged down the steps with his barking terrier in tow, then sprang at Gunhild. Despite his feeble body, vicious elbow jabs poked her waist when teeth sunk into her ankle. Gunhild screamed as her weight buckled on top of the man. After landing, she crawled on all fours and grabbed a rake off a hook on the wall. She swung it fiercely towards the dog when a red-faced and breathless Trond sprinted through the garden gate. As he took in the scene, his eyes widened in terror and he took a giant leap, arching the mail bag in the air. A thunk resounded as the missile crashed on the property owner's head. Then he grabbed the hedge trimmer in the shed, turned it on and made threatening motions towards the dog. The growl of the machine caused the terrier to slink back.

"Lock up your dog, lady, or I'll call the police right now!" Trond yelled. Cowering, the woman on the porch moaned but obeyed. "Oh dear! I think this may be a misunderstanding."

"A misunderstanding? We have an injured, innocent woman on your property. Harassed and attacked by your husband and beast." Trond knelt and checked Gunhild's leg. "Let me support you to the mail van. I'm taking you to the hospital."

Gunhild looked at him, dazed. "But what about people's mail? It won't get delivered on time."

"Screw people's mail when my woman's life is in danger; eh, I mean a woman's life." Trond straightened with an air of dignity. "Lean on me," he commanded. Gunhild did, but ever so gingerly. She'd already crushed one male and the one next to her might not withstand her full body weight either. But his heart was massive. She'd lean on that solid organ.

LaRae relished the bustle of traffic, gawking tourists and street vendors, then leaned on Matthias' arm. "Take our picture with the Slovak graffiti artist and include the troll design behind us on the brick wall, will you?" A natural at navigating the city, her agent organized the group and told the boys to wear their Norwegian flag caps in the photo shoot. Afterwards, they rode the tram up the mountain to the national ski jump stadium, a venue able to accommodate 70,000 spectators. Everyone except Amanda and Wallie undertook the narrow climb up the steps to the jump point. Winded, they perched on the narrow platform. A dizzying panorama of the slope and metropolis unfolded below. The day passed fast with fun-filled cultural activities. In a partially carved log structure above the city they devoured meatballs, cranberry jam and stewed peas. The children and Amanda agreed to hire Matthias' assistant to babysit for the night.

"How are you getting us into the most posh nightclub in Oslo?" LaRae savored the nutmeg flavor of the meat.

Matthias winked. "I have friends in high places."

At the hotel, Amanda vanished into the bathroom. When she emerged two hours later, LaRae saw her sister's jaw go slack. "Rae, do you think we will dance around a gypsy fire?"

"No?" She looked up from a wrestling match with her nephews.

"That skirt consists of fabric remnants patched together in the boonies of India. Plus it has tiny mirrors, probably a Hindu religious symbol for reincarnation. Great for nursing babies on the homestead or swinging a tambourine. Tonight requires different bling. Take advice from fashionista Big Sis, okay?"

"Fine." Haphazardly throwing clothing in a bag while tearing herself away from certain people had required a momentous effort. Amanda took on the task of dressing her with the same zeal she'd exhibited while orchestrating Barbie dress-up parties. Only this time it was not the doll who got to wear the skimpy, body hugging silver lamé dress and matching heels. When

LaRae caught a glimpse of herself in the elevator mirror, she blushed at the amount of leg showing.

In the lobby, Matthias whistled and seized her arm; "Relax, I'll introduce you and show you the right moves when we dance." As they passed through the security of the club, laser beams pierced the darkness and halos swirled. Blue lights flashed on and off to the beat of the music, reminiscent of cop cars in full pursuit. A writhing humanity gyrated in a storm of thunder and lightning.

Christopher and Amanda hit the dance floor, bobbing to the beat. LaRae thought their dancing old fashioned but they laughed and her sister made flirty moves on her husband.

Matthias's arm cradled her bare shoulder, presenting her as a new celebrity to the Oslo designers, sculptors, and actors. A Nordic model with no bra caused LaRae to study the floor. She couldn't tell if the person her agent introduced next was a man or a woman. All the while her mind scrambled through excuses why she wouldn't step onto the dance floor. The moves happening left nothing to the imagination and body parts normally concealed slipped out.

Don't judge. Focus on having a good time.

"How about we drop your sister and husband off at the hotel and go to my apartment for a night cap?" Matthias offered as they exited. "I'd invite them but the babysitter needs to go home."

LaRae pictured the two of them enjoying late night drinks and figured they probably wouldn't play dominos. And though art was an inexhaustible subject, she doubted the gleam in Matthias' eyes was due to her paintings. "I'm sharing a room with the kids and am afraid Amanda and Christopher will have to sleep in separate rooms if I leave. I hate to split up the happy couple. Have you noticed the sparks?"

Matthias frowned. "No. I guess I've been too busy managing my own."

Cheeks aflame, LaRae seized his arm with both hands. "I am so appreciative of everything you've done for me and my family." She leaned in and kissed his cheek. "Thank you for being so kind. But we've kept you from work. I'll touch base with you after everyone leaves."

Her agent sighed, then smiled. "The night is still young. My author friend is celebrating the release of his latest crime thriller at a new tapas bar. If I pay the babysitter big bucks will you come?" Matthias wiped his forehead with a monogrammed silk handkerchief and wiggled his arched eyebrows. "My friend does not serve cheap wine."

"I see how you succeed. Perseverance is a great character trait. But no thanks. My blistered toes are begging for immediate attention." His gaze wandered to her pink toes strapped in bejeweled sandals.

"I'm good at first aid." She giggled and as they arrived at the hotel she wiggled her fingers in farewell.

The breakfast buffet offered pickled herring, brown goat cheese and boiled eggs. Amanda shunned the fish and chose a bowl of yogurt and muesli. They settled at a table and ate. LaRae spoke over a cup of coffee. "I forgot my phone charger in the rush to get packed. I need to buy one today. My phone's dead, and the realtor is calling."

"Thanks, Rae! If my hubby is merciful, he'll lend me the Visa and take the kids to this fabulous playground we read about. What say you, darling?" Amanda turned her doe eyes to Christopher.

"Depends on what's on the menu for tonight." Christopher eyed his wife's pink sun dress. "Wouldn't mind last night's dish."

His wife slapped his arm. "Find us a mall, sis. Even better, dig up the most exclusive one in town. I'll prove to both of you I have mastered window shopping."

LaRae looked at Christopher and burst out laughing.

Cora shook her sleep-deprived head. "Weird. I sent multiple texts while everything was happening and asked for her prayers. Then told her we'd found him. I also left voicemails. This is so unlike her."

Toralf nodded.

Cora sighed. "I don't want to bring Matthias into this, but may have to in order to find out if LaRae is okay."

"Wait till the afternoon, dear. I booked a room at the Sheraton. Lars Gunnar is stable and you'll be five minutes away if they need you. Remember, you haven't slept a wink."

"It's taking way too long to receive a diagnosis. The tropical medicine expert comes in tomorrow. He's ordering additional tests."

"Let's grab a shrimp sandwich from the nearby cafe and then get you situated. Lars Gunnar is so drugged up, he'll remain asleep."

"All right." She leaned into him. "I rarely tell you how much I like you. You are a real friend."

The man nodded. "I can say the same about you, Cora dear."

Gunhild scowled at her Crochet Club friend. "Do you mean to say Lars Gunnar went missing and no one told me? I am offended! Here I was, worrying about a ridiculous, willful cat while the boy's life was in danger! Did you put crab in the fish soup? Crab gives me indigestion."

Gerda shook her head and harrumphed. "Rumors of the unfortunate neighborhood drama are circulating, the story growing more fantastic with each retelling." Gerda poured soup into a porcelain bowl and sprinkled pepper and salt.

"So, the rumor is that I was rummaging through a neighbor's shed because I believed he had stolen my lawnmower? Have people lost their minds?" Gunhild asked.

"It's bad. I'm doing my best to set everyone straight. But more fodder got added to the gossip mill by the mailman kidnapping you and shirking his delivery duties."

"What do you mean, 'kidnapping' me? Of all the hogwash I've heard so far! That man made me swoon. He swooped in like a knight in shining armor. It was the most gallant thing I have ever witnessed. He clubbed my aggressor on the head using the only weapon on hand."

"Our mail, that is," her neighbor interjected laconically.

Gunhild waved dismissively. "Never mind, he risked his life for me. That monster had its fangs bared about to attack again."

"A miniature terrier," her friend interrupted again.

"Can't you see the seriousness in this situation? If it hadn't been for Trond, I might not even be here. The beast has rabies." Gunhild put on a dramatic pout.

"All I know is my mail was so late I couldn't cash the retirement check at the bank today. The other confusing element is why you ventured into Mr. Lund's backyard? We all know the man has been off his rocker since that Nazi shot him. That bullet's still rattling in his brain and has turned his poor wife into a nutcase too."

Gunhild sighed. "Out of all the yards on our street, I couldn't have picked a worse one."

"Are you avoiding my question?"

"What question? Please make me a cup of hot chocolate. It'll ease the pain. Trond thinks I should keep the foot elevated until he sees it."

Her neighbor choked. "The mailman is coming to see your foot? Since when is he tending you instead of your own doctor?"

"He wants to make sure it doesn't swell too much. That's all."

"I worry more about swelling in other places right now. Like your brain."

"I can hear you mumbling while ransacking my cupboards! I take three teaspoons of sugar. Not worth drinking if it isn't sweet," Gunhild yelled.

"So why were you in Mr. Lund's shed?"

Gunhild sighed in exasperation. Gerda was like a dog with a prize bone. "Staying out of the way."

Her neighbor returned with a steaming mug. "Out of whose way?"

Gunhild felt her face deepen a shade. "Trond's way."

"Why? Everyone knows you rush to the mailbox to see him. Why would you avoid him all of a sudden?"

Gunhild sipped the cocoa offered her and sighed. "I had rollers in my hair and old house shoes on. I was even wearing that terrible housecoat I use for cleaning the bathroom. I hadn't brushed my teeth after eating leftover Roquefort cheese. It's the stupid cat's fault. He's missing but I refuse to fret. I'm begging the Good Lord that LaRae doesn't call to check on him. She may take the perfume back. I thought Trond would be scared off for good if he saw me unkempt. You know what his first wife was like."

"A dry stick in buttoned-up immaculate funeral clothing."

Gunhild's head snapped back. "Do you think he likes my style?"

Her friend looked her over before answering. "If the man risked his job and life according to you, what do you think?"

Gunhild pushed herself up with her arms, heaving her body out of the chair. "Help me put on toenail polish, will you? I can't reach my toes but prefer my feet to look decent. If Trond gives me permission to travel, I'm seeing our poor boy in the hospital tomorrow. Do you fancy driving us there?"

"It'll be a breeze compared to giving you a pedicure." Her girlfriend guided her to the bathroom to stick her feet in the tub.

CHAPTER 33

LaRae watched her sister on the move. Although raised in a backwater town by an uber frugal mother, Amanda didn't give away a hint of her simple upbringing. A squeal broke the monotony of the generic mall music.

"The latest Versace scarf collection! My friend plans on buying knock-offs in New York this fall. Knowing her, she'll pass them off as the real thing. I must get a genuine one to prove it's always worth going for quality." Amanda sniffed. "Oh, check out the matching belts!"

Upon entering LaRae looked at the wide selection of colors. No gift of prophecy was necessary to picture what the next hour would look like. Discreetly she headed for a nearby leopard print chair.

"Look; is lavender too girlish? What about black? Such a classic. But I come across as somber. Brown makes me appear drab, doesn't it? Spells 'frumpy housewife', especially with my bloated breasts." Amanda rolled her eyes and put on the purple one. "Look! Pastel pink, your color, Rae. Why are you just sitting there? I need a shopping partner, not a spectator! Oh, you don't have an income to afford brand name goods! Sorry. We can swing by H&M afterwards."

Mother in heaven, forgive me! LaRae faced heavenwards before rising. A minute later, she strode towards the glass counter and scrutinized the merchandise pulled out by a voluptuous blonde. "Do you know what, Mandy? Green looks sexy on me. You're right. I *do* need to shop, only I hate that shade of pink!"

The store clerk's fake eyelashes swept over LaRae and she whipped out the matching patent leather belt.

LaRae cinched it at the waist. "Nice! I'll take it with the matching foulard."

The smooth fabric caressed her neck. "The yellow and brown accents pull out the shades of your highlights, it's lovely. And the green matches your eyes." The clerk held up a mirror.

"I agree. Mm. I may spring for a designer clutch, too. Why don't we stick with the same color?" While her sister watched slack-jawed, LaRae pulled a stack of Norwegian paper bills from her wallet and paid for the purchases, hoping it was an angelic smile playing on her face. "Red, Sis."

"What?" Amanda's eyes bulged.

"Red is your color. Brings out the blue eyes and blond hair. And it's patriotic. Says fun, but can be serious. Sassy, yet determined. Passionate but steady. Christopher loves you so much in red he might overlook the charge on the next credit card statement."

Her sister perked up. "Right. Rae, you may become my partner in mischief after all."

They exited the store and meandered past a fountain. They stopped to examine local silver jewelry when Amanda caught sight of a Christian Dior storefront. "Let's check the display, I swear I'll not go inside!" Exclamations of full-blown admiration from Amanda followed. "I'd love to just touch the fabric of that gown. Restrain me!"

LaRae grabbed her arm. "I desperately need to locate the Apple Store and get in touch with people back home."

"Your cell plan doesn't allow for overseas calls."

"Back home in Mandal." The spontaneous wording flustered her. LaRae caught sight of her reflection in a storefront window they were passing. A tanned, skinny girl with a few sun- bleached strands added to her brown curls looked back at her. The face tilted at an angle queried: Where do you belong?

She sighed. Why did this tiny, Norwegian coastal town with white clapboard houses come to mind?

"Can we at least grab a skinny latte from Starbucks before we do boring technical stuff?"

LaRae agreed and they sat down at a bistro table, sipping from paper cups while people-watching.

"Look. That's an oil sheik, I know it!" Amanda spilled coffee on the newspaper left at their table. Two veiled women trailed a man in a white headscarf, a variety of exclusive shopping bags dangling from their wrists. "When do they wear the stuff they're buying? Imagine wearing a Christian Lacroix under a burka?"

"Lower your voice."

Unfazed, Mandy switched her train of thought. "And as for you? I changed my mind about Norman when he suggested you go through fertility testing before marrying. So unromantic. I have found a better match for you in your new male acquaintance."

LaRae reared backwards.

"Don't freak out. It's our secret. He's adorable! The things he can teach you! No need to squirm. I saw him making eyes at you. What's a double-wide compared to what he possesses?"

LaRae rose; an accelerated pulse throbbed in her ears. "First, let me make one thing clear. I never have nor will pine away for Norman. That was a fabrication of your own imagination from the start. Secondly, there is nothing between Lars and I." She swallowed the lump in her throat. "Thirdly. If we were an item, I wouldn't care what he had to offer. I'd decorate a mud hut with palm leaves and live on coconuts!" Tightening her lips and squaring her shoulders, she left the cafe and marched down the white marble hall.

"Wow. You've become a spitfire!" Amanda trailed after her. "Who is Lars?"

LaRae flashed a sideways warning. "Nobody. There's the store."

Her sister huffed. "I don't care about your Mr. Nobody. If

you're smart, you'll notice what's staring you in the face. An opportunity of a lifetime."

"What might that be?"

"A perfectly charming, wealthy man bending over backwards to impress you. My guess is he'd buy you that Christian Dior creation we salivated over. Especially if he starts mass producing your work. I wouldn't mind coming back next summer for a fashionable city wedding, hobnobbing with his in-crowd."

"Aha. I see. Thanks Amanda! The tech is calling me."

"Blow me off. Buy the charger and let's get going. Christopher gets antsy. I need to pack since we fly out early."

They took the tram to the park. The boys had shed layers of clothing and ran beneath an umbrella shaped sprinkler. Wallie's stubby legs carried him towards LaRae. Snot, grass, and smudges of food smeared his face. She tossed him in the air. A glob of saliva fell on her chest. "Will you bring Tiger home to Lorenzo, Aunt Rae? They may fight over who is your favorite."

"Hi Mickey! That's a great name for him. I hope he'll like it."

"Of course. Anyone can see his stripes come from the tiger family."

LaRae laughed. "I'll miss you guys so much!"

"We will miss you too. But, look! Is that an ice cream man?"

"Yep. And I'm treating you. Race you?"

Both boys beat her to the stand.

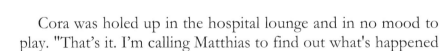

Cora was holed up in the hospital lounge and in no mood to play. "That's it. I'm calling Matthias to find out what's happened as soon as this doctor appears!" She put her cellphone on the table with a bang.

The intake nurse handed the person next to her a clipboard and responded. "It won't be long now."

"You said that over an hour ago. What if my son dies while everyone takes their merry time diagnosing him?"

The girl, dressed in scrubs and wearing clogs, rolled her eyes at her colleague behind the desk.

Help Lord! You're letting the apple of my eye get touched.

A doctor wearing glasses perched on a hook nose appeared. "Are you the mother of Lars Gunnar Pettersen, Ma'am?"

"I sure am. What's wrong with my child?"

The physician stroked a salt and pepper goatee and looked down on his tablet. "He is suffering from the Giardiasis parasite. The symptoms got out of hand because he avoided treatment. We started the right meds but we need to monitor him till tomorrow morning, if that's okay?"

"By all means, Doc. Keep him the whole week. He is a terrible patient. You may have to send him home in a strait jacket if you don't want him to move about."

He closed the portable computer. "I recognize the type and will have a serious talk with him. He's not contagious, so you can visit. But limit the amount of people. It's crucial that he gets rest."

Cora nodded vehemently. Upon entering Lars Gunnar's room, she rushed to the bed and held him tight. "Son, don't ever do this again! Next time you hike make sure you're healthy and bring a working cellphone. And to hide that you're sick? Do you think I was born behind a barn door? I knew you were ill the moment you walked into the gallery pasty white beneath that tan."

Her son squirmed. "You're right on both counts. I was wrong to storm off. I'm really sorry for causing so much trouble. How can we thank everyone who searched for me?"

"First on the agenda is getting well. I'm demanding that director of yours extends your stay into a sabbatical. Why did he fly you home without seeing a doctor?"

"He ordered me to go straight to a tropical medicine expert here. But you know me; I'd rather keel over in the woods and let the bear have me than take medicine."

Cora smacked her tongue against the roof of her mouth. "This is how I became an intercessor, Lord. Bull-headed men."

A knock interrupted the scolding. Gunhild and Gerda trudged in, arms laden with snacks and magazines. "Where's my boy?"

Gunhild limped across the room, engulfing Lars Gunnar in her bosom. "You went missing and no one told me." Her eyes drilled Cora.

"Oh my goodness! I'm so sorry I forgot to tell you girls!"

"We know."

Lars chuckled. "On the bright side, she saved you from worrying over nothing. Do I see my favorite milk chocolate?"

Cora snatched it away. "No sweets for him until that nasty parasite dies. Doctor's orders. If you don't obey, he'll prescribe coffee enemas."

"Real suffering, ladies."

"I'll mail you a goodie box after you leave. With my contacts in the postal system, we'll take care of you." Gunhild squeezed him again.

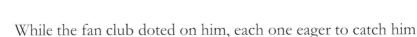

While the fan club doted on him, each one eager to catch him up on the latest news, Lars' mind was racing. *I'm stuck. Incapacitated. Why, Father? Is this the only way you get my attention?*

He stared at his mother, still furious at her meddling. Though unintentional, her portrayal of what was going on had turned already murky waters opaque. *Your mother is human. At times humans draw wrong conclusions.* He sighed. What now though? Was this terrible mess a relief to LaRae? Perhaps she was giddy receiving Matthias's attention and probably lavish gifts. If so, Lars would look like a complete idiot convincing her he was a free man. Did he even have a right to barge in and demand she listen to him?

The bell signaling the end of visitation dinged.

"I'm checking out of the hotel then picking you up at ten AM. Your duffle bag is in the closet. Put on clean clothes and don't misplace your wallet." His mom kissed him good night as did the other women.

Back in her room Cora showered, brushed her teeth and checked her phone. Two missed calls from LaRae. She dialed her number and the girl's sweet voice answered.

"Forgive me! I forgot my charger, and the phone died. I feel terrible. I can't believe you went through this trauma and I wasn't there! How is Lars? In shock? What's the diagnosis?"

"Slow down, Rae! He caught a serious fever in Africa. After being hospitalized he developed other symptoms. He needs to take his medication religiously."

"I hate this! Is it okay to drop in?"

"What do you mean, is it okay? Of course. Come on. We'll return to town by eleven in the morning. Toralf is moving a bed downstairs, setting Gunnar up like a king ruling over the living room so he can receive guests."

"I'll hop on the express bus after dropping my family off at the airport."

"That's my girl. I have things to share with you, but would rather do it in person. Did you accept the offer to lodge with Matthias?"

"I'll be in town till Sunday. I prefer talking face to face, too. See you tomorrow."

"Goodnight Sweetheart." Cora undressed hating the fact that LaRae dodged the last question.

It was a full-on rush to make it to the airport. Not forewarned about traffic, the family had not allowed extra time for sitting in line. "Here, this is for Uncle Walter." LaRae handed Amanda a package.

"What did you get him?"

"A moose T-shirt. Norwegian chocolate."

"I'll keep it with me inside the airplane. Uncle Walter will be glad to hear from you. Said he worried so badly about you he got an ulcer."

"Really? He hid that pretty well."

The goodbyes were quick and before LaRae knew it, she was on the way back to her little house. The "For Sale" sign in the yard was an eyesore and reminded her of how much she was in transition. She picked up Tiger from Gunhild and held him tight, hoping she wouldn't have to give him up too. Looking around the house, she decided to pull an all-nighter, packing up her belongings. She called to book a moving van to Oslo. During the bus ride today she'd decided to live in the big city till December. Come January, she'd finish up her education at Northwestern. The mirror showed a harrowed face. She put on two layers of foundation, a coat of lipstick, and heavy mascara hoping the make-up mask would help conceal her raw insides from Lars. A good friend did not shy away because of tension and discomfort, not during times of sickness. She added eyeshadow and a pair of big hoop earrings while addressing her mirrored twin sternly.

"Stuff the emotions. This is not about you. It's about a sick friend who has gone through traumatic times."

Cora's doorbell reverberated, and her finger froze on the brass button. Since when did she treat her friend and the house that was a second home to her like strangers?

The house's sunroom had her paint supplies on the shelves and the walls hosted her art. The kitchen had become her playground where she had kept on cooking despite mishaps and scary-tasting food. And she'd slept in the bedroom upstairs. After a late-night painting session, Cora had tucked her into the guest bed and served breakfast in bed the next morning. Embarrassed, LaRae had apologized about the inconvenience. And Cora had looked at her strangely and put the question to her straight. "Have you never been served breakfast in bed?"

"Not unless I was sick. Mom worried about us spilling and messing up the linens. Food was not allowed outside the kitchen and dining room."

"Well, in this house we take turns serving each other breakfast in bed. It's meant to be a happy surprise where you smile and gobble down food to your heart's content. And if you spill, I possess a new-fangled invention called a washing machine." She had winked at LaRae. "I miss treating someone to my crepes. I think we should train you in this art by having you come and stay over on Saturdays. What do you think?"

LaRae had giggled. "Will it make me better wife material?"

"It'll put you right at the top of the candidate stack."

And that's how a new habit had been established. LaRae had learned how to serve a soft boiled egg and pair it with seasonal flowers from the yard to make Cora's breakfast tray special.

"LaRae! Why are you standing out here ringing the doorbell like some sales person?"

Cora had her painting apron on and was sporting her pink bandana.

"I was just making sure Lars would get a heads up in case there's medical care going on in the living room."

Cora shook her head in consternation. "There's no medical care going on. The patient has gone AWOL. Come on in and grab a paint brush before we both lose our minds."

The sunroom was bright and airy, and LaRae put a mini canvas on her easel. *He is with his gorgeous fiancé.…*Though her hand shook, she smacked a dab of black on the virgin white surface.

"Let's work in silence for a minute. I need to let off steam before I blow a gasket. That boy is a stubborn goat," Cora hissed through clenched teeth.

"Suits me fine. Can I borrow your cadmium red light?"

"Help yourself."

Gracious strokes filled in the spaces on Cora's canvas, her brush performing an intricate dance of feather-like movements, then changed to staccato rhythms of small strokes only to move on to covering larger swaths with bigger brushes. LaRae blushed at the red blob bleeding down her own canvas as if it had suffered an assault by the black smear.

"I literally don't know where Lars Gunnar is."

"Really?" *Snuggling with you know who.*

"Uh, huh. He left a note for me at the clinic."

"Weird."

"Said he had unfinished business. He apologized, knowing I'd be upset. The nurse admitted he persuaded her into discharging him ten minutes early."

"I guess he is an adult."

"That's exactly what the Lord told me!"

LaRae couldn't stand it any longer; "Do you think he is tying up loose ends with Ania?"

"There are no loose ends, honey. All is tied up neatly." As if for emphasis, Cora plunked down on the nearby daybed and crossed her arms.

LaRae put her brush down and shut her eyes to stop the tears from seeping out. "Congratulations. I'll head on home now. I've got a lot of packing to do. I'm moving tomorrow."

"Hold your horses, girl! How about you and I enjoy a good cup of tea for old times' sake?"

Grudgingly, LaRae accepted and set about cleaning their brushes while Cora set the pine table in the sunroom. It reminded them both of that first time they'd enjoyed a meal in the sunlit space. It had been a dramatic yet wonderful moment of getting her childhood and adult hurts out in the open. As they sat down, Cora poured the tea out of her ceramic pot. Then she added milk from the cow pitcher and a spoonful of raw honey from the beehive jar. LaRae was quiet.

"So how are you doing? We've talked of everyone else but you," Cora's blue eyes bored into her young friend.

LaRae avoided her stare and fixed on a sparrow flitting to the bird feeder outside. *When did my own budding wings suffer an attack of paralysis?* Annoyed, she swiped offensive wetness from her face with the back of her hand and answered. "Okay."

"I owe you an apology." Cora touched her knee.

"Why?"

"I misinformed you. By mistake. I thought Lars was in love with Ania. But I was wrong."

The silence stretched taut in the room. Cora stirred her tea. "He didn't come home to propose to her. She's just a good friend."

Again silence filled the room except Tiger showed up and scratched the back door. When he resorted to pitiful meowing, LaRae looked at her friend. "May I?"

"As long as you keep an eye on him. He's still a rascal in my eyes."

She opened the door, and the cat sauntered in, then jumped on the daybed and curled up in LaRae's lap.

"Lars Gunnar was mad at me," Cora said.

"Why?"

"That's for him to tell. But he was hurt you took off without saying goodbye. He is only here for ten more days."

LaRae stroked the cat. "We named him," she said and pointed to the purring animal. "Tiger. I thought you might find it fitting."

The older woman nodded and sipped her tea. "I am not disappointed about Gunnar's decision. I had second thoughts about him marrying Ania. He needs a different temperament."

"Why is that?"

"He needs someone who understands his passion for the Third World and his desire to make a difference. Whoever marries him will have to be ready to take that on. It's a lot to ask. Dangerous jungles with a high risk of disease. Robberies. Not to mention primitive campsites. There was no Wi-Fi at the last camp. They even slept in tents."

LaRae tossed her hair, sensing a flush creep into her cheeks. "I do not think those things would be a hindrance! If the girl loved him, she'd be able to embrace his passion as part of who he is. You have raised a remarkable son, Cora. I'm not sure you realize what a great man your son has become!"

But Cora didn't respond; instead she excused herself, saying she needed to refill the teapot. LaRae stared at the kitchen door, wondering what the strange tapping sounds were about. Little did she know Cora was dancing a jig in front of the kitchen sink.

"Please Lord! Make me the happiest mother in the world!" she prayed before composing herself. With a serious mien she re-entered the sunroom. "Thank you dear. I appreciate your kind words. There's only one problem."

"What? I'm sure there are many girls who'd love to date your son. For all we know he might have found someone suited to him already."

"Oh, now that you mention it, I think one of the traveling

nurses is interested in him. Gunnar kind of mentioned it. Ella something is her name."

"Really? So he is dating then?" LaRae moved, and the cat fell with a thud. It wheezed in indignation but got ignored.

"No. He is not interested."

"Oh."

"Well dear. I need a nap. I'm not chasing you away. Feel free to stay."

"What's the problem with Lars Gunnar that you mentioned?"

"The problem is this: if he is anything like his father—if he fixes his affection on a girl—he'll be all in. Head over heels. Loyal to a fault. A big romantic is trapped within that macho body."

LaRae stood up, furrowing her brow. "Do you consider that a problem?"

"Only if a woman takes advantage of him. You know what some women can be like. Manipulative and cunning. Squeezing a man to the max."

LaRae picked up Tiger and paced the length of the room, bouncing him until the cat growled. "Then again, the right woman might just consider him the greatest gift God could ever give her."

Cora cleared the table. "I hope and pray you are right, dear. I will ask for that. I'll see you later, 'tuste jenta'." After a peck on the cheek, her mentor disappeared.

LaRae stared out the window. Ripe plum trees swayed in the breeze and the dark leaves of the rhubarb plants trembled. The news filtered into her consciousness at a snail's pace. She walked to Great Aunt's house, grabbed her bike and headed towards the beach.

Lars is free. Lars is free. With every pedal push the chorus reverberated within her head. She greeted walkers and bikers enthusiastically while muttering: "Lars is free." As she sprinted up the rocky path overlooking "Sjøsanden", she repeated the magic mantra. When dusk fell, she rode through Mandal, affectionately taking in the storefronts and subtle changes in the flower boxes. The tourists had vanished and the geraniums had been replaced by decorative cabbages and pansies. The crisp air caused a delicious shiver down her spine. Until a thought hit. Cora didn't exactly read every situation right; *What if Lars' unexpected disappearance meant a change in his affection towards Ania?*

CHAPTER 34

She forced herself to stay busy with packing yet her vigilant eye stayed glued to Cora's house. No perceptible movement took place nor did the light switch on upstairs. At 1 AM she crawled into bed. Sleep came slow as molasses. At last a fluffy cloud carried her across a landscape of dense jungles, mountain ravines and a patchwork of fields.

A vibrating noise disturbed the carefree float. She rose and grasped the dancing cellphone off Great Aunt's chest, admiring the fresh coat of turquoise she'd added during a late afternoon thunderstorm. Cora's chirping voice interrupted her furniture study.

"Good morning sunshine! I have a surprise for you!" Cora lilted.

LaRae's throat constricted. "Lars is back?"

"No. Having lost his last shred of common sense, he is doing business in the big city. I'm taking you for an escapade. We've done nothing fun in a long time."

"All right, how shall I dress, army fatigues or ball gown?"

"Ha, ha. Grungy rags. Dress warm. I'll pick you up in an hour."

The Volvo, waxed to a brilliant shine, rolled up. "Toralf had the car detailed while I pitched fits in the hospital. Although this is a surprise, I won't blindfold you. Get your camera out." Cora sped east of town and coasted down a dirt lane towards patches of ocean. The bright green larch needles dipped and swung above smaller hazelnut shrubs and blueberry bushes. Two black and white swallows clipped a cerulean sky. Through the open window sparrows twittered. "Here we are. I figured you haven't explored the sheep farm yet. The property belonged to my husband's uncle." Cora parked.

"Oh! The location is stunning. The rear lawn ends on a shale beach?" LaRae got out and snapped a photo.

"The house has the typical gingerbread trim of whitewashed Swiss style homes constructed in the 1800s." The stoop, framed by an A-shaped tile roof, revealed Lisa dressed in scrubs and putting on shoes.

"Welcome! I made waffles and coffee and the fridge is full. So nice to see you. Here," she handed LaRae a full glass of milk. "Raw. Packed with good bacteria and enzymes. I'm still howling with laughter about Sven pulling a hamstring while rock-and-roll dancing at your house. God knows the man needs to loosen up. Can we repeat it next year?"

LaRae laughed. "If you hire me as a shepherdess, yes. I need a livelihood. This sheep milk tastes grassy by the way."

"It's from Rosa, our cow. I'm sorry to leave you two alone. I'm going to work."

"I hope it goes smoothly." Cora waved at the departing car and undertook a tour of the property. Winding trails led up pinewoods to tall granite bluffs.

"Let's hike," LaRae plucked a blueberry and ate it.

"No." Her friend pulled out a key from her fleece and headed towards a shed behind the barn. Moss-covered flower boxes were decaying in the windows and ivy engulfed the entire structure.

"Oh, a former guest house. So quaint." LaRae came to an abrupt halt in the doorway and gasped. "A potter's shop! Is that a working kiln? How come it's here?"

"I so love the passion of youth! You look alive, Rae! Despite its holes, that mustard sweater suits you. When I was newly widowed, Lars Gunnar and I lived here with my husband's uncle and wife. After brooding inside their house for a year and refusing to budge, his uncle built me this workshop. In the beginning I only came out here to cry. Then I threw clay. And by 'throwing' I don't mean on the wheel." Her seasoned artist friend pointed to the walls. "After the initial sadness, anger spiked. This was a safe place to deal with it." Cora lifted a sheet of plastic off a big block of clay on a plywood shelf. With her other hand she seized a jar of tools and placed them on the work bench. "Enjoy your surprise. You heard Lisa. There's food inside their house. I'll pick you up tonight." Like a cat who'd just caught a mouse in its paws, Cora grinned impishly, then sauntered to her Volvo and drove off.

LaRae approached the porcelain sink and filled a bucket with water. The pungent smell of damp earth tugged and her fingers itched to dig into the dense, grey substance. Grabbing a wire cutter, she cut off a chunk of clay and pressed the cool matter against her cheek.

"I missed you. What do you want to be?"

With her head tilted sideways she inclined her ear towards the clay. "A pitcher? Oh, a sugar bowl? I see. I'll do my best."

The hard block yielded into a rough wedge shape. She picked it up, slamming it into the work bench. With a tight grip on the wire cutter, she cut the wedge in half, checking for air bubbles. After dusting off the stool she rallied her five senses. It felt oddly right to wrap her legs around the spinning wheel in a perfect isometric pose. Arms raised, she flung the clay with force on the center of the wheel, then used her right foot to spin the wheel into motion. Her hands dipped into the water bucket and she cupped the clay, squeezing it steadily and evenly, engaging her core for extra strength. The tower shape emerged and she used her palm to push it back down. In expectation, the round lump, now malleable, lay still, waiting for her touch.

"Here we go. Have no fear, I've got you." The words fell on the shaky places inside. As a torrent sucked her up in its grip, she chose to surrender to the hand molding and shaping her own soul.

Little more than 120 miles away, Matthias double-checked the new haircut in his rearview mirror. Despite the designer jeans and Italian loafers, the insecure school boy inside begged him to turn back. But temporary insanity had gripped him and he pushed on. The 100 red roses in the passenger seat made his allergies act up, impeding his sight and breathing, but they did not deter him from his trajectory. Today he was not a man of leisure but of action. Upon arriving, he tapped LaRae's front door but only stillness met him. With a sigh, he turned and took swift steps to Cora's house and rang the doorbell.

Cora opened the door. Matthias smiled.

"Hello, darling. So glad to see you. Is LaRae here? Her house is vacant."

His client stared at him dumbfounded. "Oh Matthias!" Her quick eyes lowered to the bouquet. "How nice! You shouldn't..."

He shuffled, babbling. Her eyes widened at his explanation and request. He wrapped up the conversation by apologizing for any misunderstandings and returned to his car still clutching the blooms.

When the afternoon sun waned, LaRae found herself in the throes of a big project. On an empty stomach, she cradled the mass taking shape, the bleating of sheep and cawing of seagulls from outside tuned out. She hummed, unaware of the approaching car and the spray of gravel. With a firm grip on the scalpel she ruthlessly sharpened the plane of the nose protruding from the half-finished face on the pedestal. She used a sponge to smooth the tall forehead, then picked up a knife to carve the eye sockets. Intent on nailing the exact crease of the lids, she didn't hear the creak behind her or notice the person peeking in.

The visitor himself however, was in tune with his immediate surroundings. A horse whinnied in the paddock and a chained dog barked. But his eyes fixed on the elegant neck of the potter at work. He opened the door further and leaned against the gnarled frame.

He couldn't quiet the voice in his head saying "I want to kiss her". As much as he tried to shove it away, the thought trespassed through some crack in his mind.

But the female form in front of him remained oblivious to the raging passion welling up. She stood up, put her weight on one leg while arching her spine, then reached her muddied arms and hands above her head. A ballerina rising from a mud bath.

Speaking to the clay, LaRae whispered "You need a fuller lip, I know. And I haven't forgotten the opinionated cleft in the chin. Let's keep you clean-shaven this time, shall we? And your eyes true to shape. Sorry. I can't make them icy blue." She took a few steps back, inspecting the emerging features from a distance.

"Hm. You're a work in progress, I grant you that. Nevertheless I love you." She sank down on the stool and leaned forward again, landing a kiss on the wet clay. "Keep this a secret; I love you. When you're finished, I'll give you to your mama for her to find comfort when the real Lars leaves to save humanity again."

The man witnessing the scene inhaled the sharp brine of sea air, steadying his grip on the jamb before pulling out of the room, making sure to close the door behind him.

A knock caused LaRae to lose her balance and fall off the stool.

"Ouch!" She pushed herself off the floor and scrambled.

"Just a minute, Cora. Please wait! Okay, enter." LaRae turned, trying to contain the smile building when her stretched lips froze.

"I, oh? I mean 'hi'. You're in Oslo. I mean you are here? Just thought... Was expecting Cora."

"Hi." Lars Gunnar entered the studio, hair disheveled, eyes sunken, wearing a white t-shirt and flip-flops.

LaRae blocked the draped mound on the table using the pose of a center tackle. If necessary, she'd die rather than allow its canvas cover to get ripped off.

"You are creating something? I'd love to see your work. Wouldn't be the first time, you know."

"I, um, it's not complete. I never show off unfinished pieces." The stool swung swiftly to her left, and she grabbed the pitcher she'd made. "I finished this. It needs to cure, then get fired."

"Nice!" He took a step closer, the delicate, scalloped-edged vessel drowning in his weathered hands. A pulse thrummed erratically in her temples.

"Is the mound behind you another sculpted head? I love the way you described the steps to doing your own head, remember?"

"My own head? Oh, yes. That head. I do remember." The male chuckle filled the cramped studio, and caused her to titter like a hyena on Ecstasy. *Get a grip.*

"Is it challenging to keep track of heads?"

"Especially when feeling like a headless chicken." LaRae's hand swooped up to cover her mouth, her fingers splashing mud on her chin.

"You do?"

"Right now, my head's feeling brainless, I admit. So sorry."

"You mean this lovely and exquisite head?" Lars approached.

Wide-eyed she placed her hands behind her, pinning the edges of the drape to the rough planks. But instead of wrestling away the cloth, his hands rose to meet behind her neck.

LaRae tried nodding but her body did not respond.

"I prefer this human one to any clay creation."

His voice tickled her like a goose feather and a shiver snaked down her vertebras.

"This particular head I could never tire of."

With a slight touch of his thumbs he turned her head sideways and examined her profile. "Utterly lovely." His index finger landed on the tip of her nose. "A stubborn tilt to this Gunther nose, yes." He touched an eye lid. "Emerald eyes that probe. Lips... Lord help me move on." He turned her head back again. "Not to mention the contents of this magnificent skull. Poetry and wisdom. Timidity and boldness. Honest, yet filled with secrets."

His stare snagged her eyes. "Will you have this emaciated and tired world traveler, LaRae? Feeble and hard-headed. He sometimes acts the coward and runs away from conflict. Or gets enraged and beats tables. But despite all his faults, he has at least figured out one thing."

"Which is?" LaRae still held his gaze.

Lars brought her muddied palms to his face, slowly kissing each finger. "I love you."

"Huh?"

"Really. I love you so madly that I refuse to contemplate life without you."

LaRae's hands involuntarily moved up to his face this time. Eyelids shut, she explored each indentation, wrinkle and form, memorizing the flesh-and-bone version.

"What do you say? Can you live with that?"

She squinted and her lips parted treacherously. "Maybe."

With a sudden move, Lars picked her up, swinging her in a circle, noses touching. As he put her down, he looked at her with a new seriousness. "Will you do me the honor of marrying me, LaRae Gunther?"

LaRae threw her head back and laughed. "If you can catch me first!"

Ducking under his arm, she hopped across the threshold and raced outside, her pursuer hotly on her heels. The wild chase ended in the sheep field where a swollen, red sun hovered above the ocean. LaRae felt herself being tackled to the ground with Lars landing on top. "Ouch!" His body weight eased when he leaned his elbows on both sides of her shoulders. She watched his eyes change from icy to smoldering blue welding flames.

"Brace yourself because I am about to kiss you."

His head descended; she felt his lips grab her. She let herself sink into an ever-deepening embrace. At last Lars rolled to the side and lying next to her, he nuzzled her head. A frustrated groan escaped from his chest. "Can we marry really quickly?"

LaRae giggled. "We'd better. At this rate we need to get married before that sun drops."

Cora agonized. As much as she respected her agent, she'd refused to divulge LaRae's whereabouts. So kindly but firmly, she'd asked him to back off for now. And when a dejected Matthias insisted on leaving her the flowers instead, she suggested he drop them three doors down. Feeling guilty and too wound up to go to bed, she lounged on the daybed in the sunroom.

By the time the Volvo pulled onto the cobblestone street, her house lay wrapped in darkness. Cora startled at the sudden noise. "Anyone here? Are you back Gunnar?" Heavy with sleep, she could barely bring herself to talk but swept off the paisley blanket. "Did you take that sweet girl home?"

"Yes Mother, indeed. Brought her all the way home. And I bear good news." Lars towered above her.

"She liked the potter's studio?"

"That she did. The news I bring is even better."

"Erna's house sold?"

"No."

"She decided to keep the house? That's exciting!" Cora pulled the slipping silk kimono tight and sat up.

"No, Mom. What's the best news I could ever give you?"

LaRae hid in the shadows of the living room, her eyes brimming with merriment.

The sunroom fell silent. Then Cora sprang up and stood barefoot, looking up at her son. "Stop torturing me. Out with it!"

"May I present to you your future daughter in law?" As Lars spoke, LaRae stepped inside.

"Oh dear God in heaven!" Cora toppled towards the supply shelf and gripped its edge. "The room is spinning. I'm so ecstatic I can't move."

"Well, we can." Lars crossed the floor and drew LaRae into his arms. This time the kiss was short but steamier.

"Ahem, son. Nice! But move no further." Cora gathered her wits and pulled LaRae protectively from him then held her at arms' length.

"You're already a daughter. But now we won't ever have to be separated. My heart is full." She drew LaRae in tight, then kissed her forehead. "Come here, son." Lars Gunnar joined the circle, his height overshadowing them. "My imagination being a wild rabbit, I've had vivid day dreams before. But I never ever pictured this moment."

That night, after Lars walked her home, LaRae slept like a well-fed, satiated baby. When she opened her eyes again, she felt as light as the dust dancing in the sunbeams of her room. After slipping into a pair of shorts and her favorite rose-pattern blouse, she knocked on Gunhild's door.

Her neighbor flung the door wide, wearing the purple velour jumpsuit. "I am engaged." Both women spoke in unison, then stared at each other while seconds flew off the clock. A hoot from LaRae broke the silence. "I can't believe it! The perfume did the trick?"

"This is too rich to be gossiping about on the doorstep. I have a fresh Roquefort cheese. Come on in. After the assault, Trond came to inspect my foot daily," Gunhild plopped back down and rested her leg on the stool next to her easy chair. "Yesterday, when he got down on his knees to tighten the bandage, he proposed. Said my pot roast tops Emeril's. And that I am the sexiest woman he has ever met." Gunhild blushed. "I attribute that to the Opium perfume. Anyway, I told him 'yes'. Will you attend the wedding?"

"I wouldn't miss it for anything in the world!" LaRae sat

down.

"But, Missy? My mind is racing right now. The photo of the wedding gown sent you over the edge and you contacted the hog farmer?"

LaRae laughed. "No. It's not Norman. I am marrying Lars Gunnar."

Her neighbor gasped. "You are marrying a total stranger?"

LaRae giggled again. "No. We have a complicated but sweet history."

"Oh, thank goodness! I thought you'd barely shaken his hand at that reception." Gunhild stared. "Even if you had just met for a minute, I still think you'd be perfect for each other," her big-hearted friend remarked before heaving herself upright and engulfing LaRae in her purple arms. "My two most favorite young people getting married. Maybe we can go to class together to learn about sex. I need a crash course!"

LaRae's eyes widened.

"Got you!" Gunhilds's rumbling belly laugh trilled out her cheesy-smelling mouth.

"Are you telling Cora?" LaRae asked.

"You bet. I'm calling everyone I know. This will be one busy day. Gerda's giving me a perm before Trond arrives for dinner at four."

LaRae stopped on her way out. "That's the biggest bouquet of roses I've ever seen." She eyed the bucket on the floor. Gunhild blushed. "I counted them. One-hundred. Found them on my doorstep this morning. That man is ruining himself."

LaRae strolled down the street to check on her intended. Only this time, she didn't ring the doorbell but entered with a holler that dwindled to a gasp. On every horizontal surface, the living room sported confetti. American and Norwegian flags draped the stairway banister. Boiled eggs in handmade ceramic egg cups sat on the table next to linen napkins and fine china. The smell of fresh coffee wafted in. Nonplussed, she headed to the kitchen.

"Not so fast, young lady! This man has waited to start his day right by being greeted properly." Lars blocked her passage, an embroidered apron tied at his waist; a dusting of flour smudged his left cheek.

"I expected you laid up, convalescing in the salon."

"Yes. But the strangest thing happened yesterday." Lars lifted the spatula and crossed to the stove where a frying pan sizzled. "I came across this miracle drug. Made me feel like a million bucks."

"So that's why you traipsed off to Oslo?"

"No silly. I went looking for you."

"Oh."

"Exactly. Except the bird had flown the coop, and I had to continue my long journey until I found you."

"Really?" LaRae tilted her head.

"Yes, really."

"Is this drug a new prescription?"

"It is. Though I haven't taken my daily dose yet. Will you help?"

"I have no experience with injections."

"It's a shot, but it doesn't require a needle."

"Mm, you'll have to show me."

"Come on over and look at this." Lars flipped a pancake in the air and placed it on a platter before pulling her close. "Your irises have tiny yellow sparkles." With a lowered head, he bent over her, his lips closing over hers. A couple of minutes later, he inhaled and opened his eyes. "Wow, that did wonders. I think this injection thing might become a lifelong habit."

LaRae punched his bicep. "Okay, you got me! If that's what you require then put a ring on it. And a gown." She batted her eyelids when a crash and clatter followed by a cry sounded from the hallway. They leapt towards the stairs.

"Oh my goodness, I fell down the steps," Cora moaned.

"Mom, what in the world are you up to? You have a man in the house. Why not ask for a hand?" Lars scolded.

A large white cardboard box and paper tissues littered the Persian rug while Cora sat midways up the staircase. Silk the color of clotted cream spilled out of the box.

"Oh, hi honey! Call me a meddling mother-in-law, but I couldn't help myself. I rummaged in the attic and found my wedding gown."

LaRae crouched and examined a row of tiny, silk covered buttons and eyelet loops. "Exquisite. Can we pull it out?"

"I'm not suggesting you wear it. You may not like it. It was tailor-made for me by my girlfriend; we based it on a bridal *Vogue* edition." With creased forehead and a wince, she descended and handed LaRae a faded magazine cover.

"Oh, so sorry. Are you hurt?"

"Just my pride. There's never anything graceful about sliding on a well-padded bottom. Comes in handy though. Gunnar, am I meddling?"

Lars Gunnar looked dazed. "Two weeks ago, I was close to dying in a straw hut in Tanzania. This scene is surreal." LaRae stepped into his arms. He let her go reluctantly to finish up the breakfast preparation.

"I'm getting a man who cooks, too?" LaRae eased into the proffered seat and bit into the thin crepe dusted in powdered sugar. She wolfed down two more buttery pancakes.

"Motivation helps one do things one has never done before." Lars eyes wandered over her body, dwelling on its various curves.

LaRae blushed and jumped up. "I'll do the dishes. Don't dry. It may be too much for you. I mean that in more than one way." Eyebrows raised, she nodded to the bed behind the plaid couch. "If you obey, I'll come find you before I go to see the realtor."

Her fiancé's mouth shifted into an unbecoming pout. "Keep the door open. I enjoy watching you work."

Cora limped to the dish washer. "My boy is head over heels in love with you. He had a conniption fit when Matthias took a shine to you."

LaRae looked up from scrubbing a doughy mixing bowl. "I'm glad it got a rise out of him. Though there was no danger."

"I couldn't quite picture it myself. Matthias will have to look for new pastures. I keep that man in my prayers."

"So do I," LaRae admitted.

The realtor checked the contract. "The buyer is serious but must pass the credit check. They're offering to pay full price." The news created a hollow feeling in her mid-section. Blurry-eyed, she left and paced the beaches.

The next Wednesday, trusting Mr. Hansen's legal work, she raised a pen and signed the dotted line without taking the time to read the fine print.

"It's a done deal. Great Aunt's house sold today."

Lars looked up from his chess game where he was playing both sides of the board. "How do you feel?"

"Sad, but relieved. Amanda was putting pressure on me to get it done. Time to divide the inheritance and move on."

"Come here, honey. Let's move on right now."

LaRae giggled. "Sounds dangerous." She motioned to his pajama clad body seated in the rumpled bed. "Mr. Hansen's coming over to keep you company."

"And chaperone."

"You're a smart man Mr. Pettersen. I'm impressed by your deductive powers of reasoning."

Lars laughed. "Enjoy the respite, woman. It won't last forever." He climbed the stairs to get dressed before Mr. Hansen arrived. While upstairs he heard the doorbell ring, voices rise and the clanging of pots. When he descended the Crochet Club and mailman Trond surrounded him. "Congratulations!" Gunhild swept him up in a hug. "You may congratulate me too!"

Cora dinged a crystal glass with a spoon. "Welcome! Refreshments are on the sideboard. Lox, herring, flat bread, lefse. Toralf is serving champagne. Let's celebrate and toast to love."

Lars Gunnar rolled his eyes at LaRae. "There goes my candle lit night *a deux*. Like our Savior, my mother feeds the multitudes. Hope you're not a part of this conspiracy."

LaRae cinched her lips to keep from smiling while moving to answer the doorbell but his aunts and uncles were already spilling in.

The cold September drizzle did not stop. It had rained for a week. Looking around the waiting room and listening to people's sniffles and coughs, Cora wanted to give the folks a lecture on the benefits of antioxidants, raw honey and apple cider vinegar. She checked her wristwatch. 2:13 PM. The follow up doctor's visit was taking too long. She flipped to the next page of the gardening magazine but halfway through the paragraph and despite her passion for living things, she lost interest in how to use beer to prevent worms. Cora tapped her big toe inside her suede leather boot, her knee bouncing in time with the seconds ticking off the clock on the wall.

Heat rose from her lower abdomen, creating a burning sensation in her lungs. LaRae, a master at keeping secrets, had gone too far. While the girl chose silence, a lump had grown in her breast. All through the wonderful summer, during her God encounter, their backyard painting sessions and midnight chats, a foreign, unwelcome growth had doubled in size. Now, after Lars Gunnar had returned to Africa, LaRae had casually brought up needing a check-up.

Cora had assumed it was the virgin deal. The doc would clear her for marital sex, put her on birth control and perhaps vaccinate her against yellow fever and hepatitis before she flew to the Third World. So LaRae had gone alone. And the next day over fried fish burgers and stewed peas the girl told Cora that the doctor recommended a biopsy.

"A biopsy?" The medical term had lodged in her throat along with a bone from the ground fish. "Dear God, no!"

LaRae's face had reddened and after apologizing for not bringing the subject up sooner, her cheeks had turned a greyish oatmeal as she confided. "I've been scared. Whenever happiness comes along in my life, it's as if a vicious cycle goes into motion and something terrible happens. I didn't want to brace myself for anything bad this time. But history seems bent on repeating itself."

"That Darling, is where you and I differ." Cora remembered her knee squeaking upon rising and grabbing the green glass bottle of extra virgin olive oil from the cabinet above the spice rack. After placing it on the dinner table, she'd opened the Bible to the Book of James.

LaRae had questions after the reading. "Anointing with oil and the laying on of hands?"

"If you agree, yes." Upon her acquiescing, Cora intended to use a drop or two of oil. But the amber liquid spilled fast and she soon stood there with a handful. LaRae had looked up.

"Go ahead and dunk me."

So she'd brought her cupped hand to the girl's forehead and as oil streamed down her temples, soaking into her wild hair, Cora had prayed, commanding a release from anything contrary to good health and life.

"Jesus. You said it was finished 2000 years ago. We say 'yes' to your finished work." After the "Amen", they had sipped tea and dug out a frozen custard to show the enemy that fear was not an option. But today, the thought of custard soured Cora's stomach. The faith that shone as bright as LaRae's oil-slicked forehead had waned. All she could see this afternoon was her son's anguish and the possible loss of a daughter. Rain pelted the clinic window. In the office the doctor was sharing the test results with LaRae while a Band Aid concealed the cut on her chest.

Annie, the nurse, emerged from behind the closed door. She walked straight to the computer, clipboard in hand, ignoring Cora even though they exchanged vegetable seedlings each spring. *Not a good sign.* Next, LaRae stepped back into the waiting room, red-rimmed eyes and with a pink-tipped nose. Her flared jeans looked big and Lars' sweatshirt swallowed her lithe body. She had lost weight, playing with her food during the last two weeks. Like a tightly wound jack-in-the-box, Cora sprang up and gathered her close. "Hush. We will talk at the bakery."

LaRae took the tissue Annie offered, signed a paper and they exited the clinic. They rode the elevator to the shopping center's first floor and sat down at the table in the coffee shop. "How bad is it? Give it to me straight." Cora seized her future daughter-in-law's hands from across the round table.

"It was a benign cyst."

"But you are crying!"

"Out of relief. Oh, thank God. I am cancer-free!" LaRae rose and jumped up and down three times in a row before approaching the barista. "Next ten customers' coffees are on me. We are celebrating."

"Happy birthday!" The clerk gave her a high five.

"Happy lifeday. I'm going to live!"

Cora rushed to join them at the counter. "Add free Napoleon cake with the coffees because the Father, the Lord God Almighty is merciful and good." A Pakistani immigrant in his twenties thanked them in Arabic and a mother with a flock of young ones confessed to a wiped-out bank account and took Instagram pictures of her munchkins delving into the delicacy.

Upon arriving home, they Skyped Lars Gunnar in Tanzania, sharing the news. Wiping away tears, his hair stood on end from raking anxious hands through the short strands. "Are you certain, Rae?"

LaRae nodded. "Not a trace of anything malignant. But something else showed up." Lars' hand flew to his forehead, eyes widening.

"What?"

"Tachycardia. A galloping heart. An uncontrollable, increased pacing of the muscle whenever I hear your voice."

Lars slammed his hand down near the camera. "Better not

toy with me like that woman! I almost booked a ticket home."

"Ah, now you're tempting me." LaRae batted her eyelashes at him.

Cora laughed over the wool sock she was knitting. "Time for bed, you two. And I for one am glad I don't have to forcefully separate you for bedtime anymore."

CHAPTER 35

Walter Gunter hated flying as much as he loathed the exaggerated airport security. Already TSA agents had confiscated his pocket knife and a half-empty can of Coke. What would they grab next? But he endured it because of the honor of escorting LaRae down the aisle. After watching her pine away at her dad's bedside and then at his dealership, he would've done anything in the world to fix the mess. But he'd run plumb out of ideas. A skinny, miserable sparrow, for as long as he could remember, she didn't even seem happy when her mother was alive. Sweat beads pimpled his temple and he wiped them with a handkerchief, aiming for Burger King before take-off. He hoped LaRae had put some meat on her scrawny bones. And as for her heading to Africa after the wedding? With Ebola and terrorism, how did anyone in their right mind consider such a thing?

"The good Lord sure makes all kinds," he muttered, swallowing the last bite of the Whopper and boarded the flight. The tuxedo lay neatly folded in his suitcase. He planned on looking sharp. If her wedding had been in Illinois, he'd have given her an Escalade. It had driven him crazy, watching her hold on to everything she disliked. Her job, car, the dreaded teaching career. But what do you give to a couple headed for a mud hut? Somewhere above the Atlantic, a thought formed in his head.

Walter exited the duty-free electronics store in the Amsterdam airport with a shopping bag full of photo equipment, including a pricey zoom lens. He had thrown in an iPad and a solar charger. Now his niece could document her experience by blogging or tweeting. And once she started, perhaps she'd pick up a pen and write like when she was little. His cousin Peggy who taught English at Dresden Elementary School had shared the girl's fantastic stories. It was probably illegal to blabber about one's students these days, but he'd remained mum. Besides, when Peggy's husband left her maxed out on credit cards and ran off to crab fish in Alaska, his cousin had become a belly dancer on exotic cruises in the Black Sea.

"Uncle Walter! Fancy running into you! We spent two days in Amsterdam but are heading to Norway on this flight too! A winter wedding, can you believe it? Who thought my sister would tie the knot with a foreigner. There is snow. They have rented horses and a sleigh for the bride and groom. It's so romantic, I'm about to die."

Walter greeted Amanda and her brood and they piled into a small plane. Upon landing they descended the stairs to the tarmac, a fierce Northern gust tearing at their coats. Above, leaden skies dropped wet flakes on the ground.

"Welcome. I am Toralf Hansen and your host for this most important event." A rotund, pink-cheeked man shook their hands in the tiny arrival hall and led them to a black van. After loading the luggage, Walter reclined in the front passenger seat, stretching his achy knees and enjoying the smooth hum of the Mercedes van. The rugged landscape called for reliable vehicles with good snow tires. When Mr. Hansen's house appeared, Amanda gasped at the home perching atop a mountain.

"It is built in a modern, minimalist design from the 60s. As a kid I dreamt of viewing the bay from above. Each room has a different panoramic view. Let me show you." An hour later they gathered in Mr. Hansen's oak paneled library. Walter sipped coffee offered by their host.

"Did my housekeeper set you up adequately in your rooms?"

"Splendidly, thank you." Walter examined the memorabilia wall.

"There is no rehearsal dinner custom in Norway. But Cora invited us to eat wild game at the local four-star hotel."

Mickey who was spinning a large globe trying to find Europe, heard the comment and pointed to a picture on the wall. "Will we go hunting for a moose first?"

"I shot the one in the photo. And tonight's meat has been caught already. But thank you for the offer!"

Drew rolled his eyes and put his finger on the tip of Norway. "Look Mickey. The size of a fly doo doo, - this is where we are."

Walter laughed.

Amanda excused herself to coax the baby down for a nap and asked Christopher to clean and dress the boys.

When his niece descended, Walter whistled. "Mandy, you're a sight in bright red. But don't break an ankle wearing those heels on the slick pavement."

She shrugged. "Uncle. Vanity before safety. How do you like my motto?"

He chuckled, shaking his grey head and returned to ESPN on the satellite TV while Amanda got everyone ready.

Smoke rose in a tiny trail and the acrid smell of burning fabric stung LaRae's nostrils. She put down the iron in Cora's laundry room and pressed the familiar digits on her phone. Cora's upbeat voice slowed her racing heart.

"Yes, Love? The gold spray worked well on the cones. They sparkle against the white damask here in the restaurant."

"Great. My sister and her family arrived safely."

"The chef says they'll serve the soup at 5:30 sharp. Tell Amanda not to dawdle. Last time she was here, she spent hours putting on makeup."

"I'll text her. By the way, I tried on the high heel shoes with the wedding gown. You were right. The extra two inches keep the hem from dragging excessively,"

"Fabulous!"

"I accidentally spilled water down the front though. I used the hair dryer to dry it."

"Oh, no! Did the bodice shrink?" Cora clicked her tongue.

"No. But can you come home?" LaRae knees knocked and her heart rate skipped a beat.

"You're hemming and hawing. What happened?"

"Just hurry, please." LaRae tightened her robe and nearly tripped in the satin heels. Name cards lay scattered on the dining room sideboard, the green and gold cursive script would decorate tomorrow's tables. Although a power team, both she and Cora had underestimated how many last-minute details would crop up. The seamstress modifying the gown had contracted pneumonia and performed the alterations late. False advertising had caused them to order 100 dripless candles, which upon lighting ran like rivulets down the brass candle sticks. At least they'd done a test run before using them for tomorrow's reception and had saved the venue's linens from getting ruined. She finished up polishing the flea market collection of candle sticks over the sink and placed them in a Chiquita banana box on the floor. A car door slammed. LaRae jerked and scurried to a chair at the far side of the kitchen table.

"What's burning?" Cora came to an abrupt halt by the laundry room. "Lord, no!"

LaRae felt her cheeks flush and eyes water. "I tried smoothing the wrinkles. Can we fix it?"

Her future mother-in-law put on her reading glasses and studied the brown, scorched mark on the skirt of the wedding gown.

The almost perfect triangle left by the iron mocked LaRae, reminding her of her incompetence in life.

Cora turned the bottom of the dress inside out. "Got 12

extra centimeters of fabric tucked beneath the hem. I'll cut out the burn and insert a panel, perhaps add antique lace to make it look intentional."

"I hate myself for messing up like this! I'm so extremely sorry!"

Cora walked across the kitchen to her chair. "Come here."

LaRae reluctantly scooted her seat back. Her friend stooped down and cradled her face.

"You may end up waltzing down the aisle in my white nightie tomorrow. But I guarantee you, this wedding will happen. Mistakes are unavoidable and the lesson you need to glean is this: Keep on going!"

LaRae inhaled a shaky breath. "Ok. But we must cut speeches short tonight so you and I can rush home."

"Yep. Lars is setting up the folding chairs at the Manor house. And meeting with the photographer before dinner. Sorry you've had no time for each other. Who'd guess a terrorist explosion in Nairobi would cause him such delay? Somali warlords called Shebbi-something are behind this too, I bet."

LaRae unwound from the grip and texted Lars an emoji. Too busy for meaningful communication, the little faces and hearts helped her stay the course.

LaRae dressed in Cora's guest bedroom where she'd taken up residence since the sale of Great Aunt's house. They rode to the hotel and upon arriving in the foyer, they stood by the entrance until the rental van rolled in.

"Sis!" LaRae ran to hug Amanda.

"Rae! Still can't believe you pulled this one on me last summer. You cheeky girl, not breathing a word to Big Sis of your secret love!"

"You're wearing a mink stole?"

"An early Christmas present."

"It's pretty. But please forgive me, Mandy? I was so scared Lars didn't love me back!"

"Well, I expect a full report of your honeymoon!"

LaRae felt Lars Gunnar's arm wrap itself around her waist.

She leaned into his side, looking up at the rugged face. But his attention was fixed on her sister. "Detailed honeymoon account? That's a tall order. Some things are better left to the imagination, don't you think?"

Amanda eyed the tall Viking, her eyes growing bigger than usual. "We meet again. I shook your hand at the art show." She extended her cheek for a kiss. "Never mind, a report on Africa will be enough to excite us. Congratulations, Bro! May I call you that? I've always wished for a brother."

"Gladly. As long as you don't 'little brother' me."

LaRae smiled as Lars whispered in her ear how much he missed her before she hugged her nephews.

"He is nicer than your new cat. I like a real uncle much better," Mickey lisped. "Do you think he'll take us on a water buffalo hunt?"

LaRae chuckled. "First you must grow taller and stronger. Eat your vegetables, even zucchini."

He nodded solemnly before joining his brother in asking for a Shirley Temple soda.

The hostess motioned for them to enter a private dining room. When seated, the servers carried in steaming platters of roasted potatoes accompanied by slices of elk roast. A creamy gravy with traces of dark brown goat cheese and a tart cranberry relish offset the gamey flavor. Baskets of fresh baked baguettes tempted between snowflake crystal votives and sprigs of holly laden with red berries. Mr. Hansen gave a speech. As staff cleared the dinner plates and brought in chocolate mousse, Cora officially welcomed LaRae's family and informed them of the next day's proceedings. Afterwards, the party moved into the hotel foyer to pick up their winter coats.

LaRae shook the guests' hands by the exit when Ania breezed by. The girl's flimsy silver strapped sandals indented the carpet pile.

"'Gull gutten' looks good. So proud of his success around the world," the former model hugged Cora. Their conversation floated through the spotty branches of a potted fern to LaRae's right.

"Your turn will come, Darling. The Father has someone special for you too. I know it." Cora patted the girl's cheek. Matthias approached Amanda with a smile. "Do you have another sister stashed away in America? Preferably a single, unattached version?"

Her sister tittered and grabbed the kids. "No, I'm sorry to say. But I have girlfriends who'd give their left arm to meet you!"

He glanced sideways. "At least we will still have LaRae's art. Painted in exotic lands, but getting displayed in Europe."

"I hope the added income gets her out of houses on stilts and caves or whatever people sleep in in those places," Amanda said and wrapped her mink tighter around her shoulders.

LaRae waved as they exited. Through the glass doors, Matthias blew her a kiss from his sports car. She watched the overseas crew, lightheaded from jet lag, pile into the van with Mr. Hansen.

But Ania remained. In deep conversation with Lars under the outside awning, she inserted a hand into the crook of his arm. He accompanied her to the sidewalk. After smiling radiantly, Ania started down the street when a thud and a cry resounded. The girl lay splayed on her back in the snow. Lars rushed to the scene and examined her ankle.

"Mom! LaRae? Please help!" His request unfroze her.

"Goodness! As if we haven't had enough drama." Cora ran alongside her, then talked to Ania as Lars lifted her up. "I'll call your parents, Honey. You need to go to the ER."

The girl bit her lip, her face paling.

"They've gone skiing." Ania groaned.

Cora turned to LaRae. "It's highly unconventional but would you mind if Gunnar takes her in my car, Rae? Ambulances are notoriously slow. I think she is passing out."

Her fiancé eyed her, his pupils black and round like the dot at the bottom of a question mark.

"Don't be silly. Of course I don't mind. Please take her. Your mom and I have to fix the dress!" With a quick peck on his cheek she helped them to the Volvo, then draped a blanket over Ania's cleavage showing beneath her loose cape. When the taillights vanished, an unfamiliar heat seared her chest. *How could you?* She wanted to yell at Cora. *You are throwing my man into another woman's arms! A luscious one in teary distress.* They climbed into the taxi and LaRae clamped her jaw shut. What kind of Christian said "no" to such a request? Back home, she gritted her teeth through trying the ruined dress on again and again. Finally Cora sighed, stating the job would have to do.

Come tomorrow I may not need the gown. An urge to fling the accusation at the hunched-over shape at the sewing machine seized her. Throughout the fitting her phone had remained silent; not even an emoji had lit up the screen. Right before midnight they finished the place cards. Too stubborn to call Lars, she crawled under the covers in Cora's guestroom, shivering despite the central heat and flannel sheets.

Lars paced the frozen beach, compact sand and ice crunching under his feet. His breath escaped in white puffs. Driftwood clogged the normally flat ground. He climbed over a slippery tree trunk pondering the changes in his life. Memories flashed before him, some making his heart pound harder. Keeping up a brisk pace, sweat soon soaked the suit beneath his overcoat and the incoming tide lapped at the tennis shoes he kept in the car for runs. After pushing to the end of the crescent-shaped shore and back again, he headed for Uncle Sven's farm. Banned from his mother's house, away from the wedding gown and bodily temptations, he'd been warned not to see his intended until the ceremony.

"Absolutely no peeking at the bride." Mother had shaken her slightly crooked index finger in the air. He snatched a leftover waffle from Aunt Lisa's kitchen counter but couldn't eat it. At last he called LaRae's number. The news would send her into distress, but there was no going back now. Bracing himself, the phone lead in his palm, he studied the muddy tracks he's made on the linoleum.

"Hello?" Her voice sounded edgy, not sleepy.

"Hi, Rae."

"Hey."

"I feel awful. I have come to a decision without telling you." The silence unnerved him. "Can you hear me?"

"Yes."

"Are you sick? Your breathing sounds labored." He waited.

"No." He rested his elbows on the kitchen counter, leaning on it for moral support when a wave of dizziness rolled over him. He instinctively straightened. A sharp pain hit his head. "Ouch! The edge of the upper cabinet connected with my skull." Upon palpating the spot, blood stuck to his finger. "Just a minute. I cut myself." He seized a roll of paper towels, tore off several sections and dunked them under the faucet. The cold stung the wound, but stemmed the blood flow. He picked up the phone again.

"I'm back." Silence greeted him. "Hey? You there?"

A feeble "yes" answered him.

With a grimace, he opened his mouth, the words tumbling out. "Okay, here goes. I accepted the Daar El Salam offer without consulting with you. I'm so sorry. Since it's your first time in an underdeveloped country, I decided it's better for us to live in a city first. We'll have running water but no air conditioning. But a whole villa to ourselves. I apologize for postponing your village and tent request."

A sob from the other end rocked him. He raked a hand through his hair, then winced as his nails hit the wound. "I get that you're mad. And devastated." The soggy shoes squished and he pried them off and grabbed the roll to wipe up the mess he'd caused. Choked laughter interrupted.

"Lars Gunnar? In response to all of this I have one question."

"Shoot."

"Are you planning on marrying me tomorrow, December 12, at 3 PM?"

"Rae. If I never do another thing for the rest of my life but marry you, I'll be the happiest man walking the earth. Will you still have me?"

"Yes!" Her answer made the nape of his neck tingle.

LaRae felt no tingles but the sharp angle in her neck loosened. She gathered the dress she had just hurled on the floor and re-hung it in the alcove by the closet. Back in bed, her muscles slowly let go. When dawn arrived, she woke to the scent of lavender flowers and running water.

Cora's head popped in the door. "Your bath awaits, dear."

"I'm spoiled. You are ruining me for a life of hardship," LaRae sighed.

"A most blessed and good morning to you, too. When finished, come to my room with your hair wet so we can carry out your idea."

LaRae soaked in the steamy tub, then washed her hair, slipped on her bathrobe and padded barefoot to Cora's bedroom.

"Homemade rolls?" she asked.

"And fresh Earl Grey tea with a tad of cream. Can't risk you fainting on the red runner."

LaRae followed Cora's hands as they dried and braided her hair. Seated in front of a mid-century vanity her frilly, feminine underwear clung to her. Last night Amanda had handed a box to her and whispered "I'll die if you march down the aisle in sensible cotton knickers. You've saved yourself for this moment for 24 years. Can the man who opens the package also enjoy a pretty wrapping?"

A rose got pinned to the braided circle on top of her head. "I hope you don't feel obliged to wear it." Cora's eyes questioned her in the mirror.

LaRae's cheeks flamed. "The lingerie?"

"No silly, the French lace is gorgeous, but none of my business. I'm talking about the dress."

"On the contrary! Besides being vintage, the style is simple and tasteful. When you first opened the box, I knew nothing in the stores would compare. Thank you for letting me wear it. The gesture touches me more than you know."

Cora crouched and squeezed both of her hands. "Daughter. I love you. Please don't allow our relationship to change because I'm becoming your mother-in-law. May we dispense with formalities? Since your own mom is not here, will you call me Mamma?"

LaRae blinked back tears. "Thank you, Mamma."

They hugged until Cora jerked away suddenly and shuddered. "Here I am, messing up your makeup and making you cry! You must keep me in line! I'm overwrought with excitement and sentimentalism."

"I'll try, but I have my own to contend with. Since Lars had to return to Africa in September and only came home five days ago, I've only had drip doses of him. It would have driven him crazy, picking green ink over black, fir over ivy, apricot cake filling over raspberry. Plus with vaccinations visits, visas applications and the photography course, the maddening pace would've left little time for romance. I am so glad The Red Cross hired me on as a media promoter so I get to be a participant, not just a tag-along."

"Being around you would have driven him crazy," Cora stated drily, rolling her eyes. "He's a wild stallion chomping at an unwelcome bit. It's why I relegated him to barn at the farm." They giggled at the thought.

The Lutheran church carried the scent of Douglas fir and red roses. White beeswax candles glowed in silver candlesticks. The rustling of bulletins got drowned out when the organ belted out Mendelsohn's Wedding March. The guests rose and turned towards the double doors. Erect, Lars Gunnar stood at the front. Watching the entrance intently, he spied her. She took his breath away. Not only because of her refined, simple beauty, but because of the green eyes and the passion he read in them. A tight silk bodice with a flared skirt enveloped her trim body. Narrow, buttoned sleeves completed the picture along with a delicately embroidered veil from Venice. The veil had been in his mother's family for generations. He studied the gown as LaRae glided up the steps and wondered how in the world one unbuttoned a creation like that?

Her curves were hidden yet intoxicating. Uncle Walter delivered her to his side. After a closer glance at her his heart throbbed in his throat. Red roses formed a circle around a braided bun piled on top of her head. She wore no jewelry, her swan neck needing no adornment. As they turned towards the priest, he took a deep breath and exhaled through his nostrils.

"You are my beloved and my beloved is mine." The reverend read the passage from Song of Songs.

LaRae glanced sideways at her groom. Pale beneath the tan, her Nordic hero was about to promise to cherish her forever. When he pronounced the vows, his pupils dilated and his blue irises smoldered. When her turn came, her voice wobbled, then increased in strength till it resounded clear as a silver bell in the nave of the church.

"You may kiss the bride," was the prompt that moved their bodies. The kiss was long and drawn out causing applause and laughter to break out. Outside, acquaintances, neighbors, and friends lined up to shake their hands. As they crossed to the waiting sleigh; well wishes and bird seeds showered them. The driver wrapped the couple in sheep skins before lifting the reins and prodding the black horses to take off to a photography site.

The former Lord Manor's house sat above the beach where swells from the North Sea lapped over the dunes. Painted white, the modest mansion looked like a venerable old lady ready to embrace the guests in her warm lap. After trading the horses and sleighs for a car, LaRae and Lars drove up past a line of people formed to greet them. They shook hands before being ushered to the buffet line. Illuminated by candles and crystal chandeliers, the long table nearly buckled beneath the weight of a smorgasbord of hot and cold dishes. Lox and pickled herring paired with traditional flat bread intermingled with tenderloin, asparagus and open-faced tea sandwiches. From a lofty pedestal in the corner a big wedding cake covered in marzipan with layers of whipped cream and bourbon-laced apricot glaze reigned supreme. LaRae piled several delicacies on her plate and sat down at the place of honor in the middle of a horseshoe seating arrangement.

Next to her Lars gobbled down a filet of pickled herring then rose and gave a speech. His words caused an eruption of laughter and smiles beaming in her direction. She smiled back, clueless to what he had said, her mind fixed on one fact alone. *I am a married woman. The man by my side promised to cherish me forever.*

A firm hand on her forearm brought her back. "Our first dance. Let's go!" Lars steered her to where her language teacher Helen served as DJ. When Louis Armstrong's raspy rendition of "What A Wonderful World" filled the room they started dancing. LaRae smiled at Lars then shut her eyes. With each step she pictured herself waltzing into new real estate. Would loved ones still get sick or pass away? Would unforeseen problems and challenges crop up? Probably. She still lived in a fallen world. For so long that fact had terrified her, alienating her into a no man's land away from people. But the deep freeze that had kept her immobile was thawing. With her satin-slippered feet, LaRae crushed hopelessness and despair. Trust trumped fear. When others joined them on the dance floor, she threw her head back and laughed. Come what may, here they were, a happy, moving, flowing stream of humanity, abandoning themselves into a river of joy.

One couple stood out in particular. The woman towered above her small, wrinkled companion, her bosom bumping his chin in rhythm to the music. Merriment lit up Gunhild's eyes as Trond looked up at her adoringly.

"We probably won't have babies since it's rather late," Gunhild had confided after their civil ceremony at City Hall.

LaRae had done her best to keep a straight face at the obvious reflection. "Because Tiger brought Trond and I together, we'd like to adopt him."

LaRae's eyes wandered to Cora who preferred the cha-cha to the polka. Dressed in fire engine red, she sparkled beside a tuxedoed Uncle Walter. Amanda was teaching Drew an intricate step. At the table Mickey gasped as pink punch from his cup sloshed onto his shirt. Seated on Christopher' lap Wallie was burying his face in whipped cream from the cake while his father visited with Matthias. At the next table Ania sat in a wheelchair, her foot in a boot, her raven hair twirled in a chignon. Matthias left a conversation with the Reverend to spin the girl's chair in circles to Sting's "Every Breath You Take."

All was well. LaRae thought of the four suitcases packed and waiting for them in the trunk of the limousine. They'd spend three days in a hotel in Kristiansand, removed from prying relatives before flying to Dar El Salaam on Tuesday.

"Whisk me away!" LaRae pleaded in a whisper as they dragged themselves towards a table of refreshments. Her request made Lars' eyes dance more than the rest of his body. But extricating themselves from the company of friends and family proved difficult. Stories and party games followed. A Norwegian wedding was a thorough affair leaving LaRae's nephews draped over the damask couch in the throes of sleep and Gunhild nursing a blister with her swollen ankle elevated. A few minutes before midnight, Cora performed a parental blessing then nodded for them to bow out.

Right before climbing into the waiting car, Lars pulled out a silk scarf from his pocket and turned to LaRae. "I am blindfolding you."

She looked up at him. "Another custom? We are far away from our hotel."

"Wait and see." Lars wrapped the blindfold over her eyes and helped get her seated. They left to cheers and the rattle of tin cans attached to the rear of the car. Ten minutes later, the vehicle slowed and came to a standstill. LaRae heard a door open and suitcases being removed from the trunk. Then her groom appeared by her side. "I'm carrying you."

"What's happened? Do we have a flat tire? If we are not parked in a puddle, I can walk." She put a leg out but got grabbed up in Lars Gunnar's arms. "Rest has improved your form." Her fingers slid over his biceps.

"Yes. My body is back to its former virility." The sly grin starting on Lars' lips went unseen to LaRae whose hands wrapped around his neck.

LaRae felt herself being carried up steps, bumping into walls and a doorway before she got lowered to a semi-soft surface.

Lars panted from the exertion. "All right, remove the scarf." She obeyed and blinked, then rotated her head taking in the surroundings. The bed was a four-poster pine with linen curtains. A huge painting depicting a couple embracing under a moonlit sky took up the space above a turquoise dresser. "Mamma's wedding gift." Lars nodded towards the art.

"Oh, it's beautiful! But where are we?"

"You are free to explore for a moment before I ravish you, my lady." Lars watched his bride slide off the bed and open the door to the hallway.

A loud exclamation pierced the air. "Great Aunt's house! How can it be? Did you rent it from the new owner?"

"You are looking at him. I have been the proud proprietor of these premises since August. I'll be adding you to the deed, Mrs. Pettersen."

She fixed him with confused green eyes. "Erna's place sold to you? I never paid attention to the purchasing party's name when signing." Leaned against the stair rail, her brows creased. "Aren't you poor?"

"I was. But Mother invested my father's life insurance in oil field equipment when I was little. She told me the day after our engagement. I got the bright idea to purchase your great-aunt's house. This way no matter where we go in the world, we have a home in Mandal."

His new bride swept down the narrow hall, squealed and

jumped into his arms. "That was the only thing I struggled with. The elbow grease rubbed into these walls and floors made the place feel like my own. Now we will remain next to Cora um I mean Mamma."

"I had ulterior motives." Lars Gunnar chewed his lip.

"Oh? It's an investment property?"

"That's a correct observation. An investment indeed. I am investing in privacy with my bride." Wiggling his eyebrows, her bridegroom's stare darted to the bedroom.

LaRae followed his gaze. "Hmmm. I see. Is that particular room first on your list to make sure it meets our needs?" "

Lars nodded convincingly.

Daintily lifting up the hem of her dress, LaRae tossed her head with a regal air. "Lead the way, my lord; the lady of the manor is nipping at your heels."

The Northern star blinked in the indigo sky above Scandinavia. Way down on the southernmost tip of Norway moon rays lit up dark bedrooms around Mandal. It was a quiet night. The only outside creatures stirring were hardy cats pawing through snow hoping to catch a wood mouse. As the clock struck an early morning hour, the huddled shape under a goose down duvet moved. A worn silk kimono was pulled off a nearby chair and draped over the rounded female form. Dark curly hair with silver streaks glinted in the moonlight. The sheepskin slippers padded softly into the sunroom with the heated hardwood floor. The woman stretched and sighed contentedly. "You wake me up again Lord. But there is no crisis this time?"

She stood by the window, a faithful sentinel, and stared at the little, white clapboard house two doors down. It loomed still in the shadows. Empty way too long, the neighbors probably assumed it was vacant still. She smiled. "Appearances can be deceiving. You and I know that Lord, don't we?"

She curled up in her rocker, bowing her head. "After the last battle, you gave me my heart's desire. How can I not help but love you even more dearly?"

The smallest house on the street turned as quiet on the inside as on the outside. Only slight snoring cut the silence. Wavy hair spilled over the pillow and a slender woman lay on her side, green eyes looking up through the window towards the starlit night. She did not stir. Careful not to disturb the spent man next to her, her words were mouthed silently but from a deep place.

"For so long I believed significance came from doing something extraordinary. I was wrong. I finally get it."

They were private words. Intimate and confidential, laced with overwhelming gratitude. While love in human form breathed down the back of her neck, LaRae closed her eyes and let herself fall backwards, letting go of fear and control. Much to her surprise, the free fall didn't lead to disaster. Instead she landed in a soft spot, a place of belonging. Before drifting off to sleep, a verse popped into her head: "The eternal God is your refuge and dwelling place. And underneath are the everlasting arms." With Lars' hand resting on her belly, she inhaled, then sank into the eternal arms of love.

DEAR READER,

Thank you for reading the first book in the "Women of Identity Series." If you enjoyed this book please leave a review on Amazon. To find out when Book 2 will be released and to receive regular updates from me, sign up for my newsletter at maytomlin.com. You can also follow my musings and meanderings here at:

Instagram: @maytomlinfiction

Facebook Page: facebook.com/maytomlinfiction/

Website: maytomlin.com

DISCUSSION QUESTIONS

1. Why do you think LaRae is scared silly about choosing an art major and following her heart's desires? Have you felt anything similar? If so, how did you deal with it?

2. When Lars is rebuffed by Norman and disillusioned with Ania, do you think he acts right by going to Africa?

3. How would you define his inner struggle?

4. Circumstances push LaRae out of her rut and the place where she is stuck in despair when she inherits the house overseas. Yet she has to choose to embrace her new experience in Norway. What do you think helps her do so?

5. What do you think of Cora's role in the story? Have you had a mentor who has affected your life positively? Do you have one wise person who you can confide in?

6. La Rae has a hard time with boundaries and saying *no*. When Gunhild coaches her, she finds the courage to become outspoken through a letter. Do you find it easy or hard to have clear boundaries? Do you believe God desires for us to acquire conflict resolution skills instead of avoiding conflict?

7. I call Lars and LaRae's wedding "the cherry on top of the cake" because it tops off her happiness. But the cake itself is her newly developed relationship with Jesus Christ when she accepts him as her Lord and Savior. Do you agree or disagree with that?

8. I often fixate on a desired cherry and forget to enjoy the very substance that keeps me alive, namely my union with Christ. Do you struggle with similar distractions? If so, what do you do?

9. Co-dependency is a term that often appears as vague as an elusive fog. A more common way to explain co-dependency is a feeling that I can only be ok if you're ok. Therefore, I'll do everything in my power to make you ok so that I can be ok. Do you think LaRae beats this habit at the end of the story?

Made in the USA
Coppell, TX
19 April 2022

76792541R00224